Eveleen's Seduction
Twelve Dancing Princesses Book Eight

Christine Young

Published by Rogue Phoenix Press, LLP
Copyright © 2018

ISBN: 978-1-62420-415-9

Credits
Cover Artist: Designs by Ms G
Editor: Christie L. Kraemer

Chapter One

London 1821

Logan Maxwell stood outside The Duchess' townhouse, his heart pounding and his hands sweating. Rarely was he nervous but asking for the hand in marriage of a lady was not something he'd done before, and he prayed would never do again.

Scarlett, The Duchess' companion, opened the door, "Why, Lord Maxwell, whatever are you doing here? It's good to see you again. It's been a very long time."

"Isn't it obvious?" he asked with a feeble chuckle. "I'm here on personal business. I want to see Eveleen."

"No, that's just not possible. Lady Eveleen is no longer in London. She left a week ago. If you'd been in town or even at your country estate, you would have heard the news."

Logan stepped past Scarlett and strode into the parlor where The Duchess sat, sipping a cup of tea, a plate of lemon bars in front of her. Anger imploded within and frustration ate at him. He'd been in Bordeaux on business. Someone should have sent a message. As it was, he wasted time pursuing Eveleen in London.

"I wondered when you'd show up, young Lord Maxwell. You can't dally with a girl's heart and emotions then expect said lady to be at your beck and call. You hurt Lady Eveleen, and I'd be surprised if she forgave you." The Duchess set down the cup. "Have a seat, and we can chat for a few minutes." She directed her next question to Scarlett. "Will you fetch Lord Maxwell some brandy or is it whiskey you like? Perhaps, you'd like some of your own Bordeaux."

Logan cleared his throat, his jaw tensing, "Brandy is fine."

"Yes, milady." Scarlett spoke to Charlotte then scurried from the room.

"Do you know where Eveleen is?" Logan didn't feel like sipping brandy and listening to the lecture from The Duchess he knew hovered on her lips. Eveleen could be anywhere.

"Of course, I do, but that doesn't mean I'm going to tell you. Have a lemon bar. They're very tasty." She pointed at the plate of confections then with a cackle of seeming delight, "Not too good for your waist line though. At my age, I eat what I please."

Logan sat, stunned at the reception, and learning Eveleen had left London. He accepted the glass of brandy, eyeing it critically. Thinking the sooner he answered to The Duchess, the sooner he'd get out of the townhouse to pursue Eveleen. "What do you want to chat about?"

"Eveleen." Her voice was curt and penetrated Logan's thoughts. "The young lady who wore her heart for everyone to see, but you, Lord Maxwell, ignored everything. Now, you want to make amends, I see."

"Of course, Eveleen. I didn't ignore her." He'd spent every minute he was in town with her. What more could he have done? He had business to run, and a rendezvous in France that couldn't be overlooked.

"You need to learn how to treat a young woman, and breaking her heart is not the way." She lectured. "What are you planning to do so you can make it up to her?"

Put on the defensive and disliking the position, he paused, thinking, "I had no idea I was breaking her heart. I believed I was courting her."

"You didn't court her, you teased her, giving her reason to think you were interested in her then leaving without telling her why or where, and this wasn't the first time you left suddenly," The Duchess accused him, tapping her cane on the floor as if making her point. "While Drake courted Ella in a completely ungentlemanly way, you did the opposite. In a way, you snubbed her. Both of you young men have a lot to learn about the female species, and how to treat them. My Duke had no idea until I taught him."

"Business, my vineyard, needed overseeing and my orchids needed tending. It was harvest time. Critical time for the grapes." He suddenly felt like an untrained boy in front of his teacher, who was boxing his ears.

The first time he saw Eveleen he found himself transfixed by the sapphire color of her eyes, and he'd known then he wanted to have her, to wrap her long strawberry blond hair around his body. Yet, responsibilities stopped him from courting her as The Duchess pointed out, properly. Over the last few days, he'd come to understand he didn't have time for courting. So, he made up his mind to wed her.

"An excuse, a bad one at that. You've always been fast with your words, young man. Seems you could think of something more original." She waved her hand in the air, dismissing his reason. "You could have told her what you were about. She would have understood, and today you wouldn't be wondering where she got herself off to."

"The truth." He bristled. Once again, he found himself on the defensive. At the ball, when he'd first seen her, he was on a mission along with Drake Montgomery to save Jarret Kingsley from discovery. Jarret would have found himself immediately married to Fayth Graham, another of The Duchess' wards, and something Jarret vowed never to do.

"Possibly," she acknowledged. "But there is more, and I believe some might say, lies of omission, or perhaps you didn't believe she was worthy of the knowledge. Eveleen is not a trinket you can toy with. This is the nineteenth century. You need to enter the modern world."

"Eveleen is a woman," he began, mystified by The Duchess' words. "Why should she know what a man is doing?"

"Of course, you are right. Why should she know where and why you go places? She is, as you say just a woman." The Duchess leaned forward, her features drawn tight. "Do you care about Eveleen, or do you just find it's the right time in your life to take a wife. Do you believe she is not intelligent enough to understand your business?"

"Both," he acknowledged having never really thought about it until The Duchess confronted him. "But, of course, she's intelligent and beautiful."

"Do you love her?" once again she questioned, tapping her cane on the floor beside her and staring at him as if had a hole in his head. "Do you love her?" she repeated. "It's an easy enough question. Yes or no."

Logan stiffened, his gut instincts clicking in, and said, "There is no such thing as love. I am attracted to her. She is sweet and kind. Indeed, beautiful, but love, no, not ever."

"Then you have your work cut out for you, because she fancies herself in love with you. If you tell her you don't love her, she will freeze, perhaps turn her back on you, and never do your bidding."

For several breath-stealing seconds he wasn't sure what to say to The Duchess. Love had nothing to do with marriage and children. Yet, he found himself flattered by The Duchess' words. "I will do whatever I need to convince her I would make a good husband and father."

"I don't think she cares as much about a good husband and father as you want to believe. She wants a man who loves and respects her. Eveleen is tender hearted and quiet-spoken, but there is a will of iron within her soul. She will not be easy to win over if you cannot find love in your heart."

No, not easy at all if he failed to discover where she'd gone. If, as Aidan had done, she left for Baltimore, he'd be hard pressed to follow her. "Where has she gone?" he persisted, realizing in his life, time was important to him and his work. Wasting the precious commodity was not an option.

"Do you think I want to make this easy on you? You're an intelligent man. You figure it out." The Duchess laughed, her age-lined face crinkling in merriment. "In order to appreciate the woman you wed, the journey must be difficult. You must earn her love and her trust."

"Apparently not, I think you enjoy watching us men falter," Logan said dryly. "But I'd appreciate any help in this matter you're willing to give."

"You don't love her. What if a man came along who could give her what she wants, love? Would you stop her?" Once again, The Duchess challenged him and all he held dear.

"Eveleen is mine," he told The Duchess vehemently. "Another man will never touch her."

"Tsk, tsk, you might believe that but does Eveleen? It's time for you, young man, to come to your senses. Eveleen is not yours. You have no claim to her. Need I remind you again, it's the nineteenth century? A woman can say no to a man she doesn't want to marry. She doesn't have to accept a man she doesn't want." The Duchess reminded him pointedly.

Logan drained his glass of brandy, suddenly needing more of the potent liquid and glanced Scarlett's way, who seemed to understand what he requested and soon supplied him with more brandy, this time setting the bottle nearby.

"Thank you," he said.

"If not love, what can you give her?"

"If I had taken her to the hunting lodge and ruined her, you wouldn't be telling me this," he shot back, realizing that was exactly what he should have done. Drake had done everything right where it came to courting. No, what he did was not courting. It was seduction.

"If she'd agreed to go with you, you wouldn't have to convince her you care for her. You'd know where she was right now. In your home, your arms and your bed most likely." The Duchess' eyes focused on him, driving home the point.

The lady had an answer for everything, and what she said had a definite ring of truth. Inhaling a deep breath of air, "I confess. You've a good argument. I spent a great deal of time overlooking her. I will have to change my ways if I wish to win her hand."

"You should have courted her and shown her affection. I believe the last time we spoke, she told the girls she didn't think you cared at all for her. You'd only given her a few brief little kisses on the cheek, and perhaps a daytime kiss to the lips. Imaginably, at least one long body heating kiss would have kept her in London. What do you think?"

"I didn't want to frighten her," he said too quickly and while that was part of the story, it wasn't the entire reason. She was tiny, fragile and delicate. He didn't want to risk hurting her.

"Pshaw...after what she saw Drake do with Ella? You can't be serious. She told me she wanted the same as Ella had, and she didn't want to settle for less. You've a lot to answer for if you want to win her hand."

"Are you going to tell me where she is or are you going to keep telling me what I've done wrong?" His patience had come to an end.

"You must prove yourself before I tell you anything." The Duchess tilted her head, slightly smiling.

"How the bloody eyes do I do that when I can't find her?" Lady Charlotte had him by the balls and she seemed to know it.

"I'm sure if you really want to marry the young lady of our

conversation, you'll figure it out." She lifted the tray of treats, and with a daring smile, she asked, "Another lemon bar?"

Instead of accepting a sweet confection, he rose and paced the room, thinking. He had courted Eveleen very gently but she was fragile as hell. Her wrists so thin, his fingers overlapped when he wrapped them around her. So, how the devil was he supposed to court her now when he couldn't find her?

As if reading his mind, The Duchess went on to say, "She is tougher than you think. Just because she is petite doesn't mean she is fragile or she'll break if you make love to her." The powdered sugar on her lips combined with her smile left a strange impression. "You should think about that."

"So, you give me the impression I should bed a woman I'm not married to?" he whispered softly, fiercely trying to understand exactly what this lady tried to tell him.

"Of course not. Don't assume anything, but I won't condemn a man who is good at heart. Make love to her yes, but I don't know why that would surprise you. I gave permission to Drake to do the same with Ella. Well," she amended, "If Ella agreed and we all know what happened."

"Your permission is pointless." His hand knifed through the air. "I plan on proposing marriage as soon as I can find her. I will court her then make love to her after we are wed."

"That my young man is a horrible mistake."

"It is mine to make."

"Perhaps she left for Bordeaux in search of her beau," The Duchess said sweetly. "If you don't court her or at least seduce her, she won't ever be in your bed."

"Then she is not there. You are only trying to tempt me with false clues. I'm sure it would please you to see me run off to France when she was somewhere else." Frustration built inside. "Or perhaps you play games, suggest one thing in hopes I'll dismiss it."

"Intrigue is beyond me. I'm an old woman who speaks her mind." She sipped her tea, her clear blue eyes sparkling with amusement and seemed to wait for him to stick his foot in his mouth.

Picking up his whiskey glass, he gulped the contents before setting it sharply on the table. "I believe we're through here."

"Scarlett." Lady Charlotte called out.

"Yes, Milady. What do you need?" She appeared quickly as if she'd been waiting at the door and possibly listening.

"Will you please see young Lord Maxwell out?"

The Duchess had out maneuvered him from his first words. Now on his way to the Montgomerie country estate, he evaluated everything Lady Charlotte had told him. Bedeviled by the idea he'd been too gentle and caring with his lady's reputation with Eveleen, he tried to figure out how to remedy the situation he'd singlehandedly created.

Striding through the gardens to the gazebo in the back of the Montgomerie estate, he flexed his hands, feeling the need to hit something. When he saw the happy couple, he knew he was about to interrupt a tryst, but they could wait. His need was far greater than anything they could be feeling.

"Sorry to interrupt," he said out of politeness. "But I've urgent business that won't wait for the two of you to finishes whatever it is you've started."

The pair didn't immediately jump apart as expected. Instead, Drake drew out the kiss, slowly removing his hand from beneath her dress, while he made sure his big body shielded her from his view, giving Ella time to adjust her bodice and hair.

"You owe me," Drake said gruffly, his voice raw and intimidating.

"Of course."

Drake's shirt fell open, revealing unfastened trousers. "Why are you here, Logan? Everything going well, I presume?"

He meant to get to the point. The sooner he knew where Eveleen had vanished to, the sooner he could marry her. "Do either of you know where Eveleen has gone? It seems The Duchess won't tell me."

Logan watched as Ella's hand touch Drake's arm as if signaling for something, perhaps not to say anything. Drake turned to look into Ella's eyes. Time ticked by while she looked down.

Ella's gaze fastened on his before questioning him. "Why do you want to know?" Ella whispered softly.

At his sides, his fists clenched and unclenched, his anger and frustration once more surfacing. "To ask for her hand in marriage."

"By the look in your eye, I don't think you stand a chance of hearing a positive answer from my cousin. You've done an amazing job of hurting and belittling her," Ella said pointedly. "What's the rush?"

His emotions and frustrations escalated to a burning inferno. This morning his plans had been simple and seemed to be in reach, but now he'd been lectured and once again he expected another round of scolding for behavior he thought had been impeccable.

"And why and how did I accomplish all you said? If I hurt her, I certainly didn't mean to," he asked, knowing full well he was jumping in with both feet and no guarantee of a lifeline.

"You really have to ask?" Drake said incredulously. "I warned you several times that you ignored her. Your chaste kisses and modest handholding would never convince her you cared. Every time you disappeared, you left without telling her anything."

He braced himself for the second round of reprimanding. "My vineyard, winery was important. The harvest had to be seen to. I had to leave. When the grapes are ready, everything else is put on hold."

"Without telling her why? Eveleen thought you were putting your life in danger by spying. She could never quite get the picture of you with your bandaged leg out of her head. You were shot while you were spying for the crown, Logan. Eveleen is a quiet and reserved person. Violence is something she's never understood. Again, I ask, what's your burning need to marry her now?"

"I didn't want to bother her with my business." He choked on the words, realizing if he respected her, he would include her in the simplest things. "If I can find her, I'll try to do better."

"You've led her to believe that you as a man, and this is a man's world, expect her place in your life when wed would be to remain barefoot and pregnant," Ella said, studying his eyes.

He bit back the retort on his lips, understanding that once again everything he said seemed to bury him deeper. "You have no idea what I believe."

"Neither does Eveleen and that's the major problem," Ella said softly. "She didn't come here looking for a husband. Eveleen arrived in

London with me hoping to find a man to love. She believed she found that man in you."

"That's an impossible feat. Love doesn't exist," Logan answered, his voice and stance firm. Yet blood rushed to his face.

"Well," Drake laughed, "we do agree on that fact. Love is poetic nonsense, but that doesn't negate the fact you badly mistreated Eveleen. What are you planning to do about it?"

While they spoke, the sky darkened and a cold wind whipped around the gazebo. "Drake, we need to return to the house before the rain starts. I don't want to get drenched," Ella said, rising from the sheltered bench of the gazebo.

"You're pregnant," Logan said "when is the child due?"

"April," Drake said. "If you will excuse us, I need to get my very pregnant wife back to the house."

Logan welcomed a quick retreat from this strange battle he fought. All he wanted was Eveleen's location, and he would leave these two to their pursuit of pleasure.

Once inside the house, Drake called for refreshments while the trio settled in the parlor.

"I don't want to take up more of your time. Just tell me where she went and I'll leave." Logan thrummed his fingers on the table, nerves drawn tight, his tolerance thin.

"Hmm..." Ella leaned forward, one slender fingertip tapping her chin. Her gaze met his. "Aidan left for Baltimore. It's possible Eveleen joined her. The two sisters are rather close."

"And Lady Charlotte told me Eveleen went to my vineyard in Bordeaux. I don't believe either of you." He stiffened, his voice rising with the storm winds howling around the eaves.

"Suit yourself." With a shrug of her slim shoulders, Ella slanted him an angelic smile.

"Logan," Drake strode toward him then wrapping an arm around his shoulder, "walk with me. We need to speak with each other man to man. You need to understand some basic principles."

Logan looked over his shoulder to see Ella, knowingly smiling at him. A ray of sun burst through dark clouds filtering through the windowpane, warming his back and sending a moment of optimism through his soul. Perhaps he had a chance of discovering her location after all.

He waited not so good-naturedly. They'd toyed with him long enough. As far as he was concerned, this game was over. "I would like you tell me what you know about Eveleen's whereabouts and what exactly prompted her departure. Hell, she could still be in one of the rooms upstairs, for all I know. If you won't open up, I'll take my leave. I don't have the inclination to waste time."

"Have I ever lied to you?" Drake asked, an edge to his voice, letting his arm fall from Logan's shoulder.

"No."

"Then listen carefully. I'm only going to say this once. Everything you've heard here is true, and I assume the knowledge The Duchess imparted to you is also fact."

"Hells bells, I'm paying attention, been listening to every word. Just get to the bloody point." Logan said fervently, wishing he had a wall to slam his fist against. His body shook with his anger.

"I don't believe you have been, but then that's just my opinion," Drake told him, his voice clear, his meaning clearer.

"What? What have you told me that I've not absorbed into my gut?" Logan asked, staring at Drake, demanding answers that didn't seem to be forthcoming any time soon.

"Eveleen left because she believes you don't care for her. You haven't done anything to make her think you are her beau. But we've told you that a hundred times and your actions have never changed. Now you come here demanding we tell you something we're not at all sure will be good for Eveleen."

"I understand that and I'm trying to figure out how to fix things with her. I'm just a confused man."

"Arrogance is not a virtue that will promote your cause with Eveleen," Drake warned. "You might have to beg forgiveness. Are you capable of that? Do you want her enough?"

"Yes."

"That was pretty weak, Logan. Do you want her enough?" Drake repeated, seeming to expect something from him he didn't understand.

"Yes, I do. Yes." Logan fisted his hands, the muscles in his jaw flexing, raw nerves ripping through his insides. This was too important to him. He wanted a wife and children and he'd never met anyone quite like Eveleen. "She is beautiful and intelligent. Eveleen is everything I've ever wanted in a mate."

"That was a little bit better, but I'm sensing reservations on your part. Aww, what could that be?"

"She's so fragile," Logan said. "And delicate as a new flower. I don't want to break her."

"And if I'm aware of the uncertainties, she is also. Eveleen might be a small woman, but she is not tinier than Ella. You have nothing to fear."

"What if she dies in childbirth?" Logan had gone over this scenario so many times he knew the nightmare by heart.

"Don't you think it's too soon to worry about childbirth? From what Ella has told me, you've barely kissed Eveleen." Drake grinned as if seeing his friend's hesitations.

"When choosing a wife, a man has to think about things like that." Logan knew his words meant nothing to Drake who had wanted only passion from his relationship."

"I'm sure she is tougher than you think," Drake said dryly with the hint of laughter in his words.

"Perhaps, I've got a lot to think about and amends to make, but I can't do them unless you tell me where I can find my future bride."

~ * ~

"No!" Eveleen turned to run, her heart pounding in her chest. If only she could reach the boat.

From behind her, a man wrapped his beefy arms around her waist, pulling her against him. Her nails bit into his flesh while she struggled against his brute force. "That's it, fight me. It's more fun that way," he growled, his voice a low evil snarl against her ear.

"Let me go." She pushed as hard as she could on his arms, struggling to shove him away, terrorized by fear, remembering when Guy,

Hunter's stepbrother, had captured her and tied her to the rock in the middle of the ocean to wait for high tide when she would drown.

His laughter echoed in the tiny clearing on the island sanctuary. "You're a pretty little thing. I like 'em little and delicate. I bet your tits are pretty too, nice and soft." With one hand be captured a breast and squeezed.

She screamed a high-pitched sound, eerie in the tiny glade.

He laughed, letting his fetid breath wash across her face.

Trying another tactic, she bent low and bit him on the arm. Wrenched against him, he ripped the bodice of her dress from top to waist. "No!" she yelled. "Stop. You've no..."

"Lil' gal, I do what I please."

Tears flowed from her eyes and down her face while time seemed to stand still. She let her mind drift in a haze, the trees and bushes all becoming one with each other.

The earth was strangely warm, the scent of grass emanating around her while her body now floated above her detached from what was happening. Her body tensed with pain yet she didn't cry out. All she heard was the throaty sounds from her attacker.

Then the man vanished and someone e lse took his place. He hauled her from the ground. His hand explored her body. She closed her eyes, wishing she could die now, or praying for a savior.

Suddenly, blood spurted around her, spraying the ground and the surrounding bushes. The man's hold dropped and when she turned, the man slid to the ground, his throat slit blood pulsing from the wound.

"Logan," she whispered, her body convulsing. Her breath seemed to stop and the ground swirled in a hazy blur. "You're here."

He caught her before she hit the ground and pulled her to her feet, his strong hands around her waist. Holding her steady, he said, "Listen to me. Go into the hut, now."

Her head moved, nodding, but she didn't know if she could make it there. Her legs shook. "Y-yes," she whispered while she fought the blackness that even now wanted to engulf her.

Her attempt to move was feeble, her legs giving out as she ended up on hands and knees shaking. She tried to crawl but ice flowed through her and her nerves screamed out in fear.

With a veiled curse, Logan swept her into his arms. He set her gently on the floor of the hut before saying, "Stay here no matter what you hear. Promise me."

"P-promise."

The door slammed shut and a strange silence echoed in her ears. Then she heard the pounding of her blood swishing through her veins and the scratchy rasps of her breaths. She tried to slow her breathing. Minutes passed. The trembling of her legs slowed. Chilled to the bone, she wrapped her arms around herself while trying to pull the fabric of her bodice together. Hesitating a second, she reached for the door and opened it.

A shot reverberated. She gasped, her hand to her mouth when Logan turned to her, his eyes darkened and brows drawn together. In a move so fast it seemed a blur, he lunged to a spot near the side of the hut. His bellow of rage terrified her and she pulled the door shut. Her heart stopped as she tried to inhale air, terrified she would not live through this day.

Scooting into a corner of the hut, she pulled her knees to her chest and closed her eyes. Tears welled beneath shuttered lashes and slid down her cheeks. No, no, no. She rocked back and forth with her repeated words. No, it can't be.

So much had happened. She'd run from London, terrified of rejection. But now Logan had returned and just in time to save her. He'd lecture her about the island and she could no longer claim its safety. Now her trembling was caused by thoughts of the man, Logan, the killer surrounded by violence and death.

She'd left, hoping he'd come for her and now he was here. He was on her island and he killed a man to save her. No, he killed two men, slit their throats as if they were animals.

A shadow covered her and when she looked up he stood, feet braced apart his hands on his narrow hips. Logan was tall, young, striking, with strong handsome features and some indomitable presence that demanded respect. His steel gray eyes could pierce her soul and they could sizzle silver in certain lights. Blond hair fell rakishly across his brow.

Even in stillness he was vital, demanding, arrogant.

Holding out a blood-splattered hand toward her, he said quietly as if nothing had just happened, "We have to go, now."

Eveleen tried to stand. Lord, how she strained to move her arm and take hold of his hand. Finally, with a whispered curse, Logan swept her into his arms. She buried her face in his shoulder, trying to adsorb his strength into her, sobbing quietly.

"I'm sorry," she said softly, trying to cling to him while holding the bodice of her torn dress together. "Why do we have to leave?"

"There might be more men. I saw a ship on the horizon while I was sailing here. When they notice two men have not returned to the ship, they'll send out search parties."

"A ship? Search parties? This has never happened on the island." She didn't have the strength to argue or question. Nothing he said made sense, but at least he wasn't yelling at her for the unescorted trip to the island.

Quickly striding down the hill to the spot where he moored his boat, he searched the ocean. Logan set her inside while he tied hers to the stern of the vessel he meant to sail to the mainland.

Eveleen watched the trail to the hut. Nothing inhabited the path except birds and squirrels. Even in the boat, with Logan raising the sail and manning the tiller, she couldn't stop her body from shaking.

Sunlight sparkled on the ocean waves. A brisk wind blew from the south and the little boat slipped quickly through the water.

Focusing on her island, she finally understood Hunter's as well as her father's fears. Today they were proven right. She gasped, drawing away when Logan reached out to touch her arm.

"It's all right. You know I won't hurt you. The two men arrived by ship and landed on the island." Logan spoke, his voice calm, too composed. "We don't know why, but I won't take chances where your life is concerned."

Who was this man who treated her as if she was a fragile flower one moment then slit the throats of two men with seemingly no care for human life? Once, she'd thought she knew Logan Maxwell. Before this day, she'd thought him easy going and carefree. Now she knew his other side, the darkly ominous and dangerous one, the spy.

She swallowed down her terror, trying to keep the fear in its rightful place, out of her mind. She didn't know what to believe. "And you think someone will look for them?"

"I believe so," he told her, turning to the island. Then he pointed. "See, there at the bottom of the trail."

A group of men stood on the beach, sunlight flashing off the steel of their swords. "What do they want?" she asked.

"Me." He gritted out. "But they found you instead."

More danger surrounded Logan than she cared to think about. A ragged gasp tore through her, and she placed a hand at her throat, attempting to breathe deeply and slowly. Closing her eyes, she concentrated on each breath of air until finally her breathing normalized.

"Why? Whatever for?"

"Because the man is mean spirited and evil. We've had our differences over the years. It seemed I purchased something he coveted. Now he seeks revenge."

Eveleen felt as if he'd said too much, more than she wanted to know. She pulled her knees tighter to her chest, as if that gesture would stop her trembling and ease the fear encapsulating her.

"How did he know I was on the island?" she whispered softly, barely able to hear herself.

"He didn't."

"Then?"

"Because he was looking for me and he had reason to believe I visited the McLellan castle. I'm sure the island was meant to hide his ship so he could survey its defenses." Logan beached the two boats.

Jumping into the water, he helped Eveleen to solid ground. Still shaking so hard, her knees gave way as she crumpled to the earth. "I cannot walk...can barely stand."

"You have to, either that or face a worse fate than those two men planned for you." His words sounded hard and dangerous.

Drawing her to her feet and wrapping an arm around her waist, he supported her. "I can," she told him determinedly, repeating the mantra to herself and one step at a time walked toward the castle.

"Is that door at the top of the steps open?" he asked, pointing in that direction.

"Yes. At least I hope so, unless someone bolted it from the inside after I left." She knew Allura, her sister, had vowed to keep it locked but the door was not bolted earlier.

He studied her as if weighing her ability to climb the steep crumbling steps. "We have to chance it. There is no time to go around the castle and enter through the gates."

Sweeping her into his arms, he strode quickly up the steps. Setting her down, he opened the door, "Thank God."

Inside the dark passageway, Logan secured the door then picked up the torch Eveleen had left at the entrance. Before she could protest, she was once more cradled in his arms.

"To the right," she told him, anticipating his question. "You can put me down now. I can walk," she whispered, her voice thin.

Yet he did not do her bidding. Instead, he strode through the tunnel. "Let me know when we reach your room."

Within a short span of time and several turns, "This is it." She wanted nothing more than to curl up in her bed and hide from the nightmare.

With a foot, he pushed it open and striding to the bed, he placed her gently down. "I'll order a bath for you. When you're done, come to the main room. I have some things to discuss with your father or Hunter. I'm not sure which man makes the family decisions."

Logan strode quickly from the room. She watched his departing back with trepidation. There was only one thing she could think of he would want to speak of with her father. Marriage.

She nodded, watching him disappear, still trembling and alarmed by thoughts of her future. He took charge as if she was his. She could never belong to a man so violent and dangerous.

As he'd told her, a knock sounded at her door, but it seemed she couldn't rise to answer it. Foggy scenes from the island floated through her mind, but all she could remember was a man hurting her, nothing else.

The servant didn't wait long, slowly the door opened. "Lady Eveleen? Your bath is ready to be filled."

At once men with buckets of steaming water entered and poured the liquid warmth into the bathtub she kept handy. Looking through fog-dazed eyes, she stared at the steaming water.

"Come," the servant said. "Let me help you from the dress. You will need assistance with your corset. What happened? The dress has nearly been ripped from you."

"I don't remember?" she spoke in hushed tones.

"Lord Maxwell?" the maid asked, seemingly horrified.

"No," Eveleen whispered, "No not him, he k-killed..." she let her voice trail off, knowing she shouldn't speak of such things in front of a servant.

"If you say so."

Eveleen stared ahead as she was disrobed and the ripped and bloodied clothing was piled in the corner waiting to be burned. The servant led her to the tub and helped her into the water.

She let her head fall against the rim and the water warm her frozen body. Her mind stilled, unraveling her future one strand at a time. Then she couldn't help herself. She found the sponge and scrubbed. A thin wail echoed from her and she wondered at the sound. But she couldn't stop herself. She felt so dirty and used. She scrubbed and scrubbed. And when the washing didn't ease the fear and the trembling and the disgust filling her soul, she pulled her knees to her chest in a tight ball and sobbed.

She would not agree to a marriage with Logan, even though she'd thought of little else for nearly a year now. She wasn't worthy of marriage. Something happened on the island, and she knew she couldn't ever marry.

"Come, Lady Eveleen. Lord Maxwell said we must hurry. What is wrong with you? Why are you sobbing? You must not think only of yourself. The men from the ship will be here soon, and we must all show a solid and brave front."

"What are you talking about?" She brushed tears from her eyes with the backs of her hands. "I can't go anywhere. I won't. I have to get clean first."

"Your Lord will be accused of murder, yet his actions were to defend you and your honor. We must take the dress to show what the horrible men did to you. Time is of the essence."

"Yes," but her hands didn't want to move. She found her servant had undone the few pins left holding her hair and washed it. Before she knew, her lady helped her from the bath.

Clothes were set on the bed, and she was surprised to see they would be considered among her best. Indeed, this was the one she wore to Allura's wedding.

"I don't need to wear such finery to meet Logan and my father in the great hall." She wondered at the clothes and the reasons behind them. It seemed she'd been caught up in the moment at hand and she had no will to defy them.

"I didn't question my orders," she said softly. "Lord Maxwell said to lay out your best gown."

"Lord Maxwell? Why? No, no, I suppose I can wear these even though I don't understand the reason behind them. Help me, this will take some time and the corset will have to be laced tight in order for the gown to fit." This was ridiculously difficult while she still trembled from the horrific encounter on the island. She couldn't close her eyes, because she saw the knife in Logan's hand and blood splattering everywhere. Keeping them open reminded her of how easily Logan slit the men's throat. He didn't hesitate one moment, just killed them. But there was something else that happened, something she needed to remember.

To save your life, you fool.

Even now she was sure Logan felt no remorse for their murder. He'd said as much when he left her. They'd hurt her she just wasn't sure her memory eluded her.

Too many minutes had passed. She heard the knock at the door and jumped with a terrified gasp her hand at her throat.

"Eveleen?" Allura asked, stepping quietly into the room and extending her hand. "Are you ready. Come, we must hurry. Even now the captain from the ship, Logan's enemy, waits in the great hall. He has accused Logan of murdering two of his men."

The servant held the remnants of Eveleen's ruined dress in her hands. "Here, take this with you and show him what was done to you at the hands of his men."

Eveleen stepped backwards, her hands at her sides while she shook her head and her entire body quivered with fear and shock. A cold sweat broke out on her body. "No, no, I can't. I won't touch it. Don't make me."

"Give it to me," Allura said quietly. "I will carry the damning evidence. This is necessary for the truth to be told and judged." She wrapped an arm around her sister. "This will be all right. Nothing will happen to Logan. We will make this alright. Don't worry. Do you want to tell me about the island?"

"I... It was..." she began but the lost memories and the petrifying fear caused her to stumble. "I don't remember much. The man threw me to the ground and tore the bodice. Then everything is muddled."

"You don't have to talk about it, but I believe telling someone what happened there would help you get over it." They entered the crowded hall and approached Hunter, who now sat in the laird's chair.

The distance between them seemed insurmountable. She turned to Allura. "A man a-attacked me. And..." she told Allura "Logan slit his throat. He put me in the hut, but I heard a gunshot. When I looked out I saw...he killed two men without thought before I could breathe," she murmured.

"The men were going to violate you; for all we know they did. From what you've told me, Logan had no choice," Allura whispered softly. "It will get better with time. It always does."

Tears slid from Eveleen's eyes. Nothing her sister said helped ease the trembling or her fears. "The violence...all the viciousness. It's not right but I thank Lord Maxwell."

"What Logan did was necessary to save your life," Allura argued vehemently. "He should not be punished."

The great hall brimmed with light and men from the McLellan clan as well as those from the ship. Chatter was loud and fierce as if each faction tried to prove its story. Only Logan and Eveleen knew what had happened on the island.

Logan and Hunter greeted the two sisters as they slowly closed the distance to the laird's chair. Eveleen cringed back when she saw Logan. She didn't want to see him, couldn't talk to him, understanding what he'd done. Even knowing if he hadn't intervened, she might be dead. All his actions had been for her. So why was she so panicked?

When he stood beside her and pulled her hand into the crook of his elbow, gentle warmth filled her. A sudden ray of sunlight illuminated her soul. She looked at him, and his smile seemed sincere and meant to encourage. This Lord Maxwell was not the man who killed so easily.

"Are you alright?" he asked, gently squeezing her hand.

"No, when I close my eyes all I see is blood and two men lying on the ground with their throats cut open. I can't stop the shaking of my body or the cold from chilling my soul as well as the horror of those few minutes before you were there." Yet the few minutes she'd spoken to Allura had indeed helped her see the situation for what it was.

"In time that will pass." Logan whispered, "For now, you need to tell these men what happened on the island. Don't leave anything out, including what I did. Whatever you do, don't lie thinking you're protecting me." They strode to the front of the room, and he motioned for her to sit next to Hunter, Allura on the other side.

Logan stood behind her, his hands resting on the back of her chair, the knuckles of his hands touching the back of her neck.

Hunter touched her hand, "Eveleen, tell these men what happened on the island."

With a slight nod of her head, she told the men and her clan everything she could remember that had been done to her and all Logan had done to shield her from further harm. "He was defending my life. They would have killed me, and him," she finished.

Allura offered the dress as proof. "Here is the dress that was torn from her body by one of the captain's men."

When she caught a glance at Allura, she saw Hunter exchange a look with her that she imagined said, *I told you the island wasn't safe.*

Allura grimaced, seeming to read her husband's thoughts. The poignant moment passed in a flash and everyone's attention turned to Hunter.

"The only crime committed here was the crime against Lady Eveleen McLellan. If your men were still alive, they'd be sentenced accordingly," Hunter said, his voice stern. "The crime's penalty is death."

"There is no real proof. The gown could have been ripped by Lord Maxwell just as easily," the captain said but his words held no truth.

"I have the testimony of both the lady involved and her rescuer. That is good enough for me. Now," Hunter paused, "I suggest you return to your ship and leave my land. Go wherever it was you were going before you stopped on McLellan land."

Hunter nodded to three of his guards, who approached the captain and his men in order to escort them from the great hall and to the small boats that would take them to their ship.

A hush fell over the room. Eveleen looked to Hunter, expecting something to be said.

Allura spoke first, "You need to tell my sister that you've approved Logan's wishes and what will happen now."

Eveleen gasped softly, fearful. "Tell me what?"

"That you will wed today," Hunter said. "I've given Lord Maxwell your hand in marriage. He has told me that time is of the essence and his return to his estate is paramount. The captain of the men who attacked you, it seems, have pirated some shipments of Bordeaux from his vineyard in France. And we know that after what happened on the island, the wedding must happen in the next few days."

Logan placed his hands on her shoulders as if to reassure but she scooted forward, not wanting to feel his touch. "No," she turned to look at him, stunned by the tension radiating from his eyes, the taut line of his jaw. His demanding expression sent spirals of fear ripping through her. "I don't want to marry you or anyone."

"Yes," Logan said calmly. "You will be mine tonight. I will protect you with my life for as long as I live. This is what is best for you, Eveleen."

"I will say no." she couldn't let this happen. She turned to Hunter, "You can't make me." He'd ignored her for so long and now he showed up and demanded a wedding on the same day she was nearly violated. He was so threatening and unforgiving. His arrogance knew no end.

"Then you will be banished from this home," Hunter told her. "I'm sure your aunt Charlotte will take you in and once more search the ton for a suitable mate. A child might have been conceived today, and Logan has told me he will claim the babe, if there is one, as his own."

"You really have no choice in this. As Hunter said, you could be carrying a child. You must protect yourself from rumors and gossip. Thank God, Logan cares for you enough to wed you," Allura said. "In time you will learn to love your new husband. Banishment is a harsh word and really has no place here. I'm sure Hunter doesn't really mean it. We are all thinking of your future as well as possible consequences."

"I can't believe you just threatened me with banishment," Eveleen rose, racing from the room, tears in her eyes.

"You should go after her," Hunter told Allura. "She needs to see reason. The wedding will begin shortly."

"I'll go," Logan said.

"No, you would do more harm than good." Allura rose, knowing where she'd find Eveleen. "Go to the church. I'll bring Eveleen."

Eveleen sat on a small bench in the garden near the church. She knew her choices were limited and understood the threat. But her sister must have known of this. She could have told her and given her time to prepare.

"I'm sorry," Allura sat next to her. "If not for the attack, I would have talked to you about Logan's wishes. As it was, there was no time for conversation."

"Why?"

"I thought you liked Logan. No, I believed you were half in love with him. When you arrived at our doorstep, well, I thought it was a lover's spat. Still do. In time you will love and forgive him just as I learned to love Hunter."

Eveleen gasped for air, her hand on her chest. "How could we have a lover's spat when I never saw the man? I came home because he didn't care about me, didn't seem to want me. Allura," she paused, "there is no way I'm with child. I'm still a virgin. Logan has not touched me."

Allura waved a hand in the air. "None of this matters. You don't remember and for now that might give your mind a chance to heal. Hunter has given you to Logan and yes, you can say no, but that would not be in your best interest."

"Neither choices are to my liking." Eveleen wiped the tears from her eyes, feeling coldness enter her heart. She understood she was trapped in a corner and there was no way to escape.

"If you remember, I didn't want to wed Hunter. He has proven to be a kind gentle lover and a wonderful father to our children. I am heartily glad father concocted the plan that brought Hunter into my life. I love him so much more than I could ever believe."

"You think this is a similar situation?" Eveleen denied the thought. Nothing similar between these two scenarios existed.

"Yes, and no. We are different people and so we will handle the marriage differently. Come, we need to meet them in the church." Allura rose, extending a hand to her.

"Tonight? It is too soon." Eveleen meant to stall for time. "Why can't we wait until tomorrow or the next day?"

"Logan must leave in the morning. So, the wedding must take place immediately. Come now, put a smile on your beautiful face."

She swallowed hard, shaking her head. "Why is it only Logan's interests everyone heeds?"

"This is more about what's best for you, Eveleen, not Logan. The haste is for him though. We mustn't waste time. If you are going to marry Logan, then lift your chin and straighten your back. Walk to the church and to the man who will be your husband with pride."

For a minute, she closed her eyes, fighting the tears and the terror wrapping around her soul. When she rose, she looked ahead, knowing she could never look back. "I will do what is necessary."

As if the organist knew exactly the moment she would arrive, music filled the tiny church. Logan stood at the altar, Hunter next to him.

The laird stepped beside her and offered his arm. He patted her hand and looked at her with love in his eyes. "Logan will make you a fine husband. He's an honest and brave man."

But he will never love me. Eveleen inhaled a long deep breath before starting down the aisle, Allura in front of her.

~ * ~

Franco, the captain of the men who died on the tiny island near the McLellan castle stood at the stern of the ship, watching the island slowly vanish from sight. Wind filled the sails as the vessel picked up speed. The day had not gone at all as he planned. Things were done he didn't condone, but when one had little money sometimes men with few scruples were hired. His retribution was for Maxwell not some young woman.

"Enjoy your moment of respite, Logan Maxwell. You have much to account for and I will find a way to make you pay. The land is mine, passed down more generations than I can count." All the wrongs Maxwell heaped upon his family simmered in the back of his mind.

Franco had hoped to ambush Maxwell and kill him. He learned about his trip to the McLellan castle through an informant posted in London. Neither his men nor he had any idea Eveleen or Logan were on the island, meaning to use the island as a vantage point and easy access to the land.

The intrusion of the couple had cost him two men. Although under the circumstances he was glad the girl was rescued. Sometimes his men had no morals or values and while he usually let them do what they wanted, this time he would have reprimanded them. He would not have tried them as rapists. The girl couldn't remember what had happened.

The bodies were eventually recovered and they would receive burial at sea with full honors. He needed to return to France and regroup, unsure at the moment exactly how he would get his revenge. The vineyard in Bordeaux would be his starting point.

Lord Maxwell had turned over damning information about his actions to the new French government. Where the government before the revolution was concerned, he barely escaped with his head. Because of this, he lost his ancestral land, his fortune, as well as his title.

Then to add insult to his discomfort, Maxwell bought his land from the government, Maxwell's newly acquired vineyard, at half its value. The loss devastated his financial situation as well as his pride. His knuckles fisted around the railing of the ship as it plowed through the ocean, spray hitting his face, reminding him of his misfortunes at Lord Maxwell's hand.

"Can I get you anything, a meal, whiskey?" His new first mate, Tate Talbot, asked after approaching him.

"Dinner and the best Bordeaux on the ship. I'll return to my cabin in a few minutes. Then we need to talk." A few more minutes on deck, watching the swells in the ocean and feeling the wind on his face would help him sort out his thoughts.

"Dinner for two?" he queried.

"For two," Franco said, once again turning his attention to the waves, thinking of his destination, Bordeaux and the business he meant to transpire while there. If he had time, he'd visit his sister and her son.

Waves and wind battled the ship. This would not be an easy crossing. His mind warred with his body. More thoughts of vengeance filled his head.

"Dinner is ready." Talbot said. suddenly appearing by his side.

"The only solution is to kill Lord Maxwell or take what is dear to him."

Chapter Two

The meal after the wedding told Logan this marriage would not be what he planned or hoped for. Eveleen rejected the slightest touch, the smallest attempt to ease her way to the marriage bed. Conversation was nonexistent. Telling her they would leave in the morning would not sit well.

The Duchess told him to court Eveleen. He would have just as much success courting a wild bear. She shrugged his hand away each time he sought to touch her. Bedding his lady tonight and consummating the marriage would take a miracle. At this point, he decided he wasn't going to try.

"More wine," he asked but didn't wait for an answer before filling her goblet, realizing after the fact another glass might not be prudent.

"Thank you," she told him in a prim voice. Silence and time passed slowly while she met his gaze, hatred spilling from their depth.

Once conversation between them had flowed easily. Many times, they laughed and chatted about everything that came to mind. Talking of their various pasts had helped him learn more about her. Even though she was quiet and a little shy, she had a rebellious streak.

"I wish this afternoon had never happened," he told her, knowing how she felt about violence and trying to understand the real terror she must have felt. After what she'd been through no wonder she held back, keeping herself aloof and distancing herself from him. Seeing him kill two men terrified her. He didn't really believe that was the crux of her fears, thinking at least one of the men had hurt her terribly.

"I wish this wedding had never happened," she told him, downing the wine and handing him the glass asking for more. "It's very good. Is it from your vineyard?"

He obliged, not really caring any longer if she drank too much. Drinking more might not be sensible. He understood the evening would be chaste. "Yes, the Bordeaux comes from my vineyard. Perhaps someday you'd like to see it."

She smiled at him, slowly leaning forward and whispering for him only, "When pigs fly."

"I deserve that and probably more." Once he thought they'd get along as man and wife very well. Now he wondered if he just made the biggest mistake of his life, marrying her without her permission. She'd said 'I do' but she was given few choices.

"Of course you deserve that." She turned away and laughed at something Allura said, sipping the newly poured glass of wine before playing with the food on her plate.

"Do you think you've had too much to drink?" Allura asked, gently touching her arm. "You will need to rise early in order to leave with your new husband. You don't want to be sick."

"No, the wine is very good. Logan made it, my husband." She began to slur her words. "I'm not rising early nor am I leaving with him, so it really doesn't matter how much I drink."

Allura shot him a heated glance, "Do something, please."

Shrugging his shoulders, he gave Allura a shake of his head. He would stop her if he thought he had one chance in hell of making love to his new wife tonight, but he didn't. Having someone who was dead drunk in his bed would not tempt him to take something that wasn't wanted or reciprocated. Now he meant to have no more surprises between them.

"Eveleen..." he began, unsure how to tell her what was going to happen early tomorrow morning.

"Yes." She turned to him, a grim expression on her face, her fingernails tapping on the table.

"We should retire soon. I plan on leaving early, before the break of dawn, in the morning." The reaction was not what he expected, but he should have anticipated her words.

"Allura already told me. Have fun, husband. I won't be going with you." She poured more wine, slanting him a look, "Don't you dare make me."

"Of course you are," Allura said, taking the glass from her sister. "Go upstairs with your husband."

"We can stay here until Eveleen finishes the goblet. I can wait." He poured another glass for himself, watching the woman he just married and wishing his wedding night had at least a tiny bit of potential. She was beautiful and fragile, probably not meant for him. He sported a dangerous and sometimes sinister past she would never accept or understand.

"Thank you, Lord Maxwell." She sipped the drink as if she meant to make it last the entire night and into the morning.

He wanted to be polite but was finding politeness at this hour and in this situation did not come easily, "You're welcome," he said, yet the time ticked by and the early start seemed to grow farther from his reach.

What did the hour matter? Sleep for him would be elusive if he slept at all. They would leave in less than six hours. Perhaps she would fare better if she did not fall asleep only to wake with a blinding headache. She could sleep in the carriage.

Eveleen turned away from him, speaking with one of his men. His fists clenched. Jealousy had never provoked him before. Now to watch his wife smile and flirt with a man other than himself sent his possessive instincts to a boiling point.

Leaning close to his wife and trying to draw her attention from the other man, he asked, "Have you ever been hung over? It's not something you would like; the headaches, the dry throat."

"Hung over?" she asked a strange expression on her lovely flushed face. "Why do you ask?"

"I see that you haven't."

"I don't know what you are talking about," she insisted.

"You should listen to your sister and stop drinking before you regret it," he whispered.

"Are you telling me to stop?" Defiantly she poured more wine into her goblet and shot him a challenging glance.

Sighing deeply, he decided this was up to her. He sat back, watching her and crossing his arms over his chest, "As long as your actions do not put you in danger, I will never tell you what to do."

"Good," she told him. sipping more wine with a tiny grimace.

If his laughter would not have resulted in more alcohol consumption, he would have let out a roar. That single look told him she drank to spite him, and he was glad she was no longer indifferent. He'd rather have her yelling and fighting him than complacent.

"You will regret this drinking when I wake you and you have to ride in a bumpy uncomfortable carriage." Unable to resist the beautiful flush, he touched her cheek. Relieved she didn't jerk away, he continued his exploration, running his finger slowly down the column of her neck. Perhaps wine had its benefits.

"So you say." She finished the wine and stood, wavering. Her hands hit the table as she tried to steady herself.

Logan grasped her around the waist, keeping her from sliding to the floor. Deciding he wasn't going to let her walk to the solar and risk a fall, he swept her into his arms. "Good night, everyone. We will most likely be on the road before any of you wake."

Eveleen's head rested sweetly on his shoulder and her hand on his arm. He meant to savor this moment until the next one. The next one might be days away. Likely in the next several days, he would be on the wrong end of her anger and disdain.

Good wishes and cheers followed their exit from the great hall. When they reached Eveleen's chambers, he set her on the bed. She was groggy, muzzled and beautifully enticing. His body ached for her, wishing she was a willing participant.

This was his wedding night, but the marriage would not be consummated. Yet he wasn't going to call her maid. Taking care of his wife was his duty. Now she spread herself on the bed, arms outstretched, inviting him to sample what was his.

Raking his hands through his hair, he pulled her to a sitting position. Always adept at disrobing ladies, he could do this quite easily. In six hours, though, she would have to be awake enough to dress herself. He was sure she wouldn't allow his fumbling fingers to do the job.

"I'm going to take your dress and underclothes off unless you can do it yourself," he told her, waiting for a response.

"Just want to sleep." She closed her eyes, leaning into him, her breasts pushing against his chest. Good lord, she could entice him with every little movement.

"Very well." He wondered if he could disrobe her with his eyes closed.

Within a few minutes, he had stripped her to her shift and pulled the covers down. Lifting her, he set her on the sheets and pulled the blankets over her.

"Sweet dreams, Evie." He kissed her on the forehead. "You most likely will be a little prickly pear come dawn."

Entering the great hall once more, he met with his men. Eveleen's trunk was loaded on one of the carriages. Allura handed Logan a small bag she had packed with enough clothes for three days.

"Take care of my sister and be gentle. We don't really know what happened to her on the island. I believe she's been through hell. In time she will come to love you. I'm sure of it."

"Thank you, but I have my doubts. The Duchess told me I should court her first, but she won't let me hold her hand and Drake told me to take her to the hunting lodge, but I won't force her to do something she doesn't want to do."

"That is good, use patience."

"Patience is not my strong suit," he mumbled between clenched teeth.

With all the details taken care of and one hour left before departure, Logan opened the door to Eveleen's chamber. Fast asleep, her silken hair spread around her, she appeared so beautiful and at peace.

Sitting on the bed, he pulled off his boots and lay down with his hands behind his head. He didn't dare close his eyes. If he fell asleep, they would never leave by dawn.

Instead he listened to the eerie silence of the castle walls, wishing that somehow this evening could be done over. Eveleen was a woman who deserved the best, but yesterday he showed her the one side of himself he'd meant to keep hidden from her forever.

He rose, knowing the hour to leave was near. Looking out the window, he saw the carriages waited for them. Their trunks were in one as was the small bag of clothes Allura packed for Eveleen. Quickly, he washed and donned fresh clothing.

Sitting on the bed next to his wife, he understood how difficult this would be. This was her home and now, she would have to make his home hers. They wouldn't even be living in London.

"Eveleen, sweetheart," he touched her shoulder, trying to gently rouse her from deep sleep.

She groaned softly, turning over trying to distance herself from him. Pulling the covers higher, she snuggled into the warmth they offered.

"Eveleen," he said again, tracing the delicate line of her jaw, "it's time to wake up." He ran his fingertip across her eyebrows then down her nose. He brushed a gentle kiss on her lips, wishing for so much more.

"No," she said, her voice sleepy. "Can't be, it's still dark." Eveleen scrunched the pillow, drawing it close to her body.

"We need to leave now." He resorted to pulling the covers from her. She would be cold and angry when she realized he wasn't about to let her sleep, at least not in her bed.

"I'm not..." suddenly she rushed to the chamber pot, losing the contents of her stomach. She wiped her mouth with the back of her hand then soaked a rag in the water he left. The cold wet rag aga inst her forehead, she sat on the floor, staring angrily at him.

His heart went out to, her but he could not give in. "Your clothes are here," he set them on the bed. "Dress and I'll meet you in the court yard. If you're not down in ten minutes, I'll come back for you."

Logan walked from the room, ready to be on his way and hoping she would not go back to bed. He met her maid on his way down the steps. "Would you check on Eveleen and make sure she gets dressed?"

"Yes, Milord."

In the bailey, he examined the carriages and spoke to the drivers, patiently checking his pocket watch while he waited for his wife.

"I had to wake her, Milord," the maid appeared in front of him, "But I believe she might have gone back to bed again."

A few minutes ago he felt sorry for her, but now his tolerance ended. Taking the stairs two at a time to her solar, he threw open the door. The boom when the wood hit the other wall must have startled her. She sat up in bed, her hair in a silken fall around her shoulders and down her back.

"What are you doing here?" she asked, pushing hair from her face. "I told you I wasn't going anywhere with you."

"Collecting my wife." Gathering the garments that had been set out for her to wear in one arm then striding toward her, he scooped her into his arms. "We are going home."

"Put me down. I am home." She pounded on his chest.

"If I thought you would obediently follow me to the waiting carriages, I would set you on your pretty little feet and let you dress yourself," he told her in the nicest tone he could commandeer.

"How dare you when my head is pounding and my stomach is rolling. Let me go back to bed."

"You chose to drink the wine," he pointed out. "And now you're paying the price."

"Let me get dressed."

"Here in the great hall?" He wanted to challenge her, make her understand she used up all her choices last night and this morning.

"Well, no," she murmured softly. "Take me back to my room."

A roar of laughter boomed, unwilling to show her the fury simmering within. "You can change in the carriage whenever the whim hits you." He set her inside and handed her the clothing he gathered earlier. The driver closed the door.

"Where are you going?" she leaned out the window.

"I'm riding my horse."

Relief swept through him. His wife rode in the carriage in front of him and fresh air filled his lungs. She could sleep, get dressed, eat, anything she wanted. He'd left a basket of food on one of the seats.

With any luck, they'd be home in three days and they could settle into marriage life.

With any luck...

~ * ~

Riding through the village near his country estate five days after leaving the McLellan castle, he remembered his thoughts. Neither luck nor weather had their best interests at heart.

Rain had sluiced from the skies one day into the journey, and it still poured in a never-ending stream. Five long nights he spent on the floor of the inns while she slept in the bed. His back ached and his leg where the bullet had slashed through him last year throbbed.

Blaming himself each night he fought the urge to take what was his. He was sure he could seduce her into his loving arms. She didn't want him and the moment to court her properly had never presented itself. Riding behind the carriage was his only solace. Now he was home and his intentions were good. He would find a way to convince her she wanted him.

They rode past the gatekeeper's cottage and the old barn. Sheep grazed in the pastures and winter crops grew in the fields. The piece de resistance was the greenhouse where he grew his prize possessions orchids and some roses as well as other flowers. When he learned lilies were her favorite flower, he planted a bed of different types.

"We're here," A moment of nostalgia swept through him then he leaned over the side of his horse and peeked into the window.

Her face pale and her eyes red from what he could only assume was crying, she said, "Good."

Opening the door of the vehicle, he swept her into his arms and carried her up the steps to the porch before setting her on her feet. "This is your home now," he gestured with a hand. "As soon as the rain stops, I'll show you around." He looked on his property with pride, knowing all he did to make this land productive.

"Thank you."

They walked inside and were greeted by a woman and a man. "This is Maida. She is the cook and lives in the gatekeeper's cottage. And this is my butler, Mr. Botch."

A little boy ran from an adjoining room. Logan gave him a huge hug. "This is Harry, Maida's son and mine."

"Nice to meet you Harry and of course Maida and Mr. Botch," she said graciously, trying to process what he just said about Harry. "Maida and Mr. Botch," she mumbled as if trying to remember.

"Just call me Botch," he told her, his voice gruff.

"Botch it is then," she smiled politely, acknowledging all the people he considered family.

"If you need or want a ladies' maid or other servants, feel free to interview anyone from the village who suits you. Maida usually does the cleaning but only in this wing. The furniture in the other wing is covered and needs nothing. You can redecorate if you like. I'm sure Maida will send you to the proprietors who can help."

"I'm sure a ladies' maid will be enough. Now, can you show me to my room? I'm exhausted and would like to freshen up."

"Botch, Maida, Lady Eveleen would like a bath and I would too. Can you arrange for hot water to be brought to the master chamber?"

"Of course, Milord," they said in unison.

His men brought the trunks into the house and into the master chamber. Logan offered Eveleen his arm.

She looked at him with a skeptical expression. After glancing at Maida and Botch, she accepted with a nod and a, "Thank you."

"This is my room. The adjoining one is for you, but I'd like to share this room and bed with you." He waited for the answer knowing she'd choose the adjoining room. Hell, he would too, in her situation.

She caught her lower lip between her teeth, staring at the floor before she looked up. "As long as I have a choice, I'll take a separate bed from yours."

"Suit yourself," his curt voice surprised him. He'd known the answer before she spoke. "Be advised, I don't plan on spending the rest of our married life in this manner. I've never been celibate."

"I don't know what you expect of me. You ripped me from my family after ignoring me for months. Within me, I hold no kind feelings for you."

"I am your family now," he gritted out, understanding this was getting worse by the second.

He stepped toward her. "We suit each other, you and I." Running a finger along the column of her neck, he was delighted by the little shiver he felt beneath his touch. At her pulse point, he felt the increasing speed of her heartbeat. *Small steps, take them one at a time and she will be mine.*

Maida entered, with several of his men hauling water for the bath. Inviting steam rose from the tub, which was in his chamber.

He sat at a small desk he kept in his bedroom for convenience. Botch entered with a tray of cheese and bread then left. Logan pulled a flask of brandy from a desk drawer and poured a glass.

"Hungry?" he asked.

"Are you going to leave? I need my privacy." One small foot tapped a rapid cadence on the floor.

He was reminded of The Duchess and her always-tapping cane. "It's my room." He shrugged his shoulders but wondered why he was obnoxious. "I shouldn't have to leave."

"It's my bath," she said, challenging him. "And you purposely had the tub put in your room."

"You're my wife." He said simply, wondering how this would proceed. "I've every right to be here."

She turned her back on him, her hand on her heart.

~ * ~

Beneath her ribs, Eveleen's heart thundered. With her eyes closed, she tried to unbutton her bodice, but her hands fumbled each button. She would not do this, not in front of him. She whirled, her fury raging.

"I'm sorry Eveleen. I will give you your privacy. Someday perhaps we will have a normal marriage. Ten minutes," he finished, his gaze lingering on her a dark expression clouding his features.

With his brandy in one hand and the bottle tucked under his arm, he exited, the door closing it softly behind him.

She could almost breathe again. Ten minutes, she had ten minutes. She tried to inhale a long breath of air. Even though he'd left, she could barely breathe. Finally, the buttons undone she slipped from the dress and the rest of her clothing. Thankfully, she'd not worn a corset or she would have had to ask him for help.

Testing the water with a toe, she found the liquid the perfect temperature. She slipped into the tub and let her head fall on the rim then quickly reminded herself she had little time to bathe.

Ducking under the water, she soaped her hair and scrubbed before using the extra bucket to rinse. With her heart in her throat expecting the door to open at any minute, she finished washing. Just as she wrapped the bath sheet around her dripping body, he entered.

"Good, you finished," he said with a crooked grin. Maida entered behind him with another hot bucket of water. "Thank you, Maida." He downed the brandy left in his glass.

"You're welcome," she said a smile on her face but a puzzled expression when she glanced at Eveleen who had frozen to the spot she stood on, not knowing what to do.

"Evie, your trunk is in the adjoining room if you want to dress." He pulled his shirt from his waistband, slowly unbuttoning it and seemed to wait for her to say something or perhaps to leave. "While I don't care if you see me naked, I don't want to intimidate you. So, choose now. Your room or this one."

"My room," she rasped from a parched throat. Still dripping wet, she fled quickly, shutting the door behind her. She leaned against the wood, closing her eyes and slowly inhaling long deep breaths of air. This was not going well, but what had she expected. She was a married woman denying her husband his rights.

Maida knocked on her door before opening it. She stepped inside, smiling. "Thought you might want some help. I laid out a couple of choices but if you don't like any of them, you can rummage through the trunk. I will have your clothes unpacked after dinner."

"Thank you and I would appreciate some help. I would like to look nice for my husband," she said, realizing she meant what she said.

She chose a dress made of white crepe spotted with white satin. The skirt was finished at the bottom by a wreath of lilies and leaves composed of green and white silk. The sleeves were short and full while the bodice was cut low, letting the curve of her breasts show slightly.

Maida tightened the corset and buttoned the dress. She needed help with it, and she wondered how she would get the garment off when she wanted to go to bed. She didn't dare ask Logan.

"I can help you tonight, if you'd like me to stay." Maida seemed to hold her breath while waiting for an answer.

"No, that won't be necessary. You have your son and I'm sure I can figure this out." Eveleen laughed softly, knowing her fingers would never be able to find all the fasteners and undo them nor could she unlace her corset.

"If you're a contortionist, you could do it. Perhaps you could ask Logan. I'm sure he would love to help you out of your clothing," Maida said, smiling once more.

"Yes, you're right, he would." It was the other things he'd want afterwards that had her hesitating. She wasn't ready for that, wishing Allura or even The Duchess had spoken to her about the marriage bed. She thought he would have courted her, and perhaps as Drake had done with Ella, proceeded slowly.

"When you are dressed, you can meet him in the parlor. I will have hot tea and honey waiting for you."

"I'd rather have wine," she said to Maida's retreating back. "If that would be possible," she murmured.

Maida turned at her comment, "Of course it's possible. Wine it is." Maida laughed.

Eveleen sat at the dressing table, brushing her hair. She drew the strands upward into a simple style. "I suppose that's good enough." Before she rose, she opened her toilet chest.

She dusted pearl powder on her face and applied a lightly colored lip balm and a bit of eye paint.

Logan waited in the parlor when she walked into the room. He rose and extending a hand, led her to a chair. "Maida told me you'd like wine. I'm pleased. This is one of my favorite red wines from my vineyard." He paused, staring at her, "You look beautiful."

"Thank you," Eveleen sat in a chair next to his. And, "Thank you for giving me privacy for my bath. I appreciated the gesture." Tonight, Logan appeared dashing in his dark pantaloons and jacket. His white shirt and neck cloth were impeccable. The sight of him near stole her breath.

Ignoring her statements, he said, "We have cheese and slices of bread for an appetizer before dinner. Maida has outdone herself tonight in celebration of my return with my beautiful wife. I hope you will enjoy the meal."

"I am hungry. When was the last time we ate? Oh, I believe it was breakfast. Hmmm... I remember another breakfast our first day out." She didn't understand why she brought that first morning to his attention. That day was one she'd rather forget.

"You were too sick to eat in the morning. How long..." she didn't comprehend what he spoke of.

"How long?"

"When did your headache go away and your stomach stop rolling?" he asked with a tight laugh. It seemed to Eveleen, Logan didn't want to remember either.

"The next day. Let's speak of things more important." Changing the subject seemed imperative, but she didn't have a single notion of what a good topic might be.

"So, what would that entail, a different subject?" he queried, leaning toward to pick up her hand and lazily draw circles on her palm.

"What do you expect me to do here, in your house?" She wanted to know her duties as well as his expectations. His touch sent a subtle w arm heat spreading within.

He sat up straighter, sweetly kissing the back of her hand. Reaching out he gently touched her chin and drew her to meet his gaze. "Our house," he corrected. "I want your approval to court you. It seems I have put the marriage ahead of romancing you. I want our life together to be normal."

"I don't know what to say." He wanted to romance her, court her? It was what she'd wanted for so very long, but now she wasn't sure if she could reciprocate the feelings. Lost memories from the island blindsided her with pain.

"Yes, would be nice."

"Then yes," Her pulse raced and heat flooded her face. She put her hands on her cheeks, hoping to cool them. They were no longer on the island. Things would be different. She should forget that awful d ay.

He smiled as if he read her mind, as if he saw the rapid beat of her heart, felt the trembling of her body. Perhaps he did.

He let his fingertip slide from her chin to a point on her neck where her pulse beat at a frantic pace. "Maybe we will succeed in putting this marriage on a proper track. Would you like that, Eveleen?"

"You just want me in your bed," she countered, not understanding why she was so perverse when he made reconciliatory gestures.

"I do want you in my bed, but that isn't all I want from this joining. There is so much more to a marriage; companionship, friendship, a person to tell my most private thoughts to."

"What would that be?" She was curious about Logan. They'd had few conversations and while she was attracted to him, she knew litt le about him, save he could kill two men without pausing to think, wipe his blade on the ground before sheathing it for the next time.

"Trust and honesty top the list then commitment and loyalty. " He lengthened the list.

"I don't think we have a problem here. I trust you and I'm always honest. I've never lied to you. Can you say the same?"

He paused a moment, seeming to think. "Trust is elusive and has to be earned. I've never trusted or had to trust a woman. I've never lied to you, but there has obviously been a great deal I haven't told you."

"You brought it up. Is trust and honesty one sided?" she asked, not imagining that fact, yet he didn't have to believe or do anything he didn't want to do. He was a man and could proceed in whatever manner he deemed appropriate. She was his wife and was expected to obey.

"Children are important to me." It seemed he needed to change the subject at hand.

"You have a son already. Harry?" She pointed out.

"I love him but he's not legitimate, and while I will always make sure he and his mother are taken care of, I'd like an heir, a legitimate one."

"You want me in your bed then, to beget heirs. No. " The heat that had surfaced earlier turned frigid. She swallowed hard, withdrawing her hand from his. "I won't let you keep me with child until you have an heir."

"Yes, and no. I want you in my bed to give and receive pleasure as well as the miracle of having a child with you. I will not keep you pregnant at the risk of your life." His eyes darkened, and for a moment his lashes closed.

Her fists clenching at her sides, "You remember Fayth, right?" She heard what he said, but he was a man and he needed an heir.

"Of course I remember Fayth. But I only saw her a few times before she ran off with Jarret Kingsley." He appeared confused as to the direction of the conversation.

"Her father wanted an heir so much he kept Fayth's mother pregnant until she finally died in childbirth," she said vehemently, wishing for a change of subject yet understanding she brought it up.

"I would never do that. Putting a woman in jeopardy because of the need for a son is not something I would do." He said indignantly.

"Then you'd be happy with just girls?" she queried softly in need of an honest answer.

"If they are all like you, yes, I would. Heaven help me if they are more like your little sister, Aidan."

Eveleen couldn't help herself, she laughed. "One can never pick and choose personalities." The easy banter between them had, as well as his dashing looks, attracted her to Logan along with his haunting steel-blue eyes that seemed to ask questions about everything he saw.

"What else should I do? How do I keep busy around here? Sitting idle and eating bonbons is not for me."

"Anything you like. I give you free hand at decorating this home. I'm afraid since my mother passed the house has been neglected. You can hire anyone you need to help."

"In the village? I really don't know where to start." She had never been in charge of a home. "It's a big responsibility."

"Maida will help you get started," he said.

"I really don't..." she stopped when Maida appeared.

"Dinner is on the table. May I leave? Botch told me he'd take care of the dishes that are left after you eat. I'd like to see my son this evening." Maida stood in front of Logan, hands clamped tightly in front of her.

"Of course, give Harry a big kiss and a hug for me. Tell him I love him." He rose, extending a hand to her.

In good faith, she accepted the proffered hand, a strange expression on her face before turning to leave.

"Do you know what we are having for dinner?"

"I believe Maida told me there is fresh trout, scalloped potatoes, acorn squash, watercress and perhaps she said beets. She wanted to fix everything in the vegetable garden."

"We won't eat half of it then," she laughed but stilled when Logan once again placed her hand in his while his thumb moved lazily and enticingly on her palm. A shiver snaked up her spine and when she glanced at him, his steel-blue eyes sparkled with unspoken delight.

They stopped at the door to the dining room. Turning her so he held her in his arms, he brushed a soft kiss on her lips then moving away, he watched her closely. She moistened her lips with her tongue before he kissed her again with gentle undemanding pressure, but it was exciting and more of a kiss than he'd ever given her before.

When he pulled her chair out, she was thankful. Her knees trembled so hard she didn't think she could stand longer. Heat rushed through her.

Again, he appeared pleased with himself. Instead of sitting across from her, he moved the plates and silverware to a place next to her. Then he waited on her, dishing up her plate with portions of everything on the table. He poured the wine into beautiful crystal glasses. He sat next to her, his leg resting against hers.

"You can drink as much as you'd like tonight." He grinned, his smile reaching her heart.

She wasn't sure how to reply, remembering the horrid day after. "I think I learned my lesson. You said this was from your vineyard?"

"I'm glad and yes. It's different from the wines we had at our wedding. Do you like it?" He smiled and sipped the red wine, seeming to study her over the rim of the glass.

She followed suit, sipping then setting the glass on the table. "I do. It's very good," she murmured softly, nervously fiddling with the silverware before daring to look at him again.

"Good. I would like to take you there, to my vineyard, to France. Would you like to see what I love?"

"You love the vineyards and your son?" But you don't believe in love or at least loving a woman? She wanted to ask.

"Not just the vineyards but growing things, watching plants grow and produce fruit. My orchids in the greenhouse," he paused as if in thought then animated he said, "I want to show them to you. I've been grafting them trying to grow different colors."

Logan was usually an extremely calm man, one not given to venting his emotions. Speaking about his vineyard and the greenhouse his demeanor changed to passion. "Yes, and perhaps you'd let me paint the orchids and if we go to Bordeaux, your grapes."

"As soon as the rain lets up, I'll show you around the estate and especially the conservatory. You can paint anything you like."

"Could we go there tonight?" Her curiosity had risen. Despite the fact she tried to hold herself aloof from Logan's charm, she was falling under his spell. Looking into his eyes seemed to mesmerize and keep her from forming coherent thoughts. "We could wear raincoats. Is it cold inside?"

Her enthusiasm seemed to please him, his smile lighting his eyes. "Yes and no. I have people who keep the fire going inside the conservatory, but the rain and the wind..." he peered outside through the window. "It's not amenable for you. I wouldn't want you to take ill."

She downed the rest of her glass and held it to him for more. "Two glasses won't do me in and I'm not one of your delicate flowers. I rarely get sick. I'm not fragile." She spoke with defiance, angry with him for assuming she had no more endurance than one of his orchids.

"Maybe I don't want to get sick. Do you play cards?" he asked as if searching for another endeavor to keep her mind off the hothouse.

"If not the greenhouse, can we sit on the porch for a few minutes? For some reason, I want to watch the rainfall and smell fresh air. I spent so much time cooped up in the carriage, I long for simple freedoms." Many nights she would go to the turrets, a blanket wrapped around her so she could feel the rain and wind on her face.

He hesitated, staring at the door as if he wished it would disappear. "If that's what you want." Striding to a bench by the front door, he opened it and pulled out a blanket. "Come on then. I only have one blanket."

She tilted her head, slightly smiling at him, understanding his ruse. She wanted to say only one blanket in the entire household, really. Her anger at his male assumptions evaporated into silent laughter. "Thank you."

Outside, Logan wrapped the blanket around them before sitting on the swing beneath the eaves. His large body next to hers seemed to dwarf her, yet she felt his warmth and his strength. She shivered but it wasn't from the cold, it was because she was growing increasingly hot.

"Cold? Should we go in?" his hold tightened while he drew her closer, pressing his lips on her forehead.

"Not cold," she looked into his eyes, moistening her lips. "Hot."

She heard the low groan emanating from him as he tucked her head beneath his chin. "You might be right. It would be warmer in the hothouse."

"You'll show me then?" Logan was an enigma, a very dangerous man who loved to grow orchids and grapes. How could that be? What else would she discover about her husband?

"Yes, only because the rain has stopped and the wind is no longer howling around the eaves." He swept her into his arms and with long quick strides made his way to the conservatory, dodging puddles as he went.

Once inside he set her down, letting her body slide against his. Leaving the blanket at the door, he clasped her hand in his as they strolled the paths. His thumb traced patterns on the back of her hand, and she felt the intimacy to the tips of her toes.

The walkways were lit with tiny gaslights. "It's beautiful," she said, awed by the dance of lights and shadows created by the darkness. "Do you come here often at night?"

"Sometimes, just to relax and think. During the day, I can show you more of what I do in here with the orchids, but look," he pointed to earth that had been freshly turned. "I've planted Lilies there."

"Lilies?"

"For you."

His hands around her waist, he lifted her to sit on a railing, separating the path from the gardens. She wondered if this was an attempt to court her. If it was, she thought she might like what he was doing.

"Evie..." He bent toward her, his tongue tracing the shell of her ear before letting his teeth touch the tender flesh.

Warm heat swept through her and a fine trembling encased her body. "Logan?"

"Hmmm... Do you like this?" Continuing the slow seduction, he placed kisses along her chin and down her neck, his lips and tongue making their presence known, his hands resting provocatively on the tiny buttons on the back of her dress.

"I do," She clung to him, holding onto his neck with her hands. Moving closer to him as his heat traveled daringly over her skin.

"Good, I like it too." He captured her lips with his mouth, the soft moist touch singing to her.

The new pressure of his hard mouth against hers startled her. Inadvertently, she moistened her lips and immediately felt the touch of his tongue against hers. His hands exploring her back seemed to stop once more at the buttons. Enchantment swirled around her, a magic of L ogan's creation.

The soft gaslights touched her, the wonderful aromas in the greenhouse affected her, the romance of the night warmed her. His kisses drew her into sensual pleasure she never knew existed.

More buttons were undone but she barely noticed. His touch on the bare skin of her back sent blood rushing through her veins. This was like nothing she'd felt before.

"Tell me to stop, if you don't like this." With kisses he pushed one tiny sleeve of her gown down her arm then turned his attention to the other one. Seconds passed while he drew away from her, gazing at her with his steel-blue eyes sizzling with emotion and in some way daring her.

"Logan, I'm breathless..." she paused, "mindless...I can't think but I do like what you're doing."

"Then you don't want me to stop?" He kissed her and with his soft lips and hot tongue traveled his way across her bodice and with each new seduction he wove her magically and mindlessly into his arms.

She should stop him, should pull her dress up before he bared her breasts. "Is this part of courting?" she asked breathlessly. "I'm so hot and..."

He grinned lazily at her, "No, this is not courting, it's seduction, Evie's seduction." He murmured as another button leapt free.

"I thought you promised to court me."

"I did, and I will."

"Alright then."

"May I look at you, Evie?" his hands rested on her sleeves, her dress now completely undone.

She watched him, her body quivering with the pleasure he stoked. His mouth descended again, the kiss deepening while she opened for him. Lips, tongue, teeth, danced in a primitive dual. She moaned softly, small keening sounds emanating from her.

"May I look," he asked again after ending the kiss. His thumbs lazily drew tiny circles on her shoulders. He spread her legs, standing between them now, her skirts rising to show the tops of her stockings and the ribbons she tied to keep them up.

"I...I can't seem...to..." she stiffened feeling unsure as well as suddenly fearful. She closed her eyes as if to forget something in the far recesses of her mind. She was shaking her head, the enjoyment of the moment turning to fear.

"May I, Evie."

She swallowed hard, nodding a yes to him, needing him, yet wanting to tell him no. As she looked down, she saw her breast slowly emerge from the fabric of her gown. Her eyes widened as her gaze shot to meet his. Then she closed her eyes again, unable to meet his eyes. Terror raced within and she stared at him, a foggy haze filling her mind. She floated in a world where she couldn't feel, where no one could hurt her.

Logan, no, but the words were only thoughts in her head. *Logan... It's the man I love touching me. And yet...*

"So beautiful. I never imagined. Your breasts are perfection, Evie. Is the rest of you as soft and divine?"

"Logan, please."

"What is wrong, Evie?"

"Papa, what are you doing here? Did you forget I promised to...why are you undressing Lady Eveleen?"

Swearing under his breath, he drew the fabric of her bodice over her shoulders and breasts. "Harry, I did forget, and I believe you need to be a little older before I tell you why I was, uh, undressing Lady Eveleen."

A ten-year-old little boy had extinguished this moment of seduction. Inhaling deep breaths of air, she could barely breathe or think. Logan charmed her, enticed her to do his bidding, and for a short time she'd forgotten the gruesome scene and the fog-filled memories left from the island.

"I would like to know now." He said seeming determined to bedevil his father. "Why?"

Logan appeared just as determined to put the conversation off to a later time. "Go home, Harry. You can return in an hour and finish the job. I will pay you the same."

"But, I..."

Logan cut him off, "Go on, do as I say."

"Fine," Harry said begrudgingly.

"It's time to go back to the house," she tried to scoot off the railing but couldn't. His muscular thighs trapped her where she was. "Please, it's late."

"Evie, I'm sorry for that but not what we did." He placed a gentle kiss on her forehead. "It's raining again. We should wait until it stops."

"Seems fitting. We're under a dark cloud that isn't going away any time soon." She said terrified of what might have happened if Harry had not interrupted them.

With a long pent up sigh, Logan helped her from the railing and turning her, refastened her dress.

~ * ~

Franco strode to the small home just down the hill from the chateaux of the Maxwell's winery in Bordeaux. Morning sunlight burned in shining rays upon the vines growing on the land. The woman who had grown up here in a different life might have owned this vineyard instead of managing it. Now she lived in the chateau as its keeper. She was Maxwell's whore.

Her son played in the yard. Her son and Maxwell's, Franco assumed. He could kidnap the bastard boy, but that would hurt the woman more than Maxwell. His revenge was solely for Lord Logan Maxwell.

Planning had never been his forte and scheming didn't seem to work any better for him. Whenever he tried to scheme, something went awry. This time, he was determined to succeed.

Perhaps he could claim his ancestral land but again, the rulings of the court had not changed over the years. The laws would still condemn him and his heirs if he had any.

"Figured out what you're gonna do?" Tate, his friend and first mate stood by his side, waiting for an answer.

"Not yet, any ideas?" He turned to the man. Frustration and anger, two emotions he always felt when he looked at the land he coveted, French land that now belonged to an Englishmen.

"Bed her, steal land from your nemesis. Surely the French government would rather have a Frenchman owning this parcel.

"Not in this case. Neither scenario will work," Franco sighed. "I defaulted twice on payments. They were more than happy to deed the land to a man who had the coin to pay the extravagant taxes. You do know they confiscated all this land from the nobles."

"Didn't know you were a noble." The man mocked, pushing his hair from his face.

"A long time ago." Franco sighed, remembering a time where wealth and privilege was part of his life. "I can't bed her. Jule is my sister and the little boy my nephew. I don't wish them harm."

"This vineyard was owned by your family before the revolution?" The man seemed in awe. "I've been sailing with a nobleman. How did you miss a date with Madame Guillotine?" he queried, clearly curious.

"I was out of the country, delivering wine to America and was warned not to reenter the country." Those times of unrest and not knowing what had happened to his family sifted through his head. When he returned, he discovered, his parents were murdered and his sister, to save her life, hid in the cellars, starved for days on end. She survived.

"You just want to hurt Maxwell?"

"No one else," Franco said. "He has what is mine."

"Kidnap his wife then."

"No, I've a better idea." Franco smiled, knowing this would hurt Maxwell both financially and emotionally.

Chapter Three

Logan's mind and body were in a turmoil, his nerves stretched thin, and the ache he felt was tangible. At one point this evening, he thought to break through the icy barrier around Eveleen's heart. He didn't miss the fact she stiffened in his arms when he bared her breasts and he knew what caused the fear, recalling how he found her on the island. For a few brief seconds, he thought her terror had been conquered.

Harry, his dear sweet son, had inadvertently stopped that from happening. Deep in his heart though, he would have stopped the seduction. One day, the boy would understand the emotions ripping through his body.

Now to rid himself of the frustrations he created. He ran. Rain sluiced from the sky and pooled on the ground beneath his feet. Logan ran until he doubled over, his lungs grabbing air from the sky. Sweat mingled with the rain, washed into his mouth and eyes, then he ran again.

Hours as well as miles ticked by while he tried to purge the sight of Eveleen's beautiful rose tipped breasts from his mind. The sweet taste of her innocent kiss, and the soft flesh his fingers uncovered. Most of all, he needed to eradicate the knowledge she feared his touch.

Hot male blood pounded through his veins. Thoughts of confronting her again tonight and seducing her until she accepted him as her husband, until she knew he would never hurt her, filled his head.

The greenhouse loomed in front of him. Entering, he made his way to his private sanctuary located in the far end. A bag hung from the ceiling. With his boxing gloves on, he punched the bag then punched again and again as minutes ticked by and turned to hours.

"Hello, Papa, would you like me to hold the bag for you?" Harry asked. "Sorry I interrupted your evening."

Logan let his hands drop to his sides, "Of course you can hold the bag. When I'm done, you can take a few punches too. And why do you think you interrupted anything?"

"I said something to mother. I hope that was alright."

"Curious? Evie is my wife but I'm sorry you saw what you did." Inwardly, he groaned not knowing how to explain to a child what he was doing as well as his intent.

"I'm not. I like her and want you to be happy. You seemed pleased with yourself until you realized I was there."

"What did you see?" Out of the mouths of children. Maybe Harry was ready for that talk and a visit to Renee, the woman who taught him how to pleasure his partner.

He shrugged his slim shoulders, "Not much but it was the little sounds I heard. At first, I wasn't sure if she was in pain or enjoying herself but the sounds you made, I knew she pleased you. Mother said—"

He interrupted Harry. "What did your mother tell you?"

Harry looked down for a moment then at his father, "She said it was about time you made love to your wife."

"Nothing more?" His heart pounded. Well, he still hadn't made love to her.

"Was that making love," Harry asked, "I thought it was more than kisses. I've seen the cows and the sheep couple, and I'm guessing it's something like that."

"What I think, is that we need to change the subject. Why don't you tell me if you like your new teacher?" He punched the bag again, quickly realizing he wasn't going to work off his frustrations with the punching bag. When he hit it, the power pushed his son off his feet.

"Geoffrey is all right. He's a bit stiff."

"Stiff, is he? Your teacher just wants you to learn to your ability. How is your math?"

"I know my numbers, can do everything he asks me to do, most of it in my head. I like to play with the numbers. Don't care about learning French even though I understand how important it is."

"My favorite subject was math also. Why don't you punch the bag?" he asked, rummaging through a few things on the table and pulling out a small pair of gloves. "Here you go."

"For me?" he jumped up and down a few times.

Logan felt love grow inside for his son and itched to see his other son, knowing he would have to tell Eveleen about him soon. The news was sure to be exposed when he least expected it. Secrets had a way of doing just that.

"I had them made especially for you last time I was in London. A man's got to stay strong and capable. You should always be able to protect yourself and your loved ones." His thoughts traveled backwards to the island and the two men he killed. If he had it to do over, there was nothing he could have changed.

The boy spent an hour hitting the bag with Logan giving his son tips. "I'm tired," Harry finally said and, "I've got to put more wood on the fire."

"I'll help then I'll walk you home."

Together they stoked the fire, "Looks like it will last a couple of hours." Harry dusted his hands together, appearing pleased with himself. "Can I wash off? I'm sweaty from the boxing."

Logan laughed. "Yes, I've need of a cold bath too." He retrieved two bath sheets from a storage area.

Stripping, they strode over the floodwall and down the steps into the running water. He had the conservatory built over the creek running through his property for easy access. After it was here, he realized the other uses for the cold water. Tonight, he needed the frigid creek to ease his sexual fantasy and cool his ardor.

"Yikes, it's freezing." Harry yelled, prancing up and down trying not to emerge himself.

"Duck your head under and wash off with the soap." Logan tossed him a bar, which Harry caught. As soon as he finished, he rinsed and raced from the chilly water.

Logan chortled, grabbing the soap from his son as he passed by and did the same. Now with Eveleen at his home, he might have to visit the creek every day. Sometimes all it took for his body to harden with need was a gentle smile from his wife. Thinking about her and letting his imagination run off track often had the same effect.

He dried then dressed. Harry waited for him at the door. The rain had stopped and some of the clouds drifted away. A full moon hovered between clouds. The chill in the night air was palpable. Watching the night sky, he savored the moments as he walked with his son.

"Here we are," they stopped in front of Harry's house. "Give me a hug and I'll see you tomorrow."

"You can come in. Mama's still awake. See, the light's on."

The door opened and Maida stepped onto the porch. "I always wait up for him." She smiled, "And of course you're always welcome here. Would you like a drink?"

He was indeed tempted by her proposition and he knew the night could be capped off with more than just a drink if that was what he wanted. Maida had never told him no, and he doubted if she would if he asked even though he was married.

"Well, I'm not in a hurry to get home tonight. Guess I'll take you up on the drink," he said. Suddenly, a wave of guilt tore through him but it wasn't enough to stop him.

"Whiskey or brandy?" she asked, wiping her hands on the dishtowel she held before turning into the room.

"Whiskey," he said stepping into her warm house. The gatekeeper's cottage had been her parent's before her. They'd passed from a fever several years ago.

He watched as she left the room, her hips swaying provocatively. Bloody hell she called to him and she'd always tempted him. He remembered that first time in the woods when he changed her life as well as his forever.

Maida was fourteen and he was sixteen. His father had sent him to a suitable widow, Renee, to teach him about lovemaking or sex as the lady called it. After that, one day when he met her in the forest then made love, Maida had become pregnant. That was ten years ago.

"Here, I brought cookies too, you're favorite." She poured whiskey into two glasses. "I'd think you'd be eager to get home to your wife." She said with a tilt to her head and a smile that told him she wouldn't tell him no if he wanted her.

"Eveleen is exhausted from the travel. She is, delicate," he said wondering why he kept insisting she was too fragile for him. If truth be told, he was sure she was anything but.

"For lovemaking?" she asked, her words sounding incredulous. "You deny yourself for no reason, but that's just my opinion."

"I always thought so but now, well, it doesn't matter. She watched me kill two men," he said, remembering the blood spattered over her and her ripped bodice, the scene horrific. He still didn't know for sure what the men had done to her. When he finally had the situation under control, her eyes were clouded over and she said she couldn't remember.

"You're trying to tell me you kept the espionage aspect of your life from her? Why? Don't you think it's her right to know?" She sat down next to him, her hands in her lap and her body pressed against his.

He felt the warmth and the subtle signals. She was willing if he was. Logan sat back, stretching one arm on the back of the couch and letting his hand rest on her shoulder, he gave confirmation to her unspoken request.

"She knew but I don't think she realized the danger even though shortly after I first met her I'd been shot in the leg. The circumstances were suspicious. Both Drake and I decided to keep the reason to ourselves."

Logan downed the whiskey and felt the heat in the back of his throat then poured another glass. He didn't want to think right now. He just wanted to feel. Holding a warm woman in his arms even if she wasn't his wife might give him some relief from the frustrations eating at him.

"How can any woman, especially one who has been sheltered her entire life, realize that?" she asked turning toward him and provocatively moistening her lips.

"I could have explained," he whispered, his voice rough, touching Maida's lips with one finger. He studied her eyes then looking down saw the rapid rise and fall of her breasts. If he wanted her, he could have her right now.

One hand rested on her shoulder, her eyes sparkling with unanswered love. He never loved her, yet whenever he came to her she accepted him into her bed. Since he'd met Eveleen, he stayed away from Maida and every other woman he ever bedded.

"Yes, but that doesn't mean she would understand. Some women are attracted to dangerous men." She leaned closer, the soft rise of her breast touching his arm.

Logan drew her into his arms and slanting his mouth across hers, he was relieved when she opened for him. Her tongue met his and she tasted of mint and whiskey. Heady stuff for a man long deprived of sexual release.

He sucked her tongue into his mouth, frantic with pent up sexual emotions. She wound her fingers through his hair, pulling him closer, seeming to need to take all of her into his mouth.

Pulling away, he gazed into her eyes. It was clear to him she wanted him. If only his wife would feel the same. Maida was beautiful but not like his wife whose sapphire eyes sparkled with intensity. But his wife didn't want him. Maida did.

Maida pulled his shirt from his waistband, running her hands up his torso. Without thought, the buttons on her dress were undone by him, baring her breasts to him. The small rose tipped buds were taut and eager for his touch.

Her breaths came quickly and her tongue moistened her lips as she waited for him to take the initiative.

They came together again. He seared a trail down her throat with the damp heat of his parted lips, teasing her flesh with the tip of his tongue. He swept her collarbone and the rise of her breasts.

She had been still but now when his lips touched her nipple, she let out a tiny moan of pleasure. Her fingers now resting on the fastening of his pants teased him.

Damn her, damn his wife and damn himself, for his desire for his wife overrode his need for relief and now it seemed to burn more fiercely. Maida was a sweet woman, but Eveleen was his life; she was the heat of the sun and the rhythm of the sea.

She loathed him, would not let him touch her intimately let alone bed her. Maida was willing and warm.

He was Eveleen's husband. If he chose he could take her to his bed, rip her clothing off, have her, sink into her and forever know her loathing. But deep in the pit of his stomach he was sure that was exactly what those men on the island did to her.

He struggled with himself and his heart, believing he was losing his mind and his heart and the searing piece of anatomy that was sweeping away his senses every time he looked at his wife or when she spoke.

Then he realized he was with Maida and he was about to commit adultery simply because he didn't possess the patience to properly court his wife. *Bloody hell, stop now you fool.*

Pushing away from her, "I cannot. We cannot do this." He pulled her bodice together before kissing her on the forehead. "I'm sorry."

"I am sorry too. When you figure out how to make love to your wife..." she let her voice trail off. "Logan Maxwell, know that I will always be here for you whenever you want or need me."

He stiffened, "You should find a good man, a husband to have more sons and daughters with. I will look into it."

"I don't need a husband. I've Harry. That is quite enough," she told him, rising and buttoning her bodice.

He turned then, swearing softly as he left the temptation of Maida's home. Accepting her invitation had been a huge mistake. Bloody eyes, he almost broke his vows. This was not one of his finer moments. Guilt raced through him.

The night was dark, and a cold wind swept across the land. When he entered his house, he gazed toward his chambers. A miracle could happen and Eveleen would be in his bed naked and waiting for him.

Laughing at his imagination, he took the steps two at a time. Slowly opening his door, he saw that half of his miracle had come true. Eveleen was asleep, fully dressed on one of the chairs in the room.

He approached her and kneeling beside her, he swept her into his arms, intending to take her into her room.

"Logan?" she woke.

"What were you doing in my room?" He was enjoying her soft curves drawn close to him yet understood she wasn't ready for him.

"I couldn't get out of my gown," she said a soft blush rising to color her cheeks.

"So you came to me for help. Don't you think that was a dangerous idea?" he asked her.

"Would you want me to ask Botch?" her eyes round, her features ashen.

"No," he said, smiling crookedly.

"Then help me, please." She struggled in his arms.

This could be a second chance for him tonight. He could seduce her into his bed. After all, he'd meant to consummate their marriage earlier in the evening. But he didn't want to seduce. He needed for her to want him and come to him with no fear or memories of the island.

He set her down. "What is it you want me to do?"

"What do you think?" she asked, her impatience clearly teetering on the edge. "You've made it clear you've a certain expertise."

"If I undress you, what do you think will happen?" he challenged her, knowing he wanted her in his bed.

"I will be able to go to my bed," she told him, turning her back to him. "And you to yours. You would never hurt me."

He ran a finger down her neck then placed light kisses where he touched her. "Together? Sounds much more inviting than separate."

"No."

"You're not going to change your mind, are you?" He let out a long-exasperated sigh, toying with one button. "It looks as if you were able to unfasten a few."

"I was, but I couldn't reach the others and I would never be able to unlace my corset."

"Why did you wear something you couldn't get out of?" he asked, truly baffled.

"Because I had two choices tonight and both of them involved fastenings in the back. Besides, I wouldn't be able to unlace my corset no matter which dress I chose." She said as if she didn't understand his question.

"Don't you have something in your trunk you could wear?" Slowly, he slipped the fastenings of her dress open and let it fall to the floor.

"You didn't have to do that," she said, bending down and drawing her dress to cover her front.

"Do what?" He meant to act the innocent. A little devil inside him provoked him to push this as far as he could. The days he spent traveling with her, sleeping nearby without her in his bed, had taken their toll on him.

"Take my dress off," she said, her voice indignant.

"I thought that's what you wanted me to do."

"Just unfasten it. I could do the rest." She told him.

"So, I gave you more help than you needed? What's wrong with that?" He tilted his head slightly, taking in the view of her curves.

"Nothing. Everything."

"Well, I suppose I can go now. I need a drink." He turned to leave, understanding he wasn't finished here.

"Stop." She'd turned and now he saw what her fragile shield didn't cover.

He whistled through his teeth. "You changed your mind?"

"No."

"What then?"

"I can't unlace my corset, and at the moment I can barely breathe." She told him.

"Don't understand why women wear these torture devices. Quite enjoyed watching Ella at the hunting lodge in her breeches and shirt, no corset and no extra clothing. Could see all of her curves."

"Will you please unlace it for me then we can both go to bed."

"Together?" he persisted.

She looked as if she wanted to stomp her foot, the expression on her face almost comical. "Don't you ever give up?"

~ * ~

Weeks had passed since that first evening in Logan's home, and between them nothing had really changed. They still slept in separate bedrooms. Eveleen stood at the parlor window, holding the curtains apart and watching Logan chop wood. He'd taken his shirt off, muscles rippling with each swing of the axe. His hair was tied back by a leather thong.

Her heart thundered beneath her ribs, and her breath caught in her throat at the sight of him. She remembered the gentle touch of his hands, and the sweet heat that swept through her when he kissed her.

She felt it now while she watched him.

"Why is he chopping wood? There is more than enough for the winter stored in the shed." She looked at Maida and wondered at the strange expression on the woman's face.

"You really don't know." Maida said, pulling her away from the window.

"No. If you could tell my why, I'd appreciate the information." She stared at the woman who bore Logan a son, who knew what it was like for him to make love to her. Strangely, she wasn't jealous.

"He will be a happier and more relaxed man as soon as you let him take you to his bed," Maida said without hesitation.

She gasped, startled by Maida's blunt words. What had she said or done that would lead her to that conclusion. "How do you know?"

"It's easy to see you have no sexual experience. I can tell when you look at him and when he follows you around the room with his eyes he hasn't made love to his wife. He treats you as a delicate porcelain doll, but you are nothing like that. He wouldn't be out there chopping wood if he bedded you."

"I don't know what you mean. I can't go to his bed. There is too much standing between us, too many misunderstandings. I..." She couldn't imagine what she wanted from this marriage. Terrors she couldn't define swirled within her, ripped through her when he bared her breasts.

"What misunderstandings?" Maida stood with her hands on her hips, forcing her to sift through her mind for a plausible explanation.

Truly, the disagreements seemed a bit trivial. She watched him kill two men as if he... as if he what? Enjoyed it? Of course not, but the deed had been accomplished with such ease and expertise, as if killing was something he did every day. Then she remembered the reasons why he slaughtered them. The deed had been done because of her.

"He forced me to marry him," she blurted out, unsure of the other issues she had with him.

"You could have said no," Maida reminded her.

"Yes, I could have but I would have been disowned by my family. They would not stand by that decision." The helplessness she felt that night seared through her mind.

"Once you wanted to wed him, once before he left you without telling you where he was going. You ran away from your destiny with this man, yet he followed you to your home and rescued you. Is that right?" Maida challenged her and she wasn't sure why.

"Yes, everything you say is true. What does that have to do with anything and how do you know this?" The answer was obvious, but she didn't want to acknowledge it.

"He's a good, kind man, gentle. Are you afraid he will hurt you?" She asked probing questions she had no right to ask.

"I was, but after that night he showed me the conservatory, well, I don't think I am." She wasn't afraid of the man. She was afraid of falling in love with a man who could not return that love, and she was terrified of intimacy.

"Then why?" Maida persisted.

"Why?" Eveleen asked puzzled.

"Why didn't you let him make love to you that night?"

"It's really not your business." She wouldn't answer to this woman, a woman who bore his bastard child. Where were all these questions leading? She suddenly didn't feel friendly to this woman.

"I see. Be advised that if Logan comes to my bed, I won't turn him away."

It seemed an icy splash of water hit her across the face. Was that why he was so late returning that night? He was with Maida, in her bed? She had no one to blame but herself.

"The candles are not getting made." Eveleen strode to the kitchen where Botch had the wax melting and the candle molds collected on the table with the wicks assembled.

Maida didn't say anything more. Instead, she silently worked. The hot air brought a fine sweat to Eveleen's brow.

"Do you have scents for these?" Her tentative relationship with Maida had been put in jeopardy.

"Scents? Well, no. What do you propose?"

"Logan loves his orchids. I'll talk to him. Maybe he'll let me have some flowers for scents and decoration in the candles. I'll be right back." She left, needing to run from the woman who shared Logan's bed and who might have made love to him because she couldn't.

Eveleen had never done anything special for Logan, and he had saved her life. Perhaps this gesture could be a first step for her as she sought ways to prove herself to him.

Picking up her skirts, she tried to stay on the driest part of the path and avoided the puddles as she strode to the greenhouse. The door stood ajar. She entered, looking around.

"Logan?" she said, stepping quickly along the path he led her down that evening. She hadn't been here since.

She turned down another path. "Logan?" Hesitating and unsure which direction to take, she inhaled deeply.

"Logan?" she called out again, beginning to think he wasn't in the conservatory as she'd thought.

Then like a God rising from the sea, she watched him emerge from behind a small restraining wall and down the steps. Water drops coated his naked body. She froze, wide eyed, her hand to her throat.

"Evie?" A wide smile on his face, Logan slowly strode down the steps and picking up a bath sheet, he wrapped it around his waist.

Quickly she turned, shielding herself from the view of his body yet wishing she dared keep her gaze on him. Swallowing hard and searching for words, she felt the touch of his hand on her shoulder. He turned her.

Moistening her lips, "Logan." She breathed his name. "What are you doing? Naked?"

His fingertip drew a line down the column of her neck. "Taking a cold bath," he said.

"Why not go home and take a hot one?" she couldn't fathom why he would do something that would feel so awful.

In his arms, he turned her shrugging his broad shoulders indifferently. "Cold was what I needed."

"Why?" she repeated.

He laughed, shrugging from his towel and slipping on his buckskins. "It's just what I needed."

"You're not going to tell me, are you?" she queried watching him don his shirt.

"No."

"All right then." She meant to find out even if she had to ask Maida.

"Tell me, what brings you to my greenhouse? Slowly he fastened his shirt, his hungry gaze riveted on her.

The heat emanating from him burned her. "We are making candles." She had an urge to run her fingers through his damp hair. Moistening her lips, she stared at him, intrigued. Having never seen a naked man, she tried to remember exactly how he appeared when he stepped from the water.

"That's nice, but it doesn't answer my question." He toweled his hair, leaving it in disorder around his face.

"I," she squinted her eyebrows. "I...I can't remember."

His laughter echoed around the chamber. "You can't remember. I find that fascinating. You were making candles. Does that help?"

"Candles, yes, can I have some of your flowers?" Her mind was nearly blank. The sight of him had stolen all her senses and every coherent thought.

"What do you want them for?" He sat on the retaining wall and pulled on his boots.

"I can grind them to use their oil for scents. When the candles burn, you smell the flowers. I thought you might like that." She wished she could see him naked again.

"You can recreate the scents? I would have never thought of that."

"So," she hesitated.

"How many do you need?" he asked.

"A dozen maybe."

"Any particular color? Come here, Evie." He opened his arms for her.

"No."

Yet she stepped into his arms, her head resting on his chest. His heartbeat was steady and strong, his scent masculine and so very enticing. When she looked up, his lips descended to meet hers in a short gentle kiss.

"You don't have to make candles. We could spend the day here, alone, with all the privacy you could ask for. I would only kiss you unless you asked for more."

"I'm sure someone would interrupt us and you would have to explain why you are undressing a lady."

"Harry." He ran his fingers through damp hair.

"Your son." She reminded him.

"The flowers, please, I need to get back. Maida will be finished if I don't hurry and none of the candles will have a flower scent about them when burned."

"You're making candles with Maida. Has she said anything?"

"About what?" Once again, she was baffled by the exchanges between her husband as well as Maida.

"The other night," he said, sounding cautious.

"No, she told me though... never mind." She had already said too much, not really knowing when he would make love to her or if she would allow it.

"Told you what? You've peaked my curiosity."

"I'm sorry. I can't tell you now." She recalled their earlier conversation about truth and honesty. "She said she wouldn't refuse you, if you came to her bed." Eveleen blurted.

A finger under her chin he lifted it until she could see into his eyes. "I won't go to her bed."

He kissed her again, a brief kiss but it reassured her. "The flowers?"

Mesmerized by his kiss, Eveleen returned to the house with a basket of various flowers, including a few orchids and roses. Quickly entering the kitchen, she discovered a dozen unfinished candles.

"What are you going to do with those?" Maida asked, staring blankly at the basket.

"We are going to make an oil, a scent that I can pour into the wax. The scent will be heavenly, and Logan will love them.

An hour later they finished the candles. Eveleen placed two in the master bedroom and the rest around the house.

When she stepped into the parlor, Botch was securing a Christmas tree into its stand and little Harry stood by, giving directions.

Eveleen stepped back, smiling delightedly. "I forgot it was almost the holidays. It's beautiful. Are there any ornaments or decorations for the house?"

"They are in the boxes over there," Botch said. "Do you want me to help?" he asked, smiling and appearing to want an invitation to decorate.

"Of course, Harry, go help Botch bring the ornaments for the trees closer," Eveleen said her hands clasped beneath her chin. The scent of the tree filled the parlor, bringing back happy memories of long-ago Christmas days.

"It's almost present time," Harry clapped his hands in delight, running to do her bidding.

Eveleen opened the huge box of ornaments, "Why don't I pull them out and the two of you can hang them," Eveleen said, thoroughly enjoying the time spent here.

When they finished, all kinds of ornaments adorned the beautiful tree. There were Christmas balls, trains, angels, Santas and so much more. Garlands adorned the windows.

All three stepped back to admire the tree. "It's so beautiful," Eveleen said, her spirits higher than they'd been since leaving the McLellan castle.

"How many days until Christmas," Harry asked, excitedly jumping up and down an infectious grin on his boyish face.

"Have you been a good boy?" Botch stepped in to ask with a stern voice.

"Oh yes, just ask mama and papa."

His words resonated in the pit of her stomach, mama and papa. A strange emotion swept through her. "I'm sure you've been good."

"I found your papa's train set in the attic when I brought down the ornaments. Do you want to help me put it around the tree?" Botch asked, seeming delighted with the newfound treasure.

"Yes." Harry clapped his hands together.

"I'd like to help too." Eveleen admired Botch and his eagerness to entertain the young man. "Do you have children, Botch?" Eveleen fit two horses onto the trains so they could pull them a tramline attached to the trains.

Minutes later the track was finished and Harry was pushing the trains with its cars and the horses hooked up in front of it.

"Choo, choo..." Harry said.

"What's this?" Logan stepped into the parlor. "You all decorated for Christmas and that's my old train set."

"It is," Botch said, "I remember helping you set it up every year about this time. With Harry and now Lady Eveleen here, I thought we should put up some of the old decorations."

"Very good," Logan said with a crooked smile while his attention was focused on Eveleen who was now on all fours, playing as enthusiastically with the trains as his son. "I believe it was a grand idea."

Maida entered, seeming surprised then slanting a smile at her son. "Lunch is ready and my, you all have accomplished a great deal this morning."

"I won't be needing you for dinner, Maida. Take lunch for both you and Harry and go on home. The Lady Eveleen and I will be leaving for London within the hour."

"To London?" Eveleen's spirits rose with the news.

"Botch, will you see that a carriage is ready?"

"We're going to London? Will I be able to see Ella and The Duchess?" Eveleen asked, surprised yet pleased with the notion of seeing both her cousin and her aunt Charlotte.

"I thought you would like to go before Christmas. Is that alright? I made the arrangements yesterday but wanted to surprise you."

"Yes, but within the hour?" I don't know if I can get ready." She was suddenly breathless yet eager to be on the way.

"Pack a small bag. Anything else you might need we'll buy in London. Hurry now. I'll have Maida pack lunch for both of us and we can eat on our way. We can talk more about this later."

"I don't have a lady's maid yet." With making candles and all that happened these weeks, she forgot.

He waved his hand a crooked smile on his face, "You won't need one in London."

"I won't?" A heated shiver seeped within. She understood what he meant. He would help her undress.

"No, you won't. Now go. We're down to fifty minutes."

She whirled, her skirts flying around her and dashed up the stairs to her room. The valise she pulled out would hold a few dresses, her toiletries and undergarments.

If they were gone for more than two days, they would have to shop. She stuffed two extra dresses into the valise. Now she had an evening dress and two-day dresses, also a riding habit.

Scampering out of the work dress she wore, she slipped into a carriage dress that buttoned down the front. She couldn't manage the corset so the garment was unpleasantly snug. Yet, she discovered even though it was snug she was more comfortable without the corset and stays.

The valise was heavy, but this time she wasn't going to keep Logan waiting. She'd wanted to clap her hands together and jump with excitement just as Harry had when we finished with the Christmas decorations.

"I'm ready." she called from the top of the steps. Oh my, " she said as the valise made its way bumping down the stairs and landing on the floor with an audible bang.

"You could have asked for help," Logan said, laughing at her as she rushed down the steps.

"Didn't want to keep you waiting." Surprisingly to her she felt more herself.

Outside he helped her into the waiting vehicle before closing the door. "If you need anything..." he began.

"What are you doing?" The wave of excitement encompassing her vanished.

"I planned to ride," he said simply as if she should have expected that.

"No," she hesitated then "I'll ride too. The fresh air will be nice. I don't want to be cramped inside the carriage all by myself."

"We don't have time for you to change your clothes."

"I can ride in this," she told him, knowing how difficult it would be just to mount the horse.

He smiled, "You don't have to prove anything. Relax and enjoy the carriage ride and have your lunch. I'll be right outside if you need anything."

She climbed from the vehicle, determined to make this work. "Do you have a horse for me?"

There were several. She was sure Logan had planned on interchanging during the ride.

"Bring her Daisy," Logan told one of the men who were riding with them. "It's not a sidesaddle."

"I can ride astride." She smoothed out her skirts then stared at the saddle. Reconsidering, this wouldn't be prudent. She didn't know what devil had pried its way into her head, but she didn't want to give in.

After several failed attempts, she successfully sat the horse. They started moving slowly but picked up the pace. The scraping of the leather and the horse against her legs was unbearable. Admitting to herself this was not something she could do all the way to London, she decided to plead fatigue.

Eveleen rode close to Logan. "I don't think I can do this. I'm sorry for taking up the extra time." That was so true, she was eager to see Ella.

"You want to ride in the carriage?"

"No, but my body is telling me yes."

~ * ~

"Ella, you're here. It seems as if it's been years since we've seen each other." Eveleen and Ella shared hugs in the foyer of the townhouse. "I wasn't sure you'd be in town."

"Apparently Logan sent Drake a message just this morning saying he hoped we would be here when you arrived. Come in. I can hardly wait to talk to you. You're married now. Oh, can I take your pelisse and bonnet?"

Eveleen shrugged from the cloak before handing Ella her bonnet. The home was much like their aunt Charlotte's. "I'm so happy to see you."

"Come into the parlor. I'll pour tea and we've scones with strawberry preserves. Are you hungry? Sit. We have so much to talk about." Ella poured and served the tea.

"No, but I'll take the tea." She watched Ella over the rim of the cup. "You still happy?"

"I am." She smoothed her dress over her swelling stomach.

"You're pregnant." Eveleen wondered what it would be like to be loved by a man and have his child growing inside. "You're so lucky." Sadness swept through her as she realized all she lost.

"Why are you unhappy?" Ella reached out to her cousin, smiling. "You should be shining with love."

"It's nothing. No, well, I've been really stupid and Logan, well, he's gone at night and he doesn't return until I'm asleep." That wasn't the entire story, and Eveleen really didn't know where to begin, wondering how much she should keep private and what she could share.

The scone that had been half way to her mouth settled on the plate as Ella leaned forward to take Eveleen's hand in hers. "That's not stupidity, Eveleen. Why doesn't he come to you?"

She fiddled with the lace on her dress before looking up, "Can I be honest with you?"

"Of course you can. You know you can tell me anything," Ella said sincerely.

"You promise what I say won't leave this room?" She looked around. "Where are Logan and Drake?"

"First, I won't share anything with Drake or anyone else, and I believe Drake drug Logan to White's for some men things. He knew I wanted some alone time with you."

Eveleen hesitated, staring at the decorations in the parlor and wondering how she was going to explain to her cousin how inflexible she acted on her wedding night and the previous days afterward.

"You don't have to tell me anything you don't want to," Ella said, looking concerned, "but I'm sure you'll feel better if you talk about it and maybe I can help."

"You're right of course." Eveleen explained about the circumstances Logan found her in on the island and the men he killed. "I was so upset, and my stomach was rolling. I no sooner came to terms with the fact I saw two men killed than I was given no choice in marrying Logan. And Ella, I think something awful happened to me that day, but I can't remember. I shut what those men did to me from my mind. I felt violated, and I don't remember anything but my thoughts soaring into the sky to dance among the clouds. Logan won't tell me, but I'm also not sure if he knows."

Ella rose and said, "This is not a time for more tea. I need a snifter of brandy. Here," she handed Eveleen a glass.

"Thank you." Tears slid down Eveleen's cheek as she wiped them away with the backs of her hands.

As if Ella sensed there was more to her cousin's story, she asked, "Are you sure you can't remember? Close your eyes and try to see what happened."

Shrugging her shoulders and looking down, Eveleen didn't want to meet Ella's gaze. "That's just the thing. I don't remember that part, and I don't think I want to. I know the awful man hurt me."

"He, as in one?" Ella asked.

Sucking her bottom lip between her teeth, her breathing escalating she waved her hand in front of her face. Then, "Just one...I think. Ella, I can't catch my breath...but Logan killed two. There might have been two men who hurt me. Allura told me I had to wed Logan because I might be pregnant."

"But you're not, so that is a good thing." Ella rose and putting her hand on Eveleen's back, she said, "Take in a deep breath." She waited, "Another... Now look around you Tell me what you see."

Eveleen inhaled another deep breath, "A lamp, the table," she licked her lips, "the painting I did for auntie, the door."

"Another deep breath. Good, what can you touch?" Ella asked.

"The fabric of my gown, the chair, my hair..."

"Breathe, what can you hear?"

Eveleen laughed softly, "You, the ticking of the clock, rain falling on the porch. My heart beating."

"Do you feel better?" Ella asked, sitting down in the chair next to hers.

"I do," she inhaled, wondering how Ella knew what would help.

"So, you were forced to wed Lord Maxwell? I can hardly believe your father would allow that."

"It wasn't my father but Hunter and Allura who were in favor of the marriage. I was told I would have to leave if I didn't agree, but Allura also told me she didn't think Hunter meant what he said." She vividly remembered that night and the turmoil, and fears.

"Allura...I cannot believe it."

Tears welled in Eveleen's eyes while she nodded. "It's true and I drank too much wine that night, not that it would have made any difference. I wouldn't have let him in my bed. I was too afraid. Things have only become worse with time." She finished the story.

"But you want your marriage to get better, don't you? You want Logan to make love to you?" Ella asked.

"Yes, but now he thinks I'm too fragile and delicate. When he touches me, I flinch away or stiffen. It's because of what happened on the island, and I'm so damn tired of making that excuse and attempting to make sense of it all."

"Pshaw." Ella used one of The Duchess' hand gestures. "Your Lord Maxwell knows better than that. You are not someone who will break. But the two of you must talk about what happened on the island. Whatever those men did to you is standing in the way of your happiness."

"It doesn't matter. Every time it seems he might make love to me, I find a reason to withdraw from him or we're interrupted. Now he doesn't even pretend." Eveleen wiped the tears from the back of her eyes."

"Have you tried to seduce your Lord Maxwell?" Ella asked with a slight tilt to her head and a crooked grin.

Eveleen sniffed back a tear, "I wouldn't know how."

"I've got the perfect solution. You just have to wear one of my nightgowns, and Logan will do the rest. I promise. Wait here, I'll be right back." Ella set her glass of brandy on a side table and dashed upstairs.

"Ella?" Eveleen had no idea what was happening here.

A few minutes later, Ella returned. "Look at this." She held up two filmy garments. "What do you think? You can wear this tonight."

"You want me to wear that, why? I can see right through it."

"That's the point, silly. Drake bought me the lavender one when we were at the hunting lodge. Since then, he's bought me several more all in different colors. I thought you'd like the green one, mint green."

"You want Logan to see through it. I'd be naked to his eyes." Eveleen felt the rush of heat to her face.

"Again, that's the point. If he sees you wearing that, he'll know you want him to make love to you," Ella told her in a matter of fact tone.

"My stomach is rolling," Eveleen said, yet strangely excited about the prospect. "But when? What if I pull back and stop him?"

"I can't answer that question. Right now. They've been gone for several hours and should return fairly soon. I'll help you get ready. Come on. Let's go upstairs." She paused, her hand on the railing. "If you want to stop him, that's okay. You have that right. He'll understand, especially if you explain to him what you just told me."

Two hours later, Eveleen sat in the room assigned to them. She wore the mint green lingerie. Ella had fixed her hair into a coif with tendrils of hair hanging provocatively around her face. She lightly painted her eyes and applied a soft tint to her lips then with burned hairpins, she darkened her eyelashes.

"You're so beautiful, Eveleen. He won't believe his good fortune. How do you feel?"

Alma, Ella's lady's maid, entered with a huge tray containing cheese and fruit also one of Logan's bottles of wine and glasses. A white fur rug lay in front of the burning fireplace.

"I'm shaking from the tips of my toes to the top of my head." Eveleen fiercely gripped her hands together, fearing her knees would buckle. "I don't have any faith in this only because I don't know how I'll react. There is no reason for tonight to be any different."

Ella took them in hers. "I have to get out of here. You'll be fine. Just let Logan do what men do. Let him seduce you and don't allow whatever it is in your subconscious to tell him no."

"What if he doesn't want me anymore?"

~ * ~

Maida paced the living room of her cottage. Logan deserved a passionate woman, one who would give him pleasure and see to his needs. Not a cold-hearted bitch who was afraid to spread her legs for her man. She was the woman for him.

Logan told her he was going to find a man for her, and that it was time she wed and had more children. She had always loved Logan, loved him from the time they were small children.

Even when she became pregnant with Harry, she knew he would never return her love or wed him. She had been his first, other than the woman who taught him what to do when making love. And she had been a virgin the fall afternoon when he found her in the woods and started kissing her.

"Mama, why do you look so sad?" Harry asked, wrapping his arms around his mother.

"None of your concern," she tried to smile brightly. "I'm just reminiscing the past and wondering what I could have done differently."

"You have to stop thinking about Papa. He's married now, and I think he's going to be happy."

"I understand, but it isn't easy to let go of him. He's a wonderful and handsome man who steals my heart and my breath each time I look at him."

Chapter Four

Logan had spent too many hours drinking and gambling with Drake. He dreaded the return home and prayed Eveleen would be asleep when he stepped into the bedroom they shared. If she were awake, he didn't know if he could keep his hands to himself, especially when he didn't want to. Touching his wife, seeing her naked, was all he imagined since the unholy marriage.

At the top of the steps, he said good night to Drake and with dragging feet he entered his chamber, loosening his cravat. With a heavy sigh he looked to the empty bed then searched the room.

At the sight in front of him his breath caught in his throat. He swallowed hard praying for strength and common sense. This could not be what it seemed. "Evie?" he whispered through his teeth. She was asleep, her head resting on the chair near the fire, but when he spoke her name, she seemed to wake up, brushing the soft strawberry blond hair from her face and sweetly smiling.

"Logan, I'm sorry. I didn't mean to fall asleep before you got here." She sat up a little later and seeming to notice the tray on the table asked, "Are you hungry? There is wine. We can eat if you like."

Beneath the filmy nightdress and robe the illusion of all her curves appeared vivid and inviting. She was not so subtly asking him to make love to her. This had to be Ella's idea. Evie would never think of anything like this without outside help. Ella must have given her the lingerie to borrow for the night.

He swallowed hard again, wishing he had not spent the night at Whites. "I'll pour you a glass of wine." He wasn't sure how to proceed; he'd never bedded a reluctant virgin bride before. Never made love to a woman who flinched at his touch.

"I, I suppose so. I..." she said, seeming unsure of herself and out of her element. She looked to the floor then back to him, their gazes meeting. Unknowing what the gesture would do to Logan, she smoothed the nightgown she wore tightly to her body.

"You waited up for me." He tried to put the words in her mouth as he handed her the wine. "I'm surprised but very glad you did. Why? You need to help me understand your intentions." Stupid question. Under normal circumstances the answer seemed more than obvious, but his past experiences told him to tread lightly. This marriage of his was not normal.

"Yes, I did." She sipped, staring at him over the rim, her eyes wide sapphire blue pools, beckoning him, quietly calling his name. "Not really, I think I fell asleep. Ella thought I should do this." She sipped her wine. "Dress like this for you."

It was all he could do to stop the groan. He sat on the floor next to her. "You're beautiful, you know" he told her, lightly running a fingertip along her cheek and delighted when she responded to his touch. At least he thought she responded without flinching away from him.

"I," she smoothed the fabric of the lingerie again, an action that inadvertently highlighted her breast and their sweet curves beneath the fabric. The garment left little to the imagination as was intended.

"Are you trying to seduce me? If you are, I'm pleased." He bent to kiss her softly on the lips. Pulling away, he watched her reaction and knew the strained expression on her face meant she still wasn't completely willing. Yet he thought he saw pleasure and when she moistened her lips she gave his heart a ray of hope.

"Yes. I think that's what I'm supposed to do. Seduce you." Her smile seemed contrived.

"You got this from Ella, did you?" he held the robe between his fingers, enjoying the silken texture, just like her skin. "I like it, but it surprises me." He held up the fabric of the robe hoping to find out if Evie was a willing participant and had a hand in this, as well as perhaps seeing a bit more of his intriguing and surprising wife. He studied her eyes and the expression glimmering within.

As if they were sweaty, she wiped the palms of her hands on the gown. "Yes, this is Ella's. She thought you might like it. Ella said Drake gave it to her in hopes of a passionate night."

"That was nice of Ella." He coughed then handed her a piece of cheese. "Is that what you want, a passionate night, little Poppet?" He truly didn't want her to do anything she wasn't comfortable with but in that garment, she tempted him beyond endurance.

"I don't think I can eat that. My stomach is rolling. I can't breathe," She pushed his hand away, inhaling a long deep breath. "I think," she stopped suddenly. For a moment, she stared at the wall then turning to look at him she closed her eyes, inadvertently plucking at the flimsy nightgown she wore.

"What do you think? A penny for your thoughts, Evie," he asked her, feeling a deep-seated joy at the prospects of finally making love to his wife. Yet, here she was enticing and alluring, waiting for his touch and seeming to panic right before his eyes.

"That. I told you I would always be truthful." She swallowed hard still looking down.

He touched her chin, lifting it so he could see into her expressive eyes when she spoke. "You did. So, what is it you want to tell me?"

"I'm afraid, and I'd really like it if you just do this and get it over with. My heart pounds and I can't seem to take in a breath of air or even two." She blurted out, eyes closed as if she really wanted him to take her without foreplay. His thoughts catapulted to the men on the island and what he believed might have happened to her.

He kissed her closed eyes in hopes she would open them if nothing else to see what he would do next. "I won't hurt you." Well, that could be a small lie, and he thought about all the times he told her she was too fragile and delicate for lovemaking.

"You've said..." She did open her eyes. Eyes that were filled with unshed moisture.

"I know what I've told you, but the words were an excuse. I didn't know if you wanted me and, my little sweetheart, if I make love to you, we won't just get it over with. That would not give you a woman's pleasure."

She finished her glass, draining every possible drop. "I need more wine." She held it out for him to pour more.

"It's false courage, something you don't need. No, I won't give you more. I need for you to enjoy what we do together tonight, but most of all you have to willingly let me make love to you," he took the glass from her, setting it on the hearth. "If you say no, I'll stop."

With one hand gently cupping her cheek, he kissed her, opening his mouth over hers, letting his tongue dance across her lips until she opened for him with a soft keening sound. He groaned as he brought his other hand to her face, holding her still so he could initiate a deeper kiss. His lips caressed hers, his tongue played with hers and he felt the shudder of her body against his.

His hard shaft pulsed against the fabric of his buckskins. Taking this slow would not be easy, but he'd be damned if he didn't.

Tentatively, she touched his tongue with hers then quickly withdrew. He groaned again, his tongue pushing inside her mouth, playing with her teeth and exploring the inside of her cheek. She cried out softly, seeming to withdraw from him, yet her innate passion enchanted him.

Her hands rose to hold his head, but she seemed to push him farther away. He trailed kisses along her jawline then circled the small pink shell of her ear. She shivered and trembled, her hands now on his shoulders, her fingers digging into his body. He couldn't tell if she pushed him away or drew him closer.

His lips and teeth feathered and teased along her neck and across the bodice of her nightgown. He sent a silent prayer of thanks to both Ella and Drake for giving him a chance at this divine moment of bliss.

While his teeth, tongue and lips enticed her, he cupped a breast with his hand, testing the curve and the feel, trying to commit this moment to memory.

She gasped and pushed away, her arms stiff trying to hold him at a distance. "Logan, I don't want you to touch me there." Her voice wavered into a thin sob.

He closed his eyes, inhaling a deep breath of air and holding himself in check. "May I ask why?"

"I don't know," her voice thinned to a tiny wail. "I like the kisses."

"Does my touch hurt you?" he asked, trying to comprehend and understanding her fear was genuine. Also believing the men who attacked her had probably not kissed her and if either of them had, it didn't seem to be the focal point of her terror.

"No."

Then, "Can I try again. I only want to give you pleasure." Through the fabric of her gown, his lips pulled a nipple into his mouth, teasing the small tight bud with his teeth. Turning his attention to her other breast, he did the same. Her tiny cry startled him. The sound was one of pure terror.

"Eveleen, perhaps this is not such a good idea," he told her through clenched teeth.

"Logan," her voice sounded anxious. "I'm terrified and don't know why. I like your kisses and the way you touch me but..."

"But?" he asked cautiously, hoping he would like the answer.

"I'm not sure. Sometimes what you do terrifies me. I don't know why. It's as if I want something I'm afraid of. Do you have to touch me like that?"

His body flinched hearing her words. "If you're going to have pleasure, I need to touch you in so many different ways." He let his hand move down her leg, lifting the hem of the fragile material.

Her legs were long and sleek and he wanted to explore every inch with his fingers and lips. He yearned to hear her moan with the pleasure he was about to give her. His fingers resting near her woman's mound, he hesitated before tracing his way down her other leg. She closed her trembling legs to his exploration, leaving him disheartened and fearful they would never be able to change what lay between them. Had she not planned to seduce him?

Her fingers wove into his hair, clenching and unclenching. He rested his hand low on her abdomen and watched as once again she drew away from him. The messages she sent were two-fold.

"Logan," she said and as he lifted his head to look at her, she moistened her lips, tantalizing him further. "Do you need to do that? I'm not sure it's something you should do."

Her question reached his heart while he pushed her gown upward, following the path with his lips tongue and teeth until he reached her breasts. Drinking one beautiful lobe into his mouth, he gave attention to the other with his fingers, rolling the dusty rose bud between his fingers. His free hand investigated the swollen bud within her woman's fold. "Poppet, you're just nervous. Relax."

"Logan... You can't mean to..." Her fingers tightened in his hair. Frantically, she tried to scoot away from him, but his large body prohibited the distance she seemed to crave. "Logan, I..."

"Aw, little Poppet I do mean to do this unless you really don't want me to. I'm going to give you your pleasure and more."

"Lift your arms, little one." He swept the dress off, her breast more inviting and tempting than any man could endure. Yet, he decided she should have her pleasure now.

"I don't want, Logan I..."

He was swept away by his passion and so eager to see the pleasure on her face he could barely contain himself. "Soon you'll know exactly what you are afraid of, and that there is no reason for that terror in the back of your mind. I'm going to teach you a woman's pleasure and you're going to beg me to do it again." Sweat broke on Logan's brow and slipped down his face. He wanted this to be perfect for her, so seamless she'd never deny him again. The need to bind her to him, heart and soul overwhelmed him. After this night she would be his in every way.

A soft keening sound filled the room; a small cry echoed in his ears. He paused then kissed her again and when his tongue met hers, he tested her readiness. Her cream was non-existent. She continued to pull away while he needed her to accept him. Everything to make this moment wonderful was missing.

When he ran his tongue across her teeth, it sent his body into tremors difficult to manage. He felt hard pressed to prolong this first lovemaking. He yearned to watch her in climax.

"Do you like what I'm doing?" he murmured against her ear, praying what he was feeling was not true.

"Logan, I..." a small cry passed her lips. "Please, Logan, no."

For a moment he paused to look at her, unsure if he read her response to him correctly. Her eyes were closed and her cheeks were pale.

Once again, he found her mouth and fashioned his to her, opening it with his tongue and pushing forward in an ancient rhythm. His fingers joined the tempo. She pushed against him and he felt her tremor, her body quivering in anticipation of her release or fear he wasn't sure.

She seemed to hold back, keeping her heart and soul away from him. Then she pulled away from him, struggling against his strength, trying to distance herself from him.

"Bloody hell, Poppet." He whispered close her ear. "What is wrong?"

"Logan, please, don't..." Her voice broke on the words. "You need to end this…or just do it."

"Good Lord." He let her scoot away from him, pulling her gown up to cover her. So much stood between them, and he had no idea how to bridge the gap. "You don't want to make love." Staring into her eyes, needing to watch her reactions, he waited for her response.

Her lips drawn tight, tears rolling from her eyes, she said, "I do want you to make love to me."

"Really," he pulled the flimsy robe around her shoulders.

"Really," she parroted. "But something is stopping me, something that terrifies me. They hurt me, Logan."

He swallowed hard, watching her reactions to him and schooled his features. "Can you tell me what that is?"

"I don't know. All I remember is the pain," the thin wail of despair tore at his heart.

"Come here, let me hold you. Would you like that?" Before that day on the island, she had never sent confusing signals to him, but he'd never touched her intimately.

Slowly, she nodded compliance, "I do like that, you holding me."

"Let's figure out what just happened, what you like and what you don't." he told her, hoping to solve the issues between them. She would have to be honest or their marriage would be a sham.

"No, I, yes, but..." she hesitated. "What do you mean?"

"I need to know what I did that terrified you so." He kissed her again, inhaling her breath with his, letting his tongue explore the inner recesses of her mouth. He pulled back, watching, studying.

Her eyes were closed, her fingers now biting into his shoulders while her breathing was heavy. Slowly she opened her eyes, moistening her lips with the tip of her tongue before drawing her lower lip beneath her teeth.

"I like you to kiss me. Your mouth on mine makes me hot and

hoping for something more, something deep down in places I've never thought of before. I like everything you do above my shoulders," she told him, touching his lips with one delicate fingertip.

Well, that pretty much makes lovemaking out of the question. "You don't like it when I touch you here?" he asked, letting his finger gently touch the hardened tip of her breast.

Her sharp indrawn breath caused him to stop.

"I think I like that it's not the same."

"The same as what?" he asked, hoping for her honesty.

"The same as the ugly man." She paused. "He hurt me, you don't."

By the sudden glazing of her eyes, he understood he pursued this as far as he should tonight. But he wasn't going to leave the issue be. In time she would open up to him.

"I'll do better next time, give you your pleasure. I want to come inside you and truly make you mine. I know you're not ready for anything like that. So, for tonight I won't pursue this farther."

She hesitated, wiping the tears from her eyes, "I want to be yours in every way. I'll try harder next time."

"I know you will," he said. But trying harder would not fix this problem; discovering the source and how to fix it would.

"You didn't hurt me. I don't know what's wrong with me."

"Did I do anything you didn't want me to do?"

She hesitated. "No, but you did things I didn't understand men and women did and..." but she didn't finish.

"And what?" He needed to know more about her feelings.

"I don't know. For a moment, I thought, was reminded of another time, but it was so different...I just can't say. I can't remember what happened. Where he...where they..." She finished, leaving him more determined.

"Seeing you gave me pleasure, but I would like to understand what you're feeling and help you understand how beautiful lovemaking can be." Observing her gave him pause to think and wonder if she'd really meant to seduce him and if her sudden withdrawal had more meaning than he wanted to give credit to.

He swept her into his arms and settled her next to him on the fur rug in front of the fire. "Wine?" he asked with a smile he didn't feel.

Not waiting for her reply, he poured a small glass for both of them.

"Logan, I'm nearly naked and..." she stared at him then looked toward her robe that would cover the flimsy negligee.

He still wore his pants. Rising, he unfastened them, removing all his garments quickly. "Now I'm more naked than you are. Remember when you saw me in the greenhouse?"

She nodded before sipping more wine. "I would like my clothes now."

"But then I'd have to take them off again before we can pursue this idea of making love with my wife." He grinned, taking her empty glass from her to set it on the hearth with his.

"Haven't we already done everything? What are you going to do now?" she asked, unsuccessfully trying to cover herself with her hands.

Before he answered her, he placed more wood on the fire. The firelight created beautiful shadows dancing across her beautiful curves.

When he sat down, he drew her to him, tucked her close to his body. "I'm going to hold you and listen to every breath and heartbeat that comes from your body."

"I believe I'd like that." Her lips were swollen from his kisses.

Her breasts pressed against his chest, and his heavy sex pulsed against her abdomen, knowing where it wanted to be. He cupped her derrière, drawing her sweet form closer to him.

"I've desired you, Poppet, yearned for you for the longest time."

"I've wanted you too but now, I don't want to disappoint or anger you. I never want to tell you no."

His heart went out to her. He tucked her head against his shoulder. "Holding you was not what I thought would happen this evening when I saw you seemingly ready to seduce me, but it's more than I expected when I started up the steps. For now, just get used to my body against yours."

"You're so different."

"I'm certainly glad of that."

"Me too, I think. Can I touch you?"

He inhaled a gasp of air, her innocence astounding him. If she touched him, he would explode. He didn't dare and yet... "If you want." He closed his eyes in an attempt for control.

Her delicate fingers wound around him as his body shuddered beneath her unknowing strokes. He studied her face, her eyes, the small smile. "Why do you shake?"

"You unman me," he murmured, sliding a silken strand of hair behind her ear while his body strained.

"I like the way you feel, hard, resilient. It makes me wonder..."

"Wonder what?" Thank god her tiny fingers now rested on his stomach. He wanted her, had to make love to his wife. Men made love to virgins all the time and they didn't break. He inhaled a swift deep breath, determined this would not happen this night. But then she wasn't truly a virgin.

She kissed him, opening her mouth to his. While he thought of her fragility, she seduced him, her fingers lying now on his nipples, while he felt every inch of her pressed against his body.

Heaven and hell all at the same time, knowing she would not be his tonight.

Enveloped in the secrecy and the enchantment of the evening, he was determined not to ruin these magical moments between them. In time this woman who would be his life-mate would want him more than life.

"Logan..." his name hovered in the intensity of the sultry night enveloping them.

His mouth slanted hungrily across hers. He nibbled on her lower lip, his teeth biting down gently and tugging it. He stroked the inside of her mouth while he tried to maintain control. He turned her sweeping her hair from the back of her neck and placed sultry kisses there.

Breathing in gulps of air in an attempt to slow the seduction, Logan drew away watching her, studying her, knowing patience was something he was hard pressed to maintain. Her kiss-swollen lips tempted him calling to his baser needs.

Her nails raked down his chest. Feminine fingers slid across his nipples in a primal dance of seduction. He held himself taut in a bid to govern his sexual needs.

He kissed her cheeks, her eyebrows, the corners of her mouth, then intensified the kiss. Lingering on sweet soft skin, dancing with her tongue, he kissed her hard.

"My sweet Poppet, tell me if you like this." He turned her again, trailing kisses down her spine stopping at each vertebra to feel her shiver. He so hoped the response was pleasure.

"Logan..."

"Do you like this?" He paused, waiting for an answer.

"Yes," was her whispered reply. "Yes, oh yes."

Logan stopped and on his elbows above her, he focused on her eyes. "Evie, are you sure. These kisses are below your shoulders." Tiny steps.

"Please Logan, they make me feel so hot and strange."

"That's the way I'd hoped they'd make you feel." He lifted her flimsy nightdress, one he meant to see on her many times in the future.

He swept her into his arms and set her on the bed face down. Straddling her, he gently massaged her shoulders and back, enjoying the soft sounds of pleasure emanating from her. Slowly, he explored, giving her pleasure in a different way, reveling in her response.

His hands caressed each arm, gently kneading the muscles before focusing on her hands and each finger. He watched her hips move as if he gave her pleasure.

His attention changed to her limbs, starting at her feet, rubbing gentle circles in the arch and slowly making his way to the apex of her thighs then turning his attention to the other foot and once again moving toward her most intimate place.

Hesitantly, he touched her, felt her dampness and knew that although she feared many things about lovemaking, she wasn't averse to his touch.

He continued, enjoying the moment and praying for so much more in their future. The quickening of her breath and the soft sounds she emitted gave him hope.

"Logan?"

"Hmmm..." He pulled her night gown to cover her even though the transparency of the thin fabric left nothing to his imagination.

"You're putting me to sleep." She murmured.

"Good, you need your rest. Tomorrow will be another busy day," he said, lying down beside her and pulling her close.

Gradually her breathing slowed and he drew her against his chest, spooning her tight against him. She spread her hands across the taut muscles of his arms, her fingers closing. Several long silent minutes ticked by. He held her tight, not wanting to ever let her go. In his arms, she pushed against him as if needing the closeness his body offered and perhaps she was one with herself now. With gentleness, he lifted her hair and buried his face in the hot silken length.

"Even your hair smells of lilies."

Logan swept his fingers across her abdomen then higher. His touch to her breasts brought the nipple to a sudden and rapid peak. He sighed softly, nestling his face in her hair and wishing.

"I wish I could do everything you want," she said, holding herself a bit apart from him. "It seems I think yes and no." She turned in his arms. Tentatively, she touched him, ran her fingers along his chest once more.

He inhaled a swift deep breath, holding her hand in his as if he meant to stop her investigation of his body. She tilted her head back, watching his face for a sign of consent or perhaps displeasure.

Instead, he let go with a masculine groan, "Do what you will, Poppet. Be as inquisitive as you want." He whispered into her ear, discovering the shell with his tongue and sending her body into tremors.

A little devil and a bit of curiosity it seemed to him sent her hand to his abdomen and lower. She wrapped her fingers around him, her breath quickening at the way he responded to her. Unable to resist, she tightened her fingers. His large hand wrapped around her, urging her to move down then up.

"Bloody hell, little darlin', I don't know if I can do this again without exploding." His fingers touched her intimately yet she jerked away.

"I want to give you pleasure," she whispered as his body responded to her seductive and so very erotic caresses.

"Not now, my sweet Poppet. Not now."

"Alright then," she lifted her hand to his chest.

"It's almost dawn," he told her, picking up a strand of her hair and holding it between his fingers. "Silken fire, and so soft, you need to sleep," he said.

"What about you?" she queried, lying so very still beside him.

"Tonight, you touched my heart and my soul. You've become a part of me I never want to let go." He drew a gentle line around her areole then down her stomach to stop on her belly. Still he wasn't sure if he truly pleased her or repulsed her.

"Logan."

He placed a gentle kiss on her lips then he closed her eyes with a fingertip. "What?"

"Even though I might want to, I don't think I can or want do this again. It makes me remember things I need to keep in the dark recesses of my mind."

Turning from her, he lifted his pocket watch from the night table. "It's almost six. Light will shine through the windows." He rose from the bed and closed the curtains. "I've errands to run. I'll be back before you know it."

Suddenly, wide-awake, she watched him dress and walk from their room.

In an adjoining room he washed and dressed. Whistling, he strode the stairs and into the kitchen. A hot pot of coffee waited on the counter. Drake sat on a kitchen chair, his booted feet propped on another one.

"You had a good night?" Drake asked as Logan poured himself a cup.

~ * ~

The bedroom door closing woke her. A new tray filled with food had been set on the night table, and all the remains from dinner that had been in the room the night before had magically disappeared.

She sat up and pushing her hair away from her face, she stretched, her body still relaxed from the gentle massage the night before. Realizing she had been naked, her mind spun backwards.

"I really and truly want to be your wife now," she said to the empty room, wishing she could have given him everything he wished for. Nightmares from the island ravished her mind. Even while she couldn't remember everything that happened, she understood those were the moments keeping them apart.

Rising, she donned the robe she wore the night before then opened the curtains slightly.

"It's snowing," she murmured happily. From the sky soft white flakes fell gently to the earth. The clock downstairs chimed twice.

"It's two o'clock. I've nearly slept the day away," she whispered, swirling when the door opened.

"Did the nightgown work?" Ella asked as she stepped through the door, greeting her cousin with a huge smile.

"I've really slept the day away?" she asked, knowing her cousin wanted more answers than she was willing to give.

Ella's grin spread across her face, busying herself pouring tea for both of them. "It must have worked or you wouldn't be getting up this late. If I remember correctly, you're an early riser."

"I am and yes, the gown did, but..." She moistened her lips, remembering all the things Logan had done and how she held back.

"Good," Ella said, "Hot tea and a pastry? You're going to need more nourishment now." She poured two cups and handed one to Eveleen. "You might be with child."

"Thank you, I am famished." She didn't know what to say to Ella. What she and Logan did was private, and she couldn't explain how different she thought of herself today than she did yesterday and that there was still no possibility of a child.

"I've ordered you a bath. Thought you might like to freshen up before Logan returns." She sipped her tea then bit into one of the pastries an upstairs maid had delivered to the room.

"A soak in a tub would be heavenly. Have you seen Logan?" she asked, needing to speak with him yet at the same time not knowing what to say.

"No, I just rose myself. Drake said he left early this morning with errands to run."

"How do they do it?" Eveleen asked. "Logan didn't get any more sleep than I did. Indeed, he'd had less."

"What sweetie?"

"Go about their business without sleep," she blurted, giving away the fact they spent the night doing something besides sleep. A slow rise of heat swept her cheeks.

"Nothing to be embarrassed about. We were doing the same things last night. Drake just doesn't seem to need as much sleep as I do."

"You know what we did?"

"No, but I can guess. Are you alright? Do you have any questions?" Ella asked.

"Probably yes, but not right now. I've a lot to think about."

"Well, I'm heartily glad the nightgown I lent you worked its wonders. Now, you should probably bathe. The Duchess will be here soon, and she wants to hear about you and your new husband."

"Auntie Charlotte? I can't wait to see her. So much has happened. Did you see the snow? I want to play in it and make snow angels." Her enthusiasm was in direct proportion to her happiness in being back in London.

Ella smoothed her skirts, seeming to stare at her expanding belly. "I doubt if Drake would approve if he found me lying in the snow, knowing I would have difficulty getting up."

"Oh, I'm so sorry. I wasn't thinking of you."

Ella laughed softly. "Perhaps Drake will lie down in the snow with me then he can help me up."

"Of course he would lend a hand," Eveleen said.

"He does seem to be indulgent where I'm concerned."

"I can't imagine Logan making snow angels. He's so stuffy and straightforward most times. I've yet to see a lighter side to my new husband." But she did see a different side of him during the night. His gentleness amazed her in direct opposition to the violence he so easily wielded.

"You, my sweet cousin, are most likely right. In fact, Drake would probably join me because he could help me to my feet. I'm going to leave now. Your bath should be ready in a few minutes. Come downstairs as soon as you are dressed."

"Oh, the water is here."

"You might want to wrap a blanket around you." Ella suggested, giving a quick warning.

Just in time, Eveleen grabbed a blanket from the bed, covering herself with it as several men hauled water in to fill the tub.

Abruptly she was alone in the chambers with her thoughts. And her reflections circled around Logan. She touched her hands to her stomach and wondering if someday soon she could give Logan everything they both wanted. If she didn't get over her fears that would never happen.

Your water will get cold if you let it sit too long. Quickly she disrobed and slid into the steaming water. Washing her hair first and rinsing with an extra bucket she picked up the lily scented soap and finished.

The hot water made her sleepy, as if she didn't get enough sleep. *Gracious, the time must be nearing three.* She closed her eyes and rested in the liquid swirling around her remembering every touch and the strange gray haze holding her back.

A familiar hand touched her shoulder. She turned, "Logan, you're back. Wherever have you been?" Then she truly saw him.

In front of her he began to disrobe. Her mouth fell open, and she said, "You can't mean..."

"To join you? Of course I can." His devilish grin swept through her with trepidation and anxiety, yet she yearned to feel the magic of his touch and perhaps the culmination of his lovemaking.

The newness of this burgeoning relationship captured her soul. "There isn't room."

"Watch." His boots lay on the floor and he kicked his pants off before he slipped in behind her, spreading his legs on either side of her body. With his hands resting on her stomach, he drew her against his hard body.

The sensation of his hardness against her back sent an inferno of heat sweeping through her. "Now, after last night? I understand some of what you want but I don't see how. And Logan..." she moistened her lips. "We have things to talk about. I've questions."

He didn't answer, instead he pushed her hair from her neck and trailed kisses along her neck and across her back. "I'll show you."

His hands worked their magic, and with the lily scented soap in his possession, found every sensitive and erotic pulse point she possessed. She heard the soft keening of her voice as he continued the enchantment of his lovemaking.

Suddenly, vivid images of the man on the island swept through her head. The man lying in the dirt, his throat slit.

"Logan, really this isn't going to work," she told him, closing her eyes while her body stiffened then shook with the terror in her mind. She heard the gunshot and saw him tackle the second man before he sliced the man's neck.

"Trust me, Poppet, and try to relax. I won't hurt you. I will see this to its pleasant end. I brought you something."

His add on had her attempting to turn in his arms. He held her still. "What is it?"

"Patience," he told her. "I'll show you when we're finished here."

She sighed, trying desperately to relax as he suggested. Unable to put together a coherent thought as his fingers, hands and mouth continued to play havoc with every nerve ending she possessed. Evie's seduction was slow and smooth. He seemed unconcerned that her body shivered and heated while he seemed unaffected.

"Please, Logan," she murmured.

"Doing this right takes time, my Poppet, lots and lots of attention to every tender spot on your beautiful body. Every inch of you is gorgeous, and I want to uncover every mystery you possess."

Despite her fears and the images in her head, she responded to the dance of his fingers on her flesh. She yearned for something...

The water in the tub moved with every twitch of her body. Some drops fell from the tub to land on the floor. "We're going to drown the rug. What if water drips through to the first floor?"

"Then we'll have company," he said nonchalantly, not seeming to care if the room filled with people wanting to see where and why water sifted through the floorboards.

"Logan," she said, indignant with his indifference.

"Well, I would care," he amended. "I'm the only man who will ever see you like this, naked." His fingers found another tender spot, an erotic spot, and her body reacted.

"I love to watch your breast sway when I touch you, here and here." His voice next to her ear soothed and enticed at the same time. She moaned, lost to his ministrations. "I do believe you are ripe and swollen with need.

Would you like me to come inside you?"

Her short sharp breaths made it impossible for her to answer. He seemed to appreciate her silence and in a quick move, he swept her into his arms, turned her and now she sat astride him, his cock now pulsing, rubbing against her intimately.

"No..." her soft wail stopped his exploring hands.

He paused, drawing his lips back, yet it was for a moment only. Before she could say anything else, he smiled and with his hands held her face.

"You are so perfect and beautiful. I'm sorry. I couldn't help myself."

After a few seconds, her head on his chest, she said, "I'm sorry too. It's just, we need to talk but I don't quite know what to say."

"It's alright." His hands soothed her back, seeming to calm instead of exciting. "You can tell me anything. I need to make this right for you."

"Can get used to this maybe, but the lack of sleep will be impossible and what you say you want, I just don't know if I can ever go there." She pushed away from him.

"Hush, I'll always make sure you can sleep and that you have time for yourself. I'm single minded."

"Seems that way," she murmured.

"That's just because this is so new to me and to you," he told her, letting his hands smooth the curve of her hips.

"I didn't think this was new to you." She pushed against his chest so she could see his eyes. "You have a child."

"Sex isn't," he told her, bringing her head closer so he could kiss her lips. "But you are very original, unique in so many different ways. I want to teach you so much, and these feelings I have for you are very new to me."

"Thank you. Was that a compliment?" she asked, letting her breasts brush across his chest while she pressed her lips to his, gliding her tongue along his, trying to make amends for what she kept from him.

It didn't seem he wanted to answer. "Time to get out of the bath and dressed." With his hands on her hips, he set her away from him.

She rose from the tub, water sluicing down her body before

wrapping a bath sheet around her. When Logan stepped from the bath, to Eveleen, once more he appeared a God, rising from the water. Moistening her lips, she was anticipating the next time he would lie beside her and try to give her pleasure. Good lord but she was as transfixed on sex as he was but for different reasons.

"What are you thinking?" he asked as he used the towel to dry his body.

"Nothing," she whispered softly, not willing to share her wayward thoughts with him.

"The truth," he prompted, striding toward then lifting her chin so he could look into her eyes.

She gazed at him. Inhaling a long deep breath, she said "The sight of you made me think of Adonis rising from the sea."

"You unman me." He kissed her lips, chuckling "Go get dressed. Chat with The Duchess and Ella. If you don't put some clothes on soon, you won't leave this room until tonight."

She laughed at his comment but wished she could remember and speak of the memories tormenting her. Turning to leave, she looked over her shoulder, amazed at her husband and the tenderness she felt for him.

"What are you going to do?" She began dressing, stopping to get help with her corset and fastening.

"You don't have a lady's maid yet. While I don't mind helping knowing I'd rather assist with the undressing, I'm not always going to be around when you need me even though I'd love to be. Speak with Ella. Maybe she can help you find someone to aid with your dressing." He kissed the nape of her neck. "There, my chores are done."

He finished dressing and left her to complete her hair and makeup eager to see her auntie. With the last touches made, she stepped quickly down the stairs.

"Eveleen." Aunt Charlotte rose from the chair where she sat and opened her arms to her niece.

She'd never felt more welcome and loved. "Auntie. I'm so glad to see you."

"Tell me everything that's happened since you left London for your home," The Duchess said.

"Well, I'd rather forget most of it." Eveleen understood this would create more questions from Aunt Charlotte.

Charlotte gripped her hand before patting the top. "Now, now, the past sometimes is best forgotten in lieu of all the good things that will come to you in the present. Let's sit."

"I can tell you that with Ella's assistance, last evening helped bring me closer to my husband but there are still issues. Even though I was sound asleep when Logan entered my bedroom, he woke me up and we..." she stopped there, unwilling to speak of the things that were private between her and Logan. "Well, you know."

"I do, my darling, and I'm so happy for you. Now, what are your plans while you're in London?" The Duchess asked.

"I don't know. I would love to visit the gardens again, but the weather is so cold. There is the snow. Oh, Ella, I would love to make snow angels." Once again imagining Logan lying on the ground and playing in the snow left her giggling.

"Whatever are you laughing about?" Ella asked. The strange expression her face sent more laughter sweeping through Eveleen.

"It must involve the men." The Duchess sent a quirky smile stretching across her lips. "I'm eager to hear what has you nearly rolling on the floor in amusement."

With a tiny shrug of her shoulders, Eveleen said, "I pictured Logan lying on the ground making snow angels with me. He's really so impeccable, manners and all, it goes beyond the pale."

Ella joined in the laughter, seeming to chuckle at her thoughts. "It's the same with Drake. He'd never play in the snow."

"You girls should challenge your men to do something different. It's only fair. After all, they've tested you with demands that were unusual and perhaps uncomfortable to deal with," their auntie said. "And both of you have met the challenge impeccably.

"Did you ever ask the Duke to play in the snow?" Eveleen asked, knowing there were so many things about their aunt they'd never expected.

"I did and his antics reminded me of a child with a new toy at Christmas. We frolicked for hours, and the memory is one of my favorites." Tears slipped down Charlotte's eyes. Pulling out a handkerchief, she dabbed them from her face. "Forgive a maudlin old lady. Memories seem to be all I have left, and I do cherish them with all my heart."

Both girls knelt by their aunt, taking her hands in theirs. "There is nothing to forgive. We love hearing your stories, and we admire you and your courage. It would be so hard to live without the love of your life. Yet you do it with bravery," Eveleen said, wishing Logan loved her and understanding she would have to settle on his affection.

Eveleen found tears brimming in her eyes, and when she looked at Ella, she also found her wiping moisture from her cheeks.

"Girls, we went from merriment to tears in a blink of an eye. We need to concentrate on what makes us happy. Now it's almost Christmas. Do the two of you have gifts for your men?" The Duchess asked.

"No," they said in unison, sitting down again.

"I haven't even thought about it," Eveleen said.

"Neither have I." Ella appeared pensive.

"I do have something to help Eveleen, but right now I'm not sure what you can get a man who has everything." The Duchess pointed out, "but I'll try to help. Your first Christmas together the gift must be meaningful."

"What do you have in mind for Logan?" Eveleen asked, suddenly curious about the possibilities coming from her auntie. However, The Duchess had her hand in most everything happening in London.

"Well," she began, pausing a finger on her chin as if lost in thought. "My son was here a few weeks ago for a short visit. It seems he won a piece of land in Tuscany, a vineyard."

"A vineyard, but what does that have to do with me?" Eveleen sat on the edge of her seat in anticipation. The Duchess always had a motive or an agenda, but a vineyard?

"Everything. Your man has one in Bordeaux. He knows what running one entails. It seems my son has no interest in learning or taking the time to make a success of a winery."

"Logan might love to have a second winery," Ella interjected.

"He might. I doubt if I have the funds to buy one for him. Everything I own is now his."

"Not everything, at least not yet," The Duchess said slyly. "You remember the funds your father sent to me when you arrived at my doorstep?"

"Yes," Eveleen said.

"They are still in the Bank of London under my name. The money is yours. If you think he'll like to have this property, I'll sell it to you for five pounds."

"Five pounds? How?"

"He gambles occasionally as all men do, and he usually wins. This time he won the title to something he doesn't care to own. He gave it to me to do with whatever I'd like. So, do you want the deed?"

"Yes, of course, thank you," Eveleen repressed the urge to jump and down and clap her hands. Yet a wave of pleasure swept through her and she couldn't stop the smile forming on her lips.

"Any thoughts for me?" Ella asked, seemingly pleased with Eveleen's pending purchase.

"Not yet, my darling, but I'm going to keep thinking. I've thought perhaps a portrait of you would be nice. You could join the other wifely portraits gracing the stairway on the estate. Take a few days to think about it."

"I do think it's a good idea. Do you really think Drake would like a painting of me?"

"He would," Eveleen said. "He adores you."

"There you are." Logan and Drake burst into the room. What was once a fairly quiet yet chatty room turned suddenly masculine and boisterous.

"It isn't like we were hiding from you," Ella said with a touch of indignation in her words. "And now you just burst in as if there is no tomorrow. We were having a serious discussion."

"No, I'm just pleased to see you and I'm sure I speak for Drake too." Logan swept Eveleen from her chair to place a hungry kiss on her lips before setting her back.

"Now, how do I beat that entrance?" Drake stood above Ella, studying her as if he meant to disrobe her on the spot. "I suppose..." He hesitated then sweeping Ella into his arms, he strode toward the stairs, stopping only to look over his shoulder and say, "We'll see all of you at dinner."

"Go on the two of you. I know you, Logan Maxwell, you're thinking about doing the same. Go on, I'll be fine. Indeed, I'll check on cook and make sure dinner will be on time."

When Eveleen looked back, her hand in Logan's, she hesitated. "You sure?"

"Absolutely, go on."

Logan didn't wait longer. In the same form as Drake, he scooped Eveleen in his arms, two-stepping his way to their bedroom. Opening the door, then kicking it shut, he let her slip down his hard frame.

"I've something for you. Well, and I've several somethings for both of us."

~ * ~

Franco approached her. She was tending the vines on his ancestral vineyard; on theirs, he amended. Her son played nearby, laughing and chasing butterflies through the vines.

Nostalgia swept through him, remembering the days of his youth. As he grew older his plans cemented. He'd always expected to inherit this estate from his family.

"Jule, how are you?" He stepped cautiously toward his sister, unsure of the welcome he might receive.

"What? Oh, you scared me." Her hand at her throat, her eyes wide, she stared at him. "Why are you here?"

"Is that any way to greet your brother, *petite soeur*?" He crossed his arms in front of him, his feet apart.

"You haven't been here in five years. Why now? What is it you want?" Her expression was wary and condemning.

"Well, I wanted to meet my nephew before he becomes a man," he told her, turning his gaze to the little boy.

"Really, again I ask, why now? You risk your life just stepping onto French soil." She wiped her forehead with the back of her sleeve.

"Let's go inside where it's cooler. We can talk there." He reached down for the basket of food she brought for the boy. "What's his name?"

She took the basket from him. "Charles, I call him Charley, and we can talk here."

"It's hot," he complained.

"Not very," she said abruptly. "It's December, how hot can it be? What do you want?"

"I need money," he told her even though it wasn't true.

"Then you came to the wrong place. I've just enough for mine and Charley's needs."

"Aww...not a penny for your big brother? Doesn't Lord Maxwell pay you what you're worth?" he sneered, understanding his words wouldn't sit well with her. "It seems he could give his whore enough money to help out her family."

"You're not my family," she told him pointedly, seeming to stand firm in her statement. "And I'm not a whore."

In her eyes, he could see the simmering anger he vividly recalled from their childhood. "No matter what you say, we share the same mother and father. We are family."

"I owe you nothing. You weren't there when we needed you. I had to hide in a cellar for days while the mobs searched for me. I nearly starved. If it wasn't for the village people, I would have died."

"I could not come back here to help. And now in order to stay on this land, you became Maxwell's whore."

Jule slapped him hard. "Go. I never want to see you again."

Chapter Five

"What do you have for me?" She pushed on his chest, distancing herself slightly from him while he had other intentions.

His lips descended hard, demanding a response, still she withheld a part of herself. The perpetual magic of Evie left him breathless and in need of something she wasn't surrendering. Yet before he lost himself in her warmth and enchantment and the desire to bring her some pleasure, he meant to give her the gift he spent hours searching for.

He placed her away, praying the tiny distance between them would result in some semblance of control for his unruly body. Yet he knew he would have to do this quickly before he swept her into his arms and into his bed.

"Evie," he began, watching her beautiful sapphire eyes widen with what he hoped was not apprehension.

"Yes."

He bent down on one knee, holding her hand in his. "I did this all wrong, our marriage, the way I treated you with no regard to your wishes. I thought I knew all the answers when in truth I knew nothing."

"What are you trying to say?"

"Will you marry me?" Logan held out a box and opening it, a ring rested inside, his heart flip-flopping beneath his ribs while his breath caught in his lungs.

"I don't understand, but yes, even though we are already wed. I will marry you."

"Thank God," he said, slowly taking the ring from its home while enjoying the exquisite sparkle in her eyes.

"Is that for me?" she asked, hesitating as she watched him slide the emerald with smaller diamonds on each side onto her finger.

"Yes," he said. "Do you like it?"

"It's beautiful."

"And it's green," he said with a broad smile brimming on his lips, feeling very proud of himself. "Now, I've three more gifts for you. Would you like to see them?"

"Where are they?" she queried, appearing to search his body for a package.

"These are for both of us, for you to wear and for me to take off." He could barely restrain his eagerness to show her. He drew a bag from beneath his coat then pulled out three tissue wrapped packages for her to open.

"Really," she said dryly. "You need something special to remove from my body? I didn't think it mattered."

He roared with laughter, "Open them and you'll understand."

She walked to sit in a chair then tearing open the first gift, she pulled out a white silken dressing gown and robe. "I understand now," she grinned at him as if anticipating the same delightful magic as he did. "The other parcels are the same?"

"Different colors." Her expression delighted him, as did the curve of her breasts that could be seen above the line of her gown.

"Thank you," she said looking thoughtful.

"You're welcome."

"Logan?"

"What?" Now he wasn't sure about anything.

"Have you ever played in the snow, made snow angels?" she asked, setting the gifts on the table beside her.

"When I was a boy." Where was this going? "Haven't really thought about anything like that for a long time. Why?"

"Tomorrow, if there's time, will you?" She paused. "Will you make snow angels with me?"

She blindsided him with the playful question, but he was falling in love with her lighter side, the part of her that grabbed him and tossed him from his area of comfort.

"Perhaps, well maybe if there's time, bloody hell, why not?" It might be fun to think of something besides his businesses.

"We could take a carriage ride to Vauxhall Gardens." Her voice reached an excitement he'd never heard from her before.

"How could I say no? Of course I will take you and have fun in the cold white stuff coating the ground." As he watched his beautiful Evie unfold petal by petal in front of him, his heart soared with warmth and enjoyment. He berated himself for not paying more attention to her before she fled to her family's home.

"You won't regret it. I promise." She threw herself at him, wrapping her arms around him.

He kissed her, dragging his lips across hers, deepening the caress until she moaned softly into his mouth. Pulling away from her a moment, "My only regrets where you are concerned, Poppet, is that I took you for granted for so long."

Her fingers clutched the lapels of his jacket. Keeping him at arm's length she drew him toward the bed. Together they fell on the mattress Logan twisted mid-air so Eveleen fell on top of him, laughing.

Running his hands through her hair, pins flew as her silken hair fell around them. Drawing a lock to test the scent, lily, he sighed, satisfied with his beautiful wife and the new life that loomed pleasantly in front of them. She touched a part of him he'd thought was long dead.

Drawing away from her, he deftly rid Eveleen of her gown and undergarments then his own, the mystery of her curves unveiled to him. He smiled, settling next to her, regarding her thoughtfully.

"You are a picture worth painting," he told her while he tried to kiss every part of her body. Then immediately regretted his words when he recalled Ella's sketches of Drake and their lovemaking.

"I could paint you," she breathed softly, the words coming out in a sigh. "Would you like that?"

"A landscape is more worthy of your artistic endeavors." He flicked his tongue across a nipple while his fingers found other erotic places, watching her sweet response. It seemed to Logan she was becoming more at ease with the attention he lavished on her, stopping only when he came to the culmination of their lovemaking.

He touched her lovingly, hesitantly, unwilling to frighten her but hoping to introduce her to one more part of lovemaking. She followed suit, her warm lips and hot tongue drawing erotic patterns on his torso.

Her head lay upon his chest, and he nestled her in the crook of his arm. "We're late."

"Hmm...late for what?" His mind had stopped, and feelings soared while he fought to hold himself in check.

"Dinner, are you hungry?" she asked, drawing pictures on his chest, pushing away to watch him, her breast touching him lightly and enticing him to introduce her to something more primal.

"Famished for you," he told her, enjoying the look on her face when she rose above him, enjoying the play of her taut rosy nipples on his naked flesh.

She hit him with a fist and he obliged her by grunting. "You cannot mean... I suppose I will get no sleep tonight either," she said petulantly, sitting up and searching for her clothing and hairpins.

"Probably not," he told her. With his hands behind his head he watched her, wondering what he could possibly do that would take her mind off the events that still haunted her.

"Are you just going to lay there and look at me or are you going to help me with this corset and the fastenings on my gown?" She dressed herself the best she could.

"Just look at you." He grinned shamelessly, pleased she no longer wanted to hide herself from him. Going without dinner then sneaking down in the middle of the night for a snack seemed the best idea.

"Logan Maxwell," she said indignantly. "Everyone will be waiting for us, and they will know precisely why we are not at the table."

"Evie Maxwell," he shot back.

"Alright then, if that's what you want, you can stay here, but I might not get to see Aunt Charlotte before we leave and she's important to me. If you don't want to eat, could you please just help me so I can go downstairs?"

He knew a good argument when he heard one. Naked, he rose from the bed and in a few minutes, she was laced and fastened. He placed a tender kiss at the nape of her neck. "I'll dress while you fix your hair."

"Thank you," she mouthed the words. "I owe you."

He was shocked by her last words. "I'll happily collect." He winked at her as he dressed.

A few minutes later arm in arm they strode down the stairs and into the parlor. "Auntie Charlotte, are you alright?"

The Duchess sat up, stretching and yawning. "Oh my, I must have fallen asleep. Are you ready for dinner?" she asked as Logan stepped forward to help her stand.

"Can't wait. What are we having?" Eveleen asked as they entered the dining room.

Charlotte yawned again, "Fresh salmon, I believe along with Swiss chard and squash. Oh, and a couple bottles of Logan's private reserve." She slanted a wry glance at him.

"Where are Ella and Drake?" Logan looked around knowing the answer, but he wanted Eveleen to know how generous he'd been with his agreement to cease their lovemaking. He could have kept her in bed with him for another hour and she would have been willing.

"Pshaw..." The Duchess waved a bejeweled hand in the air. "They won't be down for at least an hour. You can count on it. They will have only cold leftovers to eat."

"Or a midnight snack," Logan added with a gruff chuckle.

It seemed the cook knew just when to serve the meal. The courses were set on the table and the wine was poured.

"So, Logan, have you been successful today with your business?" The Duchess asked, appearing to know the answer to the question she asked.

Logan's fork stopped midway to his mouth. He set the food on his plate. "What do you know about my endeavors?" Where The Duchess was concerned nothing would surprise him.

"Not a lot," she began. "However, what I do know is that White's and Almack's have agreed to serve substantial amounts of your wine on their premises. Where else have you been?"

"Is that all?" he queried, biting into the fresh salmon on his fork, relieved she didn't know about his queries regarding Franco.

"No, I've learned there are numerous other establishments around London who will serve some of your special Bordeaux." She smiled, sipping the topic of their conversation then grinning over the brim of her glass.

"What don't you know?" Logan asked dryly, now observing the intriguing older lady who was related to his wife.

"Well," she paused to eat a bite, chewing slowly. "I have my informants, the intelligence tree put together by my late husband the Duke, gives me fresh insights to all the goings on in the town."

"A valuable friend," Logan said, understanding how fortunate he was to be on this lady's good side.

"Don't you forget it. By the way," she turned her attention to Eveleen. "have you had a chance to give him your gift?"

"Gift? He queried, having never thought she would give him anything and eager to discover the surprise.

"Yes, it is for Christmas, but I plan on waiting to see if he will like it. I want to give it to him in private." She tilted her head to one side and smiled at him.

Ella and Drake rushed into the room, Ella a bit disheveled. "Sorry we're late," Ella said, waiting for Drake to pull out her chair.

"What do you want to give in private, Eveleen? You can't leave everyone wondering," Drake said.

Ella smiled prettily at Logan, "I know what it is."

"Well then, Eveleen, you best tell all of us because Ella can't keep a secret." Drake kissed her forehead.

She tossed her napkin at him. "I can too. It's Aidan who can't keep a secret."

He dodged the missile and sat down. "Tell us."

"Tell us," The Duchess said. "You won't regret anything."

"Then," The Duchess said, wiping her mouth with her napkin, "Drake will explain what we've done to keep everyone safe and our fortunes intact."

"The deed is upstairs." Eveleen said. "Should I go get it?"

"It's not necessary. I assure everyone it is valid and paid for," The Duchess said, setting her fork on the table before focusing on everyone around the table. She let her chin rest on her hands, an all-knowing grin on her face.

Logan watched Eveleen, saw her hesitate even while she inhaled a long deep breath of air. He didn't understand why she seemed to vacillate.

"Go on, you can tell me. I'm sure I'll love it," he said.

"Do you want the long story or the short one?" she stared at him, tapping a nervous staccato on the tabletop.

"Either will do." He tried to encourage her but knew this would be so much easier in the privacy of their bedroom. He didn't know why The Duchess wanted this done publicly. Well, they were among friends.

She moistened her lips and looked at The Duchess who smiled at her before turning her attention back to him. Before she spoke, she moistened her lips. "Well, Auntie's son, William, won the deed to a vineyard in Tuscany. He doesn't want it and he gave it to Aunt Charlotte."

"I didn't want it either," Charlotte said with a slight shrug of her shoulders. "Go on or I'll die waiting for you to tell him." She waved her hand at Eveleen.

"Aunt Charlotte thought you might like another winery so she sold it to me. It's your Christmas present." Eveleen swallowed, her hands shaking. "I know I don't have any money. What was mine is now yours, but it was coin I had in the Bank of London from my father under The Duchess' name. So, I hope you don't think I spent your money without permission."

The Duchess seemed to bristle at her words, "That stuff about the husband owning everything is ridiculous. Why my late husband, The Duke, made sure I had a bank account in my name and those pounds were solely mine. You should do the same for Eveleen," then she turned to Drake, "and you for Ella."

"Lady Charlotte," Logan began, clearing his throat before he spoke, "It was her coin and she had every right to spend it on me if she wished or on herself. I just hope you didn't spend too much."

He felt her hand on his leg, her eyes wide and imploring. "I hope five pounds was reasonable."

He let out a roar of laughter, "You're making a joke."

"No, that is what auntie sold it to me for. She didn't want the land after all. Do you like the gift?"

He held both her hands, "I love it and I adore your thoughtfulness. Thank you." He kissed the backs of her hands, his sudden joy overwhelming him.

"And that probably brings us back to the business at hand. Drake, do you want to begin?"

"Of course," he said "and with the same questions as Lady Eveleen. Do you want the short version or the long one?" Drake asked, grinning shamelessly.

"Everything that is necessary for Logan and Eveleen to understand and that is definitely not the short version. Maybe a tale somewhere in between," The Duchess said.

Drake swallowed his bite of salmon before downing his glass of wine and pouring another. "My friend, who will remain nameless for the moment, caught a pickpocket and her dog at Vauxhall. Needless to say, he believes this little guttersnipe is an heiress."

"Why would he think something so ludicrous?" Logan knew from this comment the longer story would most likely rule the day.

"It seems, and I won't speculate how, he found a scar on her derrière. That mark was a family crest, one he knew quite well. Comes from a wealthy family who met misfortune over eighteen years ago."

"Whose was it?" Drake clearly had his interest now. "Do I know this family?"

"Again, until there is proof, I don't want to reveal names, but I'm sure as the tale continues and when you weave all the information together, you will be able to guess." Drake stood and now paced the small room, hands behind his back. Anticipation as well as tension scorched the room.

"So, you have reason something nefarious has happened. Does this have anything to do with Ella's abduction last fall?" Logan clasped his hands in front of him, leaning back on his chair and watching Drake pace.

Drake stopped facing his audience. "It does, the abduction got me thinking. Ella and I remembered a family who actually lived close to the Hepburns. They had a baby girl and soon after that the father died in a freak sailing accident. The little girl was no more than a few months old when her mother supposedly committed suicide by poisoning herself."

"And the baby disappeared never to be seen or heard of again," Eveleen said, her eyes wide.

"Yes, and the father's brother and wife inherited everything since they were the closest kin still alive." Drake stopped, turning to gaze pointedly at Logan.

"And your brother not only threatened you, but abducted Ella with the purpose of selling her to the highest bidder," Logan said, beginning to realize where part of this was going.

"I don't want the same thing to happen to Ella and myself. Grisham, my brother, has not been found, but the one-eyed man was killed in Paris. Grisham's wife is a threat as long as her husband is still alive. We," he graced The Duchess with a nod, "and Ella and I have come up with a strategy. In lieu of the encounter at the McLellan castle concerning Franco, I believe you, Logan and Eveleen, should partner with us."

"What kind of partnership would this be?" Logan's interest was moved even farther.

"My will and assets will name Ella first then all of my children in order as heirs. If all of those heirs are somehow gone then Logan, you, then Eveleen and all of your children in order will be named as heirs. If Jarret ever returns to England and he is willing, the same will hold true for him. At the end of the line will be The Duchess then her son. The document will obviously be an ongoing piece of work."

"What do you all think?" Drake asked, sitting down again and seeming exhausted from the story as well as the remedy.

"The tale and your proposition are a lot to take in." Logan rubbed his chin thoughtfully. "I wouldn't mind including all of the cousins and sisters in this plan of yours as well."

"So you agree?" The Duchess asked, her age-lined face lighting with a beautiful smile that seemed to erase years off her age.

"This will take an army of solicitors to accomplish this," Logan said before turning to Eveleen, who he realized had turned a ghostly shade of white. He couldn't help but wonder at her sudden change of mood.

"I believe this is wise. The stories about the child and her mother..." Eveleen paused, "My mother knew her and she told us to always be wary. She'd spoken of the woman and I wasn't very old, but every time her name and the baby's name was brought up mother cried."

"So, you and Ella both believe there is some truth to this story," Drake said, seeming to study the close-knit group of friends.

The girls nodded, tears slipping from Eveleen's eyes. "With all my heart," she said.

The Duchess tapped her cane on the floor and rose. "It's getting late and a great deal has been said here this evening. You should all retire for the night and think about the best way to go about this, and," she paused, "do what you all do best, provide more grandbabies for me. Wish me goodnight."

Both Ella and Eveleen rushed to their aunt's side, "Goodnight, Auntie," they said, each giving her a hug as well as a kiss on the cheek.

Logan reached for Eveleen's hand, a smile in his heart. "Let me thank you for the gift."

Inside their room, Evie turned in his arms, "Do you really like the gift? I just didn't know if it was too much."

"I told you the truth and I'm amazed and pleased." His lips found hers.

Evie pushed away, "I want to give the deed to you." She rushed to her toiletry chest and pulled it from a hidden compartment. "Here," she handed the document to him.

"Thank you." He studied the title to the land in Italy. It seemed to be legitimate, "Tuscany, I've always wanted to see it. I'll have this verified tomorrow. Now, kiss me and love me as if we never heard that horrible story of betrayal and lies." *As if you were never violated on that island you thought was safe.* He drew her close, his lips finding hers and his fingers destroying her hair and the fastenings on her gown.

She became an aggressor in the game they played, undoing the buttons on his shirt and dragging it down his arms.

Pushing, pulling, unlacing, desperate to be naked together they finally fell onto the bed.

The loud crash against the wall set Logan's fighting nerves on edge. His mind and body stiffened, ready for battle if necessary, yet he waited for confirmation of an enemy.

Instead, a feminine giggle filtered through the nearly paper-thin walls. "Drake, wait until..."

"Can't stop."

"But they'll hear us."

"No, they won't."

Eveleen's laughter brought Logan's attention back to Evie. "You think that's funny?"

~ * ~

Two days later Eveleen stood by the window in the parlor, watching the snow as it drifted lazily to the earth while waiting for Logan. The promise of playing in the white stuff coating the ground had been replaced with business the last few days. She drummed her fingers on the glass pane.

Three hours ago, she received a message to be ready at two o'clock. Well, it was now two fifteen. He was late. Turning from the window, she wandered through the empty townhouse, missing Ella and Drake.

The plan to meet her cousin and husband at Vauxhall Gardens did not seem to be materializing. The long sigh escaping her lips as she swept dust from an end table defined her momentary unhappiness.

Eveleen had barely seen her husband the last few days, and with the cloudy dark skies, depression settled in her heart. All her best intentions and attempts to find things to do were met with failure.

"Evie? I know I'm late. Will you forgive me?" Logan strode into the room, packages in hand. He bent to kiss her before dropping the bundles on a chair and pulling her into his arms for a more magical kiss.

Dragging herself from the enchantment he never failed to weave around her, she said, "I was afraid you weren't coming, but now that you're here, of course I forgive you."

"I'm sorry I haven't been around the last few days. I hope to make up for my absence so well you'll be sick of me." He handed her one of the packages. "Open it." He crossed his arms, watching her intently.

"For me?" She loved surprises and this one she didn't expect. With the paper torn and the ties undone, she pulled out a pelisse lined with fur and edged with ermine. Another bundle contained a muff made of ermine and the third boots lined in the same manner.

"Yes, for you. I don't want you to freeze today while you're making snow angels. Do you like them?"

"I do," she clutched them to her bosom. "Does this mean we're really going to Vauxhall? Are Ella and Drake going too?" All her dismal thoughts vanished suddenly swept into happiness and excitement of the moment.

"Yes, and yes," he said, taking the garments from her. "Let's get the boots on first."

She sat down and gallantly he slid her shoes off and slipped the boots on her feet before lacing each one. The fur lining warmed her feet as she wiggled her toes inside.

"Thank you," she told him while he covered her shoulders with the pelisse and handed her the muff.

"I believe you're ready." He extended his elbow and they left.

Outside, snow fell softly around them. He helped her into the carriage before joining her inside.

"I can't remember a single time when you actually rode in a carriage with me." She said, trying to think backwards in time.

"There was one time. When Aidan and Blade left together that evening from the gardens and it ended very badly for the couple."

"Oh my, yes, I recall. I feel so sorry for both of them. Anyone who watches them can see how much in love they are." She hurt inside for Aidan and all the times Blade told her she was a little girl. It wasn't fair and it wasn't right and she didn't blame her cousin for fleeing to America. So distraught about Logan, she almost went with her.

"Love doesn't exist," he reminded her pointedly, "perhaps infatuated is the right word or in lust."

Infatuated, was that the way he thought about her? Lust, not love? She shook the idea from her head, not wanting to cast another cloud of darkness on this day. "Do you think Blade will follow Aidan?"

"Most likely, just as I would have followed you to Baltimore if you'd gone there. I'm so glad you didn't," he told her, slipping his hand inside the muff to join with hers.

His calloused hand spoke of the hard work and diligence he spent each day. If he didn't love her, what did it matter? He treated her with gentleness and respect. He cared for her deeply and expected the same in return. Love was just another word.

"I'm glad you found me and decided to marry me." Speaking of her feelings was difficult. She wanted to tell him how much she loved him but knew what he would tell her. Love existed only in fairytales.

"Evie, you understand why I couldn't spend more time with you the last couple of days."

"Yes and no, it's always business and after our dinner the other night with The Duchess, I see how you're selling the wines to establishments here in London. I'm sure that takes a lot of time, and I know it's important."

"I have done that and more, but most of the hours were spent with Drake. We were trying to set up the line of inheritance so no one could challenge what we've done and benefit from some loopholes in the documents. Everyone should know you are protected. Drake and Ella's situation is more dire than ours simply because you are my only next of kin."

"I forgot about that. I missed you, Logan, missed seeing you. When we are home, even if we don't talk, I see you outside or I can find you in the conservatory. What about Harry? His mother could seek your fortune if we have no children."

"I'm sure that in time we will have children of our own. Most of the work with the solicitors is done. All that remains is including Jarret and hopefully Fayth in the wills. Have we heard from them?"

"Not for a while. Storm wrote that Hadden was going to America to bring Fayth back to England. While Storm tried to understand Fayth and her motivation, she doesn't believe Jarret treated her in a gentlemanly way." Yet those very words reminded her of how Drake had treated Ella. Without a chaperone, he brought her to the hunting lodge. What was done behind closed doors only the two of them knew. Yes, she had a strong suspicion their time was spent in bed, but Logan knew more than he would say.

"We're here," he said, and not waiting for the driver to open the door, he did it himself and leapt from the carriage. Holding out his hands for her, he placed them on her waist and helped her from the carriage.

When they walked through the park, the fallen snow crunched beneath her feet. The sun poked its head from behind the clouds sending sparkles alight on the snow.

"There they are." She pointed to Ella and Drake and rushed to meet them. Ella and Evie hugged. "I've missed you."

"I've had so much I've wanted to talk to you about," Ella said then turning to Drake, she laughed, watching him with a twinkle in her eyes, "Time to make your snow angel."

Drake looked at the snow then back to Ella then, "I don't suppose I can put this off to the next snowfall."

"Of course not," Eveleen answered for Ella. "And you, Logan, I'm waiting." With hands on her hips, she tapped one foot, grinning.

"After you," he waved a hand at the ground.

Eveleen laughed delightedly and lying on the ground, she ran her arms and legs across the snow. She stopped and sat up. "That was fun. I can't remember the last time. Logan?"

He contorted his face in what looked like a grimace. Even though he hesitated, he followed suit and soon a second angel was formed. "Are you happy now?" He stood and drew Eveleen into his arms, kissing her soundly.

"Yes," her breathless reply seemed to make him beam. They both turned their attention to Drake. Ella sat on her snow angel.

"Well," Ella patted the ground near her, smiling at her ever so reluctant husband.

He scratched his head. "I suppose if it gets me a kiss and maybe more, I can do just about anything."

A moment later with the deed accomplished, Drake drug Ella into his arms. Rolling over her, he kissed her soundly to the applause of a few onlookers in the gardens.

"Drake," laughing she beat his shoulders with her fists. "This isn't proper. You have to stop before there is more talk about us."

He roared with laughter, "You should know I'm never appropriate and neither are you. That would be so boring." He rolled with her, snow cloaking her pelisse and hat.

Seeming to like what Drake was doing, Logan gently tackled Eveleen to the snowy landscape. She laughed, picking up snow in one hand and tossing it at him.

"Oh, you don't play fair." He loosely packed a snowball and tossed it at her, missing as she anticipated and ducked.

"I don't need to be treated like a girl. This isn't my first snowball fight." She packed snow and threw it, hitting him in the chest.

"Doesn't appear that it is." He reciprocated and the game continued until they were both quite breathless.

With a quick look to Ella, Eveleen signaled to her cousin and snowballs flew at the men. They laughed, running from the onslaught of missiles directed their way, hiding behind a tree while they fashioned more weapons.

The two men appeared on either side, and they were bombarded even as they emptied their arsenal. Laughing again, they raced from their hiding place to see other people had joined in the snow fight.

"Look what you started." Logan stood behind her, his hand on her shoulder as he put the cold wet snow on her neck.

"Oh! That's not fair." She shivered from the cold wetness, pushing away from him.

"It's a fight. Everything is fair," he whispered, and seeming to take pity on her, he brushed the snow from her body.

"I want to find privacy. Do you?" he asked her, retrieving her muff and handing it to her.

Moistening her lips, she nodded, wondering what he intended yet she had a pretty good idea. "You don't mean to do it here?"

"Only if you want to," he teased.

Her breath caught in her throat. "It's too cold."

"We will warm each other." He grinned and winked.

One hand on her elbow he guided her down a path then another and finally they saw no one. Finding a rock to sit on, he pulled her onto his lap and kissed her hard and deep.

Determined to meet his deviltry with her own, she slipped her fingers inside his coat and finding the fastenings on his shirt, she undid enough to slip her hands inside to meet hot flesh.

"Evie!" he gasped. "Your hands are freezing."

"I know and I thought you could help warm them up. Isn't that what you just said?" She smiled sweetly at him.

"Little devil," he whispered. "You can warm your hands on me any time as long as I can heat mine as well."

"Don't think that will be possible with all the clothes I have on."
She wasn't about to tell him her secret, which Ella had wickedly passed on
to her.

"Hmm...there are other tender places, hot places, I can put my
hands. If you're willing." He drew her pelisse around them, making a tent
of sorts with the two of them inside.

With her eyes closed, she rested her forehead against his as his
hands rested on her ankle and explored the length of her leg.

"Logan, they're freezing." She shivered as he made his way higher.

"Naughty," he whispered next to her ear. "Very naughty, my little
Poppet." His cold hand rested on her belly.

"I thought you would say nice." Her head fell back, bearing her
neck to the tender ministrations of his lips and tongue.

"Nice and naughty," he laughed, wondering if he could let his
fingers concentrate on her most pleasurable points. When he touched her
center, she flinched. "May I?"

"Logan, I want you to but..." She held her breath.

"It's just a little thing, but I'll stop if this scares you."

"I don't know,"

He found her swollen bud and touched lightly, watching her eyes.
When she didn't stop him, he concentrated on moving slowly. "I would
have never thought you would do such a thing as wear no underwear, and
I'm pleased you will let me touch you here. Are you sure?"

"It was Ella's suggestion." She breathed in deeply, trying to control
the raspy breaths he caused by giving her pleasure.

"Nothing on beneath the gown and petticoats, I will forever be in
her debt." He groaned as she raked her fingers down his chest.

"Don't tell her. It's our secret." She was suddenly afraid he might
say something in passing that would forever embarrass her.

"Our secret," he murmured. "Look at me." She opened her eyes just
as the climax that had been building reached its zenith.

"Logan, what is happening?" She clung to his shoulders, her nails
biting into his skin. She gasped with sweetly painful pleasure. Eveleen
forgot everything but the waves of fire that shot from her breasts deep into
her belly. "Please," her shriek was mindless. He'd never done that before.

She'd always pushed him away.

"Yes. Oh, yes, my beautiful Poppet." With an inexorable stroking, he saw the final, violent spasm of her release.

"Logan!"

He smiled and used his fingers in her secret erotic parts and the ripple of her spasm spread. Her thighs tightened and she felt a spasm of such unexpected force that she wondered if she would survive it. The thing was, though, she didn't care. She just wanted those incredible feelings to keep pounding through her and she cried out again and again.

Logan drew her close, holding her tight while her body fell limp against him. "I will always wonder what isn't beneath your gowns. If I had my way, you would never wear your undergarments."

"I will keep you guessing. Now, what about you?" She rested her hand on the bulge beneath his buckskins.

"When we are home, you can see to my pleasure." He nipped her ear, further tantalizing her.

"Very well," she began to fasten his shirt. "I don't think I ever want to leave. I'm warm and you're in my arms and I'm so sleepy."

Her last words caught his attention. "Keep your eyes open, Poppet. Never fall asleep in cold weather. You say you are warm but..."

"I am warm, my hands my body and my heart. I'm not in danger," she told him, trying to adjust and smooth her skirts. "We should find Ella and Drake."

"They passed by here a few minutes ago." His voice seemed calm.

"While we were, where I was..." she panicked.

"I can assure you they saw nothing, besides even if they did, my guess is that they just came from making love also." Then he bent close to whisper. "Do you think she took her own suggestion?"

"Now you're being naughty. You shouldn't be thinking about things like that about another woman," she berated him.

"Be assured I only care about what you are wearing. Now let's catch up to them and say our goodbyes." He set her on the ground and arranged her pelisse to sit on her shoulders before handing her the ermine muff.

"There you two are," Ella said.

"Didn't know if you were going to show up or spend the night,"

Drake said with a lighthearted chuckle.

"I wanted to say goodbye. We're leaving," Eveleen turned to Logan for confirmation, "in two days."

"Right," he said.

"Will you be coming into town?" Eveleen asked even though she was sure of the answer.

"No," Drake said. "I've finished all my business here. Ella visited the orphanage and made some donations. She arranged for the smaller children to be taught to read."

The cousins hugged and said their farewells. "Until next time." Eveleen waved as her cousin's coach left.

As if feeling or at least understanding her pain, Logan wrapped an arm around her, hugging her. "I'm sure we'll be in town again soon. Perhaps they could pay us a visit."

In the carriage, Eveleen let her mind wander, reliving her past and imagining her future. She wanted to visit his vineyard in Bordeaux and hoped he'd allow her to go with him when he introduced himself to the Tuscany vineyards. Having never thought about traveling, she was suddenly excited to see other parts of the world. Perhaps she could visit Aidan in Baltimore.

"What are you thinking?"

"Trust and truth," she murmured. "I'd love to visit your vineyards and see Paris maybe while we are there go to Tuscany." Telling him her wishes made her vulnerable and wary yet at the same time relieved of a burden.

"I think we could arrange that. Before we go to Bordeaux there's something I should tell you." He smiled, brushing a wayward lock of hair from her face and gently kissing her forehead.

"What is that?" she asked, suddenly eager to learn something about her husband. Perhaps he would take her with him when he left on business.

The vehicle stopped. "We're here," he said appearing relieved as he assisted her from the carriage.

She raced ahead of him up the steps to the door. Once inside, "Logan, I need to change my dress. The bottom is wet. I'll be right back down. We can have some hot chocolate to warm us up."

"Do you need help?" he asked, with a smile and a wink.

"No but you can put the milk on the burner to start it heating." She raced up the stairs, feeling the chill of her damp clothing. Tempted to put on one of the filmy nightdresses Logan bought her, she changed her mind, settling on a velvet day dress with fastenings in the front.

Per Ella's suggestions she'd skipped the corset and was glad Logan had not chosen to warm his hands on her upper body. She shivered again, recalling the afternoon's pleasure, satisfaction for her but not for Logan. Yet Logan had never felt the same type of pleasure. Maybe it was time she put her fears to rest. Dressed and with freshly pinned hair and new makeup, she strode quickly toward the staircase.

The sound of voices, Logan's and a woman's, stopped her. Before she rounded the corner, she listened but couldn't quite make out the words. Peering around the bend she saw a woman with a gun pointed at Logan's heart.

She stifled the horrified gasp threatening to spill from her lips. Eveleen picked up her skirts and raced to the bedchamber. A few minutes spent rummaging in her trunk, she retrieved her slingshot and found four nicely rounded pieces of ammunition made for the weapon.

At the top of the staircase, hands sweating yet her gaze focused on her prey, Eveleen let fly the small projectile she loaded. Before the paperweight hit its mark, she had the weapon loaded with another trinket.

Her first attempt hit the gun, knocking it from the woman's hand and eliciting a startled gasp. Then she recalled the words she overheard the woman saying, "He has our son."

He has our son. He has our son.

She held back the pain the words caused her. His past not his future, yet his past haunted her and created scenarios she had to find a way to live with. Did he have more than one son from another woman?

Logan held the gun now and looked at her with amazement and pride. "Where did you learn that?"

"On the island," she told him, wondering if she should tell him she was an excellent marksman with a bow and arrow too. She and her sisters used to spend hours practicing, but her cousin Christel was the best shot.

"I'm pleased. This is Jule Bouchard. Did you hear anything,

Eveleen?" he asked, his tone suddenly brisk and threateningly harsh.

Slowly, she nodded, moistening her lips while her hands trembled now just seconds after such clarity and steadiness. "I did."

Logan cleared his throat several times plainly appearing hesitant to speak, "Eveleen, Jule keeps my vineyard in Bordeaux running when I'm not there. When I first met her, we had a brief affair. Our son Charley resulted. Now I've just learned he's been abducted by her brother who covets the vineyard. The same man whose men attacked you on the island."

She sank into a nearby chair, tears threatening, unsure of anything about her husband. "How many children do you have?"

"Only two," he said.

"That you know of." She waved a hand, dismissing the questions she had that could be answered later. "Someone has your son. You must do something about that."

"Yes," Jule said. "Franco has my son and he won't give him back until Logan hands over the vineyard."

"I won't be blackmailed."

"Even for the life of your son?" Jule questioned.

"You and I both know Franco will not harm his nephew," Logan said.

"You know about my brother? When?" Jule sank into a chair, her face resting in her hands.

"It was not difficult to figure out." Logan said. "When he first became threatening, I had a few of my men search for information about him. I discovered he was delivering wine to America when the first nobles were executed. Learned too that he never returned to the estate to see if you were safe or that the peasants near the vineyard let you hide in their homes while your parents were taken prisoner and later beheaded."

"You knew all that and you never told me," Jule said, her voice filled with reproach.

"I believed when the time was right you would explain your situation and be honest with me. Instead, you show up at my home threatening me."

Eveleen watched and listened, consumed by the information about this woman and her brother Franco. The man who searched for Logan at the McLellan castle and wanted to have him prosecuted for the murder of the two men who attacked her. Now he held the life of Logan's son over his head.

"I also know the French government foreclosed on the estate when he failed to pay the taxes after he purchased it. I then bought the land. It is mine. Jule and her brother will never own the estate again."

"It is my brother who covets the land," Jule said.

"You should have come to me for help, not with a gun to my head," Logan told Jule.

~ * ~

Franco paced the deck of the ship docked downriver from London. He didn't believe for a moment Logan would care enough for his bastard son to give in to his wishes. He had hoped though.

Another plan, his second plan, would have to be put into place. He didn't like it, but if he controlled the burn and made sure the fire hit only the newly planted vines when he regained the title, he wouldn't lose everything.

"Uncle Franco," the little boy tugged on his jacket. "When can I see my mama? Where is she? I miss her."

When I'm good and ready. "Your mama is visiting a friend in London. We might sail without her, if she doesn't do what she's been told."

Tears formed in the boy's eyes and he started to wail. "Mama, I want mama. You are a mean man."

He nodded to one of his crew to take the boy below. Charley struggled against the strength of the man and his caterwauling echoed into the cold night air until the hatch was closed.

"The boy, what do you plan to do with him? You can't mean to keep him on board this ship." His first mate stood beside him. They both stood with feet apart, staring into the distance.

"You trying to be my conscious again?" Franco asked while he reviewed his new plan as well as possible options.

"Someone has to be, sir," the first mate said. "You know Lord Maxwell will use his considerable means to retrieve Charley. Once he knows you've kidnapped your nephew, he'll be outraged. We're in London now. He could have the bow street runners take you into custody"

"He doesn't know I'm Charley's uncle." Franco rocked on his heels, more determined than ever to get back what was rightfully his.

"You don't know that and the two of you are family. Any harm done to Charley is not right," he challenged.

"Only if he married her, which he didn't. We're enemies." If Franco could, he'd kill Logan Maxwell he would, but then he would have killed Charley's father. Frustrated by the circumstances, Franco pounded the railing of the ship with his fist.

"Sir, if you had stayed and fought for the land as your parents did during the revolution, you would be dead now. In my opinion you should forget about the past and look to the future."

"But I'm not dead," Franco growled low in his throat. "I'm very much alive and I want my inheritance," he said, tired of this conversation. He wasn't the kind of man to leave the past behind him and focus on the future.

"You will never be happy if you stay on this course. Let me take the boy back to his mother. Lord Maxwell will see Jule is returned safely to her home in Bordeaux."

"Go on then, take the *petit garcon*. He is driving me crazy with his constant whining. I need a moment of piece to put my thoughts together. We sail as soon as you return."

Franco stared after the pair as they walked down the gangplank and hailed a carriage. As soon as his first mate returned and they reached Bordeaux he'd put his plan in motion.

Perhaps if he burned the old vines instead of his original plan, he would bring Lord Maxwell to his knees.

Chapter Six

On his country estate, Logan rose early and dressed, kissing his sleeping wife on the forehead before he strode downstairs ready to put a few finishing touches to the Christmas presents around the tree.

He bought a stocking for Evie when they were in London and so many presents for her and Harry he lost count. Maida was going to receive a few gifts even though he knew she'd protest.

Whistling, he pulled out the box of Christmas stockings and hung them on a line over the fireplace, filling Harry's with a few wooden trains and horses then lemon and peppermint candies.

In Maida's stocking, he placed kitchen gadgets including some new butter paddles and a rolling pin. When in town he ordered two day dresses and a nicer evening gown although it wasn't very practical. He knew she would enjoy it.

At the midnight hour he finally finished wrapping all the gifts. Now looking over the tree he stepped back and admired his handy work and a job well done. Turning from the tree to the kitchen, he wanted to get breakfast started before Maida arrived. She wasn't going to lift a finger this morning, and he knew that would have her protesting.

Maida made the eggnog the night before and it now awaited the whiskey and brandy, a virgin form was for Harry who loved this drink.

Before he had all the potatoes chopped, Maida stepped into the room.

"Well, I knew I had to get up early to beat you to the kitchen, but I didn't expect you to rise this early." She walked through the room as if she owned it and pulled two aprons from a drawer.

"You're not doing anything this morning," Logan told her while she tied an apron around his waist then fastened her own.

"I am. You can't possibly fix breakfast for all the workers and your family by yourself and you know it, Lord Maxwell."

He waved a spatula at her, "Alright, but when this is done, you're not doing anything else."

One eyebrow rose, "Dinner? Who do you think will cook the ham and roast beef? The vegetables and pie?"

"Well," he paused, "I'll help with that too, and at least we won't have to worry about lunch."

"I can help. Is there another apron? I make great pancakes." Eveleen stepped into the room, Harry behind her.

"St. Nicholas came," the boy said excitedly. "The stockings are full and he left so many presents. Can I open them?"

"You can open the things in your stocking, but the rest of the gifts won't be opened until after breakfast. You have to learn the gift of patience," Maida said, brushing the top of his head with a matronly air.

"Okay, Mama." Head bowed he walked into the parlor. "I'll wait for the big presents."

"A child on Christmas day with patience. That's a tall order," Eveleen said, spying a plate overflowing with cinnamon rolls on the counter, she asked, "Can he have one of these?"

"Yes," Maida said.

"I'll take him one then." Eveleen pulled a plate from the cupboard and poured him a glass of eggnog.

In the parlor, she handed Harry the food. "St. Nick was good to you, wasn't he? What's in there?"

"Candies and a train and a horse, I can't wait to see what's in the presents." Harry pulled a piece of the roll off and stuffed it his mouth.

"You be good and we'll have breakfast soon."

He nodded, icing and cinnamon on his face while he played with the train.

Logan watched Evie when stepped into the kitchen. The potatoes, bacon and eggs were cooking and Maida had started the pancakes.

"You didn't leave much for me," she said, busying herself with the little things such as the maple syrup, honey and other condiments.

"My employees and their families are coming for breakfast. You can make sure there are enough plates and silverware for each one. The eggnog is ready except for the alcohol."

"Do you do this every year?" Eveleen smiled and seemed to appreciate his efforts.

"Yes, it's one of the best parts of Christmas." He pulled Eveleen into his arms then swinging her in a circle, set her on the floor and kissed her.

Two hours later, they sat in front of the Christmas tree, sipping eggnog. Evie was curled in his arms, her feet on the couch. She was on her third glass of eggnog, and Logan didn't have any doubts he could ask her for anything and she'd say yes. Yet, they still had not bridged the gap between the wonderful foreplay between them and actually making love. Except for that one time at Vauxhall Garden, she always pulled back or flinched away when he touched her intimately.

Harry played with his train set, not really caring too much for the new clothes Logan had bought for him in London. Maida, as he expected, protested each gift even when she smiled with every unwrapping.

He made Evie wait to unwrap the items in her stocking because some of them were meant for his eyes only, and he wanted to enjoy each precious moment between them.

"Come on, Harry," Maida rose holding her hand out to her son. "It's time to go." And to Logan, "We'll be back around four to start dinner. At least that meal won't be as much work."

"Go rest," Eveleen said, "I'd be happy to cook dinner."

"That's not your job." Maida protested.

"It's Christmas and I enjoy cooking."

"I didn't know you could, cook, I mean," Logan said, wondering what else he didn't know about his beautiful wife.

"Father let us do whatever we wanted. I liked to spend time in the kitchen and our cook appreciated the help," she said then shrugging her slim shoulders, "I've never done anything by myself though."

"Perhaps you should come back," Logan said, feeling the brunt of her wrath when she punched him.

"I can do it. We can do it," she said. "Take the day off with your son and enjoy the moment. If all else fails, we can have breakfast for dinner. There are certainly enough leftovers."

Maida and Harry said their goodbyes, and for Logan it wasn't soon enough. Like a child he could hardly wait to watch Eveleen's eyes when she opened the packages he painstakingly shopped for and purchased for her.

"Let's see what's in your stocking," he said, wrapping an arm around her and walking into the parlor. "I've some other gifts for you too."

"When did you do all this?" she asked, gazing into his eyes then to the Christmas tree where at least a dozen unopened presents waited to be unwrapped.

"In between business transactions."

She sat down, stocking in hand. Pulling out the items she found sheer stockings with floral decorations at the top as well as satin garters, a lacy nearly see through corset and undergarments. "Thank you," she said, staring at the items.

"I can't wait to take them off." He brushed a quick kiss to her lips, thinking perhaps he could leisurely put them on first.

"Here is something for you, Logan. I didn't think it appropriate with Harry in the room, although I'm sure you'll be teaching him how to use these fairly soon. Drake helped me pick them out."

Slowly, he opened the first gift, a hunting knife encased in leather with a strap for his waist as well as his leg. "You realize this isn't just a hunting knife."

"I figured as much since Drake picked it out, the two of you are much the same," she said, shrugging. "I have to learn about the man I'm married to, and all his different sides."

"Are you sure? I know the pain the violence has caused you."

"Yes, I am," she told him adamantly. "I'm trying as hard as I can manage to get over the things that happened to me on the island."

He opened the next one, "A gun. I'm overwhelmed."

"Drake told me it was the best and you would love it," she told him, her voice a bit stiff.

Drawing her into his arms he held her next to him, understanding how precious she'd become to him in such a short time. "Thank you," he said, "You didn't have to do so much."

"Neither did you. I wanted to get you something you'd like." Her cheek rested against his chest. He wanted to always keep her close and safe. She snuggled into him, her breathing deepened.

He was not surprised that she slept so easily. He'd kept her awake most the night and he was surprised to see her so early to help with breakfast. For a moment, he closed his eyes, remembering how difficult their first couple of weeks had been. At least they'd formed a loving alliance, but he needed to take their relationship to a deeper level. He just didn't know how to bridge the gap between love and terror.

Maida poked her head into the parlor. "We're leaving, but I will come back around four to cook dinner."

"Thought the two of you already left."

"Had to clean up first." Then she vanished.

He wasn't a man to do nothing but he supposed holding his wife in his arms was something he should cherish for as long as possible.

"Logan?" she pushed away from him, gazing into his eyes.

"You're not asleep."

"I was for a while. I don't know," She blinked sleepy eyes while she pushed hair from her face before looking at the clock. She'd been asleep at least two hours. "What do you want to do?"

"You have to ask?" he laughed softly.

"If we go upstairs, we'll never make it back down to cook dinner," she told him indignantly.

"Don't be angry. I asked Maida to come back."

Ignoring him, "I'm going to fix a pot of tea. Do want anything?"

He watched her walk away from him, her back stiff, her hips swaying. Bloody hell but he never wanted to lose her. Despite the fact he believed she'd given her heart to him, so much was missing, the closeness they should share wasn't completely there. Everything, every word, every gesture and thought lacked intimacy. A chasm seemed to separate them. He didn't know how to bridge the gap.

She returned, having guessed his preferred drink, brandy. While he watched, she poured his drink and sat down on the couch next to him.

"Are you angry?" His fingers drummed on the armrest while silence penetrated the small room.

"No, I most likely would have burned everything. The cook never let me do anything. I sat in the kitchen telling her my worst fears and my happiest moments. She was the only one I could talk to besides Aidan, who never really listened because her head was always in the clouds."

"What are your fears?" This was the first chance he had to see into Eveleen's life. So many times she kept her thoughts to herself.

She stared at him, her face turning ashen, her head shaking. It seemed to Logan she wished she could run from the room.

"How are your orchids?" she asked, a tiny smile gracing her pale features. "Have you managed to create any new varieties?"

"You don't want to talk to me? The cook has your ear while your husband does not." His wife, he was sure, was afraid of their lovemaking and afraid of talking about her feelings as well as the moments on the island that seemed to snatch her away from him. He always knew she was shy and easily embarrassed, but this was taking it farther than he wanted to allow.

"No," she said, turning her attention to the rim of her teacup. "I don't like to talk about myself and you are always so busy. My childhood fears were silly and childish."

"I work hard," he said, defending himself when he understood the truth of her words. "I don't mean to leave you alone and yet my farm and my vineyard are important to our well-being."

"I understand and now you own a second vineyard."

"You're lonely," he surmised, wishing he could do something to change that. "There is Maida," he told her before he had time to think.

Her breath drew in long and slow, her lips pursing together and looking extremely uncomfortable, "You want me to confide in the woman who has born you a child and who you seem to rely on for so many things, a woman who told me if you came to her bed she wouldn't refuse you."

"You can't be jealous." His words left a stunned expression on her face. "You're my wife."

"It's a title." She told him, some bitterness to her tone. "And it's my fault we haven't shared the same intimacies."

He was taken aback with her comment. For at least a few months since their marriage he thought their relationship had improved. "It's more than that to me." His hand tightened around his brandy glass.

She set her cup down and staring at the ceiling, she said, "When I close my eyes, I see the men you killed. When you hold me in your arms, I can't forget how you wrenched me away from my family without my consent. I am trying, Logan, but there are worse things in my head too."

"Is that why you almost always seem to hold yourself away from me, not just physically but emotionally as well?" The question left him thinking with no answers.

Her slim shoulders shrugged while she looked down, still holding herself from him, "I don't know. I suppose I'm afraid."

"Of me? Of sex with me?" He thought he spent so much time initiating her, yet again she still held herself slightly apart and reserved.

"No, yes, it's just that I see...and however vague I can't erase the images and the sensations from my head."

"Have I hurt you in any way?" he kneeled beside her, taking a tiny hand into his.

"Just when you give me no choice. When you assume you know what I want and what I think," she said softly. "When I see you at Maida's home, a tender smile gracing your face."

"She needs help with things." He shouldn't have to defend his actions.

"Why hasn't she wed?"

Once again, Eveleen gave him reason to think. "I don't know. She hasn't found a man she can love."

"So now love exists," she countered, her cheeks regaining color.

"Perhaps for other people." He sounded sheepish even to himself.

"She loves you. That's why she hasn't found a man to wed," Eveleen said, taking her hand back and rearranging her skirts.

"Of course, Maida doesn't love me." His attention was caught by the sound of a door closing and a movement in the hallway. *Maida.*

"Ask her." She turned her head and nodded toward the kitchen. "Why would she continue to do everything for you if she didn't love you. And why haven't you hired more help? You have the money."

"I told you that you could hire anyone you wanted." He defended his actions, beginning to understand she would have to go to Maida for help if she hired anyone from the village.

"I have a lady's maid now with the help of Ella. Hiring people from the village would require Maida's influence," she told him, her back stiff, even while he watched the slight trembling of her hands.

"Do you want me to tell Maida to leave?" This conversation needed more clarity and now with Maida nearby, it needed to be curtailed.

"No, she is here. Let her finish the meal. We can send food home with her. I see Harry didn't come with her. Is he safe by himself?"

"Yes, he is ten after all, nearly a man."

"I'm going to refresh myself. I'll be down when she is gone." Eveleen left the room, her back stiff.

Logan stared after her retreating back, watching and wondering how exactly he would right this. What would he tell Maida, a woman who had been a childhood friend and never anything more?

Time seemed to fly as he searched for a solution to this problem, while knowing a similar situation existed in France where he had another son. If she were to tell him Jule loved him, he'd most likely agree, but Maida...

Maida had never given him one indication that she might want him in anyway but sexually.

And he never pretended to want to wed any woman who was not a lady and Maida was help, nothing more. Besides, love didn't exist.

The object of his thoughts stood in front of him. "I've started dinner. It should be done in an hour or two."

"You're early. It's too soon to start dinner."

"Where is Lady Eveleen?"

"Refreshing herself," he said, looking at Maida with new insight.

"I'll go see if she needs anything," she offered, turning to do just that.

"No," he said, startling Maida then too curt, "Sit."

Eyes wide, she did as he asked. Her hands folded in her lap. "What is it?"

"Why haven't you wed?" he asked, wondering if she would deflect or answer truthfully. Then he remembered other boys and men in the village who had tried to court her, good men.

She stared at him as if he was crazy. "There has been no one interested in me and my son."

"Really," he rose, pacing the room, his thoughts reeling. Then he confronted her, meaning to challenge. "What about Oliver, Oliver Flynn? Two years ago, at least from my viewpoint, he seemed more than willing to care for the two of you."

"I didn't want to leave you without anyone to see to your needs," she shot back, seeming angry and hurt as well.

"Oliver Flynn is still single," he suggested. "Perhaps you should take another look at the man. He works hard and can provide for you and Harry. He has a nice home."

"What are you telling me?" she said stiffly. "Do I no longer have a job here?"

"If you wed, you don't need one, but Harry can always have a job in the greenhouse."

"I'm leaving." She gathered a basket of food she put together for herself and Harry. "I'll leave you and your wife to finish your dinner. Do you want me in the morning?"

"I do but Eveleen and I will be making another trip to London to find a cook and a few other people."

"I would find people in the village for her," she offered.

"That's just the point. She doesn't want your help. I will send word to Oliver that you are still interested in courting him if he is." His voice wavered. This was the end of an era, but it had to be this way and Maida needed to accept a new life.

A few minutes later Evie entered the parlor where he waited.

"Thank you," she told him.

"You were listening?"

"From the stairs, yes," she said.

"I've solved one problem, but we have more pressing issues to deal with. I don't want you to fear me in any way. We need to discover some way where you won't equate my touch to those of the men who attacked you."

The knocking at the door ended their conversation.

"Who is it?" she asked, stepping forward. "Maida wouldn't come back after that and she wouldn't knock."

"Stay in the parlor," he warned, understanding the person on the other side might not be friendly.

A wounded look crossed her face. "Why?"

"For your safety."

Cautiously and with his hand on the hidden knife at his belt praying he wouldn't have to use the weapon in front of Evie, he opened the door.

"Sir?"

"Yes," he recognized one of his men who crewed the ships coming from Bordeaux.

The man handed him a message. "The last shipment of wine was stolen."

~ * ~

The eerie silence encapsulating the entryway sent a wave of shivers down her spine. With this news he would leave. After everything she told him, she was almost glad she wouldn't have to sleep in the same bed with him tonight.

All her fears were laid out in front of him and the vulnerability she felt was overwhelming.

He would leave and the loneliness assailing her was raw, ripping into her heart. Her mixed emotions confused and frustrated everything she believed in and had wanted her entire life.

They were speaking in whispers, and it was just a matter of time before they walked out the door. She held her breath, her hands clasped tightly in front of her, praying she was wrong.

The man left and Logan turned striding toward her, his hand outstretched. "Should we figure out how to cook the dinner?"

Surprised, she said, "Yes. I thought you would leave."

He smiled at her. "There is nothing I can do tonight. The ship and the crew were unharmed, but the wine was stolen."

"Franco?" she asked, understanding the man coveted the land Logan owned and now he seemed willing to do anything to accomplish the feat.

"Yes, it's the fourth shipment he's stolen. I have to put a stop to him. Piracy on the high seas is frowned upon and the punishment is death."

She stiffened, not liking the direction of his thoughts. "You're not going to kill him, are you?"

"No," he said, patting her hand. "I'm going to let the French government do the job for me. What Franco doesn't understand is that I don't need to ship my wine, don't need the proceeds from this vineyard to survive. He will never own the land."

"You have that much wealth you can speak so casually about lost cargo? What about all the establishments in London you contracted with?" she asked, stunned by his simple revelation.

He let a breath of air out slowly, "Perhaps it is time to share something about myself."

"Perhaps."

He pulled out a chair at the dining room table for her. "My father, although a nice man, was a wastrel."

"He gambled?" she asked, watching as he sat down across from her. Maida had set the table, even pouring glasses of wine before she left. The dinner simmered on the stove and would be ready soon.

"No, he invested when he should have saved. My father had no sense of money. The only inheritance remaining when he died was this estate."

"That's why your businesses are so important to you. You're obsessed with regaining your fortune." She looked away, not intending to use such a strong word.

Tapping his knife on the plate, he seemed to think for a few minutes, "I suppose one could say that. I was fixated on that aspect of my life but no longer."

"Now that you've built a small empire don't you think you could relax and enjoy life?" she knew the truth though. Logan would never change any more than she could.

He smiled, lifting his glass to her before shrugging. "I enjoy my orchids."

"And how much time do you spend in the conservatory?" She knew the answer.

"Very little," he admitted.

Changing the subject, "Did you mean it when you said we were going to London to find help?"

"I did until I received the message about my stolen wine. We can see to it when I return."

"Return," she choked on her wine. "You're going to France then. Without me." She stiffened, confirming what she'd thought earlier. He had told her he would take her and now he reneged on his promise.

"Yes, I am going to France without you. This trip is too dangerous." His tone changed to curt, and a dark shuttered look crossed his face.

She wanted to go with him but waited for an invitation she knew wouldn't come. "In the morning, I presume."

"Dawn."

"To Bordeaux? Will you be sailing as soon as you arrive in Dover?" she questioned, understanding he would want to answer.

"Why the sudden interest? I didn't think you would care." He leaned forward, resting his forearms on the table.

"I guess I was just wondering how long I would be here alone, in this remote farm with Maida as the only person to talk to." Her stomach rolled at the thought. This was her home and seeing the woman he fathered a child with fawning over him, sent her in a rage she didn't understand.

"I could arrange a carriage to take you to London. I'm sure The Duchess would love the company," he offered. "It's what I was planning before this last minute and necessary decisions."

"And leave my home, our home to Maida. Logan, she thinks she is in charge of everything that goes on here. Even when I try to take over some of the chores, she finds a way to insinuate herself into our lives, your life. I don't feel comfortable here when you're gone."

"Maida is no longer a problem. She is to wed soon." He waved a hand in the air, noticeably frustrated. "But if we are both gone, someone must oversee the home and the farm."

"Why can't you hire someone," she persisted.

He set the fork down, "I will but I can't do that by dawn." Then he rose, striding from the room.

He left her with her heart in the pit of her stomach. She would never make him understand how she felt, not when she couldn't satisfy his basic needs.

"Well," she muttered, getting up from the table and turning off the stove, "The meal won't get eaten tonight." She was no longer hungry.

Another commotion in the entry brought her to the front of the home, a dirty pot in hand. "Auntie." She set it on a table and enveloped The Duchess in her arms.

"No, they won't clean themselves but I took it upon myself, understanding the goings on here, to hire staff for you." She turned to Scarlett. "Will you please introduce everyone?"

As if the new help waited in line, Scarlett introduced each person one by one, beginning with the new cook and the scullery maid.

"I don't know what Logan will say."

"Pshaw, he'll be happy you finally have suitable help. He's told you that you can do what you will, so..." She waved a hand in the air.

"Are you hungry? There is dinner left uneaten."

"I'm famished," she said, starting for the dining room. "Scarlett, you can join us as soon as you have everyone settled and informed of their duties.

In the dining room, Charlotte dished up generous helpings for herself and Scarlett.

"Thank you," Eveleen said as she sipped her wine and for the first time this evening felt a weight lift from her shoulders. "How did you know?"

"Ella," she bit into a piece of ham. "She told me you were able to hire a lady's maid but nothing else." She leaned forward, waiving her fork in the air. "I know a bit of what is going on here."

Eveleen let a small sigh of relief slide from her lips. "Of course you do. You know about Maida and Harry."

Charlotte patted her hand. "I make sure I know everything about the men and their extended families in my charges' lives." She sat back, hands folded on her ample stomach. "Now, it has come to me that Logan has had multiple cargoes stolen from him. He is on his way to France, isn't he?"

"Tomorrow morning, at dawn," she admitted with a long sigh. "Auntie, where is this all going?"

"You need to travel with him and I'm here to make sure you arrive at his ship before he can set sail. I've brought men to accompany the carriage to keep us safe and a second carriage for your maid and Scarlett. I will escort you to Dover. The two of you will never consummate your marriage if you are not together."

"A carriage can't possibly..." *She knows about that, too.*

Tapping her cane on the floor. "Go pack a valise and we will start our trip now. With so much to do tonight, I'm sure Logan won't miss you."

"Auntie, he will come to bed and find me gone." Eveleen's heart beat out of control.

"He won't." Charlotte was shaking her head, a grin on her face. "I've made sure there are blankets and pillows in the carriage. You'll, we'll be able to sleep."

"What if he sends me back?" Eveleen didn't like the idea of his rejection. She didn't want to make the trip to Dover only to return the next moment humiliated.

The Duchess tapped her cane twice. "I've a plan for that too. Now listen."

"Yes, Auntie." Charlotte's transformation to The Duchess always made her smile and sometimes it terrified her.

"It's really very simple."

"Simplicity is your strong suit," Eveleen said, waiting for the answer to at least one of her problems.

"When the carriage stops in front of his ship, you will get out, bag in hand and walk up the gangplank. The carriage will leave so he has no alternative but to keep you on board."

"You really believe that?" Eveleen asked, clearly thinking she might have become a bit crazy. Logan might very well delay the sailing just to find another carriage to escort her home.

"Of course I do." She turned to the cook who entered the room. "Please pack us a simple breakfast and a lunch. I don't know how long it will take us."

"Yes, mam," The cook turned to the kitchen.

"Now, go put your things in a bag and we'll be off. The men I've hired will have the carriage ready for us."

"Logan is sure to see the coach sitting in front of the house." She was still hesitant and unsure about this insane plan.

"No, he's in the village speaking with some of the men who live there, the ones who have helped him in the past. He won't be back until he's ready to leave. It won't be easy since it's Christmas. Now go, hurry. If we are to beat your man to Dover, we must start now."

With much too many reservations to count, Eveleen rushed up the stairs to her room. Hastily tossing clothing and toiletries into her valise, she closed it and stepped quickly down the steps.

The Duchess sat in the entry, tapping her cane and holding two baskets on her lap. She rose as Eveleen approached.

"I don't believe I've had this much fun since my husband, the late Duke, swept me off my feet and on numerous adventures just like this one. Are you ready?"

"I don't know." Eveleen had second thoughts and third ones.

"My dear niece, trust me, everything will turn out just as you'd like it. Now, you'll have time to think about the best ways to handle Jule and her son."

"I haven't done well with Maida," she whispered softly.

"Oh, but I believe you've accomplished more than you think here. If anything, Logan is a fair man and if my research proves true, he's never cared for Maida as anything but a friend. Now Jule, on the other hand is a different story."

"Jule? He loved Jule?"

"Now, I wouldn't go that far. Logan would never admit love even if he felt it for the girl, but Jule lived with him for over a year and she still resides inside the chateau believing she has a claim to it."

"She was his mistress?" Eveleen didn't really think Logan was the kind of man who'd keep a mistress, but in his earlier days anything was possible.

"Yes and no. As it turns out Jule was a French speaking infatuation. He lusted for her."

Lusted? There was that word again.

Arm and arm, the unlikely traveling duo stepped down the stairs to the carriage. The coachman helped them inside, and a few minutes later the vehicle began to roll forward.

Charlotte handed her a covering and a pillow. "Now, get your rest.

You're going to need it come morning. Fortitude does not come easily, and you will need lots of it when we arrive in Dover unannounced. As you can see, if you look out the windows we are well guarded. Your Lord Maxwell can have no complaints about that."

"What are you going to do after you drop me off?" Eveleen leaned against the cushioned seat.

"I'm going to stop at an Inn in Dover then sleep and eat until I'm ready to travel to your estate then back to London. I've a friend who lives there who I'd like to see."

"Good, I'm glad you'll take some time for yourself and sleep." Eveleen wondered how much rest she'd get.

"There's a good chance your man won't be on board when we arrive. You need to pretend you're Fayth and you've every right to the captain's cabin," The Duchess advised.

"I understand. He wouldn't put me off the vessel," she said thinking out loud.

"Of course not, you're his wife."

She sighed softly, her breath fogging in the cold air. "I wish he thought so, but all I've done is disappoint him."

"I thought Ella solved the intimacy problem with that filmy negligée, but then I saw the two of you together and knew by the way the two of you reacted to each other the marriage had not been consummated." It seemed Auntie Charlotte was having trouble keeping her eyes open.

"Go to sleep, Auntie. If there's time, I'll tell you about it in the morning." Eveleen was loathe to talk about her failures, but The Duchess might be able to help.

Those words woke her aunt. She sat up, brushing flyaway hair from her face. "No, there is no time like the present. I can sleep when I'm dead." She chortled at her comment.

Eveleen looked down, letting her lashes fall before she stared at The Duchess. "I don't know what's wrong. He wants more from me than I know how to give. When I'm in his arms and my eyes are closed, I see the man who attacked me then the men he killed. I can't get past that."

"In the defense of your life," The Duchess reminded. "He killed them to save you."

"In my defense," Eveleen echoed. "Yet no matter how many times I say those same words to myself, it doesn't help. I'm grateful and so very indebted but terrified at the same time."

"The solution is simple. Don't close your eyes. Focus on his eyes instead. Look into their depth and see how much he cares for you. Look at the man you love."

"It can't really be that simple."

"Perhaps it is. You'll never know unless you try. If my guess is correct, he just wants to give you your woman's pleasure. He wants to watch your beautiful face when you make love. It's my experience a man likes to watch his lady reach her pinnacle when he's deep inside and one with you."

"I don't understand."

"Of course you don't, but I've every confidence you will." Aunt Charlotte leaned against the side of the carriage, a pillow beneath her head. "Just keep your eyes open," she murmured.

It seemed one moment she was awake and the next second Aunt Charlotte snored deeply in sleep.

With her eyes open, Eveleen listened to the sounds of the vehicle as it rumbled along the road. What if The Duchess was wrong and Logan went to bed. She forgot to leave a message. Her nerves stretched thin; she imagined every worse-case scenario.

Sunlight began to filter into the carriage. Sounds of seagulls and the smell of sea salt littered the air. Aunt Charlotte still snored softly on the opposite seat. Eveleen sat up, stretching her muscles before patting her hair into place.

They had to be close now and what would Logan do when he saw her? She shivered, rubbing her arms, trying to ward off the sudden chill sweeping through her. He could send her home.

Her knees trembled and her hands shook. She rubbed her hands up and down her legs, thinking she could stop the throbbing and ease the ever-growing apprehension.

"Eveleen?" Aunt Charlotte yawned.

Pushing away from the side of the carriage and placing her hand over her aunt's, "We are almost there?"

"I can smell the sea," The Duchess said, beaming.

The Duchess tapped the roof of the carriage. It drew to a stop.

The driver hopped down and sticking his head in the window, he asked, "What can I do for you?"

"How much longer?" Charlotte asked.

"Ten minutes," he said.

She waved him away. "Good, go on."

"How are you, my dear." She leaned forward and patted Eveleen's hands. "Ready to make things right with your husband?"

"I'm terrified." She knew this would take a great deal of courage. "He's going to be angry, furious, ready to throttle me."

"Stiffen your backbone, my dear. You can do it. McLellans are made sturdy. Your mother would be proud of you. You know, she was a bit like you, shy and quiet. Kept things inside of herself. Liked to paint."

With a little wistful sigh, "I wish I could have known her."

"Me too, my dear, me too. You didn't have very many years with her. Now, no more of this maudlin stuff, you've got to get your life in order. Be strong when you approach him. You are in the right."

"I understand and I'll try." She had no idea how to chase away her fear of intimacy. Telling herself to trust him was not enough. Telling herself to relax when he touched her intimately didn't work. She paused thoughtful, it did once and she was so cold and afraid someone would see what they were doing she never shut her eyes. How would keeping her eyes open make a difference?

"Good girl. Now one more thing, you need to find a way to keep Jule from his bed. If you are having trouble satisfying him, he could turn to her. Suggest to him that he should find someone for her to wed just as he did for Maida. It will make your life there so much easier." She stopped, gazing out the window for a second, "And get her out of the chateau."

"I'll try," she said, having no idea how to broach the subject let alone get him to do her bidding.

"Promise me you'll do more than that. Promise me." For emphasis she tapped the cane on the floor.

Eveleen understood The Duchess was behind this and she would keep driving until she promised her. "Of course, Auntie. I promise."

"Good, then I can rest easily. Oh, by the way I believe we're here. Give this old lady a kiss on the cheek and take one of these baskets. Remember, don't look back, only forward. This will be the beginning of your future."

When the coach rolled to a stop, Eveleen leaned toward her and gave her a quick kiss on the cheek. Then, grabbing her valise and one of the baskets, she let the driver help her onto the road.

Almost as soon as she stepped on to the ground and the driver regained his seat, the carriage whisked away. She inhaled a long deep breath, praying for the needed courage and without looking back, she walked up the gangplank to meet her future.

Logan stood in the middle of the ship, his hands behind his back, a strained expression on his face when he noticed her. She held her breath, gazing at him and wishing he'd say something. The best-case scenario, he wasn't here when she arrived. Unfortunately, that didn't happen.

A few feet in front of him, she stopped and waited, taking long deep breaths in hopes to slow her heartbeat. She tried tilting her head flirtatiously and smiling.

"Lady Maxwell," he began, "I hope you can explain yourself. You knowingly put yourself in danger by coming here. Why would you do such an incredibly stupid thing?"

"No," she said, backing up a step, her heart stopping. "I did not put myself in danger. As you can see I'm fine."

"No?" he paused and stared at her long enough to make every muscle in her body twitch. "You mean to tell me that traveling through the night is not dangerous." A muscle ticked at the base of his jaw, his hands now at his sides were fisted. His anger wilted her courage.

"The Duchess employed men to accompany us and guard the carriage. She believed the journey was safe. Who am I to argue with her?" Her knees began to tremble again and a wave of nausea swept through her.

Her lady's maid stepped beside her. "Is there a place I can put your things and mine for the trip across the ocean to Bordeaux?"

"The two of you are not staying." His voice became harder than she'd ever heard it before.

Eveleen remembered The Duchess' words. She stiffened her back and thought of her future, their future. She couldn't keep Jule out of his bed if she wasn't with him. "Where do you propose we go?"

"Back where you came from. Our home where no harm can come to you or London where you can visit with Ella." His voice seemed to waver a moment as if he suddenly realized the carriages bringing the women here had vanished.

"That's not possible unless you've a carriage and men to guard us and take us home," she whispered softly, trying to hold on to the minimal courage The Duchess had given her.

~ * ~

The Duchess cackled as they drove away from the docks. She didn't think she'd ever concocted such a wickedly delightful plan. Everything had been thought of, not one thing had been left to chance. In a matter of minutes, Eveleen would have all her wishes granted.

Opening the basket of food, she munched on the scone and strawberry preserves that cook packed last night. When she finished the scone, she rummaged further, discovering thick slices of ham and cheese, which she ate with her fingers.

"Delicious," she licked her fingers then tapped on the roof of the carriage, hoping to bring her companion to her carriage.

"Duchess," he opened the door.

"Bring Scarlett here from the other carriage. I need someone to talk to."

A few minutes later, Charlotte's friend and confidant since the duke passed on sat across from her, grinning and chattering nonstop.

"We did a good job, didn't we?" Scarlett asked, grinning. "She is now with her husband and can protect her rights."

"We did. Now it's time to settle at a nice Inn and have a real breakfast then sleep for a few hours before we visit with the McLellan. I haven't seen him in such a long time." The Duchess had other plans with the laird she wasn't telling her companion just yet. Her matchmaking had one more step to complete before she was finished for the day.

"I'm exhausted from all this plotting and planning." Scarlett yawned, eyeing the basket of food.

"Forgive me," Charlotte handed the packed breakfast-lunch to her friend. "Did you sleep well?"

"As well as can be expected under the circumstances." While Scarlett ate, Charlotte lifted the curtain and focused her attention on the passing scenery. The carriage traveled up the hill from the docks to the town. A castle guarded the port and stood sentinel over the community of Dover.

The inn was warm and inviting. Meals were ordered and rooms purchased. Over a pot of tea and hot food, Charlotte prayed this would work out for Eveleen. If this ploy didn't play out in the manner she planned, the fault lay entirely on her shoulders.

"You're worried about her, aren't you?" Scarlett seemed to read her mind. "You know Lady Eveleen will be fine. Even though he hasn't told her he loves her, he does."

"Yes, but I'm more concerned about Jule. She has divided loyalties in this, and Logan must find her a suitable mate or there might well be hell to pay." Charlotte leaned back crossing her arms over her ample bosom, remembering some of the trials she and the Duke had during their marriage.

Chapter Seven

"Then, I guess you're going to France. You can put everything in the captain's cabin." He turned to one of him men and nodded for him to take the bags into his room.

"I'd like the basket," she said quickly and asking Brann, her new lady's maid. "Did you have anything to eat?"

"Yes," she curtsied. "The Duchess made sure we were all taken care of before we left. I'll just sit over there." She pointed to a spot on the deck.

Logan stepped into the conversation. "All the cabins below are empty," he said gruffly. "You can pick one and rest or do whatever you want. We should be arriving in Bordeaux sometime tomorrow."

He wasn't sure how he felt right now. Relieved nothing happened to his wife on the roads to Dover and happy to see her even though it was unexpected, or terrified something might happen to her in France. He had too many mixed emotions where Evie was concerned.

Confronting Franco was the focal point of this mission and that could prove treacherous. He wanted to end the man's constant intrusion in his life and make sure the French government was aware of his proclivitie s.

Eveleen now stood at the railing, her hands closed firmly around the wood. He approached her cautiously, hoping to have a peaceful discussion.

"You should go inside. It will get cold out here once the ship starts moving." He hesitated, wishing she were tucked away safely at his estate.

"Where inside?" She turned to him. a strange expression on her face, one he couldn't read. "One of the cabins below? Do you really abhor my presence that much?"

"I don't dislike anything about you," He said softly. "I treasure you."

"Liar." Her attention remained focused on the ocean as the ship's sails rose on the masts and began to catch the wind.

"I suppose there is one thing," he reluctantly admitted, "but I'm hoping that together we'll find a solution." On this voyage he had no illusions of solving any problems between them.

"The Duchess gave me advice," she told him, her voice whisper thin almost blown away on the wind. "I pray it might help me...us."

"Advice about what?" he asked skeptically. What could The Duchess know about her issues with their lovemaking? A slow heat rose to his cheeks. "You didn't tell her?"

"Not really. No, I told her nothing. She has a way of ferreting out thoughts and ideas from us without actually knowing what happened. I think she reads minds as easily as sipping her tea and eating lemon bars."

"I see," He leaned against the railing, staring over the churning water, his mind reeling, unsure how he felt about The Duchess knowing the intimacies of his marriage, which were supposed to be private.

"You, we are going to the vineyard. What will we do there?" she asked, turning to meet his gaze.

The sparkle in her inquisitive eyes never failed to steal his breath and leave him wishing for so much more. "Probably nothing while we are at the estate. I plan on taking an overland shipment of wine to Paris."

"You want Franco to attack the shipment."

He didn't answer. The less she knew the safer she would stay. Shivers seemed to wrack her body. "You need to go inside, Eveleen. You're cold. I'll walk you to my cabin. Get some rest. I'll see you later."

She stared at him, tears welling in her eyes. "The Duchess hired staff for your home."

"Our home," he corrected her. "And good, we needed people. I'm guessing they had to come from London not the village."

She slowly nodded her head, "The Duchess understood, understands, everything. I'm still trying to accept Maida and her son as part of your life. I only wish you would have told me sooner."

"I'm sure she comprehends," Logan agreed reluctantly wishing he knew Eveleen's aunt a little better. He'd heard so many rumors and innuendos. Half of London feared her and bowed down to her. The rest seemed to regard her power, curiously happy they'd done nothing to capture her interest.

"How long will we stay?" she asked.

"We should be in Bordeaux tomorrow or the next day depending on the winds. We'll stay in the town and start for the vineyard in the morning. It's not that far, but I don't want to travel in the dark. What advice did she give you?" His curiosity was getting the better of him and if her suggestions worked, he could breathe easier.

She smiled, reaching out to touch his face. "Don't close my eyes."

"Keep your eyes open. That sounds a bit simplistic." Yet her smile gave him pause to think, and the touch of her fingertip against his skin sent a rush of heat throughout his body.

"Yes," Eveleen turned away from him, wrapping her arms around herself. "That's all. Do you remember Vauxhall and what you did, we did? I never shut my eyes because I was frozen and terrified of someone rounding the corner and seeing us."

"I do remember. For the first time you let me touch you intimately."

"You did." She moistened her lips, looking away from him.

He didn't know if she was cold or still terrified or perhaps shy. "Let's go inside where it's warmer. No one needs me out here. We can check out what the new cook packed for you to eat and perhaps explore your aunt Charlotte's proposal."

"I am cold." She let him put his arm around her waist and guide her to the room he called home when he was on the ocean. "I'm not at all sure I'm ready to explore any proposals." Nervously, she gripped her hands together.

He opened the door for her and let her step inside. And with a quick shrug he said, "We don't have anything else to do."

"It's nice." She sat down at the small dining table near the window. The ship had pulled up its anchor and was heading into the sea. She ran her tongue across her lips, keeping her gaze away from him.

"Do you get seasick?" he asked, suddenly concerned as the ship dipped into a small swell.

"I don't know." She blinked a few times, tilting her head slightly as if in thought.

His hands rested on her shoulders, gently massaging tight muscles.

He'd made her this way, tense and wary. He would give anything to change this.

"Perhaps we shouldn't eat." His suggestion made his stomach growl and he looked at the basket with longing. Neither one of them had eaten much the day before.

She opened the basket, and said, "Help yourself. I'm going to try a little something. Perhaps a slice of cheese."

Logan pulled out a ham sandwich, relishing the food but feeling guilty as hell. "I'm going on deck." Sitting next to her with hours in front of him and afraid to touch her or make love to her, left him shaking with need. Perhaps with distance between them, he could begin to understand his wife.

Advice to keep her eyes open, how the bloody hell would that stop her terror? No other woman had ever feared him, but now his bloody wife couldn't return his passion, wouldn't let him make love to her.

Frustration at the situation ate at him, stripped his nerves raw. He left the room, swearing under his breath and cursing the circumstance on the island that created this situation. If he'd been there sooner...

Maybe he wasn't as gentle with her as he should have been. After all, he didn't know the extent of the abuse that day. He thought hard about what he'd seen, her bodice ripped open, the man adjusting his trousers, and that sight sent him into a bloody rage.

She needed to tell him what happened to her even if he knew she wouldn't want to talk about it. If keeping her eyes open kept her from reliving those horrific moments, maybe The Duchess' advice would work.

This gave him an entirely different prospective of that day and the nights with her afterwards.

A few minutes later he saw her standing at the bow of the ship. The warm pelisse he bought her in London was draped over her shoulders. She had to be cold. Her face was ashen in color and he worried about her.

He stepped behind her, "Evie?"

She turned, a half-smile gracing her face. "Logan."

"What are you doing outside?" From behind her he wrapped his arms around her and pulled her against his chest.

"I lost what little I ate. I thought if I watched the horizon, with fresh air caressing my face, I would feel better."

"You have good instincts." He rested his chin on top of her head, bracing his feet to steady them against the rise and fall of the ship.

"When will we reach Bordeaux?" she asked, letting her slender body settle against him.

"Tomorrow," he said. She must have forgotten a previous conversation or she just searched for something to say. "Evie, we have to talk about that day." Against his body he felt her stiffen.

"I don't see why. I don't remember much. Don't want to remember for that matter."

"I know but..." he let the sentence trail off. The drive to know what happened came from his selfishness. If she didn't want to relive that day and if remembering brought her pain, why would he push her to do just that?

"The ordeal of that horrific afternoon seems to fill my soul even though I can't recall anything but the dead men, the blood and their lifeless eyes. Why can't I forget? And what happened that has me terrified when you touch me in certain places."

"Because you haven't remembered yet. I know men who have had horrible experiences, shocks that changed their lives forever. No one knows why some people can survive traumatic events and others don't. Why some withdraw and others seem to go back to normal lives."

"I want to be normal," she whispered softly. "I don't want you to suffer from something I don't seem to have control of. I promise I'll try harder. Maybe together I can put the past where it belongs."

"Hush, I'm not suffering. I only want to help you, us so we can live the rest of our lives the way a normal married couple does." He wanted all that and more. Not so long ago, he made plans to take Eveleen to his chateau in Bordeaux. Now, because of the possible danger to her, that was the last place he wanted her.

Her laughter was soft and nearly nonexistent then he heard a soft sigh that sounded like despair. "Normal, once a few months ago all I wanted was to be married and happy like Ella. I wanted children. Now I don't know what I want, and the possibility of children seems so far away."

"I believe you want me," he said, turning her in his arms. She placed her head against his chest. "You like my kisses, I think."

"I can hear the beat of you heart," she murmured her head just above his heart. "You're so strong and handsome. You could have any woman you set your eyes on. Why me?"

"Because there was always something about you that called to me. The first time I saw you I knew I wanted you, had to have you, make you my wife. I never felt that way about another woman," he told her, understanding how true those few words were. In so many ways she was different.

"Why didn't you tell me that a long time ago? I would have waited for you in London and never gone home. Why?"

He felt her tears on his shirt, knew the trembling of her tiny form. "I should have protected you better. The time never seemed right. I didn't believe for a moment you would leave the city."

She shrugged as if giving up on him.

"You have to talk to me. This time I want you to close your eyes and tell me what happened." He set her slightly away, needing to see her face and her changing expressions.

She closed her eyes. Seconds ticked by slowly at first then faster while he waited. Then she shook her head and opening her eyes, she said. "All I remember is the moment you slit his neck and made me go into the hut. Then I heard the shot and I looked outside and you tackled the second man, sending him to the ground then once again blood splattered everywhere. When I looked at myself, I was covered with blood."

"Very well, go back farther. What did you do when you stepped on the island?" He held his breath, hoping she at least recalled the first seconds leading toward the violence.

"I looked at the rocks my cousins and sisters left there, all but the marble one, Allura's stone. Hunter took it back to the castle to prove he'd been on the island and it was never returned."

"Good, what next?" he asked. "Think about it. What happened after the rocks?" Intensely curious and eager to put an end to her fears, he was afraid he pushed her too hard.

"I walked up the hill to look at the huge rock in the ocean." Shivers racked her body.

"Why?" he asked, striving for more patience than he'd ever possessed. "You're trembling."

"I almost died there. Hunter's stepbrother kidnapped Aidan, Christel and me. He tied us to the rock and was going to let us drown when the tide came in. Blade and Hunter rescued us."

"Thank God you didn't die." Nausea rolled in his stomach. She'd been through more in her short life than he ever could have imagined.

"No, Hunter and Blade got there before the water was over our heads. I don't know why I wanted to relive those moments."

"It's just like this time. Talking about what happened can heal the mind and soul." He slipped a piece of hair behind her ear, cradling her in his arms. "What happened next?"

"I..." she moistened her lips. "I felt hands around my neck and then everything went black. I..." She let her forehead fall against his chest. "I don't remember." A sob tore through her, breaking his heart.

He smoothed his hands up then down her back, hoping to console her as memories slowly returned. "That's good so far. How do you feel?"

"Abused, molested. He hurt me, Logan. I don't know exactly. I can't recall what he did, but he did things he didn't have the right to do. Things I never would have said yes to," she said, her voice a thin pain filled wail.

"How did you get back to the hut?" He wanted to take this one step further. No, he wanted everything out in the open. If they left anything unturned now, she might withdraw further into herself.

"I don't..." she rubbed her temples, closing her eyes, grimacing as thoughts seemed to encompass her soul.

"Think," he told her. "You can remember. I know you can."

She closed her eyes again, silence except for the sound of the sails filling with wind.

"He drug me back to the hut. I tried to resist but he was stronger and when we got to the little cabin, he pushed me. I fell to the ground. Then he ripped my dress and was on top of me."

He watched her swallow while her ashen face seemed to get whiter. Puling her close he tried to sooth her. Yet anger threatened to overcome rational thought. "It's okay. You're remembering and that's good, but we should take a break for now. Let's talk more later."

She nodded, seeming relieved to stop the conversation. Her body shaking against his, she said, "Thank you."

He held her while they watched the horizon, letting the movement of the ship soothe battered emotions.

"Sail ho," rang from above.

He felt her stiffen against him as she turned to look. "Franco?"

"I doubt it. We're not carrying wine so he has no reason to risk his ship and lives of his crew. Could be anyone bringing cargo or passengers to England. We are getting closer to Bordeaux."

"No, we won't be on land so soon?"

"But when we are you will have to find your land-legs." He laughed softly, pulling her closer and enjoying the rush of warmth from her slender body and soft bountiful curves.

"What then?"

"Are you wondering where you will have to sleep?" he asked, knowing he meant to keep her close but also realizing he would not get much rest. The transportation to his chateau needed to be arranged, and the afternoon would have slipped away by the time they made landfall the next day.

"Yes, no, I'm curious but I'm exhausted so it really doesn't matter."

"You're not hungry?"

"Starving, but at the moment I can barely keep my eyes open. I don't know which to do first."

"Perhaps you should think twice before stealing away in the middle of the night in a carriage that is not conducive to restful sleep." Good God, but she could have been robbed or worse. The Duchess had a lot of accounting to do next time he saw her.

"You still angry with me?"

"No, but I hope and pray you don't ever do something so foolish again. I enjoy your company but had I understood what you were up to, I would have worried myself sick." And that was the absolute truth.

"Without The Duchess' influence, I would have never embarked on this journey, but I'm glad I did. I've always wanted to see France."

Her words warmed his heart. If anything, this journey opened his eyes and taught him a few things about his wife. "Look," he pointed south. "There's land. We're going to stay close to land as we travel west then south toward Bordeaux."

He ushered her to his cabin and to the bed. "Rest, sleep tonight, I might join you later." He doubted if he would. With so much to think about, there would be no time for sleep.

The next afternoon they watched in silence as the land drew closer and the smoke from the chimneys could be seen. Sailors busied themselves on the deck, with the lines and the sails as many of them came down. Crew on the docks worked to bring the boat to its proper mooring.

Favorable winds had brought them to the Bordeaux docks sooner than expected. Yet even now the sun dipped below the ocean and a full moon hovered in the darkening skies.

He didn't want to risk an overland trip to his chateau in the night. Highwaymen took what they wanted, besides he didn't want to risk Eveleen's health. She was exhausted after the overland trip to Dover and little comfort in his bed with the rolling seas.

By the time they walked down the gangplank it was almost midnight. She clung to his arm as if she couldn't walk by herself. He heard her heavy sigh of fatigue.

A carriage picked them up and took them to the inn he often frequented. Once inside he ordered food and drink. He carried her up the steps to their room while one of his men followed with her valise.

He set her down. "You can refresh yourself and join us downstairs for dinner."

She nodded and said, "I'll be right down."

~ * ~

Eveleen yawned and stretched. Sun beat in through a window. Her stomach growled its discontent. Looking back the last couple of days, the last time she ate was about thirty-six hours ago.

The last conversation she remembered was agreeing to freshen up and meet Logan downstairs. She'd fallen asleep instead.

"Logan?" A quick glance at the room told her he wasn't here. And a quick look at herself told her he had undressed her down to her underclothes. Even though he'd seen her naked, this was so new to her a blush crept up her body.

The door opened and he strode inside, a tray in hand with a steaming beverage and a platter of food.

"That looks and smells divine." Her mouth watered, anticipating the hot breakfast.

"I'm glad you like it." He set the platter on a small table in the corner of the room then pulling out a chair, he gestured for her to sit.

While she found the robe he must have set out for her and donned it, he poured the hot chocolate and dished food on her plate until it was filled with soft-boiled eggs, hash browns and bacon. The amazing aroma filled the tiny room and her stomach growled again.

"Are you going to eat?" she asked, forking a piece of egg and dipping a slice of bread that also arrived on the platter into the yolk. She chewed, savoring the flavor and the sustenance.

"I already have. We are only about an hour away from my chateau. Take your time and eat. Once you're ready, come join us." He walked to her and bending over placed a quick kiss on her cheek.

Something inside her wished he would pull her from her chair and kiss her passionately. Instead, business like, he turned on one heel and left the room without a look over his shoulder.

"Take my time," she paused for a moment between bites. She finished eating then dressed. It seemed the day was sunny but cold so she dressed for the weather before she slipped into the warm pelisse he bought her before they made snow angels.

Picking up the valise, she opened the door and it seemed Logan meant to pamper her. One of his men waited by the door to take her satchel.

"Lady Maxwell," he reached for the bag, which she handed to him. "Allow me to help you."

Suddenly, her heart raced and a tingling of energy swept within. Heart speeding, she moistened her lips and inhaled a deep breath before she descended. She was about to see his chateau in France. Waiting for her at the door was Logan. The smile he sent her way melted her heart and helped her believe there was a future waiting for them.

With long strides he met her midway and offered his arm, politely saying, "Eveleen." Waiting outside was a carriage and several wagons filled with goods or supplies of some kind.

He helped her into the vehicle and followed, sitting opposite her. Lines along his brow were clearly etched on his face. She understood his concerns but didn't know how to ease them. With every breath, she wanted to satisfy him as a wife and a lover. Yet that incident on the island haunted her soul. Keeping her eyes open just didn't seem to be a plausible or constructive idea. When she talked about what happened that day, it didn't seem to help either.

She closed her eyes, letting the rhythmic sway of the carriage soothe her battered nerves. Logan seemed to need time to think also.

The carriage rolled to a slow stop. "Are we here?" Eveleen asked, looking outside the carriage window.

"Yes, do you like it?"

The chateau was magical. The front entrance was flanked by two turrets and set in the insider corner of the right-angled floor plan. Logan helped her out, and for a few seconds she looked in awe at the building.

"You own this?"

"For six years now. I fell in love with the ageless beauty the first time I saw it. Come, I'll show you around."

"I'd like that," she said, her heart in her throat and wondering when Jule and her son would present themselves. The Duchess had insinuated the woman lived in the home unlike Maida who lived in a cottage away from the main house.

In the front entrance Jule met them. "*Bien venue*, welcome," she said, staring at Logan with a brilliant smile as if she didn't exist.

"What are you doing here in our home?" Eveleen remembered The Duchess' words and decided to make sure the woman understood what was expected of her.

"I live here," she replied, tilting her head but not even glancing Eveleen's way. Instead, she concentrated her attention on Logan.

"Not any longer." Eveleen said. "I trust if you have belongings here, they will be moved to the stone cottage."

"I won't. Except for a few years during the revolution, I've lived here since I was born. I won't move by your say so." She looked once again to Logan, seeming to think he would contradict his wife.

Eveleen crossed her fingers, praying Logan would back her in this. She didn't know how she would proceed if he didn't.

Logan cleared his throat, hands clasped behind his back. "I've allowed you to live here because I had no reason not to. Now I have a wife and your presence here would not be appropriate. It would also make her uncomfortable. I would like you do as she asked."

Jule gasped, her face turning red. "I don't believe you said that. What about Charley?"

"He's your son. The boy will go with you."

"Charley is your son too." Her hands defiantly fisted at her sides, her eyes clearly angry.

"And I will always support him, but it's time you found your own way and a husband who will give you more children," Logan continued.

Eveleen breathed a silent breath of relief. At the moment, she didn't need to say anything more. Her gaze shifted from Jule to the beautiful and ornate decorations in the home. She'd never seen anything to compare.

"I work here, help tend the grapes and I taught you everything you know." She tried to defend her position.

"Since the child was born, you've done little with the vineyard and no, you gave me my first knowledge, but I've researched the new techniques of which you know nothing about. I know more about growing these grapes than you learned in your childhood. Much has changed."

"I've done my fair share."

"It seems Jacque has done most everything for the past five years. I've supported you and our son without hesitation. I've let you live in the chateau. It stops now."

"How will I survive?" Now she cast Eveleen a look of hate.

"Jacque has been interested in you for a long time. I believe it is way past time to wed, and Charley needs a full time father not someone who is here a few months a year."

"He has one, a father," she injected.

"A biological one, not a real father. You understand very well I spend only a few months each year at this vineyard, perhaps less. From here on out your credit at the dressmakers in town as well as the other business you frequent will be cancelled. The only funds you will have are the ones meant to be used for Charley."

"I have seen to your needs," she protested.

"And I paid highly for that, but now I have a wife, a cherished wife. I've sent one of my men to locate Jacque, and we'll see if he's amenable to the idea of marriage to you."

"When?" Eveleen asked, wondering if Logan had been prepared to dislodge Jule from this home even before she confronted his mistress.

He picked up her hand and kissed the back. "Before we started the last leg of our journey, I sent one of my men ahead to seek out Jacque and bring him here. While I appreciate your sternness, I don't want Jule living here any longer."

"How dare you," Jule said, clearly angry with him. "Without even asking me, you're planning the rest of my life."

"I did what needs to be done," he said, his voice taking on a tone Eveleen had never heard before. "And you need to wed and live a new life, have more children if that's what you want. You can no longer live in the past. Your parents lost their lives, and it is my understanding you lived with Jacque's family and they protected you from those who would have harmed you. He fell in love with you a long time ago."

"But I don't love him," Jule wailed, her protest reaching deaf ears.

"Doesn't matter," Logan said curtly with a wave of his hand, "Love doesn't exist. He will be a suitable husband and father and he will care for you."

"Lord Maxwell," the voice boomed through the tense quiet of the entryway. "It's good to see you."

The two men hugged and slapped each other on the back, seemingly best of friends. "Good to see you too, *mon amie*."

"Your man told me you wanted to talk with me at the chateau. What about?" he looked at the others present, his expression turning to a scowl when he noticed Jule.

"It's not private by all means. I wanted to know if you were interested in wedding Jule if she would say yes."

His jaw clenched tightly. "I didn't think you'd..."

"That was a long time in the past. I'm a married man." He let the last statement hang.

"I see." Jacque ran his hands through his hair. Then, after another few seconds of thought, he approached the lady in question. On bended knee, he took her hand in his, "Will you do me the honor of becoming my wife?"

She stared at him and it seemed an eternity passed before she glanced at Logan then back to Jacque. Her hand shook as she slowly almost reluctantly said, "Yes, I will since it doesn't seem I have a choice."

Eveleen would have loved to know what she was thinking; perhaps a way to get out of the marriage.

"Good," Logan said, patting Jacque on the back. "That is taken care of. We will plan the wedding two days from now."

"We can't possibly wed in two days. There is too much to do. No, we must wait," Jule protested.

"Why not? What is there to do? All we need is a priest and a few witnesses. Both are easy to procure." Jacques challenged his soon to be wife.

"It will take longer than that for a dress. I'd like flowers and a nice reception. If I have to wed, I want a real wedding," she protested.

Smoothly, Logan said, "There are pre-made gowns at the dressmakers. I will pay for the fitting and make sure all is ready."

"I would like to wear my mother's dress," she said, seeming to concede. "Where will we live?"

"In my home. It will have to be good enough for you. You won't regret this. I promise," He said calmly and seeming to understand she was giving up the chateau, once her family home for his meager lodgings.

She nodded slowly then breathing deeply, a wan smile gracing her face "I'll see to our belongings, Charley's and mine."

Eveleen watched her stiff departing back and, for a few moments, felt sorry for her. But the woman assumed things that weren't to be.

"Thank you, sir," Jacques said. "I've loved her since we were kids, which was why my family rescued her and hid her in the cellar when the revolutionaries were looking for her. She would have lost her life along with her parents."

"I should have understood your feelings sooner," Logan told his friend. "I did nothing but keep her hopes of becoming my wife alive. In my defense, I was lonely."

"Where is she to stay until the wedding?" Jacques asked.

"She may stay with you or in the adjacent stone cottage. It matters not to me. I leave the place of residence up to you and Jule."

Eveleen didn't want Jule even that close but chose to remain silent. This was between the men. She accomplished all she set out to do. Jule would be away from the chateau and her husband.

"For her safety, I'd like her to stay with me, but I will understand if she chooses the cottage. Perhaps you could leave a guard or two outside the door. I don't trust her brother."

"Done, if that's what she decides."

The two days passed in a blur. Despite her reservations and inherent dislike of the woman, Eveleen helped to make Jule's wedding everything she dreamed of. Nostalgia over her marriage sent tears to her eyes. A picture-perfect wedding day would have been nice. She had been deprived of most everything Jule demanded now.

"Ah, well," she sighed softly as she gave consent to the purchase of flowers. "I can never get the day back, and there are more important things in life to dwell over."

"How are the plans coming?" Logan strode into the parlor, a grin on his handsome face. "What did she say she needed; flowers, dress, food and what else?

"Slowly," Jule said, a slight bitterness to her voice. "I'm still not wanting this marriage."

"But you'll say yes," Logan urged, seeming to regard her closely. "I would not have you at the altar and deny the groom."

Jule slanted him a fierce glare. "Do I have a choice? Would you put me in the stone cottage for the rest of my life if I said no?"

"You'll be happy with Jacque. I promise," he said softly. "He loves you. And if you refuse to wed Jacques, I will find someone you would deem more suitable."

"That remains to be seen," she said stubbornly. "So, you will not give up on this notion that I wed?"

"No, I won't. Jule, you have two hours until the ceremony, until Jacques is your husband. It will be small and intimate with the closest of Jacque's family as well as Eveleen and myself will be there."

"Franco was not invited?" she queried, her eyes wide.

"His presence causes too many questions. You are aware he has pirated several of my ships. He is not welcome in my home under any circumstances. You will have to put this thought aside and concentrate on all that is positive happening here," Logan said, his voice strangely calm.

Eveleen watched, fascinated by her husband and his easy way with words. Despite everything, except for Charley's best interests, Jule as well as Maida were no longer part of her life, and she thanked Logan for the part he played. Maida was wed and soon Jule would be also.

"I'm trying," Jule told him, "but it's not easy. Franco is my brother after all."

"If there is nothing else, I will see you in a couple of hours. I will walk you down the aisle and give you away. Eveleen will serve as your matron of honor. Jacques family will make up the rest of the witnesses."

"Again, I have no choice in this," Jule said bitterly.

"You do not. If not Jacque, you will marry someone else as I told you before." With that said, Logan strode from the room without a second look.

"We must finish here." Eveleen directed her lady's maid to finish dressing Jule's hair and makeup.

When Jule finished, Eveleen forced herself to admit she was beautiful and once again she questioned Logan's choice of brides. Unwanted chills swept down her spine, her stomach rolling. Jule could give Logan everything she could not.

Eveleen and Jule stood in the entrance to the parlor. Jacque stood beside the fireplace, a man Eveleen had never seen stood to Jacque's left and a minister standing to his right waited to perform the ceremony. No music played to usher the bridal party to the waiting groom.

Eveleen, bouquet in hand, walked toward the minister and took her place. Then Logan with Jule on his arm brought the bride to the groom.

"Who gives this bride?" the minister asked.

"The father of the bride's child," Logan said then sat on one of the chairs set out for Jacque's immediate family.

To Eveleen, the wedding was vivid and clear. Unlike her wedding each word rang loudly and seemed to echo in the room. She realized the extent of the vows she made when she married Logan.

Very few of their pledges had been kept, yet in ways it was not all her fault. When the promises were said and Jacques kissed Jule, a weight lifted from her shoulders. Unless there were other children in other places, she felt freedom from her husband's past lovers sweep through her.

Drinks and food had been set out for the reception. Jacques family milled around, visiting and talking for more than an hour.

"Thank you," Jacque shook hands with Logan. "This is the culmination of my dreams and I owe it to you. Even though Jule doesn't love me, my heart holds enough for both of us."

"You're welcome, but it took me long enough to figure it all out." Logan laughed. "Take good care of Charley and if you need anything for him, let me know."

"You don't owe me anything." Jacque seemed to bristle.

"My child will have whatever he needs, and if that means providing something for your future unborn children, for fairness sake, I will do that."

"We will see. Let the time and circumstances dictate those indefinable things. I've never asked you for anything I didn't earn and I don't plan on starting now," Jacque said as they left followed by cheering family and flying rice.

Logan stepped beside Eveleen, taking her arm in his. "Would you like to go for a walk and hold a personal celebration of their marriage?"

"Can we look at the grapes?" She was eager to see what seemed to draw so much energy and time from her husband. These last two days had been so filled with wedding plans she'd had little time to see the vineyard.

"That was my thought. Get your pelisse. It's cold outside."

The coat hung by the door. With his help, she slipped her arms through the sleeves and buttoned it. After putting her hat on and grabbing her muff, she said, "I'm ready."

She wondered what he really thought of the wedding and if he'd miss Jule in his bed. Waiting for him to open the door, she wrapped her arms around herself, as if she could hold in all the insecurities assailing her.

Stepping outside, a chill bit into her exposed flesh, but sunshine filtered through a light splattering of clouds. The sunlight uplifted her spirits and gave hope for the future.

"Where should we go first?" She accepted the proffered arm as they walked down the steps.

"I want to show you the old growth vines. Don't know how long they've been here. They produce the best grapes. Their roots go deep into the ground and can soak up nutrients and water the new vines can't. The old growth is the heart of the vineyard."

They stood at what seemed to be the beginning of the rows. Rolling hills filled with grape vines was all she could see. "It's strangely beautiful even though the vines are barren."

"I love this scene," he said, a hint of nostalgia in his tone.

"Why did you purchase this land? You've no connection to France or the aristocracy who owned these lands. I can almost understand the animosity Franco and Jule hold where you are concerned."

He paused for a moment, his arm circling her and pulling her closer then with a heavy sigh. "As I believe you know, my father nearly lost everything we owned. I've worked my adult life expanding the Maxwell fortunes. When I heard this land would be auctioned, I made sure I was the one to purchase it. Jule and Franco would have never retained it. The government would never sell it back to the same aristocratic family who owned it before the revolution."

"Have you ever taken time out of your life, to play or relax?" She turned toward him, needing to see his eyes when he answered. "Other than the day we made snow angels."

For a moment he gazed into the distance then laughed. "Our snowball fight that day in Vauxhall Garden. I will always remember the time fondly. You looked so dear with snow in your hair."

"Yes, yes, you did play and I did take advantage of your warm body." She remembered her frozen hands on his flesh as well as his gasp of surprise, and she also remembered his attempt to ease all her fears and insecurities.

"Don't ever think I didn't enjoy every moment," he said, touching her chin with a finger and gently lifting.

She stared into his eyes and saw the signs of desire building within them. She knew he wanted to kiss her but now yearned for so much more. "I enjoyed most of that day too."

"Let me guess, no, I suppose we've been over some of the problems plaguing our marriage. When we return to London, would you like The Duchess to plan a reception in celebration of our marriage? I know I've denied you something that should have been yours, and perhaps if we had begun our relationship with a bit more joy, we would be able to work through the fears."

"Perhaps," she sighed, having wished for those same things. "I know aunt Charlotte would delight in the planning, but I'm not sure I want that. Let me think about it." A reception this late in their marriage might be fun, but it also might be bittersweet.

"We don't have to decide anything now. Will you let me kiss you?" he asked, still gazing into her eyes.

"You understand you don't have to ask," she said, appreciating the gesture though.

"You're wrong. May I kiss you?" he asked again.

"Yes." Watching him she moistened her lips, preparing for the pressure of his mouth against hers then closed her eyes.

Suddenly, she felt him withdraw.

"Open your eyes, Poppet," he murmured.

His breath whispered across her lips as her eyes opened and she watched as his mouth met hers, his hands on both sides of her face. His tongue seeking entrance and his lips dancing against hers, touching, withdrawing then moving with swift determination to encompass hers.

She responded, closing her eyes briefly then, "Keep your eyes open, Poppet," he said, momentarily withdrawing from her.

Her body melded with his, the romantic play and sexual dance between them incredible. The ballet was magical and ethereal at times primal as she tried to become one with him. Infinity and beyond, his eyes sparkled, shimmering with desire, the heat encompassing her exponentially.

He pulled away with a nip and a soothing touch to her lips with his tongue. "What do you feel?"

"Hot," she let her head fall into his hands.

"Any fear?" he queried.

"Nothing but joy."

"Good, who am I?" he asked as he continued the passionate sexual dance with his lips on her heated flesh, setting an inferno flaming inside her body.

What a strange question. She closed her eyes for a second, wondering how he wanted her to answer.

"Who am I?" he insisted.

"Logan," she said still wondering at his intent yet gazing at his face, memorizing the handsome angels and planes.

"Who am I?" he persevered.

Shaking her head, she stared, confused with the query. "My husband?" she finally said in question.

"We should continue this later in privacy," he told her, once again bending to take her lips in his, stealing her breath.

"Hmm..." she sighed, gazing at the chiseled features her husband possessed. Her hands rested on his well-muscled shoulders. This kiss all but consumed her. Molten fire rushed throughout her limbs and deep into her belly. She could feel the pulse of his heart, or hers, and it was as if drums pounded in her head. The intimate sensations were delicious, mesmerizing, so engulfing that he was moving again before she realized it. Searing sensation remained. His lips parted from hers, touched them again. His hand stroked her cheek, her breast.

When she closed her eyes, he reminded. "Evie, you must keep your eyes open. Always."

Her lashes flew open. He swept her into his arms and swiftly carried her the distance to the chateau and up the steps to the master bedchamber.

~ * ~

Franco sat on the edge of a stream, tossing rocks into the water. His sister gave up claim to the family home. She married a commoner and now her future was settled forever for her and her children.

"*Va te faire foutre,* Lord Maxwell, kiss my ass," he muttered watching ripples from the rock spread across the water. Except for his first mate and a few men who manned his ship, he was alone. The money from the sale of the wines he spent gambling and on prostitutes. Severe depression slipped into his head. He searched for another way to destroy Maxwell."

Maxwell must have stopped shipments from Bordeaux to Dover. Now his source of money had dried up and his eyes and ears inside the vineyard was nullified. He was going to have to do something drastic.

His first mate towered above him. "The fish is fried if you want to eat." He held out a bladder of wine. "If he ships overland to Paris, we can waylay him and take the delivery."

"The suggestion has merit, but I'm sure the wagons will be heavily guarded and he'll likely be watching for such an attempt." Yet the thought of stealing from Lord Maxwell again had merit. In reality he'd like to rob him blind.

"You could set fire to the vineyards." Tate offered again while he placed fish on two plates.

"And ruin the grapes?" It was a fleeting thought. "Never would I do such a thing. Circumstances would have to be more dire than they are now." Outrage swept through Franco. They were his grapes and somehow he'd find a way to buy the land back. Putting an end to Maxwell's financial hold on the vineyard would come first.

"You could set the young vines on flame. I noticed about an acre of new land and new grapes. That would make a statement without ruining the crops." Tate offered the idea.

"That goes against all I've ever believed in or wanted for this land." But he desired it back at almost any cost. Yet Maxwell seemed to have an iron hold on his property and resources well beyond anything he could afford.

"You must be willing to go to any length if what you say is true. Maxwell won't give in easily. You tried kidnapping his child. Kidnap his wife. Hold her for ransom."

"He'd kill me," Franco mused thoughtfully. He stirred the fire with a stick, embers swirling into the night sky and remembered the two men. Maxwell had slit their throats easily. Emptying the skin of wine, he found another and drank deeply.

"Not if you took him by surprise. We could figure this out, set a trap. I'm sure he would give you the land in exchange for the woman he's supposed to love."

"We don't even know if he's going to take a shipment to Paris, but perhaps I can get Jule to spy for me." Jacque, Jule's husband was loyal to Maxwell. She'd have to go against her new husband but if he understood his sister, he knew she resented the marriage Maxwell forced her into.

"He will. The only question is when. Talk to Jule. Unless this new husband of hers is a miraculous lover, she'll help you."

Franco thought on all Tate said and everything swirling in his head. Every scenario involved risk, every situation could provide all he ever wanted. His ancestral home and land should be in his name. Even if he could get the land from Maxwell the French government might never allow him possession.

"What if the government discovers who I am? They could confiscate the land again. The hatred of the old nobility still runs strong and pure. The only reason Jule lives now is because Jacque has always loved her. Upstart commoners," he spat into the fire causing a slow hiss.

"A risk you can either meet face to face or you can sail to America and start a new life. You can begin again. We can begin in a new land."

"Not something I planned," he said. "The chateau beckons to me. It is my heart's desire."

"Perhaps it's time to put the past where it belongs. I'm growing tired of the fight," Tate let out a long slow sigh.

"*Merde,* Tate, you enjoyed the pirating as much as I did. You thrived on it. Rob from the rich, Lord Maxwell, and give to the poor, us." He roared with laughter at the little ditty.

"I need more wine. Do we have any?" He rummaged through their bags, drawing out another skin of wine. "We need to go into town and buy more."

"I'll do it tomorrow."

"Good, good, I wouldn't want to be recognized," he laughed. "Last time I was in town I was sixteen and with no hair on my face." He let his head back and swigged the wine.

If he took the Lady Maxwell, he might have to check out what made Maxwell want her for a wife. She was pretty little thing in a mousy way. He rubbed his crotch realizing it had been at least a week since he had a woman in his bed.

"Did you see the young girl down the road? Think she'd be willing to have a little fun?" Franco asked, meaning for Tate to get her and bring her to him. "I'll share with you."

"She was only about fifteen but ready for some fun, I dare say." Tate said, seeming eager for a dalliance this evening. "I'll be back before you can finish that wine. Perhaps I can confiscate more than one girl."

Franco grinned, undressing her with his imagination as his first mate left the clearing. The bedrolls lay on the ground, his breathing increased with the anticipation.

Biding his time until Tate returned, he set up lean-tos for privacy, close enough to the fire to stay warm but far enough away from each other. He knew Tate wouldn't return with two women.

Restless, he stirred the fire before adding more wood. Sitting back, he watched flames, picturing the vines up in flame. Shivers wracked his body while the fire heated his face.

He didn't know how much time passed but he finally heard horses approaching. Unwilling to take a chance, he pulled his pistol from his breeches and waited to see who approached.

"Franco, I'm back," Tate slid from his horse before helping two girls from their horses. "Brought us each one. The little lady you asked for was hold up tight in her house. Didn't want to risk her daddy's wrath so I went to a brothel just outside town.

"Good, what did it cost you?"

"Just the promise of a crate of Bordeaux," Tate chuckled while he wrapped his arm around one of the women. "I see you got some places for us. You didn't waste any time."

Franco approached the other lady, "What's your name, sweet one." He reached out for her hand.

"Rose," she said.

"You're not very old." He stroked her arm, stopping at the neckline of her low cut gown to trace the bodice. "Come on. You want wine?"

160

She looked to the other girl who nodded. "Yes," her voice nearly a whisper sent heat coursing through his body.

"You a virgin," he asked while he handed her a cup of wine. "Drink."

She didn't answer but took the wine he gave her and drank as if searching for courage. "What do you want me to do?"

"Just be yourself." He took the cup from her and walked with her to his bedroll.

Chapter Eight

Settling Evie on the bed and resting on one elbow, he looked down, watching the myriad expressions flowing across her beautiful face. "We need to finish what we started on the hill. You must remember to keep your eyes open and know I won't ever hurt you. Do you know who I am?"

Laughing softly at what seemed to her an absurd question, she said, "My husband, Lord Logan Maxwell," she nodded, catching her bottom lip between her teeth, her eyes wide and her lips gleaming with moisture. She giggled, "Do you know who I am?"

"My beautiful and charming wife."

Needing to taste her lips and feel the sweet texture, he lowered his head and whispered, "Good, now keep your eyes open and watch me. Look into my eyes and on my face, understand how I feel about you." He was done with her fears. They would end tonight and she would be his wife in every way.

"And what is it you feel?" she queried softly keeping, her gaze riveted on his eyes. "I'm not sure I know or understand. You need to explain."

"You are precious and fragile, delicate, but you are also strong and capable of withstanding many hardships." Her unique scent, lilies and innocence constantly intrigued and fascinated him. She was always ready for an adventure.

His lips touched hers gently, reveling in the softness he encountered. For a moment, he felt her resistance, tasted the salt of her tears. When he looked at Evie, her dark lashes lay against her flesh.

"Open your eyes, my sweet darling." To his ears his command sounded harsh. He wanted to bury his face is the silk of her hair and breathe in the soft scent of swirling around Evie.

"I don't know if I can." Her fingers bit into his shoulders.

A sob tore through her, but he could not let this go, would not allow her to spend the rest of her life in terror of him, imagining and not remembering exactly what happened on the island.

"Remember, Evie," he whispered, lifting his lips just a breath from hers. His voice was low, rich, deep. Demanding, pleading for her to heed his wishes and live up to all she could be.

She inhaled on a ragged little sound, her pulse beating a rapid staccato at the base of her neck. "I want you, need you and have yearned for you since the moment I saw you, but the essence of you always seems to elude me. Let's change that tonight."

"I want to change this, but I'm not sure I want to remember. The knowledge will change me and I'm terrified of that."

He touched her lips once again then once more. Tasted them, pressed past them, felt the desire in him flame wildly as he took in the sweetness and warmth of her. He wanted to see her face flush with pleasure. Her fears needed to be swept into her past.

She was in his arms and he could have her, but nothing would be complete until she remembered everything that happened that day when she risked her life for a simple pleasure.

He lifted his lips from hers. Thought himself insane. Her sapphire blue eyes were focused on him. Her lips were damp from his touch, still so tempting, inadvertently inviting him to take what she offered and damn the consequences.

He smiled ruefully, hating himself and the question when he asked, "Did he kiss you?"

She shook her head, her wispy strands of hair whipping aground her face. Before she answered, she moistened her lips, "He ripped my dress and...and I remember his hands on my breasts...and his mouth. But it wasn't a kiss. He was cruel." In the safety of his arms she shuddered, her body trembling as he tried to calm her terror.

"Did he hurt you?" A wave of fury swept through him, his body shaking with the urge to kill the man who dared violate his wife. Too bad he'd already done just that, slit his throat. If he could have a second chance, he would torture both men until they died in terror.

Her eyes widened and with tears slipping down her cheeks, she nodded. "Yes."

He slowly slipped the sleeves of her dress down her arms, freeing her beautifully rounded breasts, just the perfect size to fit in his hands. The rose-colored tips invited him to taste and to touch. Then focusing on the task at hand, he asked, "He ripped your bodice."

Once more she nodded without answering, her shoulders trembling, tears filling her eyes.

"I'm not going to do that, tear anything from your body. I won't touch you without your consent." Gently he worked the bodice of her gown to her waist, freeing her arms. "You can touch me as long as you keep your eyes open and remember who I am."

"My husband," she murmured. "My..."

Quickly he slipped his shirt over his head and set her hands on his chest, inviting and encouraging her to explore his body.

"And I will always be your husband and you my wife. You can touch me anywhere you want." This was so damn hard. His body shook with the restraint. He needed to take his time and teach her about the beauty of lovemaking.

He ran a finger seductively around one areola to the other then back. What if this didn't work? What would he do then? *You will keep trying until Evie is able to accept you completely as her husband.*

"Logan, I..."

"Do you like this?" He flicked the hardened peak with a finger. It had to work and if his seduction didn't this time, he would keep trying.

"Yes," she moaned softly, her hands rested on his chest, her nails scoring his flesh with tiny marks.

The most seductive touch he could manage, moving lower, unbuttoning the fabric of her gown so he could touch her stomach. Spreading his fingers so he spanned her hipbones, caressing every inch that was uncovered. Softly, gently, over the rise of her hip. He drew circles with his fingertips and felt her hips jerk and arch in response, a silent invitation.

"Did the man do this?" he asked. "Did he seduce you gently? Touch you in erotic and evocative places? I want my touch and the memories of what we do here to haunt your dreams at night; nothing else, only the pleasure of this moment and ones to come."

She licked her lips, closing her eyes for a moment then as if realizing what she'd done she opened them. Wide and innocent, her blue eyes gazed at him with unspoken desire. "No, he hurt me and I fought him but he grabbed me more tightly. He did horrible hurtful things to me, but I'd rather not say. I remember now." She broke down in heart wrenching sobs. Tears slipped from her eyes.

He knew first hand now that he had not reached them before he completely defiled her and he swore. The depth of her pain was horrific, and he didn't know how he would convince her he meant her no harm.

He held her close, waiting for her to stop crying trying to absorb all her pain into his body.

"Will you let your husband give you pleasure, no pain? I promise. Your choice," he said, praying she would give consent for her virtual seduction.

"With my eyes open," she murmured, sniffing back the tears yet smiling at him to give him the answer he sought.

His fingers threaded into her hair. His lips silenced her, praying what she said was an agreement. "Was that a yes? Do you want me to make love to you, come inside you and bring you the greatest possible pleasure?"

"I think so," she whispered, yet for a moment she looked away.

"I think so is not a yes," he told her.

"Yes, I want you."

Still, she stiffened, pushing him away as if he was her assailant, shaking her head slightly when his mouth rose above hers, connected with her.

"Evie, do you know what you're doing to me?" he groaned, his voice husky with desire. "Please, I want to see into your eyes and I need for you to know it's me giving you sensations you'll want to feel again and again. It's me touching you intimately, loving your body as it should be worshiped."

"I won't close them no matter how tempting. I promise," she told him yet her voice shook with either fear or desire. He couldn't be sure and so he waited.

"Good," he finished on a breath. "I'll make sure you regret nothing. If you want me to stop or don't like what I'm doing, tell me."

He swept an arm around her, bringing her fully against him. The length of his body shuddered hard, shaking his determination to his core. He found her lips. Caught them, held them. Stroked the rim of them with his tongue, parried between them. She would stiffen now, push him away. He expected none of this evening to be easy.

To his delight, he heard a delicate moan rumbling in her throat then a soft purr. Her hands pressed upon his shoulders, pausing, went still. Her fingertips dug into his flesh, explored the width of his shoulders and his neck.

Holding him, leaning into him as if she desired his caress, her eyes still open, she gave encouragement. "I want you."

"That's what I needed to hear."

He drew her tightly into his arms, afraid to let her go, terrified if he did he would lose her forever. He kissed her lips, stroking her back softly, feeling the sensual curves and planes of her soft body. He broke from her lips to touch them again, his tongue tracing the shape of them before slipping deeply into her mouth once more. He caressed the silky skin of her back, sweeping the length of her spine, creating erotic swirls once more at the base of her backbone with his fingertips, stroking the curve or her hip, the rise of her derrière.

She was different tonight with her eyes open, brighter, more cognizant and intense. The terror didn't seem to lay dormant, waiting for release at any moment. He did not deny that she had always yearned for him, but had to admit to himself she had never been able to fully return the passion he tried so hard to ignite within her.

There was always some elusive factor keeping her from accepting him, holding back the passion he knew simmered deep inside her and at times so close to the surface he could taste her hunger.

He had touched nearly every part of her. "Do you want more of this?"

"Only if you do," she moistened her lips once more.

Determined to release the demons lying inside, he trailed his kiss to her earlobe, along her throat. He lifted the mass of her hair and kissed the nape of her neck then shuddered, sighing deeply, burying his face within the strawberry silk and kissed the blond cloud falling around her, enjoying the scent and silken feel of her hair. He moved her, shifting the fall of her hair once again and pressing a kiss against her upper spine.

"You are so soft," he whispered. "Is there any part of you that is not soft?"

"I..." It seemed she didn't know what to say.

Laughing tenderly, "I thought so, every part of you is soft and sensually sweet, my Poppet."

He lavished her shoulders with his caress then moved lower against her spine, his fingers dancing fire while his lips delivered their liquid heat, down to the very small of her back, over the rise of her hip. He paused, sensations sweeping through him in a staggering manner from the taste and feel of her as she suddenly sighed and shuddered.

He held her in his arms once again. Her eyes met his; very wide, soft, dazed and strangely imploring.

"You are soft too." She touched his mouth with a fingertip, blinking her stunned look of amazement settling in the deepest part of his heart.

He coughed, chuckling at her words. No one had ever called any part of him soft. "I believe hard or tough might be a more appropriate description of my body."

"Your lips are soft," she challenged.

"We're going to do this right tonight, you know," he said, tenderly brushing locks of hair from her face, studying her and trying desperately to read her mind.

"My eyes are open, and who would have thought the answer was so easy," she murmured. "Always open and no terror will fill them and push you away from me."

"That is what I needed to hear, little Poppet."

He continued, capturing her mouth and feeling at long last the duel of her tongue with his own. An urgent hunger seared through him. His hand moved fervently over her breast, discovering the peak pebble hard. He delivered his kiss there, teasing the tight bud, treasuring the sweetness and amazing scent of the small bud, suckling upon the fullness. She shifted beneath him magnificently. Even as she did so, yearning gripped his loins tightly, a fierce heat swept through him and he moved against her, his hands never still. There was a greater demand to his touch now, an urgency that filled his body.

She could always awaken his desire. But tonight, she was a breath of magic in his arms. Perhaps she could put that one horrible day in her past, perhaps the passion lying just beneath the terror danced narrowly close to desire. Maybe in the past months they had just been building to this.

But she was responding to him too. She was liquid and supple in his arms. He stroked her breast, and she rose against him, and he whispered soft words to her, reminding her who he was, "I'm your husband and I will always give you pleasure. Feel the touch, my Poppet. Here, and here...feel it become a heat that begins a swirl inside of you, deeper and deeper, here." He stroked her upper thigh, set his leg over the rise of her dark blond triangle. "Here," he whispered then slipped a finger deep and hard inside her. "And here..."

"Logan," her body arched in response, begging for more. In the past his touch had made her flinch away from him. "Should you do that?"

"Poppet," he breathed into her mouth so amazed at the sweet response, "look at me. Yes, and soon I'll do so much more."

She inhaled swift and deep, trembled against his touch then shifted as if she would remember things best left on the island. If the fires were not sizzling through her then, they were running rampant within his body. Still, he took his time teaching her memories that would fill her mind and soul, erasing that horrific experience.

She was stretched out on her back. Her flesh was damp with an exotic sheen, touched by the gold candlelight. Her hair was a tangle. Her limbs were long and beautiful, and her breasts were rising and falling in a rush. Her eyes were soft glazed as if he had taken her quite by surprise. Perhaps he had. And perhaps it had been building as he had said, and perhaps tonight he would erase all the nightmares haunting her.

"You are mine, Evie, as is your passion and the wild sweetness waiting for us to discover together.

An anguish ripped through him. He wanted her then and there. But he needed more tonight, too, than he had ever needed before. He wanted those blue eyes to fill with the hunger he knew lurked behind the midnight shadow of her lashes. He yearned to feel the bowstring quivering of her slender form, the fervent tempo of her hips. It wasn't time to seize hold of her, not yet.

He rose above her and softly caressed her lips with just the breath of his own. He drew a pattern between the valley of her breasts with his finger. He followed it with his tongue. He lowered himself slowly against her. Wherever he caressed her, he kissed her. Lower and lower until he lay between her legs. Touching her, parting her, stroking her, kissing her.

A soft, fervent cry escaped from her. Her fingers tugged upon his hair. He caught her hands and held them within his own. She moaned softly. Her head began to toss, her body to writhe.

With her eyes wide open, she knew who touched her, understood how sweet this enchantment could be. Perhaps their marriage had been fraught with issues, but magic surrounded them tonight.

Beyond the open window of their room, the night breeze stirred softly, making their flesh seem all the more searing. In the midnight black sky, the stars rode the heavens. They seemed to also dance within the room. They poured down upon them in bursts of radiant light. Bloody hell, she was beautiful, alive with her passion.

He grinned roguishly. All the torments of hell could take hold of him now and he would endure them gladly. He found her swollen bud, the center of her greatest sensuality and toyed mercilessly upon it, laving, teasing, demanding with the caress of his lips and tongue. She began to tremble, and the silver gleam of light upon her began to shimmer with the growing undulation of her hips. "Please," she whispered suddenly, "I need you."

And she did indeed need him. The sensations inside her seem to grow until she arched wildly against him. Sounds of her rising passion filled the night, soft, desperate, breathless. Sounds he delighted in hearing and prayed would continue. It seemed she spiraled out of control and to Logan it was achingly sweet.

Then he was atop her. Her eyes shimmering with wonder in the gleam of light, her naked body lush and full begging for him. She cried out softly, closing her eyes for a moment then seeming to remember, her lashes flew open. His body slid into hers and he did not touch upon her maidenhead, confirming his worst fears. Until now he'd held at least a sliver of hope she might not have been violated.

"Oh," she whispered.

"It's your husband, my Poppet."

Her fingers fell upon his shoulders. She shifted beneath him, seeming to encourage him. She gasped and arched to meet him. Her gaze met his, locked on him as if he was her lifeline.

He moved, demandingly. His arms held his body above hers. He thrust into her. And into her again, his gaze locked with hers. He moved faster and faster, his face fraught with tension. She cried out, unable to keep the pleasure inside. Her hands fell upon his shoulders. Her fingers raked across them. She was pulling up to him, meeting his thrust with a rhythmic arch of her own.

Her lips fell upon his shoulders. She covered them with ardent kisses. Her fingers played upon his back, massaging, digging, gripping. He thrust hard against her just as sensations seemed to split and explode within her.

She gasped, clinging to him as the force of her climax seemed to seize her. For a moment, it appeared she was so absorbed with the ecstasy she didn't realize he remained above her, that the heat spilling from his body was filling her own.

He fell to her side, slick with sweat, breathing hard.

She shuddered, gazing at him, sudden tears warming her eyes. "Good God, I never imagined such a piece of heaven."

"Heaven?" he asked with a soft smile, relieved this had gone so well. He had known he could bring her to this, even though she had been immersed with the ghosts haunting her nights.

"Yes," she lowered her lashes, seeming suddenly shy.

"All your nightmares have been vanquished because you love me," he told her, slipping a strand of hair behind her ear and bending toward her to once more brush her lips with his.

Beneath him he felt her stiffen. His self-satisfaction vanished.

"Love doesn't exist," she quoted him, closing her eyes. "Love is for poets and fools."

He felt the icy slap as if she delivered the blow herself. Pain swept through him. If he didn't know better, he wanted her to love him. "Yes, of course you're right. Love is a word that has no meaning."

~ * ~

"Evie, Evie. You have to wake up. Now."

She came awake from a deep unconsciousness. There had been a strange cocoon of comfort in her sleep. Last night, she had given everything to him, and he taught her how sweet lovemaking could be. She had longed to feel peace with herself and her husband. Now she understood the demons holding her apart from him.

Love didn't exist.

She had drained herself with the preparations for Jule's wedding and her surrender to his seduction of her. Now, all she yearned for was sleep. She was exhausted.

"Go away," she murmured. "I need to sleep." She pulled the covers more tightly around her, snuggling into her warmth.

"Evie!" His voice had been gentle at first. Now it rang harsh and cold, penetrating the elusive warmth she tried to maintain. Without saying anything more, he yanked the covers from her, letting the chill of the early morning sweep across her naked flesh.

Slowly she opened her eyes, staring at him, questioning. "Please, just let me rest, one more hour."

With sunlight slanting on his form, he was so striking. Yes, he'd done things to her she had never imagined. Now when he touched her, she remembered only her husband and her body heated with newfound desire.

She pulled the sheets up and hugged them tightly, determined to do what? Perhaps protect her heart. She would never tell him she loved him even though she yearned to do just that.

"You have to get up." His voice still sounded urgent. Once again he tugged on the sheets covering her.

"I don't see why. There is nothing for me to do here," she told him petulantly, still wishing she could hide in the covers and not divulge the new emotions, physically and mentally sweeping through her.

A smile curved his lips and he gazed at her, his eyes seemingly on fire with desire. "I do like you there. In our bed. Evie. Very much so. And more than anything I would love to join you beneath the covers. Especially after last night and the bridges we built together. You were wonderful. Extraordinary." He stroked her cheek.

A flood of heat rushed to her cheeks. "You were extraordinary too," she whispered softly.

He chuckled, smoothing her hair, "Must have been my devastating charm and insight. Perhaps I should cast duty aside and crawl back into bed with you. Ah, Evie we have so much to share but now is not the time. As much as I wish the fact was not true, duty takes precedence right now."

She wanted to remember how beautiful his lovemaking had been, but his arrogance in assuming she loved him angered her. He told her love didn't exist. Those words would haunt her forever, and a small measure inside wanted revenge.

"Logan," she began as she started to waken then... "What duty?"

But she broke off. She swallowed hard as he suddenly pinned his arms on either side of her, bracing himself as he studied her eyes. For a moment she thought he had second thoughts and would kiss her.

"Evie, I won't go back in time. I won't see the fear in your eyes and feel your body stiffen beneath mine or tremble with fear." He spoke quietly. "Everything I longed to find was there within you last night. I won't let you wallow in your nightmares. Together we found a way to span the infernal gap that has separated us for months."

She felt a trembling deep within. She was terrified of the surge of emotion that flowed through her. She didn't mean to argue with him. There were times now when it seemed he wanted to give her everything she ever yearned for as well as find satisfaction in their relationship. At other times though he challenged her, he touched a part of her she never knew existed.

This morning she needed to be alone with her thoughts. She was suddenly very afraid, terrified for her heart. Because she did love a man who could never return those feelings.

"What is it you need that you come in here and wake me so rudely?" she asked, and she saw the blue of his eyes glitter and harden but couldn't seem to stop the challenge. She didn't even understand where the words were coming from save the fact he didn't love her and never would. She could only assume they came from a place of pain deep inside.

His brow arched. His lip curled. She wondered fleetingly whether he was amused or furious. She hadn't meant to be so bold. She hadn't meant to insolently defy his wishes.

"When your mind is in a better state, I'm sure I'll understand this exchange. Together, we found there does exist a match to strike the fire within you and between us. By God, Evie, I swear I'll not let that flame go out." He said his words soft yet determined.

"I don't want that either," she admitted quietly, wishing he hadn't stormed in here and woke her without a thought. A bit more gentleness would have gone a long way to soothe her wounded pride.

"Then perhaps we should try our hand at lovemaking again tonight and see what transpires between us."

"Perhaps we should, but you still haven't told me why I need to rise so expediently. Why you stormed in here and demanded without explaining why." She was more than ready to start the day. His touch upon her, his scent aroused her as did the mere sight of him.

He sat on the side of the bed. "So, you want to be more amenable now. I didn't realize you would wake in a bad mood. The new vines we planted last year were on fire. Look out the window. Smoke still billows into the sky. You must get up and help the servants prepare to feed and give medical aid to the men who are working the fire. I'm sorry. If I could let you, sleep I would."

"No," she sat up, reaching for the dressing gown near the bed. She had acted like a sullen child wishing for something that would never be. She would have to make do with what he was able to give and nothing more. Ella admittedly loved a man who could not return that love, and she seemed splendidly happy and enchanted by her husband. "What do you want me to do?" Even now when she really looked at him, she saw smeared ash on his face and smelled the acrid scent of smoke.

"Dress first," he said, his voice calm as if the situation were not dire. "The fire is nearly out. I waited to wake you as long as I could, knowing you needed your sleep."

"Who? Who would do such a thing?" she queried softly, sure she knew the answer. The man, Franco, was despicable. Would he stop at nothing to run Logan off the land?

"Don't know," his voice stiff, "but..."

"Franco." she finished for him, rummaging through her clothes trying to find something appropriate to wear. "We both know who would set fires, the man who pirated your ships, Jule's brother, Franco."

"I believe so," he paced the room, running his fingers through his hair. "Is there no end to this devilry? No matter who he manages to eliminate or how many vines he burns, he will never own this land. The French government will never allow it nor will I."

She managed to dress in record time, leaving her corset and some of her underclothes behind in her haste. Only the most necessary garments were thrown on.

"What can you do to stop him? Is there anything?" She looked in the mirror, drawing her hair into a topknot before turning her attentio n back to Logan. The situation between the two men seemed to be at a standstill.

"Catch him," he told her simply. "Give him over to the French Government and let them decide his fate."

"If that feat were something easy to do, he would already be in the hands of the French government. Do you have something planned?" He opened the door for her.

"I do."

"Good, tell me about your strategies later."

Skirts hiked, she raced from the room and down the steps to see the first floor filled with his men as well as the servants. She looked at him as if searching for some direction then sensing the needs of a few men in the far corner, she headed that way.

In that crook, a servant had piled bandages and bottles of whiskey. Several men had burns. While Eveleen watched, one lady bathed the burned area in whiskey before bandaging the wound then continued on to the next person.

She observed for a moment then realizing cook had the situation and the burn victims in control, she moved on to the men who had other injuries.

Hours swept by as men were tended to then released to either go home or return to the fires.

Food and drink had been set out for the firefighters who milled around the first floor.

Hours later, Logan found her handing out bread and cheese. He wrapped his arms around her waist, pulling her close. And whispering in her ear, he said. "Come, you need to rest. Have I told you how proud I am of you? You didn't need to spend all day helping my men."

"Because I am your wife, they are also my people. These folks need food and rest too. They've worked hard for us," she told him, enjoying the brief time in his arms and reminded of the possibilities of the night to come. "Is the fire out?"

"Yes, let me help you." He didn't wait for an answer but handed out food to those in line, wishing them well and thanking them for all their assistance.

"I'd like that." Her heart did a little flutter, anticipation sweeping through her. Last night changed her life forever.

She watched him, laughing with his men, enjoying the tales and jokes they told. His men loved and respected him. When the last man passed through the line, the sun hung near the horizon.

"Most of the town came out to help," Eveleen said, brushing hair from her eyes, the hair she'd quickly drawn into a knot this morning was gradually slipping from its pins.

"They did. This vineyard provides most of the families who live in Bordeaux with their livelihood. It's in their best interest to stop the fire. I'm not sure what the town would do if we and some of the other vineyards in this valley didn't exist," he said, watching the exodus from his property heading back to town.

"I thought I saw Franco in the crowd, but I had to be mistaken. He wouldn't dare be so bold, would he?" She glanced at him, hoping to see denial in his expression.

"You did see him. He showed up for a brief time then left. I was too busy to confront him." He stepped away from the nearly empty table to clean his hands with a towel. "Come on, the last man has been fed and we have the evening servants who are just now arriving. I'm sure they won't mind helping with the cleanup."

He took her by the arm and led her outside and down the steps to the lawn. Arm and arm they strolled along the grass lined path in silence.

Smoke still billowed down the hill where the fire had been doused. A sudden violent chill swept through her as she gazed over the countryside, and she had an intense desire to go home to England and Logan's small farm.

She knew they wouldn't return until spring or early summer. Their plan was to visit the vineyard in Tuscany that she had gifted him with. Survey the land and take stock of the people. Perhaps he would sell the land, or perhaps he would keep it. If he decided to work the land, they might remain there through the summer.

"What do we do now?" She knew the answer wouldn't lead them back to England, understood Logan would never go back until he silenced Franco.

Jacque appeared from seemingly nowhere, slapping his thigh with a pair of working gloves. "Don't mean to interrupt but we've got to stop him, Jule's brother, or he'll always plague us."

"And your wedding night?" Logan laughed. "Must have been a hell of a night. Do you know where her loyalties lie?"

"*Merde*," Jacques said. "It seems it was over before it began, and for sure Jule has always been loyal to you. I pray that her allegiance will remain with me, her husband. "

Eveleen felt heat rush to her cheeks. She had enough trouble coming to terms with the seductive and erotic things Logan did to her let alone imagining the same between Jacques and Jule. Placing her cold hands on her cheeks, she turned away to let the men visit.

The lingering scent of smoke clogged her lungs. She coughed, wishing Jacques would leave, but it seemed the two men had a lot to talk about. Words floated around her, yet her mind didn't assimilate anything. She heard words like, Paris, wine, guillotine and French soldiers. Nothing seemed to make a coherent sentence.

"I want to take wine to Paris. We'll need a couple of wagons. I'll defer to you as to the route, preferably the fastest path we can take and one with the fewest chances of ambush."

"I'd like to go," Eveleen interrupted, realizing she didn't want to be left behind, in a land where she barely spoke the language and trusted no one save her husband.

Logan stopped his conversation and focused his attention on her. "That might not be wise or safe. We can speak about this later." He seemed to dismiss her and her statement.

She bristled inwardly but said nothing more, trying to listen and gain as much information as possible.

"As to the route?" he turned his attention back to Jacques.

Jacques glanced between them, his eyes resting on her for a moment then back to Logan. "The best and fastest course would be through Poiters to Tours, to Orleans then on to Paris. There are buyers in Versailles if you want to cut a few kilometers off the journey."

"How long will that take?" Logan wrapped an arm around her drawing her to him, running his hand the length of her arm.

She leaned into his warmth enjoying his strength and the innate power emanating from him. She closed her eyes. After last night she no longer needed to keep her eyes open to know who he was.

Jacques shifted as if pausing to calculate. "Probably a month if the weather holds and we don't run into any problems. It's not an easy trip. Have you thought about taking a ship?"

"A month." Logan repeated, seeming to mull over Jacques words. "Perhaps a sailing vessel would prove easier, but going by land just might take him by surprise. We'll need a crew we can trust. Do you think we could hire men from the village and surrounding area?"

"I believe so. Their allegiance would be with us. Not many liked Franco and his family. How many?" Jacques asked.

"Twenty-five at least. I'd feel better if we could put together a crew of fifty." His hand encircled the back of her neck, massaging the tight muscles.

She moistened her parched lips, believing she knew the words she could use to convince him to take her along. Now wasn't the time. Visions of enticing him when his guard was down came to mind and immediately she flushed at her wayward thoughts. Could she seduce him to her way? The wicked idea swept through her mind. Of course she could when she knew she was right and if he meant to deny her.

"Don't know about fifty." He ran his fingers through his hair, staring at the path leading to the village. "Maybe, if the pay were right I'm sure we could come close."

"Good, tomorrow after all this has died down and the men have time to rest, see what you can do. Offer them half the profit from the shipment of wine if we reach Paris without any loses. Now, go have a proper wedding night. I'm sure Jule is waiting breathlessly for your attention."

Jacques ran his fingers through his hair. "I wouldn't say that, but eventually I pray she will."

The two men laughed and shook hands then Jacques left. She stood next to her husband, her body slowly heating as he erotically made little forays on her body. Touches meant to ignite and entice even though no one watching would know what he did.

"Do you want to take up where we left off last night?" he asked with a wicked grin as he brushed soft moist lips on her cheek.

"Not right now," she said, looking down, hiding her eyes from him, realizing he could read her every expression. It seemed he knew everything she thought.

"What would you like to do then, play cards?" he laughed. "What would we play for?"

"I don't have money," she said, understanding full well he had told her she could keep all the money The Duchess supervised in the Bank of London. He also told her he'd give her an allowance, but to date she'd seen nothing.

His breath tickled her ear, "There are other things besides coin to play for."

"What then?" By the look in his eyes she realized she fell into a trap of his making.

"Why, our clothes," he laughed, brushing his lips along her earlobe and seeming to delight in the obvious tremor slipping through her body.

"I wear more clothes than you do."

His lips ran the length of her neck then back to her ear. "Not today. Remember, I watched you dress."

She cleared her throat, pushing the inferno that began to infiltrate her body and soul. "I cannot possibly do such a thing."

"Even with your husband?" he asked, catching her by her shoulders and turning her toward him.

"You have a trip to organize, barrels of wine to load on wagons. You—" His lips silenced her.

He shifted away from her lips, inches away to whisper, "And a wife to bed but I must relieve her of her clothes before I can do that. I can't think of a better way to accomplish her disrobing than to gamble. Lady luck is always on my side."

"You have to undress too," she blurted without a thought.

"Exactly what I'd like my wife to say. Of course..." he paused, "we could skip the cards and go straight to the bed."

Wanting to experience the erotic tempest and the end result of his lovemaking again yet unwilling to admit to the desire churning inside, "Cards, we could play cards. I'm really very good." *And when he touches me, I'll keep my eyes open. I wonder if I'll have to do that the rest of my life.*

"We shall see just how good you are." Drawing her close, he deepened the kiss, and she responded, desperate to accept all he offered.

"Is Jacques happy with Jule?" She didn't mean to change the subject but her curiosity got the best of her.

"I assume so." Logan leaned lazily against a tree, his arms crossed in front of him while he seemed to study her. "Why?"

She didn't want to answer and searched for a way to change the subject back to something more agreeable to her. "We should go back to the house."

"Why?" he asked again, a slant to one eyebrow and a grin seeming to stretch from one ear to the other. "You eager to lose to me? I want to see you naked; the sooner the better."

"It's getting dark and there's a chill in the air. I'm so confused right now I don't know what I want?"

He reached out to touch her chin, still grinning. "Open your eyes, Evie. We've already made it through the hardest part of your seduction."

"What kind of cards do you want to play?" She stepped away, her eyes wide and her insides yearning for everything they had last night. Part of her wanted to scream skip the cards, the rest of her was still frightened of the emotions he elicited in her.

"Faro?" he queried, "but I'm not sure there are cards in the chateau.

Perhaps we could play a different game."

At the look on his face she gave a startled gasp. "What do you have in mind?" This wasn't going the way she thought it would, but then nothing had since she met Logan.

"I ask you something and you answer the question. If you don't want to answer, you have to do what I ask," he said, seeming to enjoy this game.

"And the same for me." If he didn't answer, she had no idea what she would ask him to do. Having him remove his clothing was too intimidating but that was his intention.

Of course, he wrapped his arm around her waist and headed toward the house. "If you want, I'll strip as soon as we're in our room," he said, waggling his eyebrows.

Heat swept through her from the tips of her toes to the top of her head. Everything he did last night rose to the forefront of her mind. "I don't think that would be wise."

He roared with laughter, seeming to enjoy this banter. "As far as I'm concerned it would be more than prudent and would save us a great deal of time."

"I plan to answer everything you ask," she told him, deliberately trying to deflate his ego.

"You're not going to make this an easy game. Perhaps, I'll just seduce you and forget the questions."

~ * ~

Franco watched the smoke from the vines wither and die. "*Merde*," he swore under his breath as the good people from the town doused the fire he and Tate had set in hopes of bankrupting Maxwell. While he watched, men raced from the small village to help the Englishman put out the fire.

"It seems since the Lord Maxwell set foot on French soil, nothing has gone your way." Tate rubbed his chin. "I tell you again, perhaps it's time to cut your losses and make a good life for yourself some place where we won't risk meeting Madame Guillotine. I have no intention of losing my head."

"We had better luck when Lord Maxwell sent his cargo via ship to Dover. His ships were easy pickins. I don't like the trend. Now he's married Jule to that man of his, Jacques. Never liked him or his family." Franco kept his gaze riveted on the smoking vineyard. His loses seemed to grow and his life in a spiraling decline.

Tate let out a long sigh, shaking his head. "We should cut our loses and forget about this land. It's not worth the strain," he said once more seeming to hope Franco would come to agree with him if he kept hearing the same words.

"Never!" Franco cried out vehemently against his friend's advice. "I will die before I stop fighting for my land."

"Be advised it may well come to that," Tate said. "I hear he's planning an overland trip to Paris. If you attack and things go awry..." he let the thought hang on the air. "I don't want to join you in the Bastille. If it comes to my life, I will leave you."

Franco understood all too well what Tate referred to. He was born of nobility and although time had passed since the revolution if Maxwell caught him stealing from him, Maxwell would turn him over to the French government and his life would be in jeopardy.

If turned over to the new command, he might well meet the same fate as his mother and father. He was sure that was what Lord Maxwell had in mind. His death.

"We will not get caught," Franco said, a grim determination sweeping through him. Right was on his side. This was his family estate he meant to take back. "We will outsmart him and take his wine again. We will do it again and again until he goes broke."

"He will not see poverty for a very long time. Maxwell does not depend on this land in Bordeaux for his livelihood. He has substantial property in England, and I've heard he was given land in Tuscany."

"Another winery?" Franco rubbed his chin thoughtfully. He'd heard nothing about this.

"Chianti seems to be the type of wine that land produces."

"Still, if he's met with adversity, he might well quit and go home." Franco wanted to believe that scenario and if he told himself enough times, it might be true. Deep in his heart he had to admit that development was highly unlikely.

"Let's get out of this rain." Tate muttered, heading for the hastily built lean-tos and shelter from the elements.

"Maybe our whores will still be there," Franco said, wishing for a soft body and a willing woman to ease his apprehensions.

"Odds are they found their way back to a warm house and bed. I'm shocked they stayed the night," Tate said.

"They didn't have much of a choice. If they are gone, they had to walk because I wasn't planning on taking them to the brothel. Still not," he muttered. In a perfect situation, Rose would be waiting for him when he returned simply because he'd not given her a choice.

"Look on the bright side. It's raining so hard no one would want to trek several miles in this. A warm body and a bottle of wine would go a long way to ease the knowledge the vines are still standing."

"What are we going to eat?" Tate said, seeming to address the more practical side of their situation.

"*Merde*, we only have left overs to fill our bellies." Wine and whores, leftovers from yesterday, but they would have to do for the night.

"You mean wine and whores. That's all we got unless we go into Bordeaux and I doubt if even I would be accepted there."

Chapter Nine

Once secluded inside their master chamber, Logan poured wine and handed her a glass. "Do you want to go first?" Despite the fact he wanted to make love to his wife, he yearned to know a little more about her.

"Answer or quest?" she asked.

He seemed to think a bit, "What are you going to ask me to do? I thought the quest was already determined." He smiled at her, sipping and letting the sweet taste of the wine slide down his throat and calm his escalating nerves.

"Only if you insist," she said. Setting her glass on the table she wrapped a loose piece of hair around her finger, studying him.

He watched the rise of her breasts as she inhaled, noticed the slight beading of moisture on her forehead. "Are you nervous?"

"Yes, of course. What do you think? I've never done anything like this. It's terrifying."

"We were naked just last night. Your body is not new to me." He was truly baffled. What he thought was a fun game, she feared.

"But you've never looked at me when I'm naked. What if you don't like the way I look?" she blurted out.

He chuckled softly. "My sweet Poppet, I've looked at every inch of you, not enough times, I confess, and my lips have touched every inch of you." And he yearned to look at her countless more.

"But..." she moistened her lips. "I've never really looked at you. Well," she paused, "except that time in the conservatory and after the bath."

"Wouldn't you like to? Now's your chance. I'm ready." He held his arms out and realized where Evie was concerned there should be no modesty. But not many weeks had passed since she was a virgin and only one night since she'd been made love to.

"What's your favorite color," she blurted with a quick sigh of relief, changing the subject.

"Ah, Evie, if you're going to ask me a question, you should ask something more important. You gave that up much too easily. My favorite color is green, just like yours. Now it's my turn. What are you afraid of?" He thought she would say she was terrified of him although he hated that thought. "Or do you want me to remove all the pins in your hair? It will be a start."

"No, I'm afraid of spiders," she told him, sipping wine before folding her hands in her lap with a smug smile. "Really terrified even though many times Christel told me to just step on them and the fear would vanish."

Slowly shaking his head, he meant to confront her in this lie. "Evie, Evie, Evie, I saw you escorting a spider outside the other day when Charley was crying. You scooped it onto a piece of parchment. Because you lied, I get to remove all the pins.

Leaning forward, he ran his hands through her silken hair, watching the pins clatter on the floor and seeing her moisten her lips with her tiny pink tongue. Then without hesitation, he brushed his lips across hers before settling on his chair, hands folded in his lap, satisfied for the moment.

"What are you afraid of?" she quickly asked as if she thought he would take advantage of her again.

Slowly, he began unbuttoning his shirt, his gaze riveted on hers. "I don't believe I want to answer your question." Once the garment was free of its fastenings, he slipped it from his arms.

She pressed against the back of her chair, fiddling with the fastenings on her bodice then running her tongue across her beautiful sweet lips. For a moment she lowered her eyes, gazing at the floor then back to him. She inhaled a long breath as if waiting for his probing question.

"What are you really afraid of, Evie?" He leaned forward, watching the play of emotions on her face and knew she would lie again. How long would she deny him the truth? Most likely until she was left with too little on her tiny frame to call herself clothed.

"You already asked me that," she protested, clearly frustrated with his refusal to leave the question by the wayside.

"And you told a lie, so I'm asking you again. It's something every husband should know about his wife." He smiled at her, sitting back in his chair and crossing his arms. "I'll ask you the same question until you tell me the truth. So...what will it be?"

She plucked at her skirt and the seconds ticked by, silence enveloped by a soft keening of a breeze swirling through a slightly opened window. "I..."

"The truth, Evie. I want to know what you're afraid of."

"Snakes."

"That's it? Snakes. I don't believe you. I overheard you talking to Harry one day. It seems the two of you had your heads bowed, studying the contents of a book. You showed him a picture of a grass snake. When he asked if you were afraid of them, you told him no, of course not. They're not poisonous and they eat amphibians so there was no need to be afraid." He watched her nervously swallow as her eyes narrowed. "You're dress, Poppet. Take off your dress. You should really tell the truth if you want the gorgeous curves of your body to remain hidden from me."

"You cannot ask for the dress. What about my shoes and my stockings?" She suddenly appeared frantic.

He didn't like the look in her eyes, but he wasn't going to relent. "Take your dress off. Take if off." Then he bent toward her and whispered, "Take your dress off, Poppet."

Her hands rested on the fastenings while her eyes remained focused on him. Slowly, the dress settled on the floor.

He smiled at her. "I find I tire of this dance of untruths you present me with. I don't want to answer a question," he told her, pulling off both boots with a quick sigh of relief. "Feels good to take my shoes from my feet." He stretched his legs and put his hands behind his head, content for the moment to let her think about the questions and the information he yearned to hear from her.

"You won't let me ask you a question?" She sounded indignant, perhaps slightly angry. Her reactions to this amused him. He'd much rather hear anger in her voice than the earlier frantic note.

She wasn't furious that she was losing her garments to him but angry that he did not allow her questions. Perhaps if she answered honestly, he would answer a question also.

"Now my dear wife and sweet little Poppet, what are you afraid of?" He leaned forward, anticipating the lie.

She grimaced, seeming to realize he would continue with this line of questioning until he was satisfied. "I'm afraid of a lot of things," she began, her words slow and whisper soft. "I'm afraid of the man on the island, of how easily you can seduce me, of never knowing the love of a man."

He inhaled sharply. The last truth hit him square between the eyes. *Never knowing the love of a man.*

He'd told her love didn't exist and just yesterday, she told him the same thing. When she said the words, he felt as if she slapped him in the face. But love didn't exist. He knew this. It was a fact and he believed it. So why was he debating this now?

She studied him as if waiting for a denial of her answer. Stunned, he had no words. Once again an eerie silence filled the small room. She waited, sipping wine, eyes wide with yearning.

"Are you going to refute what I just said?" she asked. "If not, are you going to remove more clothing, or do I get to ask you something?"

"You can ask," He was sure she would want to know what he feared, but she didn't. Instead she veered to another equally probing question.

"What can't you live without?"

Tempted to say her name, he felt suddenly uncomfortable. There were a lot of things he didn't want to live without, but he would certainly survive and pick up the pieces if he lost his home, but his family, his children...they could never be replaced. What about his wife, Evie, could he replace her? There were other women, willing women to become the wife of a wealthy lord. He didn't want another wife, or a willing woman save Evie, and at the moment she wasn't completely willing. Yet the challenge intrigued him, and there was something about Evie that set her apart from all the women he'd ever known.

"I can't live without my work, my farm, my vineyards and my family." He wasn't going to make himself vulnerable by naming names. There it was, another fear, weakness. He didn't like to be seen as weak. Franco, by his presence and constant attacks, left him exposed and vulnerable. Not liking that feeling he meant to end that.

Her lips pursed together and her shoulders slumped a bit before she suddenly straightened them and lifted her chin in seeming defiance. "Am I part of that family?" she asked, challenging him to answer a question he wasn't comfortable with.

"Yes, of course." He rose striding around the room, wondering what little devil on his shoulder prompted him to start this game. He needed to change the conversation away from himself, and it was his turn to query.

Before he figured out what he wanted to ask, he refilled their glasses. It probably wasn't the best ploy when looking for coherent thoughts and honesty as well as bedding his wife.

He grinned, downing his glass before pouring another and asking, "Of the seven deadly sins, what's your weakness?"

Her tiny gasp of surprise left him wondering what exactly she would tell him. Beneath her chemise, the slight sway of her breasts and the hard tips of her nipples mesmerized him.

She crossed her eyes in concentration. "I don't know. I've never thought about it before." Then she held her hands up. "Wait, I'm thinking. I'm not going to remove more clothing until I want to."

Her comment sent a smile to his face. "Maybe we should use a timer, a minute per question or this could go on all night. It's been a long day, and I find our bed very inviting" He smiled, wishing he dared run his finger along the softness of her neck then down her arm.

"That's unfair."

A tear formed in her eye and Logan felt an immediate sense of remorse. "Perhaps you shouldn't answer."

"No, I choose to tell the truth and after some thought I know what it is." She whispered.

"And..."

"Envy," she told him. "For as long as I can remember, I've envied Aidan for her free spirit and the ability to say whatever she liked. And Allura, she is so beautiful. I've always thought if I was half that stunning I'd be happy. Instead, I'm quiet and reserved and..." she paused. "And Ella, I envied her the beautiful wedding and the ease which she and Drake had between them. You know, he doesn't love her either." She brushed the tears from her eyes with the back of her hand.

He knelt beside her, taking her hands in his, realizing that again this strange notion of love was mentioned. "You are the most beautiful woman I've ever seen. Much more beautiful than any of your sisters or cousins. For me, some of your charm comes from the way you are quiet and reserved."

Her slight smile left him uneasy. "Liar," she told him. "That isn't a question, but you should probably remove something from your person. I think perhaps your socks would be nonthreatening."

"Don't break the rules," he waved a finger at her. Yet taking his buckskins off would put him one step closer to his ultimate goal. Even if they were naked, they wouldn't make love unless she wanted to.

"I thought you wanted..."

He interrupted. "I want to see you naked, completely naked. I didn't say anything about me, but I do want you to get used to seeing me without clothes."

"So," changing the subject again, she said "what is your sin?"

"Pitch the question back to me?"

"Absolutely."

"It's a toss up," he said, realizing the truth of the question. He had more than one sin but he'd settle on one.

"And..." She smiled, tilting her head.

The radiance of that tiny expression sent a bolt to his heart. "Pride," he told her. "It sometimes gets in the way."

"Why doesn't that seem like a sin?" she asked. "You are a proud man and that in a way attracts me to you."

"Too much pride is a sin." He understood how that very sin had perhaps created some of his problems with Franco. Yet he admitted the man would have never accepted anything but his entire estate, the vineyards, the chateau.

A knock on the door distracted them. He quickly tossed her a blanket before answering.

A servant stood at the opening, a tray of food in his hand. Logan accepted the platter and brought it inside, setting it on a table, "And more wine."

The door behind the man closed with a soft snick. Evie chose to keep the blanket draped around her. As the seconds ticked by, he ignored the cheat and poured another glass of wine. She'd wake with a headache and sick stomach, just like the night of their wedding. Perhaps he would too. For the time being, this would be a night he would cherish.

"I'm famished," she said. "I don't remember when I last ate, sometime this morning I suppose."

"Eat then. We'll leave for Paris in the morning."

"We should go to bed," she said then stopped the slice of cheese halfway to her mouth then amended, "We should sleep."

He shrugged, chewing his food thoughtfully. Before speaking he waggled his eyebrows at her. "Can't go to sleep in our clothes. So, on the other end of the spectrum, what's your virtue? If you don't know I could tell you."

"Does that mean if I say something you don't agree with I have to remove an article of clothing?" she asked.

"Yes, I know all of your virtues. Perhaps you should remove something even if I agree."

"Well, that's making up your own rules," she said, her voice indignant.

"So, how do you see yourself?" he probed, wishing she would say something ridiculous.

She sighed, pushing at the heel of one shoe with the toe of the other. "I'm obviously no longer chaste and I haven't abstained. I don't think I possess one of the seven virtues."

"Your shoes."

"What?"

"Take your shoes off, or would you like me to remove them? If I do, I might remove more of your clothing." He traced a line around the top of her stocking, wickedly touching the tender soft skin of her upper thigh, smiling when he felt her shiver and heard the soft moan.

"But I don't possess a virtue," she protested while he slipped the shoes from her feet and followed that by rolling down her stockings.

"Two lies, my Poppet. Keep that up and you will be just the way I want you. Naked. What are your virtues?"

She wrinkled her nose at him, a very endearing sight, and he almost laughed. "Give me time to think," she tried to put off answering. "Why don't you tell me your virtues while I figure out what you want to hear."

He couldn't help himself and let out a roar of laughter. "No, I don't believe we should do this out of order. It's your turn to answer or remove an article of clothing."

"I've only one article left." She picked at the thin chemise she wore. The garment did nothing to hide her curves or the fact her nipples were tight buds waiting for his attention.

"Then it would be best," he leaned forward, whispering, "that you tell me what I want to hear."

"What are the virtues. I'm not sure I remember all of them," she told him, gently touching his chin.

"Ah a ploy to waste time and to put off what is inevitable, but I'm okay with that. Let me see, the seven virtues are..." and he listed them.

"Well, obviously neither chastity or abstinence are virtues I possess." She paused, her gaze meeting his. "And this is your fault."

Leaning back and crossing his legs before sipping the wine still in his glass, "I don't regret that."

"No, being a man, I suppose you have no remorse." She smiled at him as if she touched on something.

Her words surprised him for a moment, and he wondered at the hidden meanings behind them. Perhaps he overthought her comment and he still waited for her answer. Not wishing to waste more time, he pointed out, "Your virtues?"

"Kindness might be a virtue of mine but..." she seemed to pause in thought.

Curiosity had him asking, "But?"

"I vowed to be honest with you, but this does not come easily." She smoothed the fabric covering her, pulling the thin garment tight against her body.

He clenched his hands, willing his body to wait. "Please tell the truth."

She closed her eyes, inhaling a long deep breath of air then let it out slowly as if taking more time would absolve her from telling him. Then, "I did not feel kind toward Maida or Jule, telling myself they were part of your life but that was in the past. Their children, your children, keep them in your life for all of eternity. My dislike of that is not kindness."

"So, what did you decide if you're not kind?" he asked, leaning toward and unable to resist her siren's call, he brushed his lips across hers.

"I'm not kind," she told him when he drew away.

"You are though. You're kind and patient and humble." His fingers found the hem of her chemise and pulling it upward, removed the soft material.

~ * ~

The expedition to Paris seemed to last an eternity and now snow fell from the sky as the wagons neared Versailles. The overland trip had gone smoothly and without incident. Until today, the weather cooperated. Now the freezing rain turned to snow and the roads after enduring a day of rain turned soggy and ruts that seemed barely there, deepened to halt the carts.

Logan guided his horse next to the wagon Evie rode in, "There's an inn about a mile down the road. We'll stop there for the night."

"I thought we'd reach Versailles tonight?" She sounded more tired than she felt as she brushed hair from her face. Stiffening her back, she tried to look positive. After all she was the one who insisted on joining him for the journey. She told him she wouldn't take no for an answer. More than anything she wanted to see Paris.

"In this weather we can't force the horses or the men beyond endurance. I know you were looking forward to reaching Versailles tonight. So was I." He pulled the rain slicker closer to ward off the moisture falling from the sky.

A brief glance upward told her the weather wasn't about to change any time soon. "Will we be able to travel tomorrow?"

"Not unless this lets up and the sun comes out long enough to dry the road." The wagon drew to a stop and, dismounting, he changed places with the driver and sat beside her.

"Do you think Franco has abandoned any idea of pirating this shipment of wine?" Eveleen was sure the man had given up any thoughts of confiscating what was Logan's.

"No, but I did expect an attack at the beginning of the journey. The closer we get to Paris, the easier it will be for me to get him to the French constables. The danger here is extreme for him."

"Well, it seems we can most likely relax a bit while we are stuck here." She watched his expression carefully.

"Relax, that's what I would expect if I were Franco. Believe we'll double the watches and do anything but let our guard down. I want the man and I don't want to lose the wine or any lives."

"You think Franco will try for the shipment here?" she asked, confused the man would wait this long. "You've sent out men ahead and behind to make sure he wasn't setting a trap and no one saw anything." For her part, she wanted to reach Paris and see the city, walk the Champs Elysees and visit Montmartre.

To Eveleen it seemed the last mile to the inn took forever. From the inside out, her entire body seemed frozen solid. Inside her muff, she laced her icy fingers together for warmth.

Beside her Logan hummed while snow settled on his face and turned to ice crystals on his facial hair. Smiling, she couldn't resist touching the tiny frozen flakes.

"Are you sorry you came?" he turned to ask.

"No, but I wish this last leg was as warm and easy as the first. We'd be in Versailles I suppose."

"You'll like the inn. It's close enough to Versailles and the frequent travelers from Paris liven it up. It's modern and the food is amazing."

With his words, her stomach rumbled. Yet even while they spoke the weather grew increasingly worse. Wind howled and sideways snow pummeled them, freezing her to the core.

"I can't see my hand in front of my face," Evie said, terror seizing her. "Where is the road?"

"Climb in the back and cover yourself with the tarp." His voice held an urgency that was new to her.

"What about you?" she asked, wishing he would hand the reins over to one of his men and climb in beside her.

He smiled but it didn't reach his eyes, "We've got to reach the inn tonight. There's no way we'll survive out here with no shelter. Stay under the tarp, and I'll let you know when we get there."

She climbed in the back and did as he asked, wondering how long. "*Merde*," she whispered softly. It was much warmer beneath the tarp; the wind didn't batter against her.

Closing her eyes, she allowed her mind to drift, recounting memories. She seemed to relive her life backwards from this moment. Flashes of their marriage and the time she spent on her island sanctuary seemed to warm her mind if not her body.

Gradually, she felt her heart and her breathing slow and a tiny warmth began to encircle her. She watched her sisters and cousins frolic naked in the lake near the McLellan castle.

Her mother, Gracie, held her in her lap, reading a story to her and her sisters. It was a fable of some sort. No, it was about Robin Hood. She'd always loved the idea of robbing from the rich and giving to the poor. Maybe that was what Franco believed he was doing.

The fire in the hearth burned bright, but she felt no warmth. Her limbs seemed numb and her fingers unmovable. Her grandmother settled beside her, sitting cross-legged and smiling. The moment seemed poignant and she felt sure her grandmother was trying to tell her something.

"Eveleen," she seemed to whisper, "this is far too soon for you to join your mother and me. It's not your time. You must fight. Keep your eyes open, sweetheart."

"No, all I want is the fire to warm me. Grandmother, what are you trying to tell me?" The dream vanished as suddenly as it appeared. Eveleen felt nothing. She was no longer cold nor was she warm.

Splendid lights of many colors played across her eyelids and danced in her head. Her mother returned, bending over her and placing a hand on her forehead then touched her pulse. "She still breathes and her heart still beats. Would you like me to read you another story? What would you like to hear?" She placed a kiss on the center of her forehead, seeming to wait for her to answer. Finally, she pulled a book from the pocket of her dress and began to read.

"The Arabian Nights: Tales from a Thousand and One Nights," she tells her. It was one of Allura's favorites, not hers. She was fascinated by Scheherazade and horrified when her husband, the King, called for her execution the day after they were wed. Logan would never have done anything like that.

Allura would say she told stories, tales that kept her alive for one thousand nights. She remembered asking Allura how anyone could think of that many stories.

She was more tired now than ever before and she realized something was terribly wrong, but she couldn't seem to find the energy to rise. She needed to tell Logan. Everything around her was dead silent. She could no longer hear the pounding of the horses' hooves or the cringing of the wagon wheels. The men's voices didn't echo through the night.

All she could hear was the broken pumping of blood in her ears. During these tense moments between rational thought and a dream world, she felt a sense of panic and the thought she might never see Logan again ravished her reflections. Thoughts of his gentleness and patience rose to the forefront of her mind. Logan, she tried to call out to him.

She believed she felt his arms around her, his body close to hers, sending an exquisite warmth inside and filling her. Many seconds seemed to pass. It appeared she lost track of time then she realized he drew her from the wagon, cradling her in his arms.

Allowing her head to settle against his chest, she tried to draw herself inside him, needing to garner some of his heat. Without opening her eyes, she sensed they entered a lighted room and felt the rumble of Logan's chest as he spoke.

From what seemed like an enormous distance, she heard his voice reassuring her and felt the brush of his lips on her forehead. "You've got to open your eyes, Evie. Open them now."

His command impossible, she did try, thought she succeeded but when he kept saying. "Open your eyes Evie, I want to see the beautiful sapphire of your eyes," she tried harder but to no avail.

He set her down while he fumbled with her coat and the layers of clothing covering her. She remembered now, she'd been in a hurry and forgot her wool petticoat and stockings.

She pushed at his hands, "No..."

"I'm sorry but this is the only way to warm you up."

"Clothes," mumbled. "Need them. Warm."

"Evie, they are wet and some are frozen together. Be patient with me and I'll get you warm. You're safe now. We made it to the inn. My men are posted outside and around the barn where we've put the wine."

Seconds later, she lay beneath the covers naked, Logan beside her. "You can't mean..." She opened her eyes and saw the concern and fear etched in his eyes.

"Put your hands and feet anywhere it's warm. Touch me." He brought her hands beneath his arms.

Against her body she felt his slight shiver when her frozen fingertips met his flesh and heard sharp hiss of his indrawn breath. Except for his small clothes, he was naked as was she, but his warmth surrounded and penetrated her body. Yet real warmth still eluded her.

"Just like in Vauxhall Gardens, you're going to warm me?" she asked with chattering teeth but also understood the gravity of this situation, sure now that her wits seemed to have returned, she almost died from the cold.

"I don't want you to go to sleep until I'm positive your entire body is heated all the way through. Talk to me, Evie. Tell me something I don't know about you."

"Y-you k-know everything there is to know." She found that as she lay next to him, her body shivered violently as if it now fought for the heat it had given up for lost. "T-the other night I told you things I didn't even know about myself."

"Of course I don't know everything. I'll start." He paused as if he tried to think of something she didn't know about him. "I love to skip rocks. I once skipped one twenty times before it slipped beneath the water."

That's nice. "Allura used to take us to the lake by the castle. Aiden would dare us all to take off all of our clothes and swim naked."

As if he couldn't help himself, he brushed his lips across her forehead pulling her closer. "I'll have to remember that. There is a lake I know of where we can swim without wearing a stitch of clothing. Would you like that?"

She didn't know if she would. She ran her feet up his leg then down before closing her eyes. "Don't know."

"Open your eyes, Evie. You can't sleep. Not now, not yet. Not until your entire body is back to its normal temperature." He explored her body, not to seduce but to create heat. "What else don't I know about you?"

She didn't want to answer any more questions. "I'm too tired to do this. I just want to sleep."

"No, you don't get away with that excuse. Talk to me."

"I like to paint. Did you know that?" She always tried to keep her hobby hidden from him.

"I didn't know that." He brushed hair from her face, seeming to study her face, gazing into her eyes.

"Liar," she told him on a whisper. "I know you've seen me painting. Does that mean you have to take something off?"

He laughed softly, "But you never showed me your paintings. I'd like to see them. Will you show me some time?"

She suppressed a tiny giggle. "You just want to know if there are any naked paintings of you or us."

"Are there?" he queried, his voice seemingly tight.

"I think I'll leave you guessing since I didn't bring any painting material with me on this trip. Would you like it if there were?" She smiled inside, remembering the sketches Ella did of Drake and of them making love. She shouldn't have seen them and confessed later reprimanding Ella that if she didn't want people to see them, she shouldn't leave them lying around.

"No."

She heard the changed timbre of his voice and shivered, knowing he couldn't help but feel her response. "There aren't. I promise," she told him, deciding to relieve his fears. Against her she felt his muscles relax.

"That's good," he said then, "you're not just saying that."

"I'm not," she whispered against his chest.

"The hot water is here. You might want to let it cool, sir," a man said from somewhere behind her. She tensed, hoping the man didn't know they were naked beneath the sheets.

"It's okay, Evie. The hot water is another way to warm you up. Besides, after the last two days of travel, you might want a bath."

"But..."

"Hush, Poppet, he doesn't know anything nor does he care."

"Liar."

"No, it's the truth. Join me." He rose, sweeping the covers from both of them before removing his one remaining garment.

On the bed she was naked to his gaze but for the first time since their marriage, she didn't have the urge or the energy to cover herself. She accepted the hand he held out to her and rose from the bed with his help.

"We are doing this together?" The thought was wicked yet she wanted to feel the glide of water between their flesh.

"The water as well as the heat from our bodies will thoroughly warm us. And I, for one, need a bath." He swept her into his arms and after stepping into the tub, let her body slide the length of his before settling her in front of him.

Her body against his chest she let her head fall backwards reveling in the gentle caress and tender exploration of his fingers. It seemed he didn't seduce, just sought to warm her. What could easily turn erotic remained laced with concern and tenderness.

His fingers closed around hers and lifting her hand, he seemed to examine and question, "Your fingertips are no longer blue. That is a good thing." Gently, he touched her chin and drew her face so he could see her. "Neither are your lips. How do you feel?"

"I am finally warm, inside and out," she told him her, voice whisper soft.

"Good." He reached for a bucket sitting close by and poured more hot water around them.

The knock on the door startled her. "Lord Maxwell?"

Quickly he grabbed a bath towel, covering the top of the tub with the fabric, concealing her.

"Come in," he said.

A servant strode through the door, a tray of food and drink in his hands. Setting the tray on a stool beside the tub, he waited. "Sir?"

"That will be all for now. Come back with more hot water in about ten minutes," Logan commanded.

Laughing, "You can come out from under the towel now." He

tugged gently on the material covering her.

"Is he gone?" She peered out from underneath.

"Yes, but he'll back with water to rinse your hair when we've finished eating and..."

"I like this, taking a bath with you," she finished for him, accepting the glass of wine he offered.

"Me too," he agreed, popping a piece of roasted venison into his mouth.

She grinned at him, feeling better now than she did several hours ago. She leaned into his hard body, enjoying the caress of his hands on her torso. They ate in silence, thoughts to themselves. Everything, life, it all seemed so precious to her, more than ever.

Time slipped by and through the window it seemed the sun had begun to set. She yawned, feeling exhausted from the ordeal even though she spent the better part of the day in a dreamlike sleep.

Once again the knock startled her. Logan pulled the bath sheet to cover them, kissing her quickly on the cheek before answering.

"Come in."

"Sir, your hot water. Anything else?" he asked.

"No, thanks," From the small table beside them Logan picked up a coin and tossed it to the boy.

Evie picked up the soap, but Logan quickly took it from her. Lathering her hair, he massaged the scented soap into her hair.

She moaned softly, "That feels so good. Where did you learn..."

"A place far, far away," he murmured, leaving Eveleen to wonder what he meant. "Close your eyes." When he finished he poured the clean hot water over her head to rinse the soap away.

He lifted her from the cooling tepid water, studying her as she rose. She wrapped one of the towels around her before she sat on the bed and watched him wash and rinse before rising from the water and as always, she equated him as if he was Adonis rising from the sea.

"What now?" she asked while he dressed.

"I'm going to check on our shipment and the men. They need to rest and eat. I'll be gone half the night with guard duty."

"And me?" she queried, slanting her head a bit and pursing her lips.

"I can't sleep. I wish you would stay here with me."

"Finish eating? Try to sleep? We both know I can't do that. I promise you the guards will keep you safe," he offered slipping his fur-lined jacket over the wool shirt.

"Can I come with you? I really don't want to stay here by myself," she asked even though she knew his answer.

"You don't have enough warm clothes." He put his hands under her arms, lifting her from the bed as the towel slid to the wood floor. "I'd much rather stay here with you." His lips brushed hers, nibbled across her bottom lip while his tongue danced across her mouth.

"I think I'll sketch," she told him, grinning. "I don't think I can ever forget the sight of you rising from the water."

"Don't you dare," he said before he vanished from the room, the door behind him closing with a soft sound.

She plucked at the damp towel before finally rummaging through the valise a servant had brought to the room. Pulling out warm wool stockings and petticoat, she found the warmest clothes.

Finished dressing, she wandered the room, taking in the plush draperies and beautiful area rug. A gold chandelier hung in the middle of the room, casting a warm glow to all of the corners. On each table she found a candle and lit them all.

She'd threatened to sketch him, but she'd brought nothing with her, no sketchpad or charcoal. Her steps led her to the window. A soft moon hung on the horizon and stars filled a cloudless sky.

What harm would it be if she joined Logan? All he could do would be to tell her she had to leave, go back to her solitary confinement in this gorgeous inn.

She had to try or regret staying alone and wanting his company. She found the warm coat he bought her what seemed like a lifetime ago and left.

Down the stairs and to the double doors, she saw no one. The inn was eerily quiet, foreboding, casting a shadow of fear in her heart.

Outside the cold air bit her exposed skin. Her heart skipped a beat when she watched a shadow of a man dart between the inn and the stables. Tempted to turn around, she drew in a deep breath and raced to the stables.

~ * ~

Logan brought a pot of hot coffee to the stable to share with Jacques and the men guarding the wine shipment. He sat down on a bale of hay, pouring them both a cup before handing the container to his men.

"What do you think happened to Franco? I expected a visit long before this." Perhaps his nemesis waited until they were closer to Paris, but that seemed foolhardy to him.

Jacque shrugged, sipping the heady brew. "I'm not too surprised. I know you had to send this shipment out well guarded, but rumor in town has it that he sold the ship to pay bills. He's destitute and it certainly would be prudent without men to try to pirate this cargo."

"Is this what Jule told you?" he asked, believing Jule might not be truthful. While he always thought he held some of her loyalty, her heart remained with her family. The difference between Jule and her brother was that she didn't live in a fantasy world. She understood the ancestral home and land were gone from her family forever.

"No, I've made a point of speaking with the men you hired for this trip. They've told me it's just Franco and his first mate, a long time friend, Monsieur Tate. He is alone and penniless."

"His crew holds no loyalty to him?" Logan mulled over what Jacques told him. The man had been successful on the high seas as a pirate but now... Now he would be even more desperate.

"Doesn't appear so." Jacques shrugged. "I hired two men who had brothers who sailed with Franco, remembering him as the aristocrat who owned the winery on the hill. They expected honor and a gentleman but were disappointed when they were not paid."

"Whew...that wine should have brought a hefty sum in any market. What did Franco spend it all on?" Franco should have been saving every possible coin if he truly looked for a way to regain the vineyard.

"Whores and gambling, mostly whores," Jacques said with a slight sneer in his tone, standing and stretching. "Need to take a look around. You going to stay here?"

"Whores and gambling..." Logan parroted amazed at the waste.

200

"I'll watch the front door," Logan told him just as three men brought trays of food and more warm blankets from the inn.

Logan rubbed his arms then stamped his feet in an attempt to heat his body. He thought of the large bed waiting for him upstairs in the inn and his beautiful wife sleeping beneath the covers.

His shrill whistle signaled for his men to gather around. They strode from various corners, chatting, morale despite the frigid weather, seemed high. Each man grabbed food and disappeared back to guard duty.

Logan wasn't hungry. His gut churned at the thought of Franco and the way he used the coin from the wine.

Jacques returned, "Everything is quiet. Seems the snow has stopped and the sky has cleared. "We should reach Paris tomorrow and rid ourselves of our cargo. Unless something happens tonight or on the road tomorrow, we'll be done worrying about the wine. Do you want me to increase the number of guards for the rest of the night?"

"No, let the men rest and keep the schedule already set up. As you said, the two would be foolish to attempt an attack without more men."

"I'm sure they will appreciate the extra sleep."

"How about you and Jule? You eager to get back to your wife?" For some reason tonight the silence between them seemed strained.

Jacques rubbed the sides of his face, grimacing as if searching for a way to tell him something. "We haven't had much time together. Did you know we were sweethearts a long time ago?"

"You told me you were sweet on her." Logan admitted wondering where this new conversation was about to lead.

"Jule and I, well, our relationship...you know she wasn't a virgin when you first slept with her."

Logan paused, his coffee cup half way to his mouth. "I suspected as much." Wind whipping around the eaves and wailing gripped the silence. His heart sped wondering where this conversation was about to go.

"We were lovers. Had been for several years. She was only nineteen when you arrived and bought her family home."

"She thought if I slept with her and got her with child I would wed her." Scenarios churned in his head and the realization hit him hard. He'd been a fool, but wasn't that idea in the back of his mind when she first approached him.

"That's true but you didn't." Jacques expression appeared strained. "I believe with all my heart that Charley is mine."

The boy is not mine. That statement explained a lot but he needed to do more. "What makes you think that?"

"Have you looked at him? Really looked at the boy?" Jacque's tone turned harsh yet Logan didn't feel animosity toward him.

"I guess not. He doesn't look anything like Jule or me." He spoke slowly all his plans for the boy's future vanishing.

"He looks just like I did at that age. My parents, as am I, are convinced he is my son, not yours."

Logan swallowed hard. While he had only a small emotional investment in his son, he believed Jacques. "Would Jule know for sure? Do you think?"

"She knows he's my child, won't admit it, but she knows. I'm not sure what to do about all this. I want to claim him."

"As you should." Logan said yet he tilted his head, listening. "What is that?" he asked as he strode to door.

As it slowly creaked open, he waited, balancing on the balls of his feet, prepared to attack. When he saw the cloaked figure slip through the door, he lunged, his hand wrapping around her mouth, her body flush against him.

"Evie! *Merdie*, what the bloody hell are you doing here?"

Chapter Ten

Quickly, he let her go, turning and staring at her as if he saw a mirage. "Bloody eyes, Evie, you're supposed to be in our room, warm and waiting for me, perhaps even asleep."

She smiled at him, touching the rough stubble on his chin. "What can I say? I was bored and I wanted to see you."

"Boredom can only get you killed if you go places you don't belong. Did you ask one of my men to escort you across the grounds? Of course not, that would be too easy." Her sudden impulsiveness terrified him. This was not his Evie who was never impetuous or unthinking.

"I figured it was safe because you were here. You weren't in the room so..." she stopped, shrugging her delicate shoulders and slanting him a tantalizing smile. "I wanted to be with you. Is that so bad?"

He cleared his throat, searching for words that didn't seem to form. Raking his hands through his hair, he strained to think of a definitive argument.

"Was I wrong?"

After another poignant silence, he said, "Yes and no." He didn't want her to think she could take chances such as this anytime she was bored. As it was, both he and Jacques believed nothing would happen tonight or even on the last leg of this trip, but he still meant to remain alert. Knowing how desperate Franco was put the journey on edge.

"Yes and no. That's certainly vague." Then she said, as if seeking a response, "I would have sketched you naked but I discovered I had no supplies. If I'd done that I wouldn't be here."

He felt blood rush to his face and was taken aback from the laughter emanating from Jacques who sat silent but listening on a bale of hay. "This is getting a bit personal. Think I'll mosey on back and check on things. Leave you two alone to do whatever it is you want to do."

"Best you do that," Logan said, clearing his throat and watching the man saunter away, amusement emanating from every bulging muscle.

"Now that I'm here, can I stay?" she asked, striding to the food tray and pot of coffee. She poured herself a cup and sipped, making a face as it touched her mouth. "That's horrible."

"Keeps a man hot when it's cold outside. I suppose if you would drink the stuff, it would keep you hot too," he said, liking the idea.

"I'm warm enough." She tossed the liquid into a far corner. "You can make me hotter."

He laughed, realizing she was coming to terms with their fledgling relationship. "You can stay until I leave, but I don't know what you think you can do. It's not exciting here by any means."

"You're here. I have someone to talk to. Which I didn't in the room." She plopped down on a bale of hay, plucking at her skirts. "For your benefit, I've put on wool stockings and a wool petticoat. See." She lifted her skirt so he could see. "This pelisse should keep me warm. Don't you think?"

"I suppose," he told her, still a bit reluctant to let her get her way in this discussion. He should toss her over his shoulder and carry her back to the room. His body hardened every time he thought about his naked wife. Her soft curves and the feel of her body flush against his.

"What would you like to talk about?" she asked, grinning a silly smile as if she knew just how handily she wrapped him around her little finger. "We could continue the questions, but of course we can't take our clothes off."

He shrugged his shoulders, trying for a nonchalance he didn't feel. "You're the one you who wants to talk."

She moistened her lips, her mind seeming to be somewhere in the rafters of the stable. "I do," she said, focusing her gaze back to Logan. Moistening her lips, she stuffed her free hand in the muff.

He laughed softly. "So, if I understand you, you want to talk but you have nothing to talk about. Is that right?" He tried for patience yet accepted the fact he had little of it where Evie was concerned. It seemed when he spoke with her, looked upon her, he yearned for only one thing.

"That's true," she told him, inhaling a long deep breath as she watched him with huge sapphire eyes that sparkled with passion even in the lantern light. "You never told me what your virtue was."

"I'm waiting." Ignoring her statement about his virtue, he leaned against a pole, legs crossed in front of him and wondering just how long it would take for her to get to the question she seemed to burn to ask him.

"You're not making this easy." She rose then and walked toward the back of the stables where his men either slept or were on guard duty then partially retraced her steps, stopping midway.

Even though she spent almost a month near these men, they all had needs that had not been fulfilled for a long time. He didn't want her wandering near them. "Come, sit, I'll try to think of something to talk about although I think you have something on you mind you want to ask."

She drew her lips together as she turned to face him and walked back to the bale of hay where she'd been sitting. "I might," she told him thoughtfully "but I'm not sure if I should."

"Do you want children?" Not waiting for her, he asked, thinking of his two sons, Harry and Charley before reminding himself he might have only one son. A little girl who looked just like Evie would be wonderful. She might already be carrying a child, reminding himself to look for the signs.

"Yes, very much so," she said, "Do you?" Her hopeful look sent a surprised jerk to his spine.

"Of course, as many as you would like." He watched for some sign from her but the blank look was not what he expected.

"You already have two sons." She sat down on the hay, looking to him as if she sought answers.

"True but I wouldn't mind more and they are not heirs," he told her, understanding it was too soon to broach the subject of Charley's parentage. Proof would be nice but...

"I don't know how to say this." She touched his chin with a tiny finger before tracing the line of his jaw. The warmth of that delicate caress overwhelmed him with desire and praying for a long life with her.

"Just say it." Now she had him intrigued. Perhaps she didn't want children. He should have found out before he wed her. Yet children did not make a difference to him. He desired her and that emotion was more than enough, besides there weren't a lot of ways to prevent children.

The whoosh of her held breath whispered in the night. "Very well. I don't think Charley is your son."

He looked at her, startled by her statement. "Why? What would make you think that?" Once again she surprised him.

"You haven't noticed?" she asked, seemingly perplexed. "Isn't it obvious? I thought it was."

"Noticed what?" He meant to hear everything she had to say. Perhaps her thoughts would be the same as Jacques. It was possible everyone in the village believed the same thing.

Watching her, she seemed to tremble either from cold or fear. After a long pause she finally blurted, "He doesn't look anything like you or Jule. He's the spitting image of Jacques."

What she said didn't surprise him overly much, yet the words disturbed him more than he wanted to admit. "What makes you say that?" His voice sounded too harsh. He wanted to hear what she thought and needed to know why.

"Never mind," she rose, "I think it's time to return to the inn. I'm sorry I brought this up."

She didn't get very far before he swept her into his arms and carried her back to her perch on the hay bale. On his lap, he positioned her to sit astride him, hoping she was in such a hurry to see him she left her undergarments off when she dressed this evening.

"Tell me more," he whispered, his lips close to hers, his hands easily finding their way beneath her pelisse and her gown only to find layers of wool protecting her virtue as well as keeping her warm. She'd told him but he forgot. He rested his head against her forehead.

"You should come back to the room with me." She touched his lips with her tongue before closing her teeth on the subject of her attention. "Perhaps we could start a child tonight." She paused, watching him, seeking a reaction. "That is if you want to."

"An invitation I would never refuse, but I need to remain here for at least another hour and you do need to get your rest. If we leave tomorrow, it will be another long day. Did you have to wear so many layers?"

Her laughter warmed his heart but did nothing to appease his increasing desire. "I thought you might want to play another game and this time I wanted to be prepared."

He framed her face with his hands and found her mouth with his, tasted her lips with his, pushed past them, felt the passion in him ignite wildly as he absorbed the sweetness and the heat of Evie.

His lips brushing hers, inhaling her breath into him, "Will you give me what we both want without games?"

"I don't like games. Don't like them at all. Never win, especially if you're playing," she whispered against him, inhaling a long breath before he deepened the kiss.

A throat clearing behind him told him his time with Evie was finished. She rested her head on his shoulder, seeming to realize the same thing. Yet, she was reluctant to leave.

He didn't set her aside but addressed Jacques. "What is it?"

"The men have reported seeing a shadow. Nothing more but I thought you should know about it."

"A shadow, Franco?" The man couldn't possibly think to attack this shipment here where the men had cover, where he would most assuredly lose his life or be captured.

Jacques slowly shook his head, "Don't know yet. He's been too elusive to capture, although one of the men nearly had him cornered but he got away. I really don't think it's Franco. Seems too small. If what they've told me is true, it's just a boy."

"Let me know when you have him, whoever he is," Logan said.

"I will."

"Good," he said, his hands still resting beneath her dress on her hips. Until Jacques interrupted them, he'd been trying to figure out how he could get her into the hayloft.

"You should stay close to your wife." Jacques gave a warning Logan didn't need to hear.

Blood heated Jacques' face to a bright red as he suddenly realized what he said and the position of Logan's wife. Jacques would know exactly what they were about.

"I believe I'm doing just that," Logan chuckled, enjoying the younger man's embarrassment. It would not be much longer, and Jacques would enjoy what he wanted with his wife when he could.

"Yes, sir, I suppose you are, in the best possible way. What now?" Jacques asked, backing away appearing as if he wanted to distance himself from the couple as quickly as possible.

"Send the men out in threes to search the area around the inn and the stables. I want the inside checked also. I'm going to stay here with Eveleen until we know everything is secure."

"Okay." Jacques left then, attending to his orders and giving commands of his own.

Logan continued to eye the ladder to the hayloft. Eveleen pushed away from him as if she wanted off his lap. "Not yet. You need to stay close," he chuckled. "You heard Jacque.

"Logan, we can't stay this way. I have to..." Her embarrassment sent a flush simmering her flesh.

"Just give me, us, a minute," he told her, running his hands along her wool stockinged legs. "When Jacques returns, I'll take you back to our room, but I'm going to have to come back here for at least another hour."

"You have to stay with me, please. I won't feel safe if you don't," she pleaded with him.

He lifted her to sit beside him and wrapped an arm around her, drawing her close. "I will post two men outside our door. You will be fine until I can be with you."

"I will worry about you and therefore I will get no rest," she told him, smoothing her skirts before slanting him a beguiling smile. "You do want me to sleep, don't you?"

"You will not sleep if I go to bed with you either." His intentions clearly not subtle and he was sure she understood as her long sooty lashes fell across her cheeks then opened.

"Maybe that is what I want," she told him, sighing prettily, enticing him even if she didn't understand what the small gestures did to his body.

His gut tightened at the beguiling proposition. "Surely you entice me more than any man should be tempted." He argued with himself, the list of pros and cons seeming astronomical.

"I try," she told him. "You've taught me many things, one of which I don't want to live without your touch upon my body."

He groaned, thinking he needed more strength than he could possibly obtain, "You will be safe in our bed tonight. Alone. I promise you though I will make up for it when we reach Paris."

"I don't want to be alone," she persisted.

The fear in her eyes suddenly evident, he told her, "You don't need to be afraid. Everything here will soon be safe."

She glanced at him then lowered her lashes again. Rising from the bale of hay, she paced the stable. "I saw that same shadow just before I entered here. The sight sent a shiver of fear down my spine. There was something sinister about it. In any case, if I don't want to go to my room, can I at least stay here and sleep?"

His heart went out to her, but he couldn't allow her to sleep in the frigid cold. Already this stay in the outdoors had changed the delicate blush of her face to ashen white. It wasn't blue yet but an extended stay would most certainly do the job.

"When we're sure the area is secure, I'll walk you to the room." He tried to reassure her but saw in her eyes that what he said had no impact on her fears.

"I don't want to go," she told him one more time. "It's not safe. I can feel it in my gut."

He didn't know how to address her fears. "I promise you all will be fine. The shadow you saw is nothing more than a servant trying to get home for the night or someone's lover."

"A normal person would not send a shiver down my spine" she insisted, obviously determined to convince him. "I felt as if something or someone walked across my grave." She slipped her hands inside her muff.

"It's the moon. Sometimes it does strange things, creates unexplainable feelings." He tried to put the reason for her apprehension on the shadows created by the full moon and the shimmering light bouncing off the earth.

"Perhaps," she reluctantly admitted.

It seemed she wanted to agree with him, but he heard the reluctance in her voice. He ran his finger across her cheek. "I will see you to our rooms as soon as Jacques returns with his assessment that all is well and the shadows are either your imagination or people returning home to a hot meal."

"I am exhausted," she said as if suddenly realizing the stress of the last few days. Holding a hand to her mouth, she tried to stifle a yawn.

"Sleep will do you good, and I will join you in an hour or so." He pulled the hood of her coat over her head, knowing heat escaped and she needed to stay warm.

"When I crawl into bed with you, I want to find you in your warmest nightwear. Promise?"

"Promise. I am beginning to feel chilled to the bone." She closed her eyes, leaning her head against his chest.

"Sir." Jacques stood in front of them.

"Thank God, I was beginning to wonder if it would be sunrise before I heard from you again." But the expression on Jacques face worried him, and he had a hunch Jacques wouldn't tell him anything while Evie sat next to him.

"We didn't find anything nefarious," Jacques began. "If you're hoping to send Eveleen back to the inn, now would be a good time. Did you want me to find someone to go with her?"

Everything about Jacques spoke of caution and held a hint of restraint. "No, I'll walk with her. I'd like to take a look around the inn after the door to our room is secured."

He rose and after slipping on his gloves, he extended a hand to her. "Are you ready?"

She accepted the help and when she wrapped her arm around his, she closed her fingers together inside the fur muff. "I wish you would stay with me." Still she persisted.

Her heart-felt plea left him undecided, but he told himself all needed rest and the journey tomorrow would go much better if he didn't wake someone an hour early so he could sleep with his wife. "I'll return before you can fall asleep. I promise you."

She laughed, smiling at him, "Liar. I'll be lucky to see you when I wake up with the sun. You'll be in bed then gone."

He couldn't refute her words as much as he wanted to do just that. As long as there was a possibility of Franco appearing he would have to stand watch. When he stepped into the frigid night air, a brisk wind whipped around the corner of the building.

"I promise I will try to see you before you fall asleep." He turned to her and pulled her pelisse closer together, hoping he could ward off the frosty chill in the air. Everything did seem serene. If there was any trouble Jacques would make sure it was taken care of.

She pointed to the moon in what appeared to be an attempt to change the subject. A thin cloud eerily floated across it before disappearing into the black night. "No wonder it's so cold. there are no clouds to hold the heat against the earth."

"What little heat there was from this day has vanished into the sky," he told her as they walked. Snow crunched and squeaked beneath their feet. When opened, the hinge on the large wooden door wailed in protest.

"Everyone is gone," she said as she seemed to search the main room of the inn. "When I left it was full, people chatting and bustling around."

"It's past time for everyone to be in bed." He studied every corner of the entryway. She was right, the place was void of people and the light from the moon filtered through a window in the entrance casting more creepy shadows into the room.

"Including you," she murmured softly. "How do you go so long on so little sleep?"

"Wait here." He left her to scour the entrance and the doors to the common rooms. Glancing over his shoulder, he saw her turn in a quick circle before walking to a chair and sitting down. She looked exhausted, her shoulders drooping from the weight of all that happened to her today.

"Eveleen. Eveleen?" He touched her but she didn't wake. He'd only been gone a few minutes. Not waiting for her eyes to open and in any case not wishing for that, he swept her delicate form into his arms and strode up the steps to their rooms.

The guard he assigned was still there. "Lord Maxwell," he said, "everything has been quiet. I haven't seen anyone since Lady Maxwell left."

"I'll send someone to relieve you in an hour. Then get some rest. You'll need it tomorrow."

The man nodded and opened the door for them. By then Eveleen was awake. He set her down and once more searched their chambers for any signs of intrusion. When he returned, Evie had her coat off and draped over a chair. She stood, her body rigid and hands clasped tightly in front of her. Her lips were drawn tight while she waited for him.

He pulled her into his arm and brushed a quick kiss across her lips. "Dress warm and go to bed. I'll be back soon."

"For some reason I don't believe you," she said softly.

The expression on her face spoke of many things, fear, disappointment, perhaps anger as well as desire. "I promise."

"I've heard that before," she told him as he backed from the room.

~ * ~

The door locked behind him. She didn't bolt the door from the inside, knowing Logan would want to slip inside quietly when he felt all was safe. Exhausted, she sat in a chair, closing her eyes and inhaling long deep breaths of air. Even though silence closed in around her, the room seemed to slowly simmer with unspoken words. Unseen movement, whispers of a soft breeze caught her attention and made her open her eyes.

The fire in the hearth had been kept alive, and now the light from the flames shifted and danced inside the shadows. Unsure of anything, she wrapped her arms around herself.

She felt as if someone stared at her yet she saw no one. Still, the unnerving feelings filled her making her pulse beat rapidly and her breaths turn to pants. Her hands and knees trembled when she rose. She turned in a full circle, starting for the door and help from the man Logan assigned to guard the room but stopped suddenly unsure.

Franco...

Panic swept through her, filling her with bone chilling terror. She searched the room just as Logan had done before he left, pulling curtains away from the walls, looking under the bed and behind chairs.

No one.

Nobody was in this room except herself. She pulled a fur throw from a chair and swept it over her shoulders in an attempt to stop the shaking encompassing her.

Once again, she looked to the door, wishing for Logan.

"I wouldn't do that, ma'am."

Slowly she turned to see a boy holding a pistol pointed in her direction.

"Who are you?" She asked, wondering if he was yet another of Logan's children.

"No one, I was taken from my family years ago. I just want to find my way back to them." The gun in his hands shook as he spoke.

"Let's start at the beginning," she said, trying to think of the best way to disarm the boy. "Put the gun down so we can talk." Her voice trembled even while she sought ways to calm herself.

He slowly shook his head, "Don't think so," his filthy hair falling across his face and hiding his eyes. She needed to see his eyes.

"Are you hungry? There is food left. You can help yourself." She hoped he would surrender the weapon in order to eat.

"No, I ate already, helped myself when you were gone." His words were short and clipped, impatient.

"I would feel a lot better if you gave me the weapon. I'm not going to hurt you. You already know that, don't you? It's why you came here," she told him, searching his face for something...what she wasn't sure.

"I believe that but if I give the gun to you, you'll tell the guard outside and he'll make me leave. I don't want to leave, ma'am. I want to go back to England with you when you return."

"From here we're going to Paris then to Italy. You're going to have to find a different way to get to England." She saw the look of despair rest on his features for a second before they suddenly vanished.

"He can't find me," he said. Moisture filling his eyes, he determinedly told her, "I won't go back there."

"Who and where is it you won't go?"

"An orphanage in Paris. They make us do things I don't want to do. We have to steal and pick pockets. The girls are taught how to become whores. Then they take all the coin."

The story sounded too familiar. "Come, sit down. I'd like to help, really I would, but I have to know more. First, what's your name?"

"Fitz." He sat down next to her.

"Fitz," she parroted. "Now, tell me all of your story. Start at the beginning and I'll see what I can do."

Before he started, he poured himself a cup of wine from the bottle sitting on the table. After taking a long drink, he wiped his mouth with his sleeve, grimacing as he set the cup on the table.

"You're probably not going to believe anything I say. No one else has." He drank again before swiping a hunk of bread from the tray and eagerly pulling a large piece from it with his teeth.

"Try me." Despite her exhaustion, the boy had clearly peaked her curiosity.

He shrugged, making himself comfortable on the chair, the pistol resting on his lap. "My mother and father were killed in a sailing accident near Dover. I was awarded to my father's sister. She was supposed to take care of me, but she didn't want me."

She sat down in a chair opposite his and poured herself a little wine. "I take it something happened to his sister."

"His sister sold me to a man who brought me to the orphanage. I escaped one night and I haven't been home since," he said, his voice bitter, venom spilling from him.

Appalled at the story, she sat back, studying the boy. "Why would your father's sister sell you?" She asked the question but she had a sinking suspicion she might know the answer.

"I don't know, ma'am," he said, his fingers tightly gripping the gun. "I just know that she did and I need to go home."

"Do you have siblings?" The ache in her gut grew. This sounded a lot like the story she heard from Ella about the girl in Vauxhall with the dog that picked pockets. But this boy was not old enough to be related.

"No."

"Was your father first born and did he inherit everything?" She posed the question to the little boy wondering if he understood what seemed to be happening here.

"He was the oldest and we lived in a grand home with a place in London too. At least that's what I remember." His eyes began to droop as well as the pistol.

"Listen, you're exhausted. You can sleep in the changing room on the couch if you want."

He shook his head, trying to sit up straight. "You'll put me out the door and leave me here. Have to stay awake."

She kneeled beside him, resting her hand on his, praying he wouldn't jerk and shoot her. "You took a chance coming to me, now you have to take another one. You have to trust Lord Maxwell and me. I promise we will do our best to right this problem and find out the truth."

His eyes widened. "Lord Tyler Maxwell? He knew my father. We spent time at his home."

"No, I'm sorry my husband's name is Logan." It suddenly occurred to her she didn't know his father's name. "It could be his father though. Now, are you going to trust me? I don't think you have another choice. You did come here," she reminded him.

He nodded and let her take the gun from him. "Can I go to sleep now?"

"No, you're going to take a bath first, and I'm going to ask the guard to find some clothes for you. Was it your shadow I saw earlier tonight when I walked to the stables?"

One more time he nodded, stifling a yawn with his hand.

Holding the weapon in her hand, she strode to the door and opened it. Speaking to the guard, she asked for hot water and clothes. Then she turned her attention back to Fritz.

"Help me move the empty tub to the changing room." Once that was accomplished, "Sit here until the water comes."

He was sound asleep when the bath was ready and she truly didn't want to wake him, but he had several layers of grim to wash away.

"Here are the clothes and do you want me to get Lord Maxwell?" the man asked as he started from the room.

"No, I want you to stay here and make sure he wakes long enough to bathe. Then I'd like you to guard the door a bit better than you did when he slipped inside. Lord Maxwell doesn't need to know until he returns."

"The boy didn't get inside on my watch. I took over just after you returned," he told her indignantly.

"Ah well, then I'll have to learn how someone fell asleep during guard duty."

The man cleared his throat, "In his defense, everyone is exhausted.

The day was excruciating to all. Sometimes we had to push the wagons to get them through the ruts."

"Regardless, Logan will want to know," she said, clasping her hands in front of her. "I will wait in the main room. Let me know when the boy is in bed. And make sure Logan is told about the boy's presence." She strode to the door, sliding the bolt home then settled on the sofa in the sitting room.

Nodding off, she woke when the man cleared his throat, "He is asleep. Do you want me to get Lord Maxwell now or just stay by the door?"

"The boy is harmless. Stay by the door."

He stepped from the chamber and Eveleen was left alone with her thoughts about the boy and Logan's possible reactions. She could have sent him away. Logan might want to return him to the orphanage, but she didn't believe he would do that.

She glanced at the bedroom door. He'd wanted her to rest and here it was, she glanced at the clock on the table, nearly two o'clock in the morning. At one time, before the boy surprised her, she'd thought that perhaps he would make love to her, come to her and hold her tight.

In any case, she should go to bed, sleep. He told her tomorrow might well be another exhausting day. She poured herself another glass of wine and sitting down near the window, watched the moon and the clouds as they slipped across the dark sky.

The stables lights were on. Of course they were, and Logan would be waiting for another wave of men to guard the shipment. She downed the last drop of Bordeaux.

In the bedroom, she quickly slipped into her flannel nightgown and wool socks. Pulling back the covers, she wished Logan were here beside her. She plumped the pillows and sat against the headboard.

She felt the throaty rumble of his voice against the back of her neck then the soft brush of his lips. Then he laughed. "You fell asleep, and I thought you would wait up for me."

"I did," she turned in his arms while he lifted her hair then let the strands slide through his fingers. "Couldn't you tell?" she asked, wondering why he didn't ask her about the boy. The guard must not have told him.

His cold hands tugged her nightgown up before resting on her skin.

She shivered, "Logan."

"I have to warm them up. What better way than to touch every inch of you," he murmured, bathing her neck with his lips and tongue then across her collarbone. His fingers fumbled with the buttons on her nightgown, slowly undoing each one while letting the backs of his fingers brush her skin.

"Once they are warm, I'm sure I won't complain."

"I want to make love to my wife," he murmured, his lips closing over a sensitive earlobe while his fingers continued their path along her fastenings.

"And I have something I need to tell you," she said, letting her head fall back so he would have better access.

"Whatever it is, I'm sure it can wait." Her gown was open, his hands closed over her breasts while his lips continued their tender and evocative assault on her flesh.

Slowly, he built a fire of desire inside her. Frantically, she pushed at his shirt, trying to touch his broad shoulders and feel the ripple of his muscles beneath her fingertips.

She wanted to tell him she was falling in love with him, needed to explain how much she needed him and wanted him. They had wasted so much time, trying to absolve all her insecurities and fears when all she needed to do was keep her eyes open.

Perhaps it was more than that though. Maybe she needed to learn how to trust him. Except for her father, the laird, and of course her sisters and cousins, she'd never really trusted anyone, let alone a man. It was difficult to be given to a man in wedlock and expect immediate trust.

He rose then, taking off his boots and his breeches. Standing in front of her for a moment before joining her beneath the covers, she inhaled a gasp of air. His body was well muscled and lean. His hair had grown and now touched his shoulders. She had an immediate urge to run her fingers through the thick locks.

Lost in the moment all thoughts of Fritz and the immediate problems his presence made, she allowed him to touch her soul with the heat of his passions.

"Didn't you say we need to sleep?" she said while she ran her fingers across his tight muscles and lower until she rested fingertips just above his arousal while she enjoyed the precious moment as she listened to him suck air.

"Then you shouldn't be touching me there," he breathed when her fingers closed around him and his hips jerked in response. He groaned deep in his throat and wrapped his hand around hers.

Eveleen had never touched him like that, had never believed she would do anything so bold. Yet she ached to continue the exploration. Her fingers held the alien male flesh, so hot and hard and smooth. She shuddered, her body quivering as her fingers explored him. She realized she had been frightened of his maleness, his strangeness, the size of him, and yet so excited she felt her body trying to move toward him, to rub against him, to draw him inside her, into her.

She had come so very far from the terror she felt the first few times he tried to make love to her. She wanted to discover more of the sweet ecstasy he could evoke.

He touched her lips, tasted them, pressed past them and she felt the desire in her flame wildly as she took in the warmth of him. She wanted him so badly. She lay in his arms and he could have her if he wished. The night was long, yet the dawn would arrive before she wanted it to.

He lifted his lips from hers, watching her, seeming to study her face. His dark gaze was on her. Her mouth was damp from his touch, still desiring more.

"Do you want me tonight? Will you surrender all that is you to me and perhaps create a child?" He smiled at her, seeming to patiently wait for her to reply.

"I do, but—"

"No exceptions tonight, no holding back, no silent protests or fears. It has to be just like before," he murmured, his fingers threading into her hair. His lips silenced any possible objection.

He swept an arm around her, bringing her fully against him. The length of her body shuddered. He found her lips again, caught them and held them with his own. Stroked the rim of them with his tongue, parried between them. She heard a low moan, rumbling from his throat. Her hands pressed upon his shoulders, drawing him closer still. Her fingertips clung to his flesh, holding him.

He kissed her lips, stroking the length of her back. He broke from her lips only to touch them again, his tongue tracing the shape of them before slipping deeply into her mouth. She caressed the muscled skin of his back, sweeping the length then back up his spine. Stroking ever closer to that part of him which fascinated her.

He trailed his kisses to her earlobe then along her throat. He lifted the mass of her hair and kissed the nape of her neck, then shuddered, sighing deeply, burying his face within the length of it. He moved her about, shifting the fall of her hair once again and pressing a kiss against her upper spine.

He bathed her shoulders with his caress then moved lower against her spine, his fingers stroking fire while his lips delivered their liquid heat, down to the small of her back, over the rise of her hip. He paused, seeming to listen to her soft feminine sigh.

Once again, he held her in his arms. Her gaze met his.

"Logan, please," she mouthed, needing to say something about the boy but unable to form the words.

"Please what?" he asked with a tender and determined voice.

"When you..." she began, trying once again to tell him about the events that had transpired when he was in the stables, but her words were silenced by the fire he evoked inside.

He didn't wait for her to speak, capturing her mouth. She felt the duel of his tongue with hers. Yearning burned through her. His hand moved fervently over her breast, teasing the peak to pebble hardness. He kissed her there and she savored the sweet sensations he aroused. She shifted beneath him, giving back the passion she received.

She rose against him, and he whispered soft words to her. "Feel the touch, my Poppet. Here, and here...feel it become a heat that begins an inferno inside of you, deeper and deeper here." His fingers danced across her upper thigh, set his palm over the rise of her triangle. "Here," he whispered then slipped a finger deep inside of her. "And here..."

An anguish tore through her. She wanted him. She wanted more tonight than she ever had before. It seemed as if this was the first time she was totally in control of her thoughts and her passion.

He rose above her and gently caressed her lips with the breath of his own. He traced a pattern between the valley of her breasts with his finger then he followed it with his tongue before lowering himself against her.

Wherever he caressed her, he kissed her. Lower and lower until he lay between her legs—touching her, parting her, caressing her, kissing her.

A fervent cry escaped from her. Her fingers tugged upon his hair.

He caught her hands and held them firmly within his own. She moaned softly in the back of her throat. Her head began to toss, her body to writhe and arch against him.

Enchantment surrounded them. Beyond, the night wind chilled the air, yet beneath the covers her flesh seemed on fire. In the endless blackness, the stars and the moon cast an eerie glow yet their light seemed to dance within the room.

He found the bud hidden within the feminine folds and played mercilessly upon it, laving, teasing and demanding with the caress of his lips and tongue. She began to shudder, yearning for her release.

"Logan, please," she cried out his name. "I can take no more." And truly, she could not.

She couldn't think, the sensations were so strong and vibrant. They were wonderful, erotic and sending her into such sweet spirals of sensations that she couldn't fight them, nor did she want to. He was whispering to her and in her mind, she was seeing things of startling beauty.

The strength of his hands, his fingers wrapped around hers, the taut muscled feel of his body, the weight of him between her legs, and the way he touched her. The things he did. The tension grew inside her, hot, wonderful, painful, and sweet. It grew until it was torment, until she arched wildly against him, and until sounds filled the night, soft, anxious, breathless. Sounds she was making herself.

Then sensations seemed to erupt. Sweet, so achingly sweet. It splintered with astonishment over her, with light then with dark—with stars across a velvet sky. It was the sweetest ecstasy within her. It was so, so exquisite. She drifted with it, reveling for several moments in the delight.

Then he was atop her. His eyes dark and wicked in the gleam of light, his naked body slick, hard, and muscled and fascinating her. She cried out, closing her eyes. His body slid into hers. "Logan," she cried out his name.

"Evie," he called her name too.

The intense erotic spiral began again, the heat strong inside. Curling, deepening. It could not happen again throughout her body, so sweet, so delicious, so wonderful.

The escalation and the yearning that led to it were so easily coming alive again. She was achingly aware of him, as if all sensation of her flesh had heightened. She felt his hair-roughened legs and chest, the hardness of his arm muscles, the rock of his hips and him inside her—the fullness of the movement, the thrust.

She gasped. The hunger was rising once more. She arched to meet him.

Her eyes wide open. His blazed into hers, and she pulled her lip beneath her teeth, her lashes falling. His face remained so taut, his length so vital yet rigidly hard. He moved, demandingly. His arms held his body above hers. He thrust into her and his gaze locked with hers. He moved faster and faster, his face taut with tension. She cried out, unable to deny the quickening within her. Her hands fell upon his shoulders. Her fingers raked across them. She was pulling up to him, meeting his thrust with a rhythmic arch of her own. Her lips fell upon his shoulders. She covered them with ardent kisses. Her fingers danced upon his back, massaging, digging, clinging.

He thrust incredibly hard against her just as sensations seemed to split and explode with her in a wild frenzy of fire and hunger.

"Logan," once again she cried out his name, clinging to him, as she felt the force of the climax surge upon her. Darkness fell. Light burst. Liquid heat swept through her once more. For a moment, she was so caught up in glittering ecstasy she did not realize he remained above her, the heat spilling from his body was filling her own.

He fell to her side, slick with sweat, breathing hard.

~ * ~

"Leave ma'am alone or I'll put a bullet through your head."

Logan turned quickly, knocking the pistol from the hand holding the gun before catching the assailant's arms in a tight hold and pulling him against his body.

"What the devil? Who are you?"

"Logan, it's okay, he didn't mean any harm. I tried to tell you about him, but..." Eveleen said, holding the covers against her naked body. "He has a story you need to listen to."

"No harm? What is he doing in our bedroom?" Too many questions swept through his head. Story? What kind of a story? His body shook with anger, his heart pounding hard.

"He's just a boy," Eveleen said, nodding with her head toward her nightdress on the floor beside the bed.

Running his hands through his hair, he picked up the gown and handed it to her. The lump in his throat and the all-encompassing fear did nothing to ease the tension building in the room.

"I can explain," she whispered, trying to put her nightgown on while keeping the covers over her naked body. "Really, he doesn't mean any harm. He just wants to go home."

"The boy can explain." Logan set him on a chair near the bed and grabbed the gun from the floor. He slipped his buckskins on and sat down to listen to this tall tale.

"I thought you were hurting her and she was nice to me. She gave me the clothes I'm wearing and a bath." He sat with hands clasped tightly in front of him, moisture filling his eyes.

"You're going to have to do better than that. No one puts a gun to my head. If you were a man..." he paused realizing he shouldn't say his next thought. He sent a quick glance toward Evie. He didn't think she knew what he'd been about to say. His heart still beat erratically from the surprising incident. Assuming his men protected the room, he'd let down his guard.

"Logan, what he has to say is important. Just let him get a breath of air." She pulled her robe over the nightgown but remained in bed, leaning against the headboard.

"He needs to spit it out." Logan strode to the fireplace and set two more logs blazing. Several seconds passed while he fought his emotions then he turned to the boy. "So...I'm waiting."

Fitz squirmed in the large chair his gaze resting on the floor. Then, "I don't have to tell you anything. Already told ma'am," he said, his voice belligerent.

Nonchalantly Logan crossed his arms over his chest. "You're right. You don't have to say anything in your defense."

The boy stiffened, his intentions clear. He wasn't about to speak up.

"Fitz, you have to tell him your story. He's not going to listen to me," Eveleen said. "If you don't, he'll put you out and leave you behind. What will you do then?"

He looked up, moisture in his eyes. "My parents were killed when I was little," he began, "But I was old enough to know them and to know what happened to my mama and papa." Fitz told the rest of his story with prompts from Eveleen.

"You tell a convincing tale for a young one. Who told you what to say?" Logan knew the boy lied.

He looked up, seeming indignant, "No one did, sir. It's the God's honest truth."

"No, it's not, although your reference to my father did give it a hint of truth. Your story is too much like one a friend of mine is investigating."

"I'm not lying," he protested.

Eveleen's face turned ashen in color. Her hand to her throat, "You really think someone told him that story about Piper?"

"The question now is what are we going to do with the boy?" Logan strode to the door, thinking he would call one of his men then changed his mind.

Eveleen rose from the bed and kneeling in front of the boy, asked, "Who told you what to say?"

"No one," he persisted.

"We'll help you if you tell the truth," Eveleen said, roughing the boy's hair back.

"Maybe." Logan didn't want the boy to lie. Franco was at the root of this, he was sure. "Fact is we know who's behind this. I'm surprised you didn't let Franco into the room while Eveleen was sleeping."

"Don't know a Franco."

Logan heard Evie's small gasp of surprise. "Of course you do. Nonetheless, first thing in the morning I'll send for the police. They can sort everything out. For now, I'll have one of my men escort you to the barn. Not quite as comfortable as the couch in the changing room, but it will have to do."

He strode to the door, and opening it, "Take the boy to the barn and make sure he's tied securely. Don't let him out of your sight. I'll wait at the door until you return."

Before he took up guard duty, Evie threw herself into his arms. Holding her tight, he closed his eyes. Evie was his life. He could have lost her tonight but for some reason, the boy didn't let Franco into the room.

"I was so careless. I'm so sorry," Evie said through tears sliding down her cheeks.

"Hush, it's alright. Nothing happened. Go back to bed. I'll join you as soon as my man gets back." His mouth met hers, a short but sweet joining. When he pulled away, he turned her toward the bed.

Without another word he took up his position in the hallway. To Logan it seemed an eternity before the man returned, breathless and heaving air. Pushing away from the wall he leaned on, "What happened?"

"The boy got away. Surprised me, he did and took off into the night. I chased after him, but he's a wily little guy. Didn't see hide nor hair of him."

Chapter Eleven

The morning dawned crisp and cold, but no snow fell from the sky and the breeze was minimal. As the sun began to rise from the surrounding hills, the wagons bearing the Bordeaux wines were on their way, headed for Versailles then on to Paris.

Logan felt restless and on edge and it seemed the guards were more vigilant than even the days before. The boy's disappearance left him with too many unanswered questions. Fitz obviously felt some loyalty to Franco or he didn't trust Logan.

The ride to Versailles took only a few hours. When the sale of the Bordeaux was accomplished, Jacques and Logan's men along with the carts started the return trip to Bordeaux. Logan rented a carriage, and they began their short journey to Paris.

She sat on the seat opposite him. The drapes were pulled back and sunshine streamed inside. Her hands were clasped on her lap; she wore a loose wrapping coat of fine black cloth. The coat was lined and trimmed with ermine. A white crepe fichu with a full puckered collar was tied with a black ribbon. She looked as if she had something on her mind, and he imagined it had to do with his treatment of the boy. As usual she chose not to wear a bonnet and her hair was pinned up, yet the wisps falling around her face were the color of the sun at its glory.

He itched to run his fingers through it and let the pins fall to the floor. If he was honest, he itched to do much more than that. When she looked at him, a soft smile on her lips, her sapphire eyes shimmering like the most glorious crystal blue lake, he wanted to lean over and pull her into his arms.

She looked so beautiful, his heart twisted with desire.

He clenched his jaw and swallowed the fierceness of his emotions, watching her as he wondered at the direction of her thoughts. She fiddled with the black decoration at her throat. Her fingers, long and elegant retied the ribbon before slowly, seductively stroking the ermine.

Just as her fingers lay last night, long and elegant upon his bare chest.

"You waste your time worrying about the boy," he found himself saying with a strange force he didn't understand.

She arched a brow. A flicker of some emotion he couldn't quite distinguish flitted across her face.

"I can't say I like the idea of him running back to Franco," she told him. "You're tense and furious believing something nefarious is about to happen. We've been worried about Franco since we left Dover. Fitz might have had some of the answers we've been looking for. What if," she leaned forward, "what if he was telling the truth."

"He wouldn't have run off."

She stared at him, meeting the challenge of his gaze. Bloody hell, she thought she understood the boy better than he did.

"The expression on your face last night would have frightened the hardest soldier."

He'd never appreciated her as much as he did now. "Perhaps you're right. I do need to curb my anger at times. I was being cautious with your life." He leaned toward her, cupping her chin with his fingers, raising her eyes to meet his. She was indeed a startling beauty. No artist could ever capture the blues and lavenders that mingled within her eyes, nor find the splendid reds and golds of her hair among oils or paints. To touch her was to stroke silk.

And she smiled...in complete confidence in her position.

She needed to understand his station and experience. The boy was a damn good liar but unlike Evie, he saw through the ruse. He drew her hands into his. A startled look came into her eyes as he pulled her across the carriage and onto his lap.

"You can't mean..." she said breathlessly.

"I can if I wish," he told her, but he saw nothing at all at the moment, nothing save her eyes.

"You've said time and again that we need to be cautious."

"Do you realize that you're are one of the most beautiful creatures

226

ever to walk this earth? No, you've told me the opposite. You are not a woman who lacks confidence except perhaps in this."

Her breath came quickly. Her lips must have been dry. She moistened them. She leaned into him and he relished the feel of her body against his. Her gaze wavered then returned to his. "I don't know what to say. I told you the truth. All my sisters are more beautiful than me. I am the least attractive."

He smiled slowly, shaking his head, finding it hard to believe she could be so naïve. "Little liar. You are not. It is the way I see you however."

"I don't want to argue with you about beauty or the boy," she pleaded, her eyes wide upon his as she seemed to search for some truth from him.

What did bother him? His fingers tightened around her hands. "Indeed, why would you think I want to argue?"

A smile curled his lips as he spoke until his words felt like a warm breeze upon her parted lips. Then his mouth formed to the sweet curve of hers. She inhaled and he drew her closer, seized by the glorious power of a sweeping desire. Her lips were sweet; the clamor of her heart was sweeter still. He plundered her mouth with his tongue. He tasted her until drums beat explosively in his head, and he knew he would lose not only his control, but his soul in this union.

His lips moved from hers. He seared a trail down her throat with the damp heat of his parted lips, teasing her flesh with the tip of his tongue. What better way to spend a carriage trip? He tugged on the black ribbon and parted the frilly fichu before he swept her collarbone, and the rise of her breasts.

She had been still, and he wondered if her fears had returned. Yet her sweet response denied that.

"We can't," she said softly "As you said, we have to be wary. Franco."

"Of course you are right. Yet one of my men rides with the driver and another follows behind the carriage." Bloody hell and damn himself for putting her life in jeopardy because he couldn't restrain his passion for her. With each day, desire burned more fiercely. Since they made sweet passionate love, his yearning was unthinking, mindless. She was amazing in his arms. She embodied the heat of the sun and the rhythm of the churning ocean. She had fought the marriage and it had taken her a long time to come to him freely and accept him. They'd been through so much. Just now she seemed ablaze with passion, alive and searing. This kiss told him so much. Within his embrace, she seemed to sizzle, to tremble, to gaze at him with eyes afire. She swept into the core of his being, heating him anew with the inferno only she could create.

"I don't..." she began hesitantly.

"Want to make love in this carriage?" he queried softly. "I'm sure we could make it work."

She scooted off his lap and back to the opposite seat. "Really, I'd like to wait until we reach Paris and our rooms. A bit of privacy would be nice."

He slowly withdrew, realizing with a few spoken words she brought him to his senses, yet the fires of hunger still burned within. Inhaling a long deep breath, he leaned against the carriage seat, his hands folded in front of him. With his eyes closed, he counted the seconds until they reached Paris and their hotel. She didn't speak to him and the silence set him on edge. Two steps forward and one step back described their relationship.

"Logan, I'm sorry, I... Stop can we stop!"

Concerned, he pounded his fist on the carriage and it slowly drew to a stop. "Evie?"

"Let me out!" She cried out...her hand over her mouth.

Logan jumped from the vehicle and helped her down, "What is going on?"

Eveleen raced a few feet and bending over, lost the contents of her stomach. She kneeled on the grass, heaving and moaning. He knelt beside her, running his hand along her back, apprehensive. Minutes ticked by until she finally sat back on her legs.

"I don't know what just happened. I wasn't sick earlier." He handed her a handkerchief and she wiped her mouth with it.

"Can you walk a minute? It might have been the sway of the carriage. I'll get you something to drink." He left her walking and strode to the vehicle to retrieve a flask of wine.

"You mean like sea sickness?" she swirled to look at him too fast.

He watched her as she closed her eyes, nearly swooning. More than concerned for her, fear for her bout with the freezing cold of the day before caused this, he brought back the wine.

"Something like that," he told her, handing her the wine.

She looked at the flask as if it was the last thing she wanted, but he had no water to offer and knew the wine would take away the bad taste in her mouth.

Eveleen drank a tiny amount. "This doesn't taste good." She swallowed hard before bending over again and losing the wine she drank in the roadside grass.

Logan touched her forehead. "You don't have a fever," he said, relieved at that but still concerned about her condition.

"How far are we from Paris and our hotel?" she asked in a whisper thin voice.

"Perhaps an hour away. Will you survive the ride?" His concern was deep and real. Tentatively, he offered her the wine again.

Moistening her lips and seeming to grit her teeth, she sipped gingerly and swallowed. She looked to him for answers, but he had none to give. With a grim look of determination, she sipped one more time then handed the flask back to him. He drank long and deep then capped it.

"I feel better now," she told him, her eyes vacant and dazed.

Beside himself with fear for her, "Is that why you look green around the edges?"

"Must be. Let's go now while I'm not throwing up." She picked up her skirts and started to the carriage only to stop and lose the wine again. "Guess I shouldn't drink the wine."

"Guess not," he helped her inside then pulled her onto his lap.

Rubbing her back, he meant only to reassure and comfort. "A little rest and a lot of sleep should help."

"If we ever make it to Paris," she murmured, nestled in close to him.

"Hush, try to sleep," he whispered to her. She stopped trembling and shook, only an occasional spasm. She blinked then closed her eyes before leaning into him sobbing softly.

His fingers moved down her back again, "It's all right, it's all right. I am here," he whispered.

She couldn't speak, could only nod and wipe the tears away.

"What is it?" he murmured. "What is it that has you so suddenly sick. In all the time I've known you, you haven't been sick a single day."

"Truly, I don't know. It just happened so suddenly," she said softly.

"Surely you must understand what is happening to your body," he said because he was beginning to realize the truth.

The carriage began to move, slowly at first and Logan prayed he would not have to stop it again. A smile formed in his heart in hopes his thoughts would come to fruition.

She didn't answer his query and he didn't press her, knowing there would be time later to discuss this. His muscles constricted as if he would move yet he didn't dare. Her fingers wound into his shirt. His closed around them. "I told you that it is all right. That I am here."

He eased her fingers from him and set her on the opposite seat. She clasped her lower lip with her teeth, letting her lashes shield her eyes. He reached to the other side, finding the flask of wine, praying this would remain in her stomach. He teased her lips with the tip of the flask and she swallowed a tiny amount. He pulled her back onto his lap, leaning against the padding and bringing her head onto his shoulder. He sipped the wine himself then lifted her head once more, and this time she swallowed more deeply. The wine warmed him and he hoped it did the same for her. She gasped and fell back again, her lashes over her eyes.

He studied her, staring down at the perfect oval beauty of her face and the softness of her skin, ashen and a bit green if that could be. Even her lips remained pale. He traced them with his finger. Her eyes flew open. Shimmering sapphire, they held fear and confusion within their depths. Her lips trembled slightly. "I wish you would have believed the boy. He needed to be believed."

"He was Franco's pawn."

"He was a boy," she persisted.

"You must be feeling better," he said softly.

Her lashes fell upon her eyes again, covering them. "I am for now."

Logan lifted the flask, studying it for a minute. He smiled with a certain irony then sighed and relaxed onto the cushioned seat. A number of questions needed asking, but he wasn't sure the timing was right. Perhaps it was too soon, perhaps it wasn't. She'd grown up with only her sisters, yet many things in the castle would have required her assistance. If she didn't know, she had to at least be guessing the same thing he was.

He needed to be wary. He did not care to test the tenacity of Franco and his man Tate, so he and his men needed to maintain their guard. It was indeed the last thing he wanted to do. Maybe the trouble from his nemesis was over or maybe it was not. They would be in Paris and he would be able to negotiate a few business deals as well as show Eveleen around the city.

He was afraid to leave her alone in the hotel. It would be like her to venture out on her own and now if his guess was correct, she would have to realize she protected another life. His fingers fell upon her hair. It was soft and tousled more than it was before. It was beautiful, still the color of the golden sun with varying shades of red.

She did not move beneath his touch. Sleep was the best thing for her. He had to proceed now in a different manner. He closed his eyes and listened to the sounds rumbling from outside.

His hand rested beneath her coat and on her abdomen while he tried to recall the shape of her. Surely, if she was pregnant, her breasts would soon be larger as would her belly. He smiled at the thought of a child growing in her womb.

"Boy or girl?" he murmured, his breath whispering across the top of her head.

"Logan?" she sat up, turning in his arms. "What are you saying?"

"Boy or girl. If we were to have a child, what would you want? A boy or a girl?" The sex didn't matter to him. If they had four girls as her father had, he would cherish them all.

"Why are you thinking about children when you have an enemy threatening you?" she asked, appearing puzzled.

"Certain circumstances have my mind spinning in that direction, children." He wondered if he gave her enough clues she would figure out her condition.

"And what could those be?" she smiled and poked him in the chest.

"You don't know? I would think a woman of your intelligence would have figured it out." He watched her eyes, saw them darken with what emotion he wasn't sure, but he knew she still didn't get the gist of what he spoke.

"It's Fitz. He was adorable, don't you think?"

He lowered his mouth to softly touch hers and whisper against her soft flesh, "Of course not. I didn't find one thing adorable about the boy who held a gun to my head. Look, we are in Paris now." He pointed to the open window.

She settled against him again, placing her hands on his arms which still rested on her stomach. "I can hardly wait to see everything."

He inhaled a long deep breath before sighing the breath out. "What do you want to do first?"

"Eat something amazing."

"The bout of nausea must have vanished," he said, heartily glad of the fact. Still, he expected another session of sickness in the morning. "What would be amazing?"

"I don't know. You've lived in France. What is the best?"

Her enthusiasm swept into him, grabbing his heart. "I'm not a connoisseur of French food or any type of food for that matter. We'll have to try everything we see."

The hotel sat close to the Seine and the heart of Paris. He wrapped an arm around her and drew her into a shadowed entryway. He could still see her eyes, expressive and inquisitive.

They secured their rooms and made their way to the third floor. It was beautiful and grand. The opulence was amazing, astounding. Once inside, she twirled around the room, slipping out of her coat then once again, she nearly swooned. Her hand to her head, she settled on a close by chair.

Logan rushed to her side, his fear for her and their child far too real for his comfort. "Are you alright?"

"I don't understand. I feel fine then suddenly without warning..." she let the words trail off.

"Take care. We will figure this out. For now, you should lie down. I'll inquire at the desk and see where to go for the best food then bring something back for you." Unwilling to reveal his thoughts to her, he helped her to the sleeping room and loosening the fastenings on her dress. eased it from her body before undoing the ties of her corset. "You really shouldn't wear this contraption any longer," he blurted unthinking.

She didn't seem to understand him. Instead of answering, she allowed him to settle her on the bed with a quilt to cover her. Tenderly, he touched her forehead. "Sleep. I promise I'll wake you as soon as I return."

Slipping from the room, he leaned against the door, concentrating on his wife and exactly how to break the news to her. She carried his child, he was sure. He pushed away from the entrance and took the downward steps two at a time in a rush to finish his errands and return to his wife.

After a brief conversation with the receptionist at the desk, he sauntered outside. A definitive chill filled the air as the sun hid behind dark clouds, snow once again threatening. He walked along the Seine, humming and looking for the restaurants the man suggested. Several places beckoned him and by the time he was ready to return, he'd purchased baguettes, croissants a variety of cheeses and meats as well as a few chocolate candies he thought she might enjoy.

Pausing at the base of the stairway, he turned, searching the interior of the building, the hair on the back of his neck standing on end. His gut told him someone watched. He always trusted his gut. Except for the occasional stop for Eveleen, the journey into Paris had gone smoothly.

Franco and his man could have followed them. Momentarily, he brushed the idea from his mind, intending to enjoy the meal with his wife. The guard outside the room would ward off these two seemingly desperate men. They should know when a cause was lost. Did they truly wish to spend their lives in a French prison? They would not but if they had nothing to lose, what would it matter?

Readjusting the bags of food, he strode toward the third floor and he hoped, his sleeping wife. At the door, his man jumped to attention.

"Lord Maxwell."

"Any sounds from inside?" he asked, hoping Eveleen had slept the time away and would waken feeling more herself than when he left.

"No, sir, everything has been quiet. I haven't seen anyone since you ran your errands."

"Good, I'm glad to hear that." Taking out his key, he let himself into the room. Silence surrounded him as he set the bags on a table in the main chamber. Before setting out the food, he took a second to look in on his wife.

She was sleeping peacefully on her side, her hand tucked beneath her face. He sat on the bed next to her, gently pushing aside the strawberry blond strands that had broken free from the confines of the chignon. She sighed slightly, adjusting her position on the bed. Nothing but tender emotions assailed him. She was so precious to him. Her life meant everything.

He rose, striding purposely into the main room, determined to make everything perfect for her. Pulling out the baguettes, cheeses and meats, he assembled them on the table. A purchase of several bottles of his wine from a store on the Avenue des Champs-Elysees finished the setting. As a finishing touch, he bought two wine glasses even though his gut told him she shouldn't drink in her condition. He planned to make sure she had only a few sips tonight, and after that he would be sure to have other beverages specially made for her.

Stepping back and overseeing the table, he brought out his last purchase, a bouquet of lilies already in a vase, which he filled with water.

"There, I believe this is perfect," he said, trying to keep his voice soft so as not to wake Eveleen. Then he realized that perhaps he should wake her. She needed food and rest. He'd been gone several hours and many more than that had passed since they ate breakfast, none of which she kept down.

"Logan, were you going to let me starve?" She stood in the middle of the doorway, disheveled, in disarray and very nearly naked. The most beautiful woman he'd ever seen.

~ * ~

"I was just going to get you," he said. "Are you cold?" He strode to her valise and rummaging through it, he found a warm robe and wrapped it around her shoulders, covering her.

"And I would have thought you, Lord Maxwell, would have wanted me nearly naked. Now you are throwing clothes on me. What is this?" She felt clearly baffled at this new side of her husband.

It seemed he ignored the question. "You must be hungry. Have a seat." He gallantly brought her to a comfortable chair. "I'll dish some food for you. A glass of wine?"

"Logan, I'm quite capable of doing those things by myself. You don't need to wait on me." Still perplexed by this new side to Lord Maxwell, she rose but he was beside her, his hands on her shoulders gently guiding her back to the chair.

"I insist," he told her, a wicked smile on his face, one eyebrow tilted slightly as if he kept secrets from her. "I want to take care of all your needs tonight."

"What aren't you telling me?" Instant concern flashed through her head, but he wouldn't be acting like this if his fears were about Franco. No, his entire demeanor would be different.

"Nothing," he murmured, once again slanting her a smile that had her mind racing.

"Logan, tell the truth. What is it that has you acting so strangely? You are just not yourself," she told him, once again rising. She wanted to sit at the table to eat, not on a lounge chair.

"Tender concern for one's wife is acting strangely?" he countered, allowing her to move from the lounge chair to a place at the table.

She squinted her eyes together, realizing this conversation was going nowhere. He layered her plate with a sample of everything he bought. She heaped the bread with cheese, beef and ham while he poured a small glass of wine.

She looked at the glass then back to Logan without saying anything. "You're going to have to explain this to me," she nodded her head at the tiny drink, "and your actions."

"After you eat."

"Then can I get a little more wine? Enough maybe to wash down the food you want me to eat." Indignation as well as frustration laced her words. "This is going too far."

"Not far enough by my mind."

"There you go again, making no sense whatsoever." She bit into her food, chewing thoughtfully even as her stomach growled.

He dished up food for himself but didn't seem to have an interest in it. Instead, he chose to stare at her. "I've a treat for you when you're finished." He leaned back in his chair, arms crossed in front of him.

"Are you going to eat?" she asked, setting her food on her napkin and resting her elbows on the table in silent protest.

"I like watching you."

"Then I'll wait for you." Her words and meaning emphatic, she followed suit by crossing her arms in front of her.

His heavy sigh sounded reluctant, but he began to eat, "Very well," he said through mouthfuls of food and wine.

"You haven't poured me more wine," she said, finishing the second and last sip he poured in her glass.

"And I'm not going to."

"Then you should have the decency to tell my why. Is there something else to drink? I can't chew another bite unless I have something to wash it down with. What the devil has gotten into you?" she continued to question.

He raked his hands through his hair but relented and picking up the bottle, poured her a full glass. "I don't think you should have this but there is nothing else right now."

"Thank you. If I eat all this food," she gestured with her hands at her plate of food, "you'll tell me what seems to plague you."

"Of course."

"Do you promise?" she asked skeptically, yet with some hopefulness she would soon get to the root of his strange actions and words.

He seemed reluctant. "I'd rather you figure this out on your own. I've never had to explain anything like this to someone...a woman."

She swallowed hard. Suddenly, her appetite vanished. "What on earth are you talking about Logan Maxwell? You have me frightened to death. I can't possibly eat now." She pushed back from the table and strode through the main room to a window that looked down on the bustling city she wanted to explore. Watching the carriages roll by and the people stroll along the walkway somehow soothed her frustrated emotion.

She felt his presence before he touched her. His work-roughened fingers gently pushing the robe down her shoulders. He massaged her neck and shoulders. She let her face fall forward, allowing his fingers ease her muscles as well as her fears yet she had so many questions.

"Please come back and eat. I'm sorry for what I said. I didn't mean to frighten you. I promise that as soon as we finish our meal, I will tell you. I just want you to get some food in your stomach. I don't think I can even recall when you ate last and kept the food down."

She turned in his arms, his hands resting on her shoulders. The feelings and emotions emanating from him were different somehow. It didn't seem to Eveleen he meant to seduce but to protect and shelter. Something else she didn't understand completely although she liked this side of Logan.

Moistening her lips, she gazed into his eyes, trying desperately to see the thoughts behind them. "I think I can do that."

"I didn't mean to frighten you," he told her again, wrapping an arm around her and pulling her close to his side as he guided her into the chamber and the dining table.

They sat down. She swallowed hard, wishing the food looked as good to her as it did a few minutes ago. Needing to find out the truth and what he implied but didn't say, she bit into the meal. Time ticked by slowly as she made every effort to eat what he gave her. She managed to finish most of it and was pleased when he accepted the fact and opened a small bag.

"What is that?" she leaned forward in an attempt to see inside.

"The treat I said would follow the meal." He opened it and let four bonbons slip from the bag. "Take your pick."

"Then you'll talk to me..." she said, skeptical of his intentions.

"Yes," he plopped one in his mouth and seemed to watch her as she chose a piece of chocolate and did the same, washing it down with another sip of the wine.

She sat back, waiting for him to talk, yet silence prevailed while he appeared to squirm in his chair. Patience had always been one of her stronger points, so she tilted her head, smiling.

He ate his second piece of candy, stalling for time. His gaze settled on her before he rose and paced the room, his hands behind his back. As if he made up his mind, he turned on one heel and strode to his chair. He turned it so he could rest his arms on the back.

"I really would have preferred you figure this out on your own."

He picked up his glass of wine and swirling the wine, watched it for several seconds before setting it on the table.

Two could play this game. She tapped her fingers on the tabletop several times then picked up her glass of wine and sipped, watching him over the rim. He seemed tense, at odds with his usual behavior, but he'd been acting that way since she got up from her nap. She angled her head slightly, blinking several times.

"Are you going to say anything?" he asked in a throaty growl, clearly frustrated his words tense.

"What do you want me to say? You were going to explain certain strange things. Why don't you just tell me?" She didn't want to guess or pretend she knew his thoughts.

He closed his eyes and with a heavy sigh said, "When was your last monthly?"

She felt all the color drain from her face. This was something she didn't expect. "Why would you want to know something like that?"

He shrugged his broad shoulders, a gesture she'd come to recognize as all male. "Because I'm your husband."

She leaned forward and speaking through gritted teeth, said, "That doesn't make any sense." Truly baffled now as well as embarrassed, she was unsure where this conversation was leading.

"When," he insisted, now seeming relaxed and in his element.

She didn't think his questioning had any merit or would lead anywhere. "I don't know. I haven't really thought about it."

"You should," he smiled, appearing pleased with himself.

She could not fathom where this was going. She had no idea the answer to his question or why he would want to know. Eveleen rose, pacing the room then swirling to meet his gaze. "Maybe when we left for Dover or a bit before. I suppose."

"Just as I thought. Before we made love, before we consummated our marriage," he told her, seemingly more delighted with himself. "Do you really have no idea what I'm inferring?"

"I don't," she said, beginning to tremble. A single tear slipped from her eyes. "I don't know why you are taking such great pleasure in tormenting and embarrassing me. It's cruel. You are cruel."

She turned her back on him, her body shaking. His hands fell upon her shoulders and turned her. "I did not mean to torment you or be cruel, but all the facts leading up to this have implied something to me and quite honestly I'm shocked you haven't put together the facts."

Flinching away from him, she strode to the window, wishing to put as much distance between them as possible. It wasn't to be. He was beside her, his hand on her shoulder, a seemingly possessive gesture.

"Evie," he began then cleared his throat, "your nausea, the other facts we just discussed, I believe you carry my child."

Wide eyed, she swiveled, her back braced against the cold windowpane. "No." her hands on her face, "I am? I never thought."

He chuckled softly. "I guessed as much. Surely with your sisters you would have recognized the signs."

She closed her eyes, allowing his gentle massage of her shoulders to ease the abounding fears encapsulating her. "No, with Allura, I didn't pay attention. She and Hunter were so in love and we never talked about anything like that. I was so young and had other interests. Christel was in another part of Scotland."

"You're truly an innocent." He brushed a soft kiss on her forehead, the heat of his lips warming the coldness that had descended on her.

"I didn't think so," she murmured as he pulled her close her face against his chest, her tears of joy dampening his shirt. She pulled her lower lip beneath her teeth, wishing she had understood these things more fully.

"Are you happy?" he queried, stroking her hair. What were left of the pins in her hair after her nap quickly found their way to the floor.

"Scared," lines creased her brow. "Frightened to death. I don't know a thing about having a baby. Do you?" She looked up in order to see into his eyes. He had a child and for the longest time thought he had two.

"Not much, I was too young when Maida had Harry to be included in anything. She was swept away to a relative's home to have the child, and of course there were stories about Harry for a while until she finally put them to rest."

"And Charley?" After all, Jule had done everything in her power to make sure Logan thought the boy was his.

"Nothing there. I was in London when the boy was born and

apparently conceived." His tone became dry and distant.

"Then how do you know so much?" She let her hand rest on her stomach.

He covered hers with his. "Talk, men talk when they drink. They laugh about their conquests and their good fortune. Things that go on behind closed doors. The lady my father took me to..." he paused in thought as if considering his words more intensely. "The lady taught me about pregnancy and how to recognize it and how to prevent it as well as how to give a lady her greatest pleasures."

"And then they keep this knowledge to themselves?" She was astounded by what he said.

"No," he told her, pushing back the strands of her hair and letting them slide through his fingers, "They assume women speak of the same things and that mothers tell their girls about the marriage bed."

Tears slipped from her eyes as she angrily brushed them away. "I didn't have a mother to tell me those things."

"I'm sorry." He guided her into the living room and sitting down, pulled her onto his lap cradling her in his arms while she cried. "I believe we have a lot to talk about whenever you're ready."

She did want to have a child, his child but this had come so soon and so unexpected. "It only takes once or twice, how can that be?" she said, brushing the tears aside and trying desperately to concentrate.

"Only once if the timing is right."

"Then I could have conceived on that first night in Bordeaux?" She ran that idea through her head several times, remembering how Allura looked before she gave birth.

"Yes," he said, "but probably not at the inn that night." he told her, running a finger along her chin. "I'll tell you everything you want to know."

"Everything," she rose. "I'm suddenly hungry." She walked to the table and sitting down finished the meal she'd begun earlier.

He followed. "Are you happy about this?"

"Now that you're no longer frightening me, yes. I've always wanted children and believed they were part of a marriage." She finished the remaining wine.

"There are two things I would like you to consider during your pregnancy." He sat down, taking her hands in his.

"What are they? Now you're scaring me again." What little normalcy she'd been feeling vanished.

"Forgive me, I really don't mean to do that."

"Well, you have," she said indignantly. Slowly picking up the last of the candies on the table, biting into it, she stared at him. "This is really good with the wine."

"First, I really don't want you to wear a corset for the duration. I don't think you like them anyway."

"Why?" Even though she felt relieved at the idea of tossing the torture device for the duration, she was curious.

He shrugged broad shoulders, "Just my gut. It seems to me if your body is expanding and there is a child inside, it wouldn't be good to put constraints around this tiny being."

"Well, I won't argue about that. But none of my clothes will fit." She could only imagine how soon the few clothes she brought with her would not wrap around her new and growing body.

"I will buy you whatever you need. There is a dressmaker here in Paris who Jarret frequents when he's here. We'll visit her tomorrow and get an entire array of dresses."

She swallowed, wondering at the cost. The dressmaker in London had been taken care of by The Duchess and previously they had sewn most of their clothing. "I hate fittings."

"Don't worry about that, I'm sure Giselle will be able to select premade clothing for at least six months, since I'm not sure how long it will be before we return to England."

"I will need different sizes. How will she know?" This was truly getting complicated.

The twinkle in his eyes didn't go unnoticed. "Every woman is different," he said, a slight chuckle in his voice. "But I think she can take a good look at you and make some assumptions. It's not just your belly that will grow. Your breasts are already larger."

"You noticed?" she felt truly stunned. "I haven't. What's the second thing you want to talk about?" She was ready for this conversation to come to an end.

"No more wine," he told her pointedly. "I hope you agree with me in this."

"I..."

"Tongue tied?" he queried softly.

"Then you must find something else to drink. When all we have is wine it's hard to swallow the food you make me eat."

"Well, you are eating for two," he pointed out.

"Of course, I'm not. Even if the child at this very moment was the size of a newborn, that is hardly the equivalent of two people. Now, why no more wine?"

"Again, just a gut feeling I've had. Think how you felt the night of our wedding and the morning after."

"Horrible," she remembered the nausea and the throbbing headache.

"Would you want our child to suffer the same things?"

Closing her eyes, she moistened her lips, understanding what Logan spoke of. "No, of course not. But one or two glasses of wine couldn't possible affect the growing babe."

"You told me a few minutes ago the child was so tiny you would not be even close to eating for two."

"Well, tea is nice," she conceded with a yawn, realizing all he said was true.

"You're tired. Perhaps you should retire for the night."

"What about you?" She did need sleep but she didn't want to go to bed without him, and he didn't look sleepy. He looked on edge.

"I'm going for a walk," he told her, taking her arm and helping her to the bedroom. Slowly, he undressed her and finding her nightgown, slipped it over her head.

"I don't need help dressing." Was this going to be the way of it until she gave birth? He would take her to the bedroom then leave. Insecurities built inside. She wasn't fat yet, and he was turning her aside. Her body trembling with unaccountable fears, she let him cover her.

Instead of sleeping, when she heard the door close and the lock turn, she rose from the bed. The lights in the room were off but one candle burned in the entrance. She retrieved it and lit two more candles.

Sitting in a rocking chair, Evie let her hands settle over her abdomen, trying to take in all the information. She carried his child and he left her. Her heart raced and her breathing labored. She closed her eyes, unable to understand the sudden distance between them. Perhaps her best course of action was to leave, sail back to London. She could find a ship to London at the docks.

She wasn't too sure where those ideas came from. The last few weeks they'd been happy. At least she'd thought so. She tried to sift through all their conversations but couldn't remember one that would leave her to believe he no longer cared for her.

She was pregnant and couldn't drink wine or wear a corset. He wanted her to eat for two. What else would he dictate? Seeds of doubt swept through her, filling her soul with insecurities.

Logan was gone, again. He vanished without a word as to where he was going, just as he used to do. She cringed inwardly, old fears resurfacing to meld with the new.

Clouds drifted across the sky as the minutes turned into hours. She stood by the window, watching the empty street below. A furtive shadow dashed along the walkway before crossing to the other side.

"Fitz?"

~ * ~

Logan visited several establishments including the police, giving notice about Franco and the part he played in the pirating of his wine as well as the burning of the vineyards. His last stop had been the dressmaker who was just closing her doors.

"Gisele, can I come in for just a moment?" he caught her with the keys to the shop in her hand.

"Lord Maxwell, of course, what can I do for you? You have a new lady friend who needs a few garments as did your friend Jarret Kingsley." She laughed, seemingly delighted with herself.

"A wife," he told her, "a pregnant wife."

"Oh, you have been busy, I see. What can I do for you?" She tapped him on the shoulder with her fan before she led the way into her shop.

"Tomorrow, I'll pay you a visit with Eveleen. She will need clothes that will last her through her pregnancy. I hope you have some premade because we won't be here for long." Nervously, he ran his fingers through his hair, glancing around the shop, searching for what he needed.

"Over here," she led the way. "We have day dress, promenade, evening, and carriage dresses for the choosing. All will accommodate an expanding body. Will she need anything else?"

"We'll stop by tomorrow. If you could set some items aside for her to look at and choose from, I'd appreciate it and make it worth your while. Before you ask, she is small," he said, following with hand gestures to help her understand.

Leaving the shop and whistling a tune, pleased with his accomplishments, he returned to the rooms he rented. A smile lit his heart as thoughts of slipping inside the covers with his wife and making love to her darted into his head.

When he stepped inside, the candlelight from the bedroom caught his attention. Walking through the sitting area, he began undressing. His jacket hit the floor mid-room and the fastening on his shirt were undone by the time he reached the empty bed.

His heart lurched to his throat as he turned on a heel, searching the room. Thoughts of Franco filled his head and fears for Evie terrified him, his body trembling with the urge to murder. As he searched for his wife, his fists and body tightened ready to fight.

When he saw her sitting by the window in the rocking chair clearly asleep, he nearly wept with relief. Striding quickly to her side, he picked her up, carrying her to the bed. After settling her gently on the mattress, he disrobed and crawled in beside her.

"Logan, you came back," she whispered softly. "I thought you left and you were no longer interested in me."

Her words stung his soul. He'd just done what he vowed never to do again. "I'm sorry, Evie." An apology was not enough. He had a lot to learn about this marriage business.

He drew her close, inhaling her scent, sweeping her hair from her neck. Her hands on his face were soft and so delicate. When his lips molded over hers, he inhaled her breath.

"Logan, I was afraid," she said when he drew away from her.

"Forgive me?" With his hands he pulled the bottom of her nightdress up her body. "Lift your arms for me." She did and the sight of her naked body left him breathless. He paused then he thought he'd never seen her more beautiful than at this moment. A soft light from the moon swept into the room. He ran his hands over her naked breasts so soft, full and already larger because of her pregnancy. The beauty of her throat and breasts and torso were bared to his eyes. Her hair cascaded all about her, and in the light of day it was the color of a sun.

He had never felt more humble, and he trembled. He had never understood that love was possible or that it could be real. Now it was his. It was more precious than life. She was life. His life. Their child grew within her. Their future stretched before them. He had more than any man could ever wish for. He smiled, holding her tight, cherishing and savoring the soft feel of her nakedness as he held her against this body.

Yet the threat of Franco still hung over his head. He had to find a way to put an end to the man who plagued his life for so long. The need to put his nemesis from his head at least for this evening was in the forefront of his mind.

"You were asleep on the chair? Why?" he asked even while she let her head fall back to give him access to her neck and breasts.

She sighed softly, her warm breath sweeping across him. "Why?" she asked as her hands wound through his hair then sliding down his back, her fingernails leaving a trail of delight.

And the need to make love to her overpowered his senses. "I want you, Poppet, but I suppose you know that." His lips descended on hers, tasting, cherishing, exploring. The small sounds coming from the back of her throat enchanted him.

They made love and she lay in his arms. He sensed when her body relaxed and she fell asleep. Left with his thoughts, he wondered if she knew he loved her, had fallen in love with this tiny delicate woman.

Love doesn't exist, he'd quoted the words so many times he believed them until he met Eveleen McLellan. He smiled, thinking of the enticing piece of baggage he'd finally brought into his bed. She'd fought him every step of the way, but that was because he neglected her feelings and she'd run from him, finding danger and a life threatening experience that changed her life.

Slumber wasn't coming to him anytime soon. He relished the woman in his arms and the feel of her body against his. Something in the room didn't feel right. The silence seemed too complete. A whisper, a bump and a low growl came from the sitting room.

His body tightened, ready to explode into action. All senses in tune with the slow stealthy slide of booted feet across the floor, he concentrated and planned the next move. Patience, he slipped his arms from around Evie, his back to the intruders.

"Get away from ma'am. Let me see your hands." The boy's voice trembled.

"Fitz?" the child's voice held memories Logan would rather forget. His men had lost the boy and once more he was sure the child held a gun. By the sound of his voice, he didn't stand as close this time. And unlike last time, he doubted the boy was alone.

"They're making me."

"Who?" Slowly, Logan turned on the bed his hands in the air. Naked, he rose from the bed. "Who's making you?"

"I don't want to do this." His hands holding the gun shook.

"Who's making you do this?" Logan asked one more time, pulling his buckskins from the floor and slipping into them. He wouldn't have trouble disarming the boy, but two grown men would be a bit more of a challenge.

"Logan?" Eveleen's voice behind him sent a shiver of apprehension down his spine.

"Stay in the bed, Evie. Whatever you do, don't move." He needed to know where she was.

"Fitz, is that you?"

"Yes ma'am, they want to hurt you."

"Then why are you helping them?" she asked, her voice behind him seeming closer.

"Evie, stay in bed. I need to know where you are," Logan said, his voice harsher than he wanted, but this could be a life or death situation. The silence behind him gave him hope she was complying to his wishes.

"Who's making you do this, Fitz?" he asked, his voice hard and directed at the boy.

The boy seemed to try to swallow down his fear but didn't answer. Logan had inched his way closer to the boy, and with a swift kick to the child's arm, he dislodged the gun. The firearm flew through the air to land somewhere behind Logan.

"Sit down, Fitz, and stay out of the way if you really care about Eveleen. Make sure she doesn't leave the bed," he told the boy, searching the darkness and the shadows for Franco and Tate.

From the murky shadows of the room, Franco appeared, applauding him gun in hand and Tate stepped from the other side. Both pointed a pistol at him. These two men were of little consequence to him. It was Eveleen he worried about. If she would just stay put, he could take care of them. Right now, he had two men and a boy to keep an eye on.

Tate circled behind him while Logan shifted slightly. The silent night air filled with tension. He sensed the pressure and the nervous energy around Franco. Even while he held the gun, his hands shook with fear.

He shivered with the urge to fight. Blood pumped forcefully through him as he balanced on the balls of his feet.

"You should leave now, Tate, before your friend drags you down. You will be in prison by dawn, and if I have my way, Madame Guillotine will visit with you."

Franco laughed, "You are outnumbered three to one. I'll have the deed to my land now."

"I've faced better foes than the two of you and come out on top." Logan moved with the two, keeping them in his sight. "What makes you believe Fitz is on your side?

"Just give me the deed and I'll let you and your wife live." Franco's voice faltered slightly.

Logan could smell the fear. "Remember the two men on the island?"

"My men you murdered?" Franco waved the gun in the air, his words slurred.

"They were better foes than you and your man, and they didn't stand a chance against me." Bloody hell, where was his wife? Where was

Evie? Where the bloody hell was Fitz? She was supposed to stay on the bed. For the first time since the men entered the bedchamber, sweat beaded on his forehead.

He needed to end this before something happened to Eveleen.

Without warning, the boy hit Tate on the head with the butt of the pistol Logan had sent to the floor. Eveleen swung at Tate. He easily pulled her to him, the gun at her head.

Logan heard Franco's laughter and knew it would haunt him forever. "Eveleen, you alright?"

Tate's meaty arm circled her throat. Her eyes wide with fear, she nodded at him.

"I'll shoot you, Monsieur Tate. Let ma'am go," the boy threatened the man, presenting another complication for Logan.

"Give me the deed and we'll leave," Franco paused smirking, "or your wife dies, tonight."

Before the words were said, Logan regretted them and knew they would deeply hurt Eveleen but they were necessary. He had to make Franco believe he didn't care about his wife, at least not as much as he wanted the vineyards.

He shrugged his shoulders, seeking an air of indifference, and gazing at his wife said, "Wife is just a title. I can always find another." He heard the small sound of distress Evie made. His heart lurched in his chest.

If Tate had not been holding her up, she would have wilted to the ground. Her eyes closed and he saw a tear seep from beneath her lashes. Ah hell, what he said would take a long time in correcting.

Keeping his gaze on both men, he inhaled then whirled and in a quick sudden motion, he side kicked Franco in the chest. Before Tate realized what had happened, he side-tackled him. Tate's arm loosened around Eveleen. She sank to the ground. Using all the boxing skills he spent years learning, he punched Tate in the face. Franco rose from the floor, the pistol shaking in his hand.

Logan dove at Franco's knees, sending the man to the floor, the pistol clattering on the ground. A hard punch to Franco's face left him unconscious. Grabbing both guns from the floor and gesturing for the boy to hand him the one he held, he sat down on a chair, the pistols pointed at the two men.

Eveleen sat on the bed, her red-blond hair swirling around her shoulders, tears falling from her eyes.

"Fitz, can I trust you?" He sent the boy a pointed look.

"*Oui, monsieur*, I want what's best for ma'am."

"You do? Or you just want to come with us when we leave?" Logan began to understand what Evie had seen in the little con artist.

"A little of both."

"If you do what I ask, I will have one of my men escort you to Bordeaux. When we leave for London if you've proven yourself trustworthy, I'll take you with us. If ma'am wants you to go with us." He looked at his wife, searching for some sign of acceptance or trust, anything that would tell him she hadn't believed what he said.

"You can trust me," the boy sounded eager. "What do you want me to do?"

"Go to the police and ask for this man." Logan strode to his jacket that was on the floor and pulled a piece of parchment from a pocket. "He told me he would be at the station all night."

"Then what?"

"Tell him we have Franco and his man and would appreciate a bit of assistance." Logan smiled, ruffling the boy's hair in a strange moment of fatherly endearment.

"I'll be back as soon as possible." He grabbed the slip of paper before racing out the door.

Logan watched the boy leave, terrified of the feelings Evie must have. A wife, he told her, is just a title. He could find one anywhere. It wasn't true.

Accepting the harm he caused and that he had to find a way to convince her he didn't mean the words he spoke to Franco, he strode to the bed where she sat.

Trying to put an arm around her, she shrugged it off then rose and stepped into the sitting area. Well, what had he expected? He followed her and sat opposite for a moment then remembering his captives, realized reconciliation would have to wait.

In the bedroom he ripped a bed sheet into strips and quickly bound the two men. With their hands and feet tied and lying on their stomachs, he left them to apologize to his wife.

"Evie..." he began.

She turned from him, seemingly unwilling to listen to anything he had to say. "I'm sorry."

"Of course you're not sorry."

"I didn't mean anything I said." He poured himself a glass of wine then without thinking poured her one. This was sobering. Consoling a wronged wife was not in his repertoire of abilities.

She turned on him, eyes blazing, anger simmering, "You don't love me. Why wouldn't you think you could easily find another wife?"

"Because I only want you, one wife, our children. No one else will do, at least not for me." His voice soft, his thoughts somber. In a few short months together they had found a way to bridge the chasm between them, and now in a dire second and the need to gain control of the danger he changed all that.

He threw the glass against the wall, glass splintering and wine spilling on the floor as well as the wall. His jaw clenched, he pulled the chair out and turning it, he straddled the back and let his arms rest on the top.

"I understand your feelings toward me and I accept them. Since I didn't die tonight, you won't have to search for a new wife." Her voice was tight and strained.

He poured himself another drink, watching her, knowing the damage he caused to her frail ego and having no idea how to correct that damage.

"I will spend the rest of my life trying to undo what I said tonight. I spoke the words to distract Franco and to gain the upper hand. I couldn't let anything happen to you. My instincts are just that, honed and refined by the British government. I act so the people I love and care about don't meet certain death before I think of the consequences." How much more callous could he have been?

"And that justifies what you did to me?" She walked to the window in the bedroom, seeming to need the distance between them.

Their fragile relationship had reached a new low. "No, yes, I would probably say the words again. It was the words or risk your life. I didn't want you to die."

The knock on the door stopped their conversation. The boy didn't wait for an invitation. He rushed inside. "They're here," he said breathlessly.

Three policemen walked through the door. "We've come for them," one said.

"Franco and his man are in the other room." Logan stepped aside, allowing the police through.

He felt a wave of relief. The tempest of the last few years was about to end. He looked to Eveleen. His gut wrenched in despair at the sight of tear streaks on her beautiful face.

"What will happen to them?"

"They will have a trial. It would help if you could testify, but you've documented their crimes and provided evidence. They will spend many years in prison if not the rest of their lives."

"Good." Logan watched the men as they left.

"Can I go with you? Did I prove myself?" Fitz asked eagerly, as he waited for the reply.

"Yes, when we proceed on to Tuscany, I will send you with one of my men to Bordeaux. Just as I said, when we return, you can come to London with us. Now, you must be tired."

Logan called for the man who stood guard outside his room. "How did these men get inside?"

The guard looked to the boy then Logan. "He said there was an emergency downstairs. I left my post, sir."

Tempted to fire the man on the spot, he decided to give the man another job. "Then you will let him sleep on the floor in your room. He won't be a problem and you will be in charge of Fitz until we return."

Logan turned to Eveleen, unsure of everything where they were concerned. He sat down next to her and wrapped an arm around her shoulder. "I don't know what I can say to make this right." He ached for her to forgive his callous words. His gut churned while sweat beaded on his forehead.

She rose, walking away from him. "I think you should sleep in the other room tonight," she whispered softly, her voice shaking with emotion.

"You can't avoid this. If you do, it will only fester and grow." He burned for this woman who seemed to be rejecting him a second time, and he needed advice but no one was there to give it.

"I can't pretend I feel something that isn't there." More tears slipped from her eyes.

He needed to understand what was in her heart, see into her soul. "I'm going to hold you close tonight, protect you from whatever nightmares you might have."

"Right now, you are my nightmare. You never forced me before but now you plan to do just that." Her voice shook with pent up emotion.

"I would never force you and you know that." His teeth clenched so hard his jaw ached.

"Then you will sleep in the other room."

"No."

"Then I will." She picked up the quilt from the bed and marched into the main area.

She didn't have a chance to spread the blanket before Logan swept her into his arms and after placing her on the bed, he came down on top of her. "Hush, just love me."

Her eyes were wide with an expression he'd seen before then they slowly glazed over. He pulled away, rolling to his back, one hand behind his head. "Open your eyes, Evie. I'm not that man."

A tiny cry of despair reached him. He rested on one elbow, gently tracing a path from her ear to the tip of her chin. "Evie, you have to open your eyes. Please." He waited while tense seconds passed, turning into minutes. "Remember who we are together."

He gently brushed his lips against hers. "Evie, it's me, Logan. You are my life and I would never hurt you. Look at me."

Slowly her eyes changed, the foggy haze seeming to cover them was gone. "Logan," his name sounded like a cry for help.

"Hush, I'm here. You left me for a few minutes just like before. Where do you go?"

"A place where it doesn't hurt," she said, reaching out her hand to touch his face.

"I..." he swallowed hard not really sure what to say. "Will you find room in your heart to forgive me."

The pause between his question and her answer seemed to last an eternity. "I know why you said those things. I understand, truly I do."

"But can you pardon me?"

"If you loved me..."

Hearing her words, he stiffened. He did love her, burned and ached for her. Her passion filled his soul. Yet he couldn't bring himself to say the words she craved. He told himself love didn't exist for so long parts of him still believed the words to be true.

It was a maze of emotions and words he couldn't find a way out of. "What if I can never say those words to you? Will you hold yourself away from me for the rest of our lives?"

She sat up, leaning against the backboard. Folding her hands in her lap, she seemed to think for a while. "Logan, I'm your wife and no, I won't flinch from your touch or go into that place where everything seems like heaven but is really hell. Just not tonight."

"This evening and into the morning I want to hold you. Will you let me do that?"

She started to shake her head no but stopped. "I can let you do that."

A weight seemed to lift from his shoulders. One tiny step now and perhaps another tomorrow, he might win her back.

She lay down, her back to him. He pulled her close careful not to take liberties despite the passion burning deep inside.

"Do you really intend to take Fitz back to England?"

Epilogue

Logan watched her from the door of the conservatory. Their trip to Tuscany and home had been bittersweet. The vineyard and winery had been more than he expected. It was beautiful and had been run impeccably. He would make a fortune on the Chianti, and there would be no one to challenge him for this land. All who had been connected to it had died.

On the return trip to Bordeaux they found Fitz had adapted to life quite easily with Jacques and Jule, but he was happy to return to England. At Logan's family estate they eventually put the pieces of the puzzle together as to who Fitz was.

Fitz's family history was rooted in the Maxwell name. It seemed he was the bastard son of Tyler Maxwell, Logan's father, and Maida's mother. He was about the same age as Harry. If he'd looked closely, he would have seen Fitz's resemblance to Maida. When Fitz and Harry stood together, they could easily be mistaken for brothers.

They also learned Franco and Tate had been convicted of crimes against the French government. Franco had met his fate with Madam Guillotine and Tate was sentenced to twenty years in prison.

Eveleen held herself aloof and even though she told him she understood why he said those horrible words, wife was just a title, nothing had been the same between them.

At night she lay by his side, rigid and unwilling to let him make love to her, touch her, cherish her. During the day she ran the household and painted then acted as if nothing was amiss between them. Before they returned, he'd never seen her paint. She told him she wasn't very good, but the delicate watercolors she created were beautiful.

He never told her but he had one of her paintings of his orchids mounted and was planning on presenting it to her. He just didn't know when. Once she let him feel the baby kick. She would have the child soon, and their lives would change again.

Admitting he'd made a mess of their marriage was easy, correcting it more difficult than he thought possible. Drake and Ella had given advice, but nothing they knew or lived with was in their repertoire. He understood the solution, but he was too much of a coward. Sitting down with her and telling her how he felt, had always felt but was too stupid to realize, was imperative and was also the solution.

Logan sucked in a long deep breath of air before starting across the yard to meet Eveleen and his fate. He wasn't all that sure he wanted to continue in the marriage he created and because of that, he had to fix it.

When he approached he saw her back stiffen. She put one hand on her waist, stretching then set the paintbrush on the easel. "What do you want?" she asked, refusing to turn and meet his gaze.

What did he want? He wanted to apologize, to place his hand on her stomach, to ease his frustration, to tell him he loved her more than life itself and he didn't know if he could live without her.

"Do you have a few minutes?" He stepped in front of her. The frown lines creasing her delicate features were impossible to miss.

"Of course."

"Walk with me." He reached out for her hand, but she tucked it away in the pocket of her apron.

"Do I have a choice?"

"Always." He headed toward the conservatory, hoping the environment inside would ease the tension and frustration. Even though he couldn't see her, he sensed her presence behind him, heard the soft footfalls.

He held the door open for her then placing his hand lightly on her back, led her toward the bench where a nearby waterfall tumbled musically on the rocks.

"Sit?" he offered.

She looked at him, her eyes wary, questioning. "I don't understand this. Has something happened?"

He ran his hands through his hair, studying her, searching for the right words, magical words that would sway her to accept him.

"I've come to my senses, actually that happened a long time ago."

You're procrastinating old man. Just tell her. "I just haven't been willing to admit the truth."

That caused a slight shift from the frown she wore, and for the first time in months, he witnessed a slight smile. "Your senses?"

"I knew this wasn't going to be easy." He sat down beside her, his heart in his throat.

"You've decided something about me?" The frown returned. She looked away from him, the waterfall seeming to be her focus.

"About you, yes." He placed her hand in his. When she tried to draw it away, he hung on until she gave up and let it go limp.

"I have work to do." She tried to stand but he couldn't allow it.

"You have servants. In my opinion you do far too much as it is. You need to take care of yourself." How the bloody hell did this become about her when he meant to talk about his feelings for her.

"I'm not used to doing nothing," she said, her voice curt. "Really this seems to me a waste of time."

"Please, Poppet, bear with me." He watched her freeze with the endearment he hadn't used in months.

She closed her eyes but didn't talk nor did she look at him.

"Very well, I knew you wouldn't want to hear anything I have to say." Sweat beaded on his forehead.

"Logan," she regarded him thoughtfully, "I forgave you the words. What more do you want?"

"Real forgiveness. You said the words but the absolution didn't reach your heart."

"Perhaps not," she admitted. "No matter how hard I try, I can't erase the look on your face and the tone of your voice when you said the words."

"I'm sorry for that and if I could take it all back, I would, but in the end I would say the same thing and in the same manner again if I thought it would save your life."

"That's just the thing. I've seen you kill without blinking, and I can't get the idea out of my head that somewhere deep down you believe it."

"Why? What has happened that would make you think I don't care for you?" His voice was harsh and demanding.

She laughed but the sound wasn't happy. "The hasty wedding to begin with. The fact that you never told me what you were doing or asked for my opinion. Your need for a legitimate heir. Do I need say more?"

"In truth, all I can think about is you. I don't care a fig about a legitimate heir. The first born whether it's a girl or a boy will be my heir."

"You just want a warm and passionate body in your bed, Logan. You've told me more than once love doesn't exist, and if it doesn't, any woman could wear the title of your wife splendidly."

"At night you haunt my dreams and in the day you're part of every waking thought."

"Liar." A tear slipped down her cheek and he gently wiped it away.

"Don't cry, I can't bear to see your tears." He got down on one knee, holding her hands in his.

"Eveleen Maxwell, Evie, my little Poppet, I love you. In knowing you I've learned that love does really exist. I don't think I could live my life without you by my side. Please forgive me and return my love." He brought her hands to his lips and kissed the back.

Silence between them lasted an eternity. Still she didn't speak, and he watched as she brought her lips together before saying, "Say that again. Say it as if you meant it more than life."

"I love you more than life, certainly more than my own. I would die protecting you."

She closed her eyes and for a moment he thought she would run then she threw her arms around him. "I love you so much. I think I have since the first time I saw you at the ball."

His mouth found hers, softly at first then demanding. He pulled her close, relishing the feel of her body against his, enjoying the moment his child kicked.

"I love you," he said again, twirling her in circles the music of her laughter echoing in the conservatory.

"You are my life, Logan Maxwell."

"And you are mine."

Coming from the Author
February 2019
from
Rogue Phoenix Press

Tavia's Deception
Twelve Dancing Princesses Book Nine

Chapter One

Tavia and Tira Hepburn along with Larena Graham were now the new charges of The Duchess or their auntie Charlotte in London England. Aunt Charlotte took them dress shopping for their presentation gowns the week before and now they appeared at one of the festivities of the season at St. Jame's Palace.

The debutante ball this evening was at the invitation of the Duke of Somerset. Tavia stood between her twin Tira and her cousin Larena waiting for a possible suitor. She swallowed her fear as well as her distaste for the marriage mart. Only her older sister, Ella had what one could call a successful season. Ella met Drake at a ball just like this one and fell in love.

This was not what she wanted as she watched the males in the room devour them with their eyes. The man approaching made her skin crawl. She rubbed her arms in an attempt to ward off the chill encroaching. Praying the man was eyeing someone else, she looked down in hopes he would take the subtle cue.

He stopped at The Duchess and bowed, lifting her aunt's hand and placing a kiss on the back. The hairs on the back of her neck stood on end. She couldn't hear what they said but the next moment, the man, twirling his mustache, stood in front of her.

"Edwin, Edwin McMasters may I have the honor of this dance?" he asked smoothly.

With a quick look to The Duchess, and the nod the older lady gave her, she understood she had no choice but to accept his invitation. When she stepped into his arms, nausea assailed her.

He was tall and thin, smelling of cigar smoke and alcohol. She counted the seconds as they moved around the dance floor. The palm of his hand was sweaty and hot. Tavia swallowed hard, wondering when she could end this politely.

"What are you doing?" Stunned she found herself maneuvered onto a dark balcony away from the debutants and men swirling around the room in their fashionable silk gowns.

"Making you mine." His mouth found hers and his tongue probed for entrance. She couldn't breathe. Trying to push him away she couldn't. She was shaking her head but he held it with hands on both sides of her face.

Inside she screamed no, but nothing helped. His tongue pushed her lips apart. She coughed, gaging from the contact. Suddenly Edwin sat on the ground his legs sprawled, rubbing his jaw.

"Bloody hell!"

Her gaze ran the length of her savior from his well-muscled legs to his trim waist and farther to the width of his shoulders. He looked at her with his steel gray eyes as if he knew what she was doing.

"The Lady Tavia Hepburn said no." The tall redheaded man offered his arm to her and escorted her back to her position by The Duchess before introducing himself. "James Macmurra at your service."

"I remember you." She blinked several times her hand to her chest, trying to catch her breath. "Thank you for rescuing me." She flashed him a smile of gratitude as well as relief.

"I'm glad to hear that. If I recall you were Jamie Lundin's partner at Drake Montgomerie's wedding." He turned to look at Tira. "And you were mine."

Recalling Ella's wedding to Drake, Tavia cleared her throat. "The wedding was a disaster."

"Let's not speak of that," James grinned at her. "May I have this dance?" He looked to The Duchess for approval.

"Of course, go on with you, enjoy." The Duchess waved them away. "You're only young once."

Heat swept through her body, anticipation at the thought of his strong arms around her left her breathless, perhaps a kiss. Broad shoulders and narrow hips, his feet planted firmly apart, she was mesmerized by his form and silver hue of his eyes. His eyes sizzled with some undefined message. She felt a sudden urge to test the feel of his red hair and beard.

She accepted his hand as he led her to the dance floor. His fingertips were calloused and her hand seemed to be engulfed by his. She stared at the floor, terrified of meeting his gaze, yet longing to do just that at the same time.

"Lady Tavia?" he asked, drawing her closer so he could position his hand on her back. They began to dance the quadrille, flying across the floor. The steps were rapid, skimming steps. He held her tighter, guiding her, managing to lead her around other couples.

The music changed to a Scottish reel with its own intricate steps. She didn't want to stop. These moments with her Scotsman were magical. He enchanted her. At the edge of the dance floor he whirled her to a stop.

"James?" She was breathing hard, and smiling at the huge man who could move with such ease and grace. "You amaze me."

"Would you like to cool off?" he nodded toward the balcony. "Just for a moment. I promise I'll be a gentleman."

Her hand rested on his chest where she felt the beating of his heart. She heard the rapid staccato of her own heart, pulsing. "I am rather hot," she waved a hand in front of her face wondering where she'd placed her fan.

Keeping her hand in his, he led her outside. The night air was chilly but against her heated flesh it felt good. He paused at the edge, bringing her hand to his lips and placing a kiss on the back.

"Do you like to dance?" When he turned to her, his eyes sizzled beneath hooded lashes.

The touch of his warm lips sent a shiver of delight coursing through her. She moistened her lips. "With you I do."

"I like to dance to the pipes. They have a haunting quality about them, and I've always loved the sound." He slipped out of his jacket and placed it around her shoulders. The scent was of leather and a bit of rose water then all James.

"Where in Scotland are you from?"

"Edinburgh I call my home now, but I grew up in the highlands. It's beautiful there. Whenever I feel lonely, I return. I've a hunting lodge I enjoy that lies by a loch. Are you cold?" He touched her forehead pushing an errant strand of hair from her face and tucking it behind her ear.

"No." She could never be cold when he stood so close.

He folded his hand over hers where it rested next to his heart. He smiled at her. "Do you want to stay out here a little longer?"

She couldn't stop the slow bubble of laughter emanating from her. "Yes, but if we stay much longer The Duchess will be here, pounding you on the back with her cane."

"I don't plan on doing anything that would cause that." If you look just beyond the drape there, you'll see your aunt. I don't believe she'll attack me unless I do something that would warrant that. I'm pretty sure holding your hand is fine even though I'd like so much more."

Her heart lurched beneath her ribs, hoping for perhaps a kiss. She and Tira had endless conversations about kissing. They both knew Ella had let Drake do things she shouldn't have done before the wedding and The Duchess let them.

"You'd like more..." her voice trailed off as he ran a calloused fingertip across her lips. Her mind spun.

"I'm not a suitable catch for you Lady Tavia. I'm a ship's captain not a lord. Your family will never agree to a match between us. So, even though I would love to pursue this relationship, I won't."

"Oh," she murmured disappointed by his statement.

"I'm leaving at the end of the week. Trust me you'll find someone suitable." He leaned against the balcony railing, holding her, gazing at her. His hands spanned her waist. She stood close to him, even closer than when they danced.

"Where are you going? I'd like to see the world, everywhere. If I could, I would love to go..." she couldn't think. The fingers of one hand left a heated path down her neck and across her collarbone. "Fayth went to Paris and Amorica lives in Maryland. Oh..." she gulped air. "Should you do that?"

"No," he said before he dropped his hands. "I should be strung up by my thumbs but I can't seem to help myself."

"Is The Duchess still watching? If she is, you haven't done anything that isn't acceptable."

Both hands were on her waist again. "I'm not about to test things. Are you hungry or thirsty?"

"We could go for a walk in the gardens," she suggested wanting to find someplace where The Duchess might not follow, somewhere he might kiss her. She found that more than anything she wanted James to kiss her.

"That's not wise. I should put you back on the floor so a suitable man might ask you for a dance."

"I don't want to dance with anyone else. I didn't come to London to find someone who will marry me. I'm going to book passage on a ship. The only thing that matters to me is seeing the world."

He coughed and again, pushed a strand of hair behind her ear. This time his fingers lingered longer than the first time. "You would put your life in danger to see the world? You can't just find a ship and book passage." He sounded shocked. "The Duchess would never let you do that."

"Why would it be dangerous to book passage on a ship?" she demanded. "People do it all the time and survive to see another day."

"Because you would have no one to protect you. I can't let you do something so foolish. Your life and well-being is too precious."

At his words she stiffened. She could do and be whatever or whoever she wanted. "You have no reason to say that. Why on earth would you think my life would be in danger if I was on a ship."

Looking away for several seconds, he cleared his throat. "You are to innocent by far. I captain a ship and have done so for several years. My crew are no more saints than I am. The risk would be too great."

"Tavia, there you are," Tira appeared on the balcony with Larena. "Do you want to walk with us in the garden? You and James?" she asked. "Gavin and Jamie are coming too."

She turned to James, a dark expression gracing his face. She was sure he was about to shake his head no but something seemed to change his mind. "Why not?"

"Why not indeed," she murmured, disturbed by his comment. He could at least act a bit more enthusiastic. Her presence with him suddenly seemed to be a burden. Still he stared at her, his eyes sizzling with some pent up emotion, Tavia didn't know how to define.

"We're bored with the dancing and Scarlett, Aunt Charlotte's companion promised to chaperone. Our Auntie is sitting, resting."

"She looks tired," Tavia skipped ahead.

"The Duchess is going home soon but said she'd wait up for us. We're supposed to remember the talk we had this afternoon before the ball about how men think." Larena said. "She'll probably have her nightly brandy and a lemon bar."

James coughed then cleared his throat. She heard him murmur, "the way men think?"

The three couples headed outside where gaslights lit the gardens, the air redolent with the scent of roses. Tavia and James strolled behind the other two couples. Their carefree happy chatter filled the silence of the evening.

James offered his arm and Tavia accepted his polite gesture. "My cousins and sisters used to visit an island near the McLellan castle," she began. "I miss those trips to the island. We had so much fun."

"Chaperoned of course," James said, as they strode past the other couples who had stopped to kiss.

She felt the distance between them growing even as she wanted so much more. "Absolutely not, none of our fathers knew about the island until Hunter, Allura's husband appeared vying for her hand in marriage. None of our father's except, perhaps the Laird McLellan even cared what we did."

James hand suddenly rested on hers. "You were impetuous just like your thoughts of booking passage on a ship to see the world. You must take care," he warned.

"Well, it's not your life. I plan on living mine the way I choose." They stopped at a gazebo deep in the gardens.

"We should probably get back to the others." He leaned against structure, turning her to face him.

"I don't want to go back." You need to kiss me. She wanted to tell him. Her hands rested on his chest as he settled her between his legs, his hands on the small of her back.

"People will talk," he closed his eyes drawing air into his lungs. "I don't want your reputation ruined before the season has barely begun."

She laughed softly, "you see, I don't care about my reputation if I'm doing something I've chosen with someone like you then I'm happy."

"You should consider what people think in everything you do." He tightened his fingers and she enjoyed the subtle pressure.

"Do you? Do you contemplate what people think of you? Or do you just do what you want or what you believe is right?"

"Bloody hell, I'm a man." he brought one hand upward to rest on her shoulder, on her bare skin beneath his jacket.

At the sensation of his calloused fingers, she shivered. Yet she meant to tell him what she thought about males dictating to her, "Women should be treated as equals. At least that's what I think."

"Why?" he queried, his finger tracing a line along her jaw.

She ignored his question, focusing on his lips instead of the conversation she didn't want to have with this man. "I've never been kissed before." Boldly she touched his chin, felt the soft texture of his beard then drew her finger across his lips.

He stopped her, holding her hand in his, "And you want me to kiss you? Why me? Why not someone who has a title before his name? You could have so much more."

"Please," she said and not wanting him to say no to her she continued. "I want to know how I'll feel when a man kisses me. When you kiss me."

"I truly don't want to tell you no, lass, but it wouldn't be right." He kissed the tip of her finger instead. "I enjoy your company more than you should know, but I'm not the right man for you."

"Ah, kiss her," Gavin said from behind them. "If she wants you then you are the right man for her."

"Kiss her," Tira laughed. "She can't be the only one of us who isn't kissed tonight."

"Go on with all of you." He growled low in his throat. "This conversation is between the two of us. There is no room for eaves droppers."

"Really, you should kiss her. We'll give the two of you a wee bit of privacy but when we finish the stroll through the garden and return, we want to hear that you kissed her," Larena said, all the while laughing.

The sound sent a primal shiver down her spine. She couldn't speak. She moistened her lips with her tongue, his gaze riveted on her mouth. "James..."

"You unman me you're so beautiful. But..." he watched her intensely, his large hand resting on the side of her face.

She was beginning to understand the power the subtleties of her body had over this man. Placing her hands on his shoulders, she leaned into him. "You can't, won't, kiss me. Perhaps I should kiss you then." She rose onto her toes, her breasts pushing against his chest.

"You play with fire, Tavia. Don't tease a man."

Was that what she was doing? Teasing him? She blinked several times, pressing into him and feeling things she'd never thought to feel. "Do you really believe I want some lord just because he has a title in front of his name? I'm not that shallow. I would take offense if you knew me better."

Her statement brought a chuckle from deep in his chest. "Do not take offense. I'm not marriage material. I spend most of my life at sea. Would you want that in a husband?"

"It's exactly what I want because I would like nothing more than to join him on his travels. Someone like you is perfect. You are perfect. We are perfect." She stated emphatically.

"You don't know me well enough to make a statement like that. I might beat you when you disagree or don't do what I ask."

She was shaking her head, tendrils of hair falling from her swept up hair. "You would never do such a thing. A man's true character is always apparent to his male friends. Drake would have never asked you to be a groomsman at his wedding if you were an evil or mean man."

"Do you have an answer for everything?" his hands framed her face while he moistened his lips, his gaze blazing into hers with unrequited fire.

"Perhaps," she spoke softly anticipating the kiss she was sure would come soon. She wanted to feel the warmth of his mouth on hers, taste the essence of who he was. He was so close she inhaled his breath.

"If I kiss you, will I be your first?"

"Yes, please." Her fingers wound into his hair. She felt the earth tremble beneath her feet but it was his huge body shaking with desire she assumed.

"I shouldn't."

"Of course you should."

"Well, well, well, The Duchess would be interested in this. She might even have you keel hauled on one of your boats."

"Edwin, I'd know that high pitched voice anywhere."

They broke apart. She was breathing hard. From the darkness, Edwin strode toward them. "You refused my kiss but you let a Scotsman kiss you. He doesn't have a title," he sneered.

"Stand behind me," with one large hand he gently moved so he stood in front of her. His hands were fisted at his sides and it seemed he rocked on the balls of his feet ready to fight, "What do you want?"

"Apparently the same thing you do," Edwin said approaching them. "Let me kiss her and I'll be gone."

"Never," James ground out through clenched teeth.

"You should let the little lady speak," he said with a sneer. "I bet she wants a real man not a Scotsman or a commoner."

"I gave you my answer a few hours ago," Tavia poked her head from around James back. "No."

"Everything alright?" Gavin and Jamie approached with the girls.

"It will be as soon as this bloody fool leaves," James said, his hand touching Tavia's she felt an inner strength permeate through her.

It seemed Edwin knew when the odds were against him. "I'll have to try another time," he said looking over his shoulder as he walked away. "I will taste her."

"I don't like the way that man looks at you." James wrapped an arm around Tavia, pulling her against his hard frame.

"He's a lord. Do you think he's more deserving of a relationship with me than you?" Tavia challenged, beginning to understand the protective nature that defined James Macmurra.

"No. He might be a lord but he's a wastrel and cad," Gavin said. "I don't pretend to understand what is going on here, but you need to be wary of that man. He owes debts to a number of my friends, and he doesn't have the means to pay. I'm assuming he's looking for a rich heiress to finance his vices."

"Then he's trying to court the wrong girl. I'm not a rich heiress." She turned to James. "You're not looking..."

"That's right, I'm not looking for an heiress. I've made my fortune and have more money than I need or could spend in a lifetime of simple living."

"Enough of that," Tira pulled Tavia from James embrace and away from the men. Larena followed. "Well," she whispered. "Did he kiss you?"

~ * ~

"Dressed up again, I see. Where are you going tonight?" Seamus O'Malley, the first mate on James' ship seemed to strip his thoughts bare as he scrutinized him.

James had been staring at the ledgers in front of him for what seemed like hours a glass of whiskey on his desk. He glanced up, knowing he wasn't going to finish anytime soon. "Don't know, Drury Lane or Covent Garden. Not sure what the ladies decided on."

"Not your cup o' tea if I say so myself. Don't see you going to the theatre for the fun of it or the opera. Who's the special lady who has you sweatn' buckets?" Seamus chuckled, rubbing his bristly chin. "Whoever she is seems she's got you tied up in knots."

"I didn't know how to tell her I wasn't interested." James wasn't interested in the theatre just a girl he had no right to court. Seems as if he was making a colossal mistake and wasting valuable time on something that was going nowhere.

"Looks like interest to me," Sean said. "You wouldn't have been starin' at those papers all afternoon. And it looks to me as if you've made no progress or is it just the little gal you're interested in and not the theater. Take her to your bed and get it over with then you can forget her and get on with your life."

"She's a lady Seamus. Someone I have no business courting. I don't have a title or an estate to offer, and I certainly can't take her to my bed." He could certainly by land or a home. He had the means. James sat back drumming his finger on the table as he let his mind wander to the possibilities.

"Don't be so noble. Love doesn't pay any attention to the things you just listed. If you're in love..." he let the idea hang in the silence of the cabin.

"Love?" he murmured thoughtfully. "I barely know her. I believe you'd call it lust." But her beauty blindsided him the first time he saw her. When she talked to him he was more entranced by the magic that was Tavia.

"We still sailing in a couple of days or do you plan on another captain for this old vessel? You know you have men who'd love to command the ship and who are quite capable. Stayin' on land and courtin' the little gal might be the right thing to do. Otherwise, by the time we get back to port she could be wedded and bedded. You'd be the loser."

His thoughts settled on Edwin, his grimy hands touching her. He was one of those men who would stop at nothing to get what they wanted. If what happened last night was any indication, he wanted Tavia.

"I can't do that." James rearranged the papers on his desk before stacking them in a pile to be read later.

"Won't?" Seamus questioned.

"It's best for her if I leave and don't look back." She wouldn't allow Edwin into her life so he didn't have that to worry about just every other suitor in the ton.

"Did she say that? Did she tell you her life would be better without you? If you tell me yes, I'll call you for a liar."

"No."

"Well then, you best be doin' some serious thinkin' about your future and the lady you're about to leave behind. You're not getting' any younger. Sometimes a man needs to settle down with a wife and children to make his life complete."

"And I see you did just that?" James leaned back resting his hands on his stomach grinning and feeling the humor.

"Had a wife once a long time ago." Seamus said. "And a little boy."

James sat up, concerned. "I didn't know. What happened?"

"She died and my boy with her. I was at sea and couldn't do nothin' about it. 'Nough said." He turned to leave then stopped. "James, we need a new cabin boy. I put the word out and told the harbor master just this morning."

"A new one? What happened to Mica?" this posed a new problem and one he'd have to deal with if they didn't find one.

"Decided he wasn't meant for life at sea. He was seasick most days and the crew teased him unmercifully."

"Make sure we find one before we set sail in two days." James followed Seamus from the cabin. Down the gangplank he hailed a cab, giving directions to The Duchess' townhouse. He settled back mulling over the conversation with Seamus.

He didn't like the idea of Tavia, finding someone else, but he tried to maintain his thoughts trying to convince himself. She would be better off with someone closer to her station in life, someone who would be there for her. Seamus' story confirmed his reservations. His first mate had been at sea and his family died. That wasn't a story he wanted to be told about his wife.

Yet no one else seemed to think the same way he did. He'd leave this to chance. If she was still a single lady when he returned, he'd court her. Satisfied with his decision he focused on the cargo and when it would be loaded. Seamus could oversee the loading so perhaps he and Tavia could go for a ride tomorrow in Hyde Park.

The carriage slowed to a halt. He strode to the porch and rang the bell, waiting nervously. This took more courage than battling a storm at sea. The butler opened the door and waited a stoic expression on his face.

"James Macmurra, calling on Tavia Hepburn." He wiped sweaty hands on his pants.

The butler stepped aside then ushered him into the parlor. Apparently, he was the last to arrive. Jamie and Gavin sat in chairs sipping brandy, seemingly relaxed. The butler brought him a drink.

"Hope this is too your liking."

James leaned against the doorframe, holding his glass aloft, "Cheers." Either of you eager for an evening of opera at Covent Garden?"

Both men laughed. "Not here for the opera."

"So, you both have eyes for your lady. You plan on marriage when this is all over?" James pursued the topic that had been on his mind all afternoon as well as last evening.

"Can't say I've given it much thought. It's too soon." Jamie said. "She'd have to be willing to leave London. I've a life in Baltimore I won't leave."

"Me neither," Gavin said. "Larena intrigues me. She says

outrageous things that take me by surprise and she makes me laugh. A man could do worse and," he paused in thought. "She's beautiful."

"You know how these things go," Jamie began.

"And how is that?" The Duchess stepped into the room then tapping her cane on the floor held each man's gaze for several seconds. As if to intimidate these men as she walked she tapped her cane.

The staccato of the cane meeting the floor seemed to match his heartbeat. James ran a finger around his collar, waiting for the lecture to begin. "What would you like us to say, in for a penny in for a pound?"

"Mr. Macmurra, you do get to the point of things. I like that. Don't want to beat around the bush, I see. You've got places to go and time is of the essence. Well, I'm not going to live forever, and I want to see these girls find men who will treat them right. I've only had the opportunity to plan one wedding and that one went terribly awry."

"I would never hurt your niece," Gavin spoke up. "I mean it."

"That's not what I was speaking of," she looked to Gavin. "If you don't have marriage in mind, you should leave here at once and let someone who does have a chance to court her."

"I didn't mean it like that. I do have marriage in mind someday," his voice assumed a strange tone.

"What about you Jamie Lundin? What are your intentions? Are any of them good?" she turned to Scarlett who brought in a plate of scones and refreshed the men's drinks.

Jamie cleared his throat. "Certainly not to hurt anyone. Tira enjoys my company and I hers but I'll return to the states in a few weeks. Perhaps by then we'll have a better idea what we mean to each other. Would you be happy with her leaving England?" he issued a challenge.

Whatever makes her happy will please me, and make the last of my duties successful where she is concerned. Then she directed her attention to James. "You know Tavia wants to travel. She wants to see what's on the other side of the sun. She believes with all of her heart that she needs to follow sunsets and chase sunrises. A bit fanciful for my taste, but I believe she sees that opportunity in you. Don't disappoint her."

"Tavia has said as much to me. She brings to life something in me I thought long dead. I'm not sure myself what that means. My ship is leaving in two days. If you'd rather I left right now, I'll do your bidding. I won't be able to court her until I return."

"Ah," she waved her hand in the air, "You don't want to go to the opera. I understand." She leaned forward and cackling, "Tonight you will escort her to Covent Gardens, and tomorrow I expect you to ride with her in Hyde Park. She has her heart set on it and as you well know I don't want to see any of my charges disappointed."

James cleared his throat. "I don't have a title in front of my name or a home in London. An apartment in The Albany is what I call home when I have an extended stay here. My suitability is questionable."

"Fine, then you won't be taking her there or seducing her into your bed. That bit of information makes me feel much better. I'm going to tell it the way it is. If you're looking for something other than a chaperoned courtship, you are seeing the wrong ladies." The Duchess told them in her most formidable voice both Scarlett and I are determined to make sure nothing untoward happens.

"You need not worry about me trying to seduce Tira. I would never bring her to my bed before we are wed, if we are wed," Jamie added hastily.

The Duchess held her glass to her lips for several seconds. James was sure she didn't swallow. When she set the glass on the end table she closed her eyes for a moment before speaking, "I remember the late Duke. He promised much the same thing, as did my nieces fathers. They were all rakes of the worst sort until they met their ladies."

"But the duke seduced you?" Gavin asked with a soft chuckle. "Who would have guessed?"

James began to enjoy this conversation and wondered where this would end up. "Of course you didn't let him." He believed the opposite but for some reason he needed to see if The Duchess would be honest.

"On the contrary, I loved that man so much I would have done anything he asked and he knew it. Oh, he was arrogant or perhaps confident would better describe him and his pride saw no end. He was a bit like the three of you only much more handsome. He had me in the palm of his hand the first time I looked into his gorgeous dark brown eyes."

James wanted to protest that he wasn't arrogant but perhaps he was. He possessed other sins but he did have a few virtues.

Jamie seemed to stiffen. "I would never seduce Tira. She's an innocent."

"Balderdash. If given the opportunity there is not a doubt in mind you would use all the powers you possess to sway her into your arms and bed."

"I like to think of myself as a gentleman," he seemed determined to convince either The Duchess or perhaps himself.

"All three of you are gentleman but you are men first. Would you expect anything else from a debutant besides innocence? They are beginners, and the girls know nothing about sex and how a man thinks. Except perhaps Larena, her sister does breed horses."

"How a man thinks?" all three asked at the same time, looking to the other as if they knew the answer.

"Yes."

"Enlightenment would be nice," James said believing he had an idea about where she was about to go. No wonder Tavia spoke her mind. The characteristic must be inbred.

"As you like. I mean to do just that." She paused in thought watching the amber liquid as she swirled it in the crystal glass.

"You spoke to the girls about this yesterday. I remember how she told me I thought with a different part of my anatomy. Wasn't entirely sure what she meant."

"The Duke, found this tiny cottage near a lake. It was beautiful and somehow we escaped our chaperone. He must have spent hours trying to figure out how to do it. That day it was raining so he hard he didn't have to make up an excuse to take me to this spot he knew of."

"The cad," Gavin laughed a loud. "A man of my own heart..." His words died away.

"Perhaps I now have reservations about your intentions toward my niece," she directed the comment to Gavin before continuing her story. "We were both soaked to the bone by the time we were in the cottage. With a fire going he set the mood for my seduction." She waved one hand in the air, "But I digress."

"To escape the chill of the night, he convinced you to take your riding habit off and spread it out to dry." James said, knowing it was something he would do with anyone of his female friends except Tavia. With Tavia he was determined to keep his hands to himself.

"Yes, well, his words made perfect sense. He did wrap a blanket around me when I had nothing but a few things on my person." She blushed recalling the events. "It seems just like yesterday." A lone tear slipped from an eye to slide down her cheek.

"I'm sorry he passed so soon. His death must have been incredibly hard on you," James said suddenly on his feet then kneeling in front of the woman everyone called The Duchess because of how formidable she was but at this tender moment she was Tavia's auntie Charlotte. He held her trembling hands in his. "I hope I'm as blessed as you were when it comes to finding my true love."

She let him hold her hands for some time before she pulled away. "I'm a maudlin fool. I'll be joining him soon enough. Which brings me to one of the points I intend to make today with you young men before you do something someone might regret."

Her emotional break down seemed to change the tone of this meeting at least for him. He yearned for a relationship like the one Charlotte described, and he wondered if Tavia was truly the woman for him. In such a short time she touched something inside him he never knew existed.

"So," Jamie said, "what are the points you want to make?" he roughed his hands through his hair seeming as touched by her story as she was.

"First," she began tapping the cane on the floor, "you three will make several promises to me right now, today, before I let you do anything more with my nieces."

"I'm sure I can promise anything you ask. It couldn't be too difficult." Gavin said with cocky air to his words.

"You might be surprised. I'm guessing you've only slept with widows and perhaps a few women of ill repute. These women don't come with family and friends who will defend their honor or even care about what happens to them. You can come and go as you please with no repercussions to yourself but women you bed can't say the same thing even if they are debutantes."

James reminded himself he had a lady in every port he visited. They were willing to have sex with him and just as The Duchess implied, he took them for granted. "What would you like me to promise?"

"There are several guarantees I need the three of you to make but the first one is that while you are courting my nieces, you must promise me you will not have sex with any other woman." She waited seemingly patient hands folded primly in her lap.

Gavin and Jamie were quick to answer, but James thought about the issues he had about courting Tavia and if he was truly wooing her it would be months before he saw her again.

"What about you, young man?" she directed her question James direction while she loudly tapped the cane on the floor as if intending to get his undivided attention.

Heat rose to his face, "Even if I wanted to, I'm not sure if I'm courting Tavia. My ship leaves..."

"I know in two days. You cannot continue to use that fact as an excuse," she harshly interrupted. It seems you must make a decision right now and in front of me and your friends. Are you or aren't you going to see Tavia? If you have a lady in every port you'll have to inform them you are no longer available. Can you do that?"

His heart thundered in his chest. He still had so many reservations and the what ifs seemed to grow faster than he could possibly explain.

"Are you courting Tavia?" The Duchess persisted.

"Yes." He knew the answer would leave him with no regrets, not until he returned and in the time he was gone she found another man.

"Can you forgo your mistresses?"

"I have no mistresses." That part was true. He didn't keep anyone.

"Then my apologies, the ladies who wait for your arrival with baited breath," she spoke softly for the first time.

"If I have Tavia waiting for me here, I have no problem promising not to see other women. I will keep that vow." With his words a weight was taken off his chest and he began to look forward to this evening.

"To the second part which will most likely be easier. Promise me you will not abscond with your lady to a cabin or to your ship in hopes of finding out if the two you are sexually compatible."

"Of course not," James was quick to say. "A single lady has no place on a sailing vessel carrying cargo. Your niece and I have already had the conversation."

"Good, my heart couldn't take another scenario such as the one, Fayth and Jarret put me through. What about the both of you." She directed her attention to Jamie and Gavin.

"I promise," they said in unison.

"Very well, Gavin, I've learned your family owns a hunting lodge. Are you positive?" She challenged the young man.

They all understood what she wanted to learn.

"I will not take her there for..." he stopped midsentence.

She smiled clearly pleased, "I would send my men to collect the two of you if you tried something like this. Drake took advantage of my wishes to see my charges happily wed. I was convinced Drake was the right man for Ella. The only one here who fits the category of suitor material is the only one unsure if he wants to court my niece." She directed her gaze toward James.

Her words shocked James. Most times confidence exuded from him. With Tavia he'd been unsure from the moment he saw her. He wanted her but knew she wouldn't desire a man who spent his time at sea, a man without a title, a man who had no place to call home save his ship.

Gavin and Jamie appeared as if they wanted to protest but wisely kept their mouths shut.

"What is the next promise?" James was beginning to sweat. The first two had been strange the next one promised to surprise him as well.

"The hardest one of all is simple because it goes against everything that drives a man." She looked pleased with herself.

She managed to pry promises from all of them. Whether they kept them or not remained to be seen. Temptations waited around every corner.

"I wait in anticipation," James murmured appreciating the elder lady more with each passing minute.

She cackled pouring herself another brandy and sipping slowly, finally setting it on the table. He found himself holding in breath in eagerness.

She cleared her throat. "I was a bit parched. Let's get this over with. I've explained all this to my nieces. Men think with a different part of their anatomy than women. Be assured they don't know as yet exactly what I meant but they are aware of the problem."

"And..." he didn't know if he was relieved or not. If she didn't explain anything about that anatomy he thought it would inevitably be left up to him.

"I told my girls men think with their cock while they thought with their hearts."

~ * ~

Their evening gowns were hung and ready to put on, their makeup was strewn across the dressing tables, powders, eye paint, soot mixed with oil for the lashes.

"Don't use too much," Larena cautioned as she applied a shiny pearl powder on her face followed by a light rose-colored blush to her cheeks. "This is so much better than a white face."

"Do you think James will kiss you tonight?" Tira asked. "He really just has to and you have to let him. A kiss from the right man is heavenly."

"I have to do no such thing. Last night I wanted him to kiss me but today everything has changed. If he does though, I won't object. I might even like it." Tavia smushed her lips together after applying a soft lip color.

"And why not? You know he's going to be gone for several months. You have to do it now so he'll remember you," Larena patted her hair into place and smiled at herself in the mirror.

"I'm leaving too," Tavia said softly, her hands shaking with fear of the unknown. "I've been taken on as a cabin boy on a ship, called the Firtha, sailing for Spain and Italy."

"You haven't!" Larena whirled on her cousin, her hands on her heart. "That can't be safe."

"I'm going to pretend I'm a boy so no one will be the wiser. Supposed to report for duty as the new cabin boy tomorrow afternoon so I'll be settled in when the ship leaves port. As soon as I'm ready, I'll have Tira take me to the docks." The closer she got to the time, the more she reconsidered.

"Do you even know what a cabin boy does?" Larena asked clearly shocked at Tavia's statement. "They might have to do something totally inappropriate. They are boys you know."

"I made inquiries." Tavia said turning her back to her sister, Tira, for help with the corset. "They wait on the captain for one and carry messages from one end of the vessel to the other. I think I'm supposed to help trim the sails too."

"Well, I guess you could do part of that. Should find out how to trim sails sooner than later," Larena said sarcastically, eyeing her fingernails, "But why would you want to? You really should stay here in London where you won't be putting your life in danger."

"You know why. We're stopping somewhere in Spain and Italy. I can barely contain myself. I'm afraid I'll say something to James and he'll tell The Duchess and she'll lock me in tomorrow so I can't get away." Reciting all the places she about to see left her breathless.

"I'm half tempted to tell her myself. This is really a fool's mission. When our auntie finds out we hid the information from her, she'll be furious. I don't have any idea what she'll do," Larena said.

"Tira and I went shopping this morning and I've breeches and shirts, bought strips of cloth to bind my breasts. No one will guess I'm a girl." She sported a huge smile feeling a new surge of confidence.

"What about your hair," Larena said dryly. Even if you keep it tucked beneath a hat you risk losing the hat in brisk wind. How will you explain that? When all your hair tumbles down your back."

"Don't put a damper on this. I've got it all figured out. Tira and I discussed this escapade at length. I'm going to cut it off."

"No!"

"Yes, tomorrow after we get up. I'm supposed to go riding with James but I'm going to feign sickness. Once Tira has chopped it all off, we're going to the docks. I'll find the ship and board. Bought a duffel bag to keep my clothes in," she said proud of herself and the efforts she and her twin made for this escapade to succeed.

"Escapade is right."

"I'm going to the states after Jamie leaves," Tira said smugly, looking to her sister seeming to ask for approval. "I'm going to stay at Ravyn's house in Baltimore and I'm going to learn how to build ships."

"Really," Larena said, gazing at the twins as if they'd gone stark raving mad. "You going to pretend you're a boy too, and leave me all alone here? I don't like it that you're all deserting me."

"I'm sorry but we're pursuing our dreams," the twins ran to hug Lorena.

"You and Gavin will get along just fine. What are your dreams? You must have some or one even."

"I don't know," Larena said. "My passion is to ease the plight of the poor. I want to fight for all the injustices that have been done."

"That's very noble. And you too would get more accomplished if you were a man," Tira said.

"Someone go peek and see if the men have arrived." Tavia said as she was putting the finishing touches on her hair.

"I'll go," Larena said and departed without a backward glance.

"Do you think she'll tell?" Tavia asked, afraid Larena would do just that. "I shouldn't have said anything. At least when you leave, you'll be with Aidan and Ravyn and Aric will visit from time to time. You'll have a home and you won't be on a ship and sleeping in the same place as the rest of the crew."

When she said the words, her adventure seemed more daunting than when she planned it. She could not sleep with the crew. She'd have to find some place on deck where she could curl up and remain safe.

The door opened and Larena slipped inside, her back to the closed door. "They are here sitting in the parlor with refreshments and The Duchess is lecturing them."

"About what?"

"Promises. She's making them promise certain things. I didn't hear what exactly but we can ask them tonight." Larena said breathlessly.

"I can only imagine. Do you think the promises are the same as the ones we made to her?" Tira asked while she finished with the fastenings on Tavia's dress.

"Probably not," Tavia said trying to remember the three promises the girls made. "They couldn't possibly be the same."

"She wouldn't though she could never make them promise not to go anywhere chaperoned or unprotected."

"No, they'd laugh at her," Larena said.

"We promised to think with our heads not our hearts where the men are concerned," Tavia said, pausing a moment. "She most likely told them not to think with their cock."

"Close enough," Tira said.

"What do you think there third promises was?" Tavia asked. "It certainly wasn't ours. We promised to stay open minded and if they did something we didn't like we had to tell them or her. Either one was fine."

Larena spoke up. "I heard her say something about sleeping with a different woman in every port. I don't know what the promise could be except not to do that."

"He really does sleep with a woman every place they stop?" Tavia's voice cracked. "Who does he have in London that he sees?"